D0629339

A Daughter
of No Nation

A Daughter
of No Nation

A. M. DELLAMONICA

A TOM DOHERTY ASSOCIATES BOOK
NEW YORK

A DAUGHTER OF NO NATION

Copyright © 2015 by A. M. Dellamonica

A Tor Book
Published by Tom Doherty Associates, LLC
175 Fifth Avenue
New York, NY 10010

www.tor-forge.com

Tor® is a registered trademark of Tom Doherty Associates, LLC.

Library of Congress Cataloging-in-Publication Data

Dellamonica, A. M., author.
A daughter of no nation / by A.M. Dellamonica. —First Edition.
pages cm.—(Stormwrack ; 2)
"A Tom Doherty Associates book."
ISBN 978-0-7653-3450-3 (hardcover)
ISBN 978-1-4668-1236-9 (e-book)
I. Title.
PR9199.4.D448D38 2015
813'.6—dc23

2015023326

Our books may be purchased in bulk for promotional, educational, or business use. Please contact your local bookseller or the Macmillan Corporate and Premium Sales Department at (800) 221-7945, extension 5442, or by e-mail at MacmillanSpecialMarkets@macmillan.com.

First Edition: December 2015

Printed in the United States of America

0 9 8 7 6 5 4 3 2 1

For Peter Watts and Caitlin Sweet,
who came together in defiance of biological reality

ACKNOWLEDGMENTS

A Daughter of No Nation could not exist if I wasn't blessed with an abundant network of generous and inspiring people. Always at its heart, and in mine, is my remarkable and brilliant wife, Kelly Robson.

I owe much to my family—Tuckers, Millars, and Robsons alike, and to my wonderful siblings: Michelle, Sherelyn, Susan, and Bill. My friends do everything from reading drafts, explaining research concepts, and providing moral support when I am flailing: thanks are due to Beverly Bambury, Charlene Challenger, Nicki Hamilton, Michael Matheson, Dawn-Marie Pares, Chris Szego, Rebecca Stefoff, and Matt Youngmark.

I am grateful to my agent, Linn Prentis; my editor, Stacy Hill; the outstanding staff at *Tor.com* and Raincoast Books; and all the editors, writers, and mentors who've guided me, including: Madeline Ashby, Ellen Datlow, Don DeBrandt, Gardner Dozois, Claude Lalumière, David Nickle, Jessica Reisman, Alexandra Renwick, Nancy Richler, Steven Silver, Caitlin Sweet, and Harry Turtledove.

When you're writing ecofantasy, it's essential to ground your magic in some faint sense of reality. My colleagues at SF Novelists helped with everything from research details to brainstorming titles. Mark Bowman and Gordon Love checked my scuba diving details. Peter Watts has shown extraordinary patience, over the years, with my arty, drama-geek approach to magicking up the laws of the universe. Ramona Roberts, meanwhile, helps with the laws crafted by people. Walter Jon Williams got me started on resources for tall ships. They're lovely, smart, generous people, and you should know that any errors in what passes for science, language, or sailing procedure within this book were made by me despite their best efforts.

I am one of those people who do much of their creative work out in a café environment, and all of the Stormwrack books were drafted in the remarkable Café Calabria on Commercial Drive in Vancouver. The space made available to writers (along with everyone else in the neighborhood) by the Murdocco family was like a second home to me. It was a privilege to work there and I still miss it. But since I moved to Toronto in 2013, I've been revising these books at the marvelous Portland Variety on King Street.

You all made it possible for me to set sail on this journey, and I owe you.

A Daughter
of No Nation

CHAPTER 1

The blond woman had chapped fingertips with ragged, oft-gnawed nails, and she was half her attacker's size. His hand around her throat obscured it entirely. The padded glove bulged like a crash collar, wedged between her chin and shoulders.

He was making to drag her away when she let out a half-strangled shriek and stomped his left foot. It wasn't much of a blow, but he staggered . . . and, better, hesitated. She jabbed an elbow into his rib cage, then wriggled free of his grip, mostly by virtue of falling at his feet.

She scrambled away at a run, screaming at the top of her lungs, "No, no, no!"

Once she reached the far end of the dojo, she spun, improvising a victory dance.

The rest of the self-defense class bellowed approval from the sidelines. The foam-swaddled attacker, whose name was Marc, put up a hand, acknowledging defeat.

"Sophie, you're next."

Sophie Hansa stretched, exchanged high fives with the blonde, and took her place on the mat.

The class was meant to help women who might otherwise freeze in a fight, to get them past any retrograde ladylike sense of hesitation over hitting someone. The idea was to make wrestling and punch-throwing more familiar and comfortable, to simulate the mock—and not so mock—fighting that little boys allegedly got into throughout childhood.

"Okay," their instructor, Diane, said. "You're not expecting trouble. Where are you?"

Sophie fought an interior sigh as a handful of improbable answers occurred: on a climb in Nepal or in a yellow submarine. Aboard the great Verdanii sailing ship *Breadbasket,* in a world these earnest women would never hear of. But six sessions in this fluorescent-lit room, with its smell of feet and tension, had given her plenty of time to come to grips with the group's expectations.

"Coming out of a bar."

"Drunk?"

"Just tipsy."

"Where's your car?"

"Parked in a well-lit—"

Diane's role was to ask questions until Sophie at least half-forgot Marc was back there, but this time he went for surprise by jumping in right away. The flat of his hand struck the small of her back. Sophie all but face-planted into the mat.

"Roll!" someone shouted.

It was too late to somersault back to her feet like some kind of cartoon warrior. She flung herself sideways instead, wheezing. He'd winded her.

Marc was already pouncing, dragging her by her shoulder and a handful of her hair.

Sophie turned her head sharply. It was enough to pull her curls out of the glove as she grabbed for his eyes with her free hand. She got a grip on the mesh mask, remembered she was supposed to be screaming, let out one breathless "No!" and went for the knee to the groin . . .

. . . and, briefly, remembered trying a similar move on a bona-fide monster, its hot, rotten breath and the slick of blood on the floor . . .

Then she flashed on the sound of her aunt's neck, snapping.

Her knee came up, right on target, and it was a good hit, hard contact.

Mark let her go but didn't pretend to collapse.

"We're over the line," he said gently.

It was true. He'd yanked her over the white chalk smear, the imaginary boundary between life and death.

"Nice try, Sophie, but he got you," Diane affirmed as Sophie sucked air past the shards of glass in her lungs. "Elke, you're up."

Yeah, Sophie thought, *I'm quite the action hero.*

After everyone had had a turn, they practiced clobbering inanimate foam targets as hard as they could, yelling "Commit, commit, commit!" with every blow. Then they stretched and debriefed on everyone's success in fighting off—or, in her case, *not* fighting off—Marc.

"Go home and be safe," Diane said finally, a benediction and a dismissal all in one.

The class was held in a San Francisco community center, a low-slung brick building painted with kids' murals.

"No ride today?" a classmate asked as they stepped out into the parking lot. Sophie suspected her classmate had a bit of a crush on her brother. She'd told the woman Bram was gay, but her enthusiasm for him hadn't dimmed.

Scanning the lot for her brother's car, Sophie shook her head. "It's cool. I'll catch BART as far as—"

A honk interrupted her.

Her heart sank as she recognized her mother.

Ambushed! She checked her phone, but there was no text from Bram.

Regina Hansa was already cracking the passenger door.

"How did it go?" she asked, as though they did this every week. Her mother had always favored car rides for parent-child heart-to-hearts. No escape that way.

Sophie pressed herself inside, through the thick air. "I got a few good shots in."

They sat for a minute in silence, her mom not going anywhere, not saying anything. It was a good tactic—Sophie never could let a silence stretch.

"How'd you find me?"

"Bram's got that creepy stalker app installed on his phone. It shows your GPS location."

"You stole Bram's phone?"

"Borrowed." Her mother held it up.

Sophie managed to retrieve the phone without snatching it. "I don't know what you're thinking, but—"

"I'm thinking that when your father and I came home from Sicily you were limping and mopey."

"I don't mope!"

"You finally defended your thesis, and then you turned down the job interview at the Scripps Institute. Then there's all the training. I'd just about convinced myself you wanted to apply to the space program. Instead I find you taking"—her mother's voice rose—"self-defense classes."

"Mom! Nobody's attacked me."

Her mother unknotted slightly.

She decided I'd been raped just as soon as she realized what I was doing here, Sophie thought.

"I'm sorry," she said. "You weren't meant to worry."

"I wasn't meant to know about this at all, was I?" Regina started the car and pulled out into the light fog.

Where to begin? "I'm taking the class because . . . I'm filling time. I already told you, I'm waiting to hear about a sailing gig."

"The one you can't tell us about."

"It's not the space program. I thought the self-defense class would be—"

"Fun?"

This was the point where she should say yes, but Sophie was a rotten liar. Instead, she let out her breath in a whuff.

"Useful? Like the extra math drills and the knot-tying and the triathlon training and all the time you spend just looking at pictures of, I don't know, sea snails and apparently trying to memorize every single species in the ocean?"

"A little training can never hurt, can it?"

"Training for what? If it's not NASA, and you haven't been attacked . . . are you *expecting* to be?"

That was getting uncomfortably close to the truth. "Mom, watch the road."

"I found the pepper spray on your key ring."

"It's not like that." Or it was, but hopefully that was a onetime outlier of a horrible experience.

"It's not enough that you jump out of airplanes and risk the bends and shark bites every time you go off to pursue your so-called videography career. . . ."

"Mom, please. More people are killed by cows every year than sharks."

"So you keep saying, but you're not a farmer, are you? If it's just a diving job, why the secrecy?"

"Talking about the secrecy is still talking about it."

"If you'd joined the DEA or some other government agency, you wouldn't be taking community center anti-rape classes. You'd be at Quantico, learning to defend yourself properly. With an enormous gun."

"Federal Agent Sophie, that's me." It wasn't a bad idea. Didn't Quantico have programs for civilians?

"It's not funny."

Her mother was trying to wind her up. Get her babbling—play Twenty Questions. Then she could start mining out the truth as Sophie slipped and dropped clues. It was a good strategy. They both knew she was something of a motormouth.

But Sophie had promised, under threat of having her memory wiped, no less.

And the truth might hurt more than her silence. She could imagine her mother's face if she broke: *I went looking for my birth parents.*

Can of worms, or what?

The temptation to spill it all rose, as it always did. "It's an incredibly cool gig, Mom. And important, okay? But I can't talk about it."

"Says who?"

"That would be talking about it, Mom."

"You used to tell us everything."

Her patience snapped. "Unlike you. What was it you'd say when I asked about the adoption? 'Confidentiality, in this case, is nonnegotiable.'"

Regina stamped the brakes, too hard, at a red light. A driver behind them honked as they both snapped up against their seat belts.

"I would hate to think you've been waiting your entire life to say that."

"What if I was? Twenty-five years ago you do a closed adoption, and whatever I might want to know about it, it's just too bad. Isn't that right?"

Regina's voice was thready. "We made a promise."

"Yeah," Sophie said. "Gave your word, and too bad for me. Shoe's on the other foot now, Mom."

Her mother rocked in her seat, clutching the wheel. Sophie fought an urge to open the door while the car was stopped, to just run for it.

She'd never been at odds with her parents before. Her passion for climbing and diving made them anxious, but they'd worried quietly . . . well, except for Dad hectoring her to finish her degree and do something worthwhile.

Worthwhile. Intellectual. Safe.

She stared at the dashboard, digging for something she could say that would help. But it wasn't just that she'd promised—hell, she'd signed non-disclosure agreements and gotten multiple, tiresome, finger-wagging lectures on the subject. There'd been threats of jail, of magically wiping her memories, even, if she blabbed.

Secrecy, secrecy, secrecy.

In a way, the promises were beside the point, because telling the truth would land her in a facility for the profoundly delusional. She'd found her parents, all right, and they weren't even from Earth.

"Now there's a supermodel on my damned porch."

The change of subject was so jarring that it took Sophie a second to make sense of her mother's words. "What?"

Captain Garland Parrish, of the private sailing vessel *Nightjar,* was sitting on their stoop.

This was going to make things with her parents even worse. All the same, Sophie found herself smiling.

If he was here, odds were good she was going back to Stormwrack.

CHAPTER 2

Parrish was dressed in normal American clothes: pressed tan slacks, a mustard T-shirt that hung very nicely indeed on his well-constructed frame, and a Mackenzie Sam jacket that had never quite fit right on Bram. His hair was in serious need of a cut: black, lamb's-wool curls hung every which way.

It was a relief. Sophie wouldn't have put it past him to turn up in full captain's uniform: breeches, long coat, and a bicorne hat straight out of a Napoleonic-era biopic. Stormwrackers rarely gave strangers a second glance, no matter how they dressed, but Parrish had obviously let Bram convince him that things weren't the same here.

He had her mother's polydactyl cat in his lap and was examining the extra toes on its front paws with an expression of delighted absorption.

Sophie hit the ground running, jumping out, dashing to the porch, and throwing herself into a hug. "Try not to talk too much," she murmured in Fleet. He smelled, ever so faintly, of cedar and cloves. "And no bowing."

"Understood," he replied, sounding flustered.

"Mom, this is my friend Gar . . . Gary Parrish. Gary, my mother, Regina Hansa."

"A pleasure, Mrs. Hansa." He didn't put a hand out. His accent was thicker than Sophie might have guessed.

"*Doctor* Hansa," Mom said, tone frosty.

"Gary's . . . uh, Gary's a friend."

"You said that."

"I knocked, but . . ." He indicated the house. Her father had probably been out back, contemplating his roses or listening to Chopin.

Crap, crap. Now what?

"What do you do, Mr. Parrish?"

"Oh," he said. "I came to get Sophie. I—"

Mom's eyes narrowed. "You're part of this sailing job she won't tell me about."

"I'm . . ." He frowned, processing, then seemed to realize it was true. "Yes, that's right."

Oh, no. Time to go. "Yes. Mom, Gary's here because—"

"So you're a biologist? Or another crazed thrill seeker?"

"You can't quiz him," Sophie interrupted, before he could tell her he was a ship's captain or, worse, mention *Nightjar*. Mom would do a Web search for the ship's registration, fail, and get even more upset. And everything he said was coming out in that accent that wasn't South Asian, which would have matched his looks, or German, which was what it sounded closest to. "He can't talk about it either."

Mom simmered for a second and went into the house. "Cornell," she called. "Cornell!"

They wouldn't have long. Sophie whispered in Fleet, "What are you doing here?"

"Bram tried to contact you, but his telephone is missing."

"Mom snagged it," she said.

"He was afraid that if Verena came, your parents might see she resembled you and realize you'd found your . . . your other family."

"Verena's at Bram's?"

He nodded, keeping one eye on the house.

"She's going to take us back to Stormwrack?"

"As soon as possible. We have . . ." He glanced at the sky, a habit-driven attempt to tell the time from the stars, but between the fog and the light pollution, there wasn't much to see. "Perhaps an hour."

"Has something happened?" She dialed a cab. She'd had her bags packed and ready to go at Bram's for two months. She hadn't dared leave them in her room.

Parrish opened his mouth to answer and that was when both parents came back out onto the porch.

United front, Sophie thought.

Her father taught Romantic poetry and the birth of the novel at Stanford, where he was one of the world's authorities on Shelley. He was as acerbic as any British-born academic, and in the last few years he'd been making a name for himself by writing newspaper columns that railed against what he'd always called sloppy thinking.

"Your mother says you've been taking rape classes," he said.

Sophie stifled an inward groan.

Just get through the next five minutes with a bit of grace. "Gary and I are going sailing. This is the trip I've been planning, the one I've told you about—"

"The one you've *not* told us about, to be precise. The one you've turned down the Scripps Institute for—"

"I could be gone awhile," she interrupted.

"You'll certainly be gone *awhile*." Her father's acidic repetition was a criticism of the vagueness. "The question is, how long?"

"I don't know, Dad. I'll e-mail when I can. I've told you I'm going to be hard to reach."

"And in danger," Mom put in.

This was the point where a sensible person would say, *No, no, it's just a sail, it's a sensitive research project. Blahdeeblah confidentiality, don't worry, it'll all be fine.* Sophie could never pull that off. She could barely lie to strangers. Trying to deceive her parents would be hopeless. "I have to do this. I have to. I'd tell you more if I could, I swear."

"You're not federal." Dad was looking Garland up and down. "International Space Agency?"

"It's not space," Sophie said. "And he can't talk about it either."

"Let him speak for himself."

Parrish pulled himself up as if he were a soldier at attention. "If it is within my power to keep your daughter safe, I will. You have my word."

Dottar. Her father's lips moved, committing the sound of it to memory. *Mai verd.*

She was saved by the taxicab, which pulled up behind Mom's car.

"We gotta go," Sophie said, tone bright despite the crushing guilt. She gave her father a hug, which he barely returned, and tried not to register how pale his face had gone. "I'm sorry, Dad, I am. I'd tell you if I could."

Her mom clung. "I just want to understand." She was tearing up. "Sophie, please. Tell us something."

"Sorry, sorry," she whispered, disentangling herself as gently as possible. "I'll be in touch soon. Come on, Par—Gary."

She could still feel her mother's grip on her arm as she piled into the cab and pulled Parrish in after her. Regina tried to muster a wave.

I don't deserve them. She was gut-achingly achurn with guilt. What to say? Could she have done that better? Looking back, she saw their faces through the cab's back window, taut with two completely different expressions of devastation.

"Rape classes?" Parrish inquired, as she settled against the backseat, trying to banish the memory.

"Don't, okay?" With that, she burst into tears.

CHAPTER 3

Bram was the elder statesman of a shared house occupied by a transient roster of graduate students, usually physicists and mathematicians, who were working their way through advanced degrees in the various Bay Area universities. The space was divided so that it had seven bedrooms and was known, on multiple campuses, as Dwarf House. To those in the know, Bram was, predictably, Doc.

The top floor, a converted attic, was her brother's domain. It had good light on clear days, wood floors, and spartan furnishings. The bed and wardrobe were tiny in comparison to the computer workstation and a big drafting table devoted to whatever research project was serving as Bram's latest obsession.

Her little brother was a bona-fide kid genius. He had been collecting advanced degrees like a hunter gathering game trophies, or a high-altitude climber bagging big peaks, since his early teens.

As she and Garland disembarked from the cab, one of Bram's roommates was just stubbing out a cigarette near the weathered fence. She got a look at Sophie's tear-streaked face, stepped out of her way, and then did a double take as she took in Garland.

"Can't talk, sorry," Sophie said, hustling past her.

Her adopted brother and biological half-sister were waiting in his room, talking quietly next to a pile of stuff: a duffel full of unbranded, plain-Jane jeans and shirts, a plastic bag jammed with medications, and a pair of fresh diving tanks. Everything was disordered: Verena had searched it, presumably.

Sophie had cried herself out in the cab, but at the sight of her brother she almost welled up again.

"How'd it go with the parents?"

"Big ugly scene." Sniffling, she handed over his phone. "They're freaking out, Bram."

"I'll do what I can." Parental inquisitions never bothered him; he'd been fighting with Dad since he was ten.

"We need to get going," Verena said. She was ratcheted tight with tension—no hug on offer there. "Last chance to come along, Bram."

"Tempting, but we can't both disappear at once." He shook his head. "I've got things going on here."

"Okay. We'll check in with you. Sophie, are you carrying any electronics?"

Sophie handed Bram her phone. "Want to pat me down?"

Verena looked like she was considering it.

Be that way. Sophie bent to repack her bags, putting her back between herself and her half-sister as she sorted through the collection of generic casual wear: hardy, easy to wash, suitable for hiking and camping.

As she zipped the bags shut, she glanced around Bram's room, checking for anything that might expose their research into Stormwrack.

For the past six months, Bram's worktable had been devoted to the world where Sophie's birth parents had been born. They had reconstructed a map of the world, using information gleaned on their last visit to lay out its enormous oceans and the tiny archipelagos that were its only landmasses. He'd told his roommates he was designing a map for a gaming project. He was a polymath; they just accepted that he'd take it into his head to design an MMORPG in his copious spare time.

Now the incriminating evidence—all their notes and speculations—had been packed away. Bram'd flipped the map to face the wall, instead displaying a photo Sophie had taken in Africa, impala grazing under the watchful gaze of a pride of lions. The broken pieces of Aunt Gale's brass watch were out of sight, too, probably hidden under his model of the TARDIS from *Doctor Who*. There was no visible sign that either of them had given Stormwrack much thought.

"Stop fussing with your stuff." Bram took her by the shoulders. "Be safe, Ducks."

"Don't call me that," she said, bumping her forehead against his. *Best you stay here. Safe and out of trouble.*

One last hug. "You better come back."

"I'm not on a one-way shuttle to Saturn."

"Yeah, yeah." He had that pale look, the one he got when he was trying to be brave. Like Dad, she thought, and guilt surged again. "Find some way to keep in touch."

Verena pulled a palm-size pewter clock from a satchel and drew first Parrish and then Sophie to within touching distance of both her and the stack of luggage. They fell silent, and the ticking of the timepiece took over. Sophie's vision swam, the temperature dropped, and there was a wobble that felt like her ankles giving. But it was the deck of a ship, suddenly underfoot and rocking with the rhythm of the sea.

Nightjar was a seventy-two-foot cutter with a crew of twenty-five. It had been enchanted so that it was ever-so-slightly inconspicuous, easily over-looked by casual observers.

They were out on the oceans of Stormwrack, the world whose existence she'd promised to keep from her parents—from everyone on Earth.

Excitement burned through her, banishing the physical fatigue from self-defense class, frying even the guilt over the scene with Mom and Dad. This entire world, unexplored, was filled with mysteries and new species. Its very existence raised questions about the nature of the universe. She and Bram were going to unlock them. . . .

"What's our position?" Sophie said. She had expected they'd be in or near the Fleet, the massive seagoing city that was the world's capital, but there were no other ships in sight.

"Northwater," Parrish said.

Verena shot him a look that seemed to say, pretty clearly, *Shut up.* What she said was: "We can catch the Fleet in a couple days."

Verena was seventeen, eight years younger than Sophie and, as far as anyone had known until recently, the only child of their mother, Beatrice Vanko. Beatrice had given Sophie up at birth, to the Hansas.

Sophie had only just met the two women, mother and sister, six months ago. They all three had dark brown eyes that seemed just a little big and widely spaced—Bram called them anime eyes—but Verena's face was more angular than Sophie's, her nose a bit sharper, her chin a fox tip. She wore her hair pulled back in a screamingly tight ponytail that made the eyes seem even bigger.

She packed away the pewter clock and turned to Sophie with an air of bracing herself for a disagreement.

"What's up?"

"You swear you didn't smuggle in any scientific equipment? Cameras, electronic measuring devices like that laser range finder Bram brought last time . . ."

"You've searched my bags. Anyway, the cameras are here; you confiscated them." Sophie wasn't offended; she was too happy to be here again, here in this puzzle of a world. "Are they aboard?"

"No," Verena replied. "And I'm to ask you to promise you won't do any research while you're here."

"That's ridiculous!" Sophie said. "I'm not promising anything."

"I told Annela you'd say that." Verena cast a last glance at the bags. "In that case, she says, we have to limit your access to information."

"Information about what?"

"About anything. About everything."

Verena was far too serious for seventeen. Today she wore a tunic that left her arms free for sword fighting. It hung to her thighs, over tight-fitting ankle-length breeches. Would that make it a kirtle? None of it was green in color, but Sophie found herself reminded of Peter Pan.

"That is just—are you going to bag my head, then? What does Annela think I'm going to do?"

"Find out a bunch of stuff about Stormwrack and then text it to the White House? Then a bunch of aircraft carriers will get in and wreak havoc—"

"Until you sink them using magic. Which would take about five minutes, right?"

Verena shrugged. "The government regards you as unreliable, Sophie. The few people who know about Erstwhile pretty much see us as an armed barbarian hoard, gnawing on the gates of civilization."

"If I'm so dangerous, why let me back in now?"

Verena gave the plastic bag of painkillers and sunscreen one last, sour look. "Court stuff. The case with Mom."

Sophie's birth parents had married against their family's wishes. Stormwrack had a lot of countries, all of them islands, all tiny by Earth standards—and when Beatrice Feliachild of Verdanii had married Clydon Banning of Sylvanna, their prenup had been as complex as an international treaty. It had allowed divorce but only until the marriage produced kids.

Beatrice wanted out of the marriage, badly enough to give up her firstborn, to hide her in San Francisco. When Sophie found her way to Stormwrack, the deception had blown up in her birth mother's face. She'd been charged with fraud, breach of contract, and bigamy.

"Basically, Mom's been denied bail," Verena said. "She's confined to the Verdanii sailing vessel *Breadbasket*—"

"Until her trial?"

"That's just it. The case is deadlocked. She's stuck here and my dad"—by this she meant Beatrice's second husband, in San Francisco—"he's losing his mind."

"What am I supposed to do about it?"

"It may be," Parrish said, "that your father, Sophie, could exert his influence to speed the judicial process."

"Ah ha. You're hoping I'll talk him into mellowing."

"His Honor did seem taken with you. With the idea of having a child."

"Why shouldn't he?"

Parrish smiled. "I'm sure anyone would be pleased."

Sophie found herself momentarily flustered.

Verena coughed. "There've been unofficial hints that if he could see you again, it might loosen the red tape."

"Of course I'll talk to him," Sophie said. "I got into all this to meet my birth relations, remember? I want to know Cly better."

Parrish and Verena shared a look: Beatrice's side of Sophie's newfound family seemed to have an extremely bad opinion of Cly Banning. But any reply either of them might have made was interrupted by a cry from the fore of the ship: "Coming up on the wreck, Captain!"

They rushed to the bow.

The derelict was sun-bleached, riding high in the water, and listing slightly. Its main deck was scorched and its hatches had been torn from their hinges. Salt, or what looked like salt, was sprayed across its boards. Bird droppings fouled the decks and the rails; the water around it had an oily look.

"Whitebirds. There must have been shellfish aboard," said someone behind her.

Sophie cried out, happy to have been startled. "Tonio!" She practically pirouetted into a hug.

"Ah, *ginagina,* it's good to see you!"

The ship's first mate was a compact and clever-looking man in his early twenties, relentlessly cheery and utterly loyal to Parrish. When Sophie had seen him last, he'd been carrying a weight of grief—they all had—over the murder of the *Nightjar*'s owner, Gale Feliachild, Sophie and Verena's aunt. Now that some time had passed, she could see more spark in him, a zest that had been dampened before.

"No Bram?" he asked, kissing her cheek. "What a shame."

"Not this time," she replied. *They all look better. Verena looked drawn, after Gale's murder, and Parrish . . .*

Well, with Parrish it was impossible to tell. The last time she'd seen him, she'd been flirting with a man she'd met at sea, and the good captain had taken it upon himself to get all flustered and run off—

"What's with this, Tonio?" Verena said.

"We spotted the wreck about two hours ago," he said. "After you and Captain went . . . you know, to find Sophie."

"Doesn't look like there's anyone aboard."

"No. She appears to have been attacked and abandoned. There've been rumors of raids. But the birds—there must have been something for them to eat aboard after she was set adrift, or it wouldn't be such a mess."

Sophie felt a little chill. "Not a body?"

He shrugged. "Maybe. But look for yourself."

She did. There were mussel shells aplenty, mixed in with the piles of salt, but nothing that hinted at human remains: no bones, no clothes.

"Why not burn it?" Verena said. "If someone raided it?"

"Looks like they tried." Sophie pointed at the wheel, which was blackened and scorched. A burned-out bucket sat beside it.

"Maybe it rained," Tonio said.

Sophie's attention had been drawn past the ship. "There's someone out there."

Tonio squinted, reaching for a spyglass at his hip. "Are you sure?"

Verena pointed. "There!"

He or she was about a hundred yards off, draped over a hunk of log, and for all they were moving, they might have been dead.

"Helm, come about!" Tonio ordered.

The figure's head came up, as if it had heard, and its log rolled. Distant arms flailed to maintain a grip.

Sophie didn't hesitate. She skinned off her jacket and jeans and leapt to the ship's rail, diving into the water. There was an exhilarating rush of air as she fell, then the silken, chilly kiss of the sea rippling through her T-shirt.

She came up, checked her direction, and swam for all she was worth, distantly registering a splash that meant someone had followed her. Parrish?

Don't go under, she thought at the drifting figure.

For six months, all those long days when she'd been awaiting a chance to return to Stormwrack, Sophie had trained. She'd upped her endurance training, going for a long run or a swim daily, and hit the gym hard, too, building her core strength. She'd defended her master's thesis in biology, renewed her first aid certifications, and got some extra coaching from a diving instructor.

She'd also gotten serious about meditation. She couldn't tell a therapist where she'd been or that she'd witnessed a murder. Meditating seemed the best way to deal with the nightmares and anxiety created by the violence she'd encountered here on her earlier visit.

The physical preparation, at least, was paying off. A satisfying bounty of healthy energy sang through every muscle as she cut through the water.

The figure in the water was a woman—no, a girl. She had lost her precarious grip on the log and was batting feebly at the surface of the sea. Her face was grotesquely sunburned.

"Stay calm," Sophie shouted in her most authoritative voice—and then, as she realized she'd said it in English, she switched to Fleet and yelled again.

She caught the girl by the arm, alert for panic—if she freaked out, they might both drown. Instead she coughed and obligingly went limp.

"You must save him," she begged.

"You're okay, you're all right." The girl had a huge bruise behind her left ear. Had someone hit her?

Sophie secured a rescue grip, confirmed that there was no "him" immediately handy to save, and saw Verena about ten yards behind her, swimming with a lozenge-shaped flotation device and trailing a rope. The crew had brought *Nightjar* around in a gentle curve that had halved the distance between them.

"Here." Verena tossed the float ahead and swam to catch up. Treading, they worked together to tie the girl to the float. Verena signaled the crew and they began to reel her in.

"She says there's someone else."

"Nobody in sight," Verena said, between breaths. They treaded and turned, in opposite directions, double-checking. "Maybe on the derelict?"

"Hope so."

The girl moaned.

"Just a kid," Sophie said.

Her half-sister blew salt water in a sputter. "Fourteen, fifteen. Here, that's a grown-up."

Great, I've offended her. Verena might be seventeen, but most of the time she seemed to act a testy fifty.

She had been warming to me, Sophie thought. Something's wrong.

Rather than sit out in the water chatting and losing body heat, they focused on getting their charge aboard ship. Parrish had the crew lower a sling and they eased her into it. Then Tonio dropped a net into the water and Verena and Sophie clambered back up to the main deck.

"Carry her to the forward cabin," Parrish said. "Sophie, we're displacing you before you're even settled."

"Doesn't the ship have an infirmary?" Sophie said. She had pulled a leg muscle during her last visit, and that time Parrish had carried her to his cabin.

A brief memory of that—being lifted in his arms, him settling her on his bunk—momentarily distracted her from here and now.

Parrish shrugged. He was keeping his eyes up, on her face, and Sophie realized she was soaked to the skin and dressed in nothing but a thin T-shirt and a pair of purple-striped bikini briefs.

"She said, 'Save him,'" Sophie said.

"Beal," he said. "Up the mast with the outlander binoculars—have a good look."

"Yes, Kir."

He turned to Tonio. "Take two crewmen aboard the derelict and make sure there's nobody aboard. Find the ship's log if you can."

Someone handed Sophie a heated blanket and a mug of heavily milked tea; Verena, too.

"Can I go with them?"

"I'll go," Verena said, a bit sharply.

Parrish said, "If you wouldn't mind looking at the girl, Sophie—our medical officer left us recently."

"Richler's gone? Sure, okay."

"Cannon on deck," Parrish ordered, and one of the other crew took up the cry.

A dozen questions rose to Sophie's lips, but Parrish had already walked away.

Never mind. Parrish had his hands full, and she probably could figure out the rest.

"Someone clocked the kid," she said to Verena. "You're making sure they're not aboard the derelict."

"Her attacker or the mysterious 'him' she was babbling about. They probably tossed the girl overboard and sailed off, but . . ."

"And . . . 'cannon'?"

Verena nodded as a rangy-looking guy, fiftyish, with huge eyes and black skin, stepped onto the main deck carrying a wooden keg full of black sand. "Krezzo."

"An . . . oddity?" Sophie took a second look. The man didn't appear un-usually brawny; there were no overt signs of magic about him. His hands were a little flat—scooplike, she thought.

"A transform. We say 'transform' if they look like people," Verena said, voice low. "Oddities have visible characteristics of animals or plants."

"Okay." Sophie committed the fact to memory.

"Also, it's insulting."

"So transforms are regarded as useful members of society, but oddities are kind of freaks?"

"Yeah, but—" Verena broke off, scowling. "Dammit, stop info gathering!"

"Stop me," Sophie told her. Verena didn't return her grin.

A female sailor called from below, "Kir Feliachild. Do you know where Cap'n means to put Kir Hansa?"

"Maybe she can bunk with Sweet for a day or two?" She looked at Sophie. "Now I suppose you want to know why the shuffle."

Sophie thought about what she remembered of the layout: crew quarters, guest cabins, and a galley between decks, with the hold for storage below. "If 'my' cabin is that double room aft . . . it locks from the outside, doesn't it?"

Verena nodded. "She got coshed on the head and dumped. It's possible there was a reason."

"She didn't look dangerous." Sophie felt a weird sense of dislocation. People weren't dangerous at home—well, they were, but not usually to her.

"*Nightjar* doesn't have a brig, and a lot of the bulkheads are mobile. The aft guest cabin has fixed bulkheads and a locking door; it essentially doubles as a holding cell."

"So maybe the girl is a victim, or maybe she did something to warrant getting tossed off a ship? What could possibly rate that?"

Verena didn't take the bait this time, just shrugged.

Sophie made her way belowdecks, through a hatch, down a ladder to the galley, then aft to the improvised brig. An auburn-haired sailor passed her going the other way, carrying her duffel.

"Hold up," she said, grabbing an opportunity to snatch out a dry pair of jeans and a shirt.

"I've got drugs in there, too." She slid into the jeans, managing the awkward transaction of freeing up the plastic bag full of pills and bandages.

The sailor tugged out a small hand towel. "Want me to fetch the medical officer's kit?"

"Definitely. Thanks." Giving up on the juggling act, she dropped the pills on the floor, toweled off, and switched into the dry T-shirt. "You're Sweet, right? The bosun's assistant?"

"Bosun now." The woman looked pleased that Sophie had remembered her name. "Of Redcap Island."

"I hear we're rooming together," Sophie said. "Sorry about that."

"You're welcome. Unless you snore?"

"Nobody's complained." Sophie scooped up the pills again and headed aft. "Nice to see you again."

The crew had pulled back the bedcovers but laid the girl on the floor leaving her also for Sophie to examine.

No point in putting her abed until she's dry, Sophie thought.

"Okay." Sophie said. "You're not bleeding, and we've already moved you once. There doesn't seem to be any harm in drying you off and warming you up."

She didn't have any scissors and found herself forced to untie the belt knotted around the girl's pantaloons and then fight the wet fabric off her legs.

She talked as she worked: "We're going to help you, it'll be okay, nobody's going to hurt you now."

No response.

The pantaloons were crudely made, of a wool spun from some kind of coarse animal hair. Goat? As Sophie pulled them free, Sweet reappeared and nudged an empty basin at her. She dumped them inside, the better to keep the floor dry.

The girl wore an anklet that looked to have been made of pieces of horn.

"Dry her legs," Sophie said. The shirt was easily unbuttoned, but working it over the sunburns on her arms was a delicate job. The girl moaned but did not wake.

"She'll be dehydrated as well as cold," Sweet said.

"Maybe we can get her to swallow some broth?" The two of them lifted her into bed. "Chicken? Fish? Warm but not hot?"

"I'll ask Cook," Sweet said. "Richler left a burn salve, if you don't have one."

"Thanks." She dug in the wooden box for it. It smelled of aloe pulp and maybe a bit of peppermint. She tried a patch of it on a two-inch square of healthy flesh on the girl's shoulder, waiting to see if any kind of allergic reaction manifested. When it didn't, she smeared the rest on the burns on the girl's arms, back, and face. Her inner arms, where she'd been cling-ing to the piece of driftwood, were less burned. Her hands bore a dense crisscrossing of what looked to be cat scratches. Sophie salved those, too.

Then she looked at the bruise behind her ear. If she probed it, would she be able to tell if the skull was fractured?

No. She wasn't a doctor. At home, she'd have long since called an am-bulance so they could zoom the injured girl off to a nice clean hospital for an MRI.

"Anything could have done this. You might have hit your head acci-dentally. A loose spar, tripping on deck . . ."

Her mother's words came back: *You haven't been attacked—are you ex-pecting to be?*

Was this going to be her life? Longing for a chance to explore Storm-wrack whenever she was home in San Francisco but then at hazard and perpetually culture shocked when she was here?

Sweet returned with the broth. They propped the girl's head up, just a bit, and took turns spooning tiny sips into her mouth. She swallowed about half the time; the rest dribbled out.

"I can sit with her, Kir," said Sweet, once they'd done all they could.

"Okay, thanks." Sophie's eye fell on a thick envelope sitting on the bed-side table. "Was this for me?"

"I meant to move it with the rest of your things."

"No problem," she said absently. The envelope had one of those old-fashioned wax seals—though the color was royal blue rather than red or black—and its paper was thick, more board than page.

Sophie cracked the seal and found, folded within the board, three sheets of delicate, onionskin paper, bordered top and bottom by rough edges that hinted they'd been cut with a paper knife. Two were blank. The third was crammed with dense black letters, elegantly formed, that had soaked through the page.

It was from her birth father.

Dearest Sophie, the letter began,

> *When I learned of your existence, it was barely spring. Now summer will soon be waning; autumn thrusts her eager face into the Northern Hemisphere, blowing cold winds ahead of her as the Fleet of Nations makes ready for its great annual cruise across Northwater.*
>
> *I have been much engaged with those in the Convene and the Watch who keep secrets for the government, ensuring them of my discretion and taking many oaths, and so I have been privileged (and astonished!) to learn a certain amount about the outland regime where you spent your youth.*

"What is it, Sophie?" Parrish was at the hatch.

"The Convene told Cly about San Francisco. About Earth, I mean."

"Erstwhile," Parrish corrected quietly. The few Stormwrackers who had heard of Earth at all seemed to think it was a remote island nation, somewhere the Fleet never sailed—and not a member of its 250 island nations. They thought it was a place someone could reach on a ship.

> *They tell me it is a place of wonders, unbelievable savagery, demonic entities, and wasteful habits, but that you, my child, were raised in comfort and security. For this, naturally, I am grateful.*
>
> *But sentiment is not my purpose. In your absence I have not been idle—I have, among other things, successfully documented proof of paternity. I may very nearly call myself your father now. The next step, if you wish to claim me, would be to have you recognized a daughter of my home nation, Sylvanna.*
>
> *I am on leave from my Judiciary duties; I would suggest a*

*short visit to introduce you to the place, and to acquaint us with
each other.*

*I await your soonest reply and enclose papers to that end.
Until then, I remain your eager servant,*

*The Honorable Clydon Eblis Banning, Duelist-Advocate for
the Fleet of Nations.*

Sophie refolded the letter. Parrish's eyes were on her.

"He wants me to meet his people," she said. "Go to Sylvanna, grand
tour, all that."

"As a starboard nation, Sylvanna—" Just then, the castaway moaned
and opened her eyes.

Sophie took the girl's hand. The red of her sunburn was more vivid
against the starched whiteness of the sheets.

"Where am I?" she managed. Her lips were cracked, her voice almost
gone. Her Fleet accent was thick, barely comprehensible.

"Aboard the sailing vessel *Nightjar*," Parrish told her. "We found you
in the water. Do you know how long—"

"Two nights and three days. They're ahead." An expression of desperation crossed her face.

"What happened?"

"You must make for Tibbon's Wash, Kirs. I beg you."

"Why?" Sophie said. "What's up?"

"My only—my beloved. His name is Rashad." She struggled to sit.
"Rashad swore that if I did not return from this voyage, he would take
his own life."

"Tibbon's Wash is home?" Sophie asked.

The girl nodded. "I sought the Queen's favor; it's the only way for us to
marry. Without permission . . ."

"Royal permission?" Sophie said. "Because you're in agriculture and
Rashad is . . ."

Parrish gave her a faint, surprised look.

"Rashad is every noble thing you can imagine," the girl protested. "He
is generous, *beautiful*—"

"But forbidden?" Sophie said.

"His parents own a great fishing fleet." She frowned. "How did you know I was a goatherd?"

"From your stuff."

"What are you called, Kir?" Parrish interjected.

"Corsetta."

"How did you end up in the water?" Sophie asked.

"Rashad's brother, Montaro, offered to make a sailor of me. To take me in pursuit of the Queen's favor. Our task was to tame a snow vulture. I'm good with animals. If I could do it, my way would be cleared."

Sophie asked, "What's in it for Montaro?"

"The vulture," she said. "We use their eggs in an inscription."

"And you had no luck?"

"I befriended the bird." Corsetta sighed. "Montaro's men took it and tossed me overboard."

Parrish asked, "And the derelict?"

"Nothing to do with me!"

Her reply was hasty; she was hiding something.

Parrish went on: "Someone attacked that ship, that much is obvious. Its crew—"

"I tried to swim to the derelict, to save myself. That's all I know. Please, Kir! Montaro didn't believe me about Rashad's oath. You must help. He'll die!"

Nightjar corrected suddenly; Corsetta involuntarily gripped the bedsheets, as if she felt about to tumble out of her cot. Parrish seemed unaffected; whatever was up, he trusted Tonio to take care of it.

"We must make for my homeland at full sail," Corsetta mumbled. She was losing consciousness again.

"We'll do what we can, Corsetta," Parrish told her. "Rest."

They left her to sleep.

Nightjar had been brought alongside the derelict, close enough for boarding; the two ships were very nearly lashed together. Tonio was overseeing a delicate operation; a lifeboat had been lowered to the derelict's deck. Long coils of rope connected it to *Nightjar*. The cannoneer, Krezzo, had set his arsenal aside and was standing ready at the rope.

"What is it?" Parrish asked.

"Another survivor," Tonio said, and his expression was unmistakably satisfied. He pointed at Verena, who was climbing into the lifeboat, holding a wrapped something in a blanket.

Sophie's breath caught. "Not a baby?"

"No, Kir, nothing like that," Tonio said.

"It's a cat, isn't it?" Parrish said.

She remembered him, suddenly, sitting on her mother's porch with Muffins, counting the cat's extra toes, looking sexy and sensitive, as though he were posing for a poster slated to go up on a thousand moony girls' bedroom walls.

"There's something I'm missing here."

Krezzo and the others began hauling the ropes, raising the lifeboat. As it rose alongside, the other members of the crew balanced it so that Verena wasn't bounced against the rail or the sides of the cutter. "I like cats—don't get me wrong. But from the look on all your faces, you'd think we'd found a bag of diamonds."

Parrish said, "Cats are hunters. They're a danger to birds, fish, small rodents. . . ."

"Sure, yeah." Cats transported by sailors had wrought their share of devastation on island ecosystems at home, too. They'd done incredible damage in Australia to the marsupials.

"Their kind is cursed. If a cat leaves the protection of its home isle, it must ever after be aboard a ship. No cat who leaves the protection of a seacraft may live."

"Huh?"

"If it falls into the sea or sets a paw on an island without cats, it dies," Verena explained.

By now the lifeboat was up above the rail—the crew guided it down to the deck, between mainmast and foremast. Tonio reached for the bundle and unwrapped an ordinary if emaciated gray tabby with enormous green eyes and a strangely mashed look to its ears. It had a thin orange collar, braided from goat-spun rags.

So much for Corsetta having nothing to do with the derelict.

"Captain," Tonio said, bowing. "May I present the newest member of our crew?"

Parish broke out into a dazzling grin and said, "Have Cook spoil him rotten, Tonio."

"Won't earn his keep mousing if you do that."

"It's string and fire," the cannoneer opined. "Feed'm up a little or he'll keel."

"Take it below. And keep it away from the ship's ferret until they're an even match." With that, Parrish turned. "Did you find anything else?"

"Derelict's stripped to the very boards," Tonio said. "Old bloodstains but no bodies. No papers, but I think she might have been from Tug Island."

"Why?" Sophie said.

"No reason you need," Verena said, before Tonio could reply.

Parrish gave Sophie the barest hint of a sympathetic glance. "Cast off the derelict."

"Yes, Cap'n!" Sailors scrambled to obey.

"Krezzo?"

"Ready!" The cannoneer scooped black sand from his barrel, molding it into two perfect spheres, as if he were a kid prepping for a snowball fight. He waited until *Nightjar* had cleared the ship.

"Fire when ready."

Krezzo cracked the spheres together—there was a sound like a thunderclap—and thrust his fists forward. Flames rushed up his arms and both globes seemed to explode out of his palms, leaving smoking trails in the still air. He had aimed for the main deck of the derelict and they punched through handily, spreading fire across it with a deceptively gentle puff of smoke.

"What about our young Juliet?" Sophie said.

"Who?" Verena asked.

"Miss True Love. Finding Corsetta here, near the derelict—it's possible she's one of the raiders."

"Couldn't she be part of their crew?" asked Parrish.

"If so, why not admit it?" Verena asked.

"She's lying about something. Maybe whole bunches of things," Sophie said, filling them in on the little Corsetta had told her.

"I do believe her about Romeo and a suicide pact . . . you say she's panicked," Verena said.

"Do we swing her by . . . what island was it?"

"Tibbon's Wash. Tibbs, sometimes. From the port side," Parrish said. "No, it's too far."

Sophie chewed on that. "Be a shame if the boy of her dreams did himself in before they had a chance to outgrow the infatuation naturally."

"There's nothing natural about falling out of love." Parrish frowned. "Her partners will have made for the Fleet, to sell the snow vulture's eggs. We'll hope to catch them and send a message on to Tibbon's Wash. But . . ."

"But what?"

"Corsetta is sunstruck," Parrish said. "She may yet die."

Her suspicion of Corsetta, paired with the adolescent high drama of it all, had made Sophie forget, momentarily that they were talking about a gravely wounded teenager. "We'll bring her through it," she vowed.

He smiled, ducking his head in agreement he might not have truly felt.

She spent the night watching the patient, keeping her hydrated and comfortable. Corsetta half-woke, periodically, moaning in her own language. Mostly it was a mishmash of her boyfriend's name and mournful protests—in her dreams, Sophie thought, her fear that the faraway boy would indeed kill himself was fully realized.

Do your parents know where you are? Are they worried?

The bruise behind her left ear was a black welt, colorful and knotty under her hair, a swelling profound enough to make her moan when she turned her head. Sophie had read that half the danger with such blows came on the opposite side of the skull—that when you got hit, your brain bounced, mashing up against the bone. If you had a hematoma, that was where it would be. Was that why her right eye was bloodshot?

If it was, there wasn't anything she could do about it. There were no books on brain surgery lying about.

The cat—Tonio had named it Banana—appeared once or twice to nose at Corsetta, further giving the lie to her claim to be unconnected to the derelict. It hissed at Sophie, mooched at the bowl of broth, then vanished again.

If you excluded potential brain damage, Corsetta's worst injury was to the backs of her hands and forearms. They'd been exposed to the sun the whole time she'd clung to that log, and the burns were terrible. If they became infected, she'd be facing double amputation.

At least nobody had forbidden Sophie her cache of drugs.

By morning, Corsetta was sleeping more easily and Verena had come to relieve her. "How's she doing?"

Sophie handed her the amoxycillin and said, "I'm giving her a couple pills every six hours with broth."

"We'll be Fleetside by nightfall. You should sleep."

"Yeah," she said, but despite the fact that she'd been sitting by a sick-bed in a near torpor for hours, she was suddenly keyed up and alert. Her gaze fell on a empty cabinet strapped to the wall. "Did Gale's books get moved—are they in Parrish's cabin?"

"We gave them away," Verena said. "You're not supposed to be snooping, remember?"

"I was hoping for something on treating burns in the Middle Ages."

"The antibiotics and that leftover salve are probably the best thing," Verena said, yawning.

Feeling frustrated, she headed back to the fore crew quarters.

Come on, Sofe, an inner voice—Bram's voice—urged. *You gonna let them stop us after you worked so hard to prepare?*

She cracked open the hatch of her temporary quarters. It was clean and spare, with a walk-in closet and a double bunk, a dresser, and a tiny writing desk. The bosun, Sweet, was sleeping on the top bunk.

Sophie's bag was neatly stowed under the bed.

A map of the world, with its hundreds of tiny islands, was barely visible in the dim light from the lantern in the corridor. She lay a finger on it, thinking about the neat, hand-drawn map in Bram's room.

His work's nicer, she thought. The sense of missing him was both an ache and, somehow, pleasant.

She went up to the main deck and checked the skies. They were nice and clear, all the undeniably familiar constellations present and accounted for.

"Morning, Kir," said the helmsman, Beal, politely.

"Hi," she said. "Um, are we making good time?"

A nod. "See there? It's the Cairn Sistrienne lighthouse."

"We're how far off it?"

He squinted, quoting distance and direction.

She memorized the numbers. "Dawn's how soon?"

"Two hours and fifteen, Kir."

"And," Cly's letter had said it was past the solstice, "how long since midsummer?"

"Eighteen dawns."

Ha, she thought, by our calendar, it's July ninth, then. "I bet you've got a sextant, haven't you?"

He handed it over without a second thought.

Since her first visit to Stormwrack, Sophie had spent considerable time working on her low-tech sailing skills; practically the only times she'd left dry land were to hitch rides on tall ships. She and Bram had practiced figuring out latitude and longitude the old-fashioned way. Now she took a sight on the North Star's position and its distance from the moon. Thanking the crewman, she made her way back to her cabin.

The little writing desk had one nub of a pencil, two fountain pens, and an old ballpoint from a gas station in San Francisco. There was no paper, but Cly had enclosed a few blank sheets with his letter.

She sat, took a second to recall the navigational math she'd recently acquired, and started calculating.

Figuring out where she was on Stormwrack itself was no great trick: people were only too happy to stick a pin on a chart for you, and if you could get a good look at the sky, you could calculate your location easily enough. But Stormwrack and Earth—*Erstwhile,* she heard Parrish reminding her—had identical moons and the same night sky, and approximately the same rate of rotation. As far as Sophie could tell, this world was home—the same planet, in other words. But was it a parallel dimension or simply a different time?

Would her world *become* this one, or was this some sort of an alternate?

With the information she and Bram had gathered on the last trip, they had already figured out that the Stormwrackers' measurement of latitude hadn't changed. The position of the equator was fixed, and you could only be so far north or south. The question was longitude: on Earth, it was counted from zero from the prime meridian, which passed through Greenwich in England. Here . . .

She scratched through the math, double-checked it, and stared up at the chart on the wall.

"North Atlantic." She breathed. "Northwater is in the North Atlantic."

She felt a surge of pride as she looked it over. Verena could stop her from carrying cameras and computers from world to world. She could hide Gale's library, but she couldn't stop her from memorizing facts or making deductions. With one landmark pinpointed, she could work out the location of the great nations and everything else.

Where's this lighthouse Beal mentioned? She found the spot the helmsman had indicated, *Nightjar*'s actual location near Cairn Sistrienne. Then she mentally superimposed the map of Earth overtop. Zero longitude here definitely wasn't located in England—in fact, it was at another lighthouse, on a nation called Verdanii. Her mother's home island.

That puts the Verdanii capital, Moscasipay, in the middle of where North America should be. Sophie put her hand on the edge of the map's biggest island.

Sylvanna's east and south of Verdanii. In terms of latitude and longitude, it's near . . . would that be about Tennessee?

Sylvanna was close to its nearest neighbor, far closer than most islands—possibly even within swimming distance, depending on the currents. *Haversham,* she read. There was a narrow and knotty-looking passage between the two, dotted with little points that might have been islets or an indication of a border.

She spent a few minutes polishing up her notes and then memorizing the numbers. She only needed a few fixed points for Bram. He could do all this comparison and calculation on a finer scale.

When she turned back to the writing desk and her page of math, words were scrawling themselves across the bottom of the page in a heavy, not-at-all-pretty hand.

WHAT ARE YOU DOING? STOP AT ONCE!

She pulled up to the desk, looked at her stub of pencil, and wrote: *Cly?*

GOOD MORNING, DAUGHTER! scratched itself across the page. WHERE ARE YOU?

Was there any point in concealing their position? No. She felt a weird rush of relief—for once, she didn't have to keep any secrets. PASSING THE CAIRN SISTRIENNE LIGHT.

SO CLOSE! ARE YOU WELL?

FINE. YOU? She was writing in tiny letters, to save the paper she'd half-covered in calculations, and was suddenly conscious that they were wasting their limited bandwidth on pleasantries.

"Dammit," she whispered. "Why didn't someone tell me the blank pages were for texting? Wait, I know: because Verena has orders to sabotage me at every turn."

IN GOOD HEALTH AND SPIRITS. SO PLEASED YOU HAVE RETURNED!

She couldn't help but smile. Her birth mother, Beatrice, had been violently unhappy when Sophie had approached her. Cly had been all warmth from the beginning.

WILL YOU COME TO SYLVANNA?

All warmth . . . and more than a little pushy.

THINKING ABOUT IT, she wrote. TALK WHEN I GET TO FLEET, OK?

OF COURSE. DON'T WASTE THE MESSAGEPLY.

ONE THING, she added. CREW OF A SHIP AT THIS POSITION TOSSED A GIRL OVERBOARD 3 DAYS AGO, NAME OF CORSETTA FROM TIBBON'S WASH. SEE IF THEY'VE REACHED FLEET?

MY WORD ON IT. SAFE SEAS, DAUGHTER. The last word was crammed in the corner, filling the last bit of blank space, which saved her the dilemma of how to sign off.

CYA L8R? LUV SOPHIE? SAFE SEAS BACK ATCHA?

She looked at the remaining blank page, but Cly had obviously decided to save it.

By dawn they were seeing wakelights, the small illuminated buoys that spellscribes dropped in the water behind the Fleet, marking its passage for anyone seeking to meet them. The lights were protein globes that floated on the water's surface, alight with bioluminescent sculptures, glowing roses, a horse, a dancer.

Parrish had given the order to bend every sail, catching every breath of wind to get them to the Fleet as fast as possible, the better to catch Corsetta's would-be killers before they could sail for home. Sophie told him about the page of paper at breakfast, filling him and Verena in on her conversation with Cly, watching their faces carefully to see what they might betray.

Parrish's mind, at least, was on Corsetta. "Good thinking. His Honor should be able to have them questioned."

"Not detained?" Sophie asked.

"I suspect Corsetta isn't telling the whole truth. If the brother, Montaro, is convincing . . ."

"They should give her the benefit of the doubt," Verena said. "She's half-dead down there."

"She's *not* telling us the truth," Sophie put in. "She and the cat were both on the derelict."

"So one lie means she deserves to be thrown overboard?"

"Of course not. But it does mean she might not have a boyfriend, or—"

"No. She's definitely in love," Parrish said.

Whatever that means, thought Sophie. "You can tell that just by looking at her?"

"Is it her sincerity you doubt, or is it the idea of love itself that troubles you?"

"Excuse me." Verena all but jumped to her feet, leaving her plate half-touched and all but slamming the galley hatch. Parrish looked after her, faintly surprised.

Sophie addressed herself to her breakfast. She was pretty sure she knew where the sudden sulk had come from: Verena's crush on Parrish was blindingly visible to everyone except, possibly, Parrish himself.

Every time the topic of romance comes up, we're gonna be walking on eggshells.

And she felt a little breakable now, to be honest. She'd thought Parrish might be interested in her, this spring, and she'd thought about him more than she might have guessed during her six-month exile in San Francisco. Now, being here, with a teenage romance suffocating in the aft cabin under the weight of whatever crime Corsetta had committed, and Verena abovedecks, pining and jealous, she was remembering a dozen reasons why Parrish was a bad idea.

Shake it off, she told herself. What are you gonna do, bring him home to Mom and Dad?

Parrish ran a hand along his chin, looking thinky. "You've learned to use a sextant."

"I was hoping to come back."

"To meet your family."

"And so I could . . . explore, you know." Could she explain, in any way he'd understand, how important a discovery the existence of Stormwrack might be?

Before she could frame the words, he asked, "What about knot tying?"

"Of course. You'll have to tell me what you call them—we have our own names for everything." Then, for no reason she could think of, she said, "Verena said you got rid of the books."

"Convenor Gracechild's orders about leaving research material lying in your path were, unfortunately, detailed and explicit."

"What does she think I'm going to learn?"

"Obviously, I can't say." He continued: "Gale's will left the library to a school on Zingoasis. Most of her possessions went to starboard communities with little wealth."

The cook brought a selection of savory cakes to the table. They seemed to finish a lot of meals on board this way, with unsweetened scones that had a bit of chocolate and pepper, or orange, turmeric-scented breadsticks. She wondered if that was a Fleet convention or something to do with the cook's home culture.

She scooped one up, burned her fingertips—straight from the oven!—and dropped it again. Parrish's gaze was making her uncomfortable.

"You say you lost the medic?"

"Richler returned to his home nation."

"And your bosun's gone?"

He nodded. "Gale's death was a significant change. The crew is adjusting. I meant to ask if you'd continue to serve as our medical officer while you're aboard."

"If I'm the best choice, sure. But I'm no doctor."

"Understood. How's Bram?"

Ha. Changing the subject. She sensed disquiet there, something unsaid. What had made the medic quit?

"Bram's good," she said. "Busy. And then she thought: Parrish won't tell tales about Cly, and probably asking about Sylvanna would constitute espionage or something.

But before she could get in a question, Parrish said, "Sophie, I've been wondering . . ."

"Yes?"

"The other night, on Erstwhile, you argued with your parents about . . . my Anglay has deficits, but it sounded like a combat class."

"Women's self-defense," she said, trying not to remember her parents' faces as she drove away. "So?"

"Are you learning to duel?"

She burst out laughing. "Can you see me trying to hold my own in a sword fight?"

The relief on his face might have been insulting. Verena had fought a practice match with a duelist on Erinth, and the two of them had been like something out of a martial arts movie. Verena's opponent had been magical—what was the term? A transform—he'd been covered in flames and used them to fight.

And Verena was on the *amateur* circuit. Sophie had seen Cly go through a magically altered opponent like a wood chipper through Styrofoam.

She fought an urge to squirm in her seat. How to explain? "It's—"

She'd been about to say, "It's stupid," but she'd promised Bram she'd break that habit.

"I did a lot of studying," she said, beginning again. "Celestial navigation, a bunch of math I was just okay on. The knots, and I've been swimming, running, biking . . ."

"Excellent preparation."

"The self-defense class was . . . okay, not a whim, exactly. It was obvious, before, that things happen here. Violence."

"Gale's murder," he said. "John Coine's attacks on Bram and your-self."

"I don't have the slightest illusion that I could ever be a fighter."

"Don't underrate yourself," he said. "You're athletic and have excellent reflexes. I wouldn't have said 'never'—"

"Okay. But how much time would I have to spend practicing, just to be as good a fighter as, say, Verena?"

"Hours. Every day, hours."

"For years. That's not a good use of my time. I'm a photographer and a biologist."

"Then why take a combat course at all?"

"All the things I like to do—climbing, diving, hiking," she said, "your life depends on the people you're with. You trust yourself to ropes someone else fixed to a rock wall. If your oxygen mix goes off and your dive partner doesn't notice, you're toast. Cooperation equals survival, you know?"

He nodded. "A duty to your crew, we say."

"If all of us are going to end up in the occasional . . . brawl? Dustup?"

"Brawl." It was an English word. . . . He repeated it, apparently just to savor the sound.

"I don't want to fold like a sack of laundry whenever you and Verena find yourselves in trouble. I don't want to be a liability. So I was . . . I dunno, trying to get comfortable with hitting people." She remembered punching practice in the community center. *Commit, commit, commit.*

It was so removed from the reality of fighting, in this world, that she half-expected him to laugh. Instead, he broke out one of those dazzling, movie-star smiles.

"You've given a good deal of thought to what might be required, were you to stay here."

She opened her mouth to answer and felt anew the surge of guilt over her mom and dad, and that competing sense of weirdness. As Bram had put it: *What the hell, Sofe, are you really gonna move to a backwater Narnia without CAT scans or DNA sequencing or the Internet?*

"Stormwrack's not as violent as all that, if it helps," Parrish said. "Fleet society has become very civilized since the Cessation."

He meant the international peace that had prevailed since the defeat of a fleet of pirates, 109 years before. "Is that so?"

"It's merely that you've fallen in with something of a specialized community."

"Spies and dueling judges."

"Speaking of your father," he said. "You won't have anything to fear aboard *Sawtooth*."

Somehow that rankled. "I said I was preparing, not that I was *afraid*."

But some little noise abovedecks had captured his attention—he gave her one of his obnoxious, polite, not-really-engaged-anymore bows and excused himself.

She listened for a second, heard him mounting the ladder to the main deck, giving orders, nothing unusual. Then curiosity overcame her: she followed. "What is it?"

"A ship," he said, pointing.

"Are we being shadowed?"

"No, it's headed away from us," he said, handing her the spyglass.

The craft was at the farthest edge of the spyglass's field of vision. It was double-masted, with a strangely spherical wheel, and smaller than the derelict they'd encountered. It was also making in the opposite direction as fast as it could.

"No name on the stern," Sophie said, wishing for her camera. "They're running without lamps, even though it's not fully dawn."

"Yes."

"They don't want to be seen."

"Maybe they're being hunted or are bound on some kind of mischief."

"Could they be Corsetta's attackers?"

"No. She said they'd headed to the Fleet days ago."

"Pirates? I thought they'd all gone legit."

"There are still raiders. Desperate people of various stripes," Parrish said.

"Exiles, outlanders, fugitives," Verena added.

"They could be the ones who sunk the derelict?"

"Perhaps," Parrish said.

"But we're not chasing them?"

"No," said Verena, "We'll note the sighting in the logs—position, direction, what have you. If someone's after them, we'll report it."

As the sun continued to rise, the morning stretched pleasantly: the wind was brisk, and though they were out in the open ocean there was plenty to observe aboard ship. Sophie began studying each of the ship's two dozen crew members, taking note of everything from scars and jewelry to turns of speech and general mood. She hunted down the ferret, which was also a transform: its tail was a live snake. It seemed to like her: she fed it bits of fish and worked to transcribe the magical blue text lettered onto its abdomen.

Corsetta was unconscious for most of the day. She appeared to be weakening; her pulse was light and irregular, her breath unsteady. No seizures yet, but her eyes were getting wandery in a way Sophie didn't like at all.

She and Sweet managed to get a little more broth into the girl during one of her more wakeful stretches. Afterward, she slept, and Sophie took advantage of the break to go below and see if her diving suit was still in the hold.

The trunk looked just as she'd left it six months before, and inside, her wetsuit and dry suit were in perfect shape. Her mask was dusty but the seals were fine.

All good, of course. As was the nylon rope and her half-dozen carabiners.

When she had come before, the trunk had been packed with electronics: DSLR camera, video camera, waterproof housings, and a smartphone, not to mention half a dozen scientific instruments of Bram's. Now all of that was gone except for the solar battery chargers.

She felt a pang of melancholy she couldn't quite account for. Neither here nor there, she thought. I don't belong here, but I can't just live in the real world now.

This was frustration at being unable to explore, she told herself. Explore, study, and record. She wouldn't be spending all this energy navelgazing if she could just answer a few questions instead of digging up more.

She opened the trunk next to hers. It was full of stuff that had to belong to Verena—clothes, fencing equipment, and an MP3 player.

"Double standards," she muttered.

The next trunk, an old wooden box, held human bones—a single skeleton, from the pieces.

She looked this over for a minute, trying to figure out why it was aboard. The bones had a few healed breaks: one wrist, one rib. Under the skull she found a ribbon-bound roll of filled-out donation forms, indicating the remains were the bones of a magically enhanced pipe player and had been bequeathed to a music school on the island Zingoasis.

Music? She tapped two of the bones together experimentally, eliciting two notes, both something like what you might get with a tuning fork.

The bioluminescent wakelights heralding their approach to the Fleet got smaller as they closed the distance between them. They grew with time, like bubbles, until they either burst or sank, so the farther away they were from having been set asea, the bigger they got.

By afternoon there were also miniature ships, maybe five feet in length and made of wood so soft that one of them splintered when it hit the *Nightjar*'s prow. The models were laden with things that symbolized summer: unripened sheaves of wheat, emptied butterfly chrysalises, and hundreds of flowers.

Next they found themselves coming upon fishing boats, first a few, then twenty, then a hundred, all abustle with activity, men and women hauling tons of protein from the water. As afternoon gave way to evening, they found themselves sailing through cold water thick with cod. Tonio and two of the other crewmen lowered a net, just for a minute, and pulled up perhaps twenty fish, great shining animals, unblemished and thrashing vigorously as they filled the air with the smell of the sea.

They sorted through them quickly, tossing back anything that weighed less than twenty pounds, and then ran them below to the galley, presumably so the cook could salt them. Sophie claimed the net when they were done, scavenging samples of seaweed, a sea jelly, two eels, and a small ray while Verena alternately fumed and pretended not to see her.

"Fleet of Nations, dead ahead!"

The winking of hundreds of aft lanterns came into view, clarifying as the sun set.

A hang glider shot overhead and a lanky teenager dropped to the ship's main deck. "Compliments to the captain and crew!" the daredevil said, bowing. "I bear an invitation for Sophie Hansa and Verena Vanko Feliachild of the Verdanii."

He held out a sealed envelope to Sophie.

"Well?"

She tore it open. "It's . . . dinner."

"Dinner with Annela Gracechild and Cly Banning," Verena said, reading over her shoulder. "That'll be fun."

"Like a root canal. Why not Beatrice, too?"

"She's under house arrest on *Breadbasket*."

"Oh, right. Why not go to *Breadbasket*?"

"His Honor wouldn't feel welcome there," Parrish said. "And you agreed to keep your distance from the Verdanii."

This was a polite way of reminding Sophie that she'd repudiated Verdanii citizenship, to the point of signing a crazily long agreement promising she wouldn't set foot on their soil or any ships of theirs unless she was specifically invited.

Sudden curiosity itched her: Wasn't that overkill?

"There's also . . ." Verena seemed to be debating. "We haven't told Mom that we're doing this."

"Beatrice doesn't know I'm back?"

Verena shook her head.

"Why?"

"She can't veto the plan if she doesn't know about it." She flushed, seeming to dare Sophie to lecture her.

"Well, we can bring guests," Sophie said. "Want to come, Parrish?"

Verena stiffened.

Parrish scratched his head, considering.

"Don't jump to say yes," Sophie said.

"Your father dislikes me."

She felt an odd rush of relief. "Right. It's not fair to ask."

"I'd be glad to attend you," he said. "I'm just not sure my presence will aid with the task at hand."

"It's not a task," she said. "It's getting to know all you guys who are my birth family."

He gave her that odd, balked look. "Technically, I'm not—"

"Shut up, Parrish. Of course you're part of the family," Verena said. "Sophie's right: you have to come. If Annela and Cly start in on each other, we may need a referee."

CHAPTER 4

They sailed into the Fleet from the rear, first passing a three-masted schooner bristling with youngish sailors, all clad in the ochre breeches and sand-colored shirts that were the navy's day uniform. The ship was laden with equipment, armed not for war but disaster: it had extra lifeboats and a range of floats, pumps for water cannons to fight fire, ladders, and a big tower with a spotlight.

"Rescue vessel?" Sophie asked.

"*Shepherd*," Verena said. They had climbed up into the rigging for a better view. "The unofficial entry point to the city."

Tonio and the sailor on watch aboard *Shepherd* exchanged a complicated series of halloos as they sailed past. Fifteen minutes later, the reason for all the rescue equipment became obvious, as they encountered the ships at the rear of the Fleet. Some were barely more than leaky rowboats, hardly fit for scrap, let alone oceanic crossings.

Bumboats, Sophie remembered. Tonio called them bumboats.

The little eight- and ten-footers were crewed by thin, perpetually sunbaked people, many of whom raised wares in *Nightjar*'s direction as they passed.

"Buy a cooking pot, Kir, finest metalwork from the Isle of—"

"Mussels and clams, mussels and clams from the Tallon territorial limit."

"Ram husks for mining magic!"

"Tunics and pantaloons, dyed on Gittamot!"

"Fortune-teller! Know your futures, Kirs!"

"Ready girls, ready boys, take your ease, ready to please—"

"Smokes and powders!" The reek of marijuana coming off that vessel made further explanation of that one unnecessary.

As *Nightjar* glided through the vast oceangoing slum, the boats became steadily bigger and, by their look, more seaworthy. People stopped hawking their wares by shouting, relying instead on placards hung port and starboard, signs with business names and pictures of whatever they had on offer. Individual shops first, but then the ships got big enough to house what were effectively apartment blocks and strip malls. In time they were passing ships as densely active as an urban street at home.

"*Gatehouse* ahead!" Tonio shouted.

"Match course and speed," Parrish ordered. "Ready to accept pilot."

"This would be where the suburbs become the city," Verena said. "If someone says between *Gatehouse* and *Shepherd*, they mean . . ." She gestured to their rear.

Sophie nodded, keeping her mouth shut. She didn't want Verena to remember she wasn't supposed to be playing tour guide.

They were coming abreast with another craft as obviously official as *Shepherd*, filled, as *Shepherd* was, with uniformed sailors. This ship was armed: a half-dozen sailors on her quarterdeck were built like *Nightjar*'s cannoneer. They stood at the ready, near barrels that, presumably, held the same sand Krezzo had used to form his magical cannonballs.

"Run out the plank!" someone called.

A rotund fellow trotted toward the rail of *Gatehouse*, looking for all the world as though he was going to run off the edge of the deck. His beard hung in a thick blue-black braid to his navel; his arm was tucked over his chest to keep it from flying off every which way.

As he approached the *Gatehouse* rail he seemed to rise, as if he'd been on a ramp, and then he sprang up, bouncing on what turned out to be a small, square trampoline.

There was a loud *buh-buh-buh twang!*

Whisks of silver light enveloped him as he shot up, straight into the air. The man curled, rolling in midflight; then he landed with a sprightly bounce on *Nightjar*'s deck and presented himself to Parrish before taking the helm.

It was evening, and by now the Fleet was little more than a collection of lanterns on rails and sails, stretching in every direction. Overhead, the stars were coming out, barely dimmed by the thousands of candleflames. The breeze coming off Northwater was chilly and invigorating.

"Kir Sophie!" That was Sweet, belowdecks, her shout muffled by the length of the ship and the heavy wood floor. "Help!"

And a shriek: Corsetta.

She and Verena clambered down, racing to the improvised brig.

The girl had held her own during the day—she'd slept a lot, managing to keep down the broth and some gruel. The burns on her arms had— perhaps thanks to the amoxycillin—seemed to be free of infection. But she'd been feverish and nigh delirious, and the head wound—

As Sophie crossed the threshold into her cabin, she saw Corsetta's skin flowing, as if it were melted wax.

The girl wailed as the crisped parts of her hands and fingers liquefied into red and brown smears. The color diffused into the general flow of her skin, melding into her tan in a way that reminded Sophie of painters mixing pigments.

"Magic?" she asked.

"Yes." Verena grasped the girl by the shoulders. "Corsetta, listen to me. Someone's laid an intention on you."

"Impossible," she gasped. "It—"

"Does it hurt?" Sophie said. "I might have something—"

"Tickles, just tickles." She said it through clenched teeth. "But, no. Nobody knows my full name—ahhhhh!"

"What about your parents?"

"Dead."

Orphaned at fifteen. Poor kid. "Okay, your boyfriend?"

Her eyes snapped open. "Rashad would *never* tell—"

"So he does know your name?" Sophie demanded.

Twisting, Corsetta groaned in a way that suggested pleasure, not pain. Sophie felt a stab of embarrassment as the girl curled in on herself.

Even so, Sophie was braced for the worst. She had seen men scripped to death, murdered by a spell that killed them from afar.

Corsetta took in a long, shuddering breath as her waxy skin flexed once and then seemed to snap into place, tanned, healthy, leaving her without so much as a pimple. She sat upright, catching at the sheets just in time to preserve her modesty, and felt for the injury on the back of her head.

Up on deck, Sophie heard the *fa-twang* of the trampoline again, the thump of someone landing above.

"I've been healed!" Corsetta said. "You're right, Kirs. My beloved must have . . ."

"Yes?"

She shrugged, not quite pulling off the attempt to seem casual. "Someone must have told him I was in danger."

Still hiding something. Whether Corsetta was an orphan or not, Sophie's sympathy evaporated.

"I will see Rashad again." Corsetta's tone was thoughtful, almost surprised.

"That's great," Verena said. Her enthusiasm seemed forced. "We'll find something for you to wear, okay?"

"To love!" She grabbed up the glass of water on the bedside table, toasting.

"Cheers. Come on, Sophie." Verena tugged her out. "Did that seem fishy to you?"

Sophie nodded. "But she's gonna live—that's good. She even gets to keep her burned hands."

"Yeah."

"You don't think it was the boyfriend who had her cured?"

"If he's Corsetta's age, he might be reckless. Or . . . I suppose his family could have beaten her name out of him."

"Why would they restore Corsetta if it's his brother who tossed her overboard?"

Verena shrugged.

"I totally think she's up to something. But she's not going to drop dead. That's a win, right?"

"Yes." There was a visible change as Verena let that sink in. Her shoulders came down and she smiled.

"If the girl is healthy, I'm afraid she's under arrest."

Sophie whirled, surprised.

Her birth father, Clydon Banning, was standing next to Parrish.

"Child—" he began, and then he caught himself. She'd asked him, more than once, not to call her that. "Forgive me. Dear one. May I?"

He opened his arms—Cly was a serious hugger—and Sophie went willingly enough.

Her birth father was a tall whip of a man, keen-eyed and lean, with an air that was both wolfish and genial. He embraced her heartily, planting a kiss on what was threatening to become his usual spot atop her head, and bowed to Verena. "Kir Feliachild," he said. "Fair seas to you. How are you keeping?"

Something in his tone, too much innocence, hinted that he knew the answer.

Verena flinched, just a little. "Just fine. Thanks. Did you say Corsetta's to be arrested?"

He flicked a hand. "The Watch detained the crew of *Waveplay,* as Sophie requested. They claim your rescuee attacked their paymaster and tried to make off with their cash box. They don't know how she ended up adrift."

"Do you believe them?" Sophie said.

Cly looked surprised. "Does it matter? Once they're all detained, the Watch will learn the truth. If she's no longer dying, there's no great import."

"It's attempted murder."

"And thus a problem for the courts," Cly said. "They can always duel it out if they're in a hurry."

"You don't care, in other words."

"Officially, I cannot. Well, Sophie, have you decided to see Sylvanna with me?"

She was, irrationally, irked. "I dunno. Have you decided to stop jerking Beatrice around?"

Awkward silence spilled from this. Cly's eyebrows climbed into his hairline.

"Oh, what?" Sophie said. "We were going to sit around a banquet table with Annela, eating mutton and crumpets, with all of you actively hating each other and nobody wanting to talk their way around to business? I'm not doing that."

Cly laughed. "Put that way, I have to say it does sound like a terrible way to spend an evening."

Parrish said, delicately, "I'm sure you both underestimate your charms."

"Yeah, right. Cly, if it happened to be the case that Beatrice could get sprung from house arrest—ship arrest?—could she be released on bail? Do you have bail?"

"We do," he said. "You understand, of course, that I have no role in Beatrice's case beyond that of plaintiff. My position in the Judiciary—"

"Yes, yes, you're unconnected to her getting confined. But if she was, miraculously, to get bail, what would you want for that?"

"Come to Sylvanna," he said promptly. "See my estate, meet my neighbors, attend the Highsummer festival, and consider a possible role within the Banning family."

"Okay. So—you let Beatrice go, then I come on a visit—"

"You visit me *while* the Judiciary reviews Beatrice's status."

Before she could reply, Sweet and the cook appeared abovedeck.

"She's gone, Kirs," Sweet said.

"Excuse me?"

"Corsetta's cabin is empty."

Cly frowned. "Did you not have her under guard?"

Parrish said, "The cabin was locked. Sweet, have the ship searched."

"She's a kid," Sophie said. "She's harmless."

"Let's hope you're right." Cly returned his attention to Sophie. "Well? Do we have an agreement?"

She bit her lip. "It's not horrifying there, is it? Women can vote and own stuff? I could invite Bram someday and he wouldn't get harassed for being . . . how did you guys put it?"

"Inclined to men," Tonio said in a pointed tone—he was gay, too. "And Sylvanna—"

"That's enough, Tonio!" Verena barked.

"Inclined." Sophie studied her birth father's face as she said it, but there

was no sign that Bram's being gay was news to him, let alone that it per-
turbed him at all.

"Invite Bramwell along, if you wish. There will be no difficulty for him,
I promise. Every adult on Sylvanna has a right to physical security, to earn
a living, and to self-determination. The latter clause of our constitution
covers romantic inclinations."

A rush of relief. "Then what are you guys all so wrenched about?"

"You'll need someone to draft an agreement." Verena's voice was tight.

"Will we?"

"You will," Verena said. To Cly, she added, "Everything aboveboard and
on the record, Your Honor."

He gave her the sort of look he might offer a beagle if it had peed on his
shoe. "Of course. And now, since dear Sophie has so bluntly noted that you
and I and your cousin Gracechild would make a thoroughly dreary dinner
party, I think I'll excuse myself and leave you all to catch up. Don't worry,
I'll send my apologies to our hostess. I believe she's fond of apricots?"

"Uh . . ." Sophie said.

"Hush." He waved airily. "We'll have time, you and I. You deserve an
unspoiled evening with your Verdanii relations."

Is that what I deserve?

"I'll draw up the document Kir Feliachild proposes so your lawyer can
examine it." With an extravagant bow, he sprang to the rail of *Nightjar,*
whistling for a ferry. He was gone a moment later.

"Jeez," Verena said. "What are we going to do with ourselves now that
you saved us from a night of Annela looking daggers at His Honor?"

Sophie grinned. "I'd say I've earned a favor."

"You would, would you?"

"Before dinner, we have some time to kill?"

Verena nodded.

"There must be a market or two in a city this size. Maybe even a mall?"

"You want to go *shopping*?"

"I so do," Sophie said.

"You're going to collect more info about the Fleet."

"What are you going to do, Verena, lock me in my cabin? Come on,
you tried. Tonight at dinner, I'll tell Annela you tried. You must be ex-

hausted with how hard you've tried. Unless you lock me up or knock me out, I am gonna see things."

Her sister gnawed her lip.

"Besides, if you don't come, I'm still going to go, and who knows what I'll find out then?"

That got her a laugh. "Okay, you win."

They ferried out beyond *Gatehouse*—into the suburbs, Sophie reminded herself—and into what looked, from the state of the ships, to be a wealthy section of the civilian Fleet. Verena directed their pilot to a gleaming white swan of a ship whose main deck was alive with the sights and smells of a fish and produce market. Men and women running the carts were dickering with white-dressed chef's assistants who wouldn't have looked out of place at home. Negotiating, clasping hands upon agreement, they'd hand over baskets of shellfish, cod, butterfish, sardines, and tuna. The fish were huge, fresh-looking, and healthy.

"Does anyone make sashimi or sushi here?"

"Yeah," Verena said. "It's not served with wasabi. Otherwise, same basic idea. You don't want the food market, do you? What are we doing?"

"First, a jeweler."

"Okay." Verena led her belowdecks into what could very well have been a cruise ship mall, illuminated by lanternlight but otherwise about what you'd expect—a long corridor with a central promenade lined with shops.

The jeweler seemed more than happy to buy the gold and copper chains that Sophie had been wearing around her neck for months, offering her a scattering of heavy coins, each minted with the image of a ship on one side and a flag on the other.

"Your name, Kir?" he said, eyeing her blue jeans with an air of caution.

"Sophie Hansa."

"Of?"

"Of what?"

He yanked back his hands, as if the chains or she were toxic. "I don't trade with outlanders."

Sophie's face warmed. She glanced around, half-expecting that everyone in the market would be staring at her weird clothes, maybe even pointing and whispering. But no—almost everyone within earshot was conducting business normally, and the one woman who'd turned to see what was going on turned away hastily, probably fearing she'd be caught giving in to the cardinal-sin impulse of curiosity.

"I'll stand for her. Verena Feliachild, Verdanii."

"Very well." He dipped his head to Sophie in a way that seemed to mean "no offense" and handed the coins over.

Maybe it'll be Sophie of Sylvanna soon, she thought. The thought came with a thrum of guilt, a sense that she was doing wrong by her parents, back in San Francisco.

"What about these?" Sophie dug out an old wallet filled with little gems: a couple of diamonds, some semiprecious stones—turquoise, amethyst—and about six opals.

The jeweler raked through them with a look of studied indifference on his face.

"What's the point of this?" Verena said.

"Getting a bit of money of my own," she said.

"Opals?"

"Gifts from over the years. Because of my middle name. They aren't heirlooms, Verena."

"Two of these might be all right for magic," the jeweler interrupted. "The rest, just for trinkets."

"Nonsense," Verena replied. "They're nice and symmetrical. They're great for spells."

Sophie entrusted the haggling to her sister, drifting on to the next vendor with her handful of coins. She paused at a blown-glass goldfish bowl. Three bright yellow creatures swam within; they were only the length of her finger but had the shape and gaping lionlike mouths of the silk dragons she'd seen at Lunar New Year's celebrations in Chinatown. As she slowed, they broke the surface, letting water stream from their tiny jaws, and began to let out a whistle, the three of them pitching their notes so they formed a chord.

She found herself smiling. She extended her hand toward the bowl—

The vendor caught her just as one of the fish made a sharp-toothed snap for her fingertips.

"Bevvies, Kir? Brighten your day, bring good fortune."

She shook her head—both to say no and to shake off the odd, soporific effect of their song. It would be amazing to have live specimens of pretty much any species, but she needed somewhere to keep them first. She crossed to what looked like a bookstore, searching through the collection of bound diaries and ribbon-bound bundles of writing paper.

"No books—these are blank?" she asked.

"Our bookseller's ma took sick," the vendor replied. "Went back to her homeland."

Had Verena deliberately chosen a market without a bookstall?

"May I ask you something?"

His face took on a suspicious cast. That wariness, again, of curiosity. Was it simply cultural conditioning, or was magic at work here, somehow? Courtesy or the customer service impulse won out. "Of course, Kir."

"I got a letter recently that came with a sheet of paper that—well, I wrote on it, and someone from another ship wrote back."

"Messageply." He nodded.

"How does that work? I want some for my brother."

"The pages must be prepared by a specially scribed paperworker and be of a sheet." He pointed out a locked case with a giant, two-ply roll of what looked like toilet paper. "The sheets are then picked apart and held by the separate parties. They are two halves of the same thing, you see."

"Sounds like quantum entanglement."

"I don't know this term 'quantum,' Kir."

Bram would be fascinated. "To use something like that to contact my brother, I'd have to send him the other half of a page already in my possession?"

"There are other ways to message. Cheapest is to scribe a pair of chitterbugs hatched of one casing. You teach them a tapping code, tell one, the other picks up the rhythm."

"Tapping code—like Morse?" She ran out a series of dots and dashes.

He nodded. "Wealthy folk prefer birds who'll talk."

Verena and Annela would definitely notice if she took up bird ownership.

Verena had concluded the swap for the opals; Sophie selected a couple journals, a pen, and a packaged collection of items, labeled in a language she didn't speak, that caught her eye because it seemed to contain the skin of a passenger pigeon. "How much for these?"

"Five, Kir."

She handed over a coin as if she knew what it was worth and waited. After a beat, he gave her a bunch of smaller coins.

Verena handed her an inconveniently heavy bag full of money.

"How much does this come to?"

"Think of it as about four hundred bucks, assuming you can learn to haggle."

"I'll give it a try."

"Where to now?"

"Tons to observe in a market, am I right?"

"You're not supposed to be observing at all," Verena said.

"What are you going to do, put my eyes out?"

Verena's objection, she thought, seemed halfhearted. Had she surrendered to the idea of the shopping trip a bit easily? That would suggest she was hiding something specific.

She started down the mall as she mulled that over, passing a cobbler and dressmaker, then heading down a level and finding herself in front of a sign that read, POWDERER."

"Powders?"

"My lips are sealed."

"For spells," Sophie said. "I bet this is inscription ingredients."

The powderer's shop was filled with clay jars, all corded and sealed with wax, and each with a tidy label written in Fleetspeak: talc, mixed coral, red coral, black coral, obsidian, whalebone, specter, antelope, basker (whatever that was) human skull, human tooth, human ash male, human ash female, quartz, red granite, black granite, agate.

There were packages here, too, like the one she'd just bought with the bird corpse. "Is this—?"

"Not answering," Verena said.

Next to the powderer's was a place that sold scales and hair, then a sanguarium.

"Sanguarium," she repeated. "Blood vendor."

A whole shop full of labeled blood samples. All she needed was permission to do research and someone to run DNA.

"Fine, yes," Verena said. "Blood sellers. Sophie, what are you up to?"

"Look, I'd have to be dead to not notice things about Stormwrack, am I right?"

"Yes, but—"

"Telling me not to do science is just dumb. Not taking any hard information home until Annela gives permission, I understand that. Not sharing what I see with anyone but Bram—I can toe the line. I hate not having a camera, but I'll survive. But I'm still a tourist here."

"It's just shopping," Verena said, but Sophie's attention had been caught by a poster, printed on a recycled scrap of sail.

It was a crude image of a small sloop with an odd, almost dome-shaped wheel and two masts.

"That looks like the ship we sighted."

"I asked the jeweler about it," Verena said. "He says it was stolen from the dockyards at Tug Island."

"Tonio thought the derelict came from Tug, too."

"There've been a few disappearances. They figure whoever made off with the sloop is sinking ships."

"We reported seeing it, right?"

"Parrish will," Verena said.

A bloodcurdling shriek, from what looked to be a feather store, interrupted them.

The creature in the front display cage was large, on the scale of an albatross—an enormous seagull with a wingspan, she estimated, of over nine feet. It was white but for a band of black over its eyes and mottled patches of brown behind its shoulders. Its feet were typical gull feet: pink, webbed, stunningly huge.

"This is Corsetta's snow vulture," Verena said.

"How do you know it's hers?"

"They're rare. There won't be two."

The vendor had a harassed look. "She's missing the girl who charmed her," he snapped at a would-be customer. "Won't lay."

"It's the eggs that are important in the inscription?" Sophie asked.

Verena nodded. "It's said that only half of their young survive in the wild. Supposedly there are gifted . . . I dunno, call them bird whisperers, who can convince them to give up some eggs in exchange for having the rest hatched in a nice warm coop with lots of food."

"Cooperative relationship, with the perk of a higher survival rate," Sophie said. "What do the eggs do?"

"Snow vulture eggs enable a human to fly," Verena said. "Not gliding, like the taxikites. They're actually winged, like angels."

"*That* I have to see."

"Good luck if the bird's not laying."

"If it's pals with Corsetta, she might turn up here."

Verena circled in place, scrutinizing the vendors, the stalls, the customers. "Yeah. They're watching for her."

Sophie wondered if that was a good thing.

"Dammit, you've got me telling you things again," Verena said.

"So? Your official job is to go back and forth and carry stuff to Erstwhile. If there are people who move between worlds, why can't I be one of them?"

"You want a visa now?" Verena said. "It's not me you have to convince."

"Correct me if I'm wrong, but if I go hitching my star to Cly's family wagon, I'm going to have all kinds of chances to apply for travel visas."

"You want to stay on Annela's good side, threatening to play the Judiciary off the Watch is not the way to go."

"I'm not trying to pick fights with anyone, Verena. I just want a chance to see—"

"See, explore, study, record—"

"—understand!"

"And then what? Publish? And what about your parents? Are you really going to spend your life here chasing every shiny science thing you see without ever telling them?"

Sophie groaned. "I don't know."

They paused in front of a small array of lumpy nuggets and toys for pets—Verena bought some treats for *Nightjar*'s ferret, along with a small sealed pot full of crickets for its snake-head tail—and lingered over a stall of felt and fabric hats, many of them inscribed, either on brim or band, with neatly stitched or painted lettering in the magical alphabet, spellscrip.

Magic on Stormwrack was all written—you took eye of newt or other ingredients, along with someone's full name, and wrote up what the locals called an intention. It could do anything from straightening your teeth to killing you on the spot. Most people kept their middle names hidden from all but a few trusted family members or friends.

Sophie hadn't known this when she came to Stormwrack six months ago, and by the time she figured it out, the pirates had gotten hold of her name.

The sisters continued past the mages and down to a deck market that was all weapons—swords and knives, maces, cudgels and whips and bows.

"See anything you like?" Verena meant the swords, but Sophie's eye had wandered further, to a stall filled with stonewood daggers. She saw a familiar blond head within the crowd.

What are the chances? she thought. A stir of feelings, some good, some anxious, assailed her. Did she want to see him? Was it a good idea?

"Sophie?"

She turned, trying to urge Verena back to the stairway. "I'm not going to learn to use a sword, Verena. I'd be a hazard."

"Fights happen."

"Maybe I'll get one of those telescoping cop batons," she said. She didn't mention the little canister of bear spray on her key ring. Verena had missed it in her search.

"That would be smarter."

Sophie had circled so her back was to the blond head, but her jeans had, once again, given her away.

"Sophie Hansa!"

It was Lais Dariach.

CHAPTER 5

Lais was a horse breeder from an island nation called Tiladene, a place where families were run as communes that owned businesses and where the sexual morals were profoundly relaxed. On her first visit to Storm-wrack, Sophie stumbled onto a conspiracy to invade the country and murder Lais: a neighboring nation, Ualtar, had taken offense at his trying to breed a spider exclusive to their microclimate.

Does everyone hate science here? she thought, as he strode across the market, giving them both a deep bow. He let his eyes roam up Verena's stiff, upright, seventeen-year-old form.

"You remember my little sister," Sophie informed him, more frostily than was probably necessary. "She's good with a sword."

"I'd better mind my weaponry then," he said, kissing Verena's hand and then sweeping Sophie into an exuberant crush. "How fares the heroine of all Tiladene?"

Lais looked like he'd been primped to model for the cover of a romance novel: he had the Hercules hair, the whole-body tan and baby blue eyes, the tight breeches and the flowing white peasant shirt. A leather vest overtop did nothing to hide chest muscles worthy of a bodybuilding competition.

He was smart and easy-going. There was nothing dark underneath his charm, just friendliness. Lots of friendliness.

"I'm hip-deep in family conspiracies and international politics," Sophie said.

"Same thing, in your case."

Inspiration struck. "And apparently I'm in need of a lawyer. Can you hook me up?"

"Annela—" Verena said.

"Annela will pick someone who's all about the government's best interests," Sophie said. "I need someone who's in it for me."

Lais beamed. "Mine's a horse swapper, devious beyond measure. Of Tiladene and feared round the Fleet. I would love to introduce you."

"Great. How do we go about—"

"You should come to dinner tonight, Lais," Verena blurted.

"Should he?"

"Sure. He knows the score, right? You spilled the truth about Erstwhile to him."

"Well, yeah. But we already invited Parrish."

"*You* invited Parrish. I get a guest, too."

Lais beamed. "I'd be honored. Verdanii hospitality is legendary. Sophie, I'll see if I can get you an appointment with Bimisi. Who are your kin, little sword sister?"

"It's Verena." She dug out her invitation. "Of the Feliachilds."

"Until later, then," he said, saluting with it before vanishing into the crowd.

Dismayed, Sophie watched him go. "Why did you do that?"

"Do what? I thought you liked him." A hint of smugness there.

"I do better with shipboard flings when they're . . . you know, now you see him, now you don't? Ever again?" Sophie wasn't sure why she was so flustered. She'd blown him off, last time she'd seen him. Though not fast enough: Parrish had caught them in each other's arms.

Verena shrugged. "Annela is extra-charming when there's a pretty new man around. It'll make dinner way more fun. Anyway, you were happy enough to be nice to him when you wanted a legal referral."

This was starting to have a vibe that reminded Sophie of her rare fights with Bram.

"Right, okay, you're right," she said, just to head off any possible argument, and without looking took another ladder down, further into the shipboard mall, looking for another shiny science thing, as Verena would put it, to distract herself.

By the time they'd finished their big shop and made their way to *Constitution* for the dinner date with Annela Gracechild, Sophie was beginning to feel that Parrish might have been right about the Fleet being a reasonably safe city. They'd spent the afternoon in what was, essentially, a shopping center. Nobody had tried to kill her or anyone else. As for the whole "running into a guy you slept with" thing, it wasn't as though that had never happened to her before.

Three cheers for less violence.

The self-defense course had, initially, been Bram's idea. He'd pitched it as part of her overall plan to prepare for a return to Stormwrack. "You're learning celestial navigation and working all these quick dives to make money so you can buy trade goods and animal specimens. You're in triathlon training and you went to that meditation seminar so you could *omm* your way through the scary stuff."

"Don't make fun," she'd said. Even if she'd wanted to seek conventional therapy after witnessing a murder and a handful of attempted killings, it was a moot point: she couldn't tell anyone in San Francisco what she'd experienced.

"I'm just saying—wouldn't it help if you learned to throw a proper punch?"

She'd assumed that deep down, the advice had its roots in Bram's persistent idea that Sophie was some kind of good-hearted pushover—that she ignored every slight, said yes to every favor, and let people walk all over her.

She wasn't entirely sure where this image of her came from. Some of it stemmed from their father and his endless picking about her intellectual rigor or lack thereof. But that was Dad: only happy when he was criticizing something. It didn't bug her the way it bugged Bram.

As Sophie saw it, she did whatever she pleased.

Whatever Bram's motives, he'd handed her the flyer for the class shortly after they'd gotten home from Stormwrack, just a few weeks after her aunt's murder. She'd bought her key-chain-size blast of bear spray and signed up for the class at the community center without a second thought.

But maybe all that badness last time was exceptional, just as it would be exceptional at home if your mom's sister was murdered and the same people came after you. It was a once-in-a-lifetime explosion of violence, not an ongoing obstacle to her physical safety and ability to explore Storm-wrack.

Yes, they'd found Corsetta in the water and someone had attacked her. There was definitely something going on there. But that didn't have anything to do with Sophie or the *Nightjar* crew, not anymore. They'd handed the situation over to the authorities, just as you would at home.

Call the cops and go on with life, right?

She spent the last couple of hours before dinner aboard *Nightjar* writing all of her observations and questions about Stormwrack into one of her new notebooks.

There was so much here to explore. What was the exact nature of the relationship between Stormwrack and Erstwhile? Was one the future of the other? Were they parallel dimensions?

Was there a way to determine the age of Stormwrack?

A year was still 365 days long. Whatever had happened, that hadn't changed. But the length of a mean sidereal day was shorter, by about five minutes, as compared to home. Stormwrackers adjusted their calendar annually, cutting off the last day of the year at midnight on the winter solstice, starting a fresh calendar as the days began to lengthen.

Sophie hadn't been able to check the planet's angle of rotation, though she'd gathered a few measurements with the sextant that Bram might be able to use.

Question upon question filled the notebook: Was there a weather office? Did anyone measure the temperature of the seas from year to year? Who made the charts?

Verena had said half of the snow vulture's young didn't survive in the wild. That implied someone had done a study. Who did studies here? Why was almost everyone so terribly lacking in curiosity? Was it just regarded as a personality defect, or was there something more behind it?

People might just think it's true, about the vultures' survival rate. They could be making all sorts of unproved assertions.

And all of that was warm-up for the big questions: How was it that Stormwrackers could use magic? When did that develop? Did all magic really use writing and inscription or were there other forms? Did that mean there was no magic before the development of writing?

She wrote: *The effects of magic persist when I go home. I still spoke Fleet when I was in San Francisco and was able to teach it to Bram. How is it that we haven't discovered inscription?*

Why didn't Stormwrackers do more science and tech? Was there some kind of agreement just to give up on development when they hit the Age of Sail and go no further? Was it on record? Or did it have something to do with the idea some of them had that steel and petroleum were inherently dangerous?

And so on.

The book filled with questions: a lifetime's worth of things to study. The problem, she thought, would be choosing. Some mysteries would yield to simple experimentation and measurement—if they could find or build the instruments. She could buy blood samples at the sanguarium and bird carcasses at the bird skin shop. Others might be researched, if she could get herself into the company of people who weren't so damned guarded with their information.

What Bram and I need is for Annela to chill out, she thought. Which meant winning her over at dinner.

Annela had been introduced to her as a cousin, though nobody had expressly told Sophie how she was related to Verena, Beatrice, and the other Feliachild women. She was in government—at home, she'd be something akin to a congresswoman. She was copper-skinned and curvy, with thick hair the color of graphite and a fondness for comfort: velvet curtains, warm rooms, lush foods.

For this particular not-quite-family gathering, she had put on a feast that had autumnal, harvesty overtones: there were fry breads, a corn dish, baked squash in abundance, ale, and slices of a red meat with a bit of a wild flavor. Venison? Buffalo?

She'd greeted them all with no sign of displeasure; she said hello to Parrish and Lais as warmly as if she'd been hoping they'd come and asked after Bram.

Politicians, Sophie thought. They can just pour it on, can't they? She decided she preferred Annela when she was pissed off.

Since Cly had opted out and Beatrice was under house arrest, it was just the five of them.

Verena's prediction that Annela would set herself to charming Lais proved true. They talked about horse racing—the Verdanii were horse crazy, apparently. Sophie let the conversation flow over her and picked out what information she could.

She'd already figured out that Verdanii was located about where Saskatchewan was, at home. So—the prairies. But instead of being the inner grain belt of a big continent, it was a landmass perhaps half the size of Australia.

This being a traditional Verdanii meal, she could draw other conclusions: fry bread was from a wheat harvest, and the horse talk argued that there were extensive grasslands there.

No creams, cheeses, or big dairy products. *No cattle?*

By the time the dessert—a custard not entirely divorced from pumpkin pie, though the crust was more in the line of an oat crumble and the glaze, atop, was a thin layer of salt caramel—had arrived, she could see that Annela had copped to what she was doing.

"Well, Sophie, if we can interrupt your examinations of us all, perhaps we can come down to business." She gestured for the servants to pour more ale.

Sophie tried to wait her out and couldn't. "You're looking for a favor, right? I go visiting Cly, he lets Beatrice have bail. He's basically agreed, so . . ."

"So," Annela said.

"Look, I'm not some whiz-bang brass-knuckles negotiator. I want Beatrice bailed, I do, and of course I want to go see Sylvanna with Cly. What am I supposed to do—pretend I don't care? That I'm gonna let Beatrice sit around pining for home aboard *Breadbasket*?"

Lais laughed. "That would be the usual mode, yes."

Annela looked like she might be fighting a smile.

"I'm not that kind of person."

"So you keep telling us," Annela said. Sophie wondered, suddenly, if they knew she'd smuggled some bio samples and a bunch of Stormwrack footage home. If they knew about the map she and Bram had been working on . . .

"What if we ditch this whole quid pro quo thing and act like human beings," she said. "I'm not out to put Stormwrack's existence on the front page of *The New York Times*. Trying to censor everything I see and hear— come on, Annela, you must see it's a waste of Verena's time."

"The value of Verena's time is very much an open question."

"Not to me, it isn't. Give me back my camera and equipment."

"Impossible."

"Last time I was here," Sophie said, "I learned stuff that was useful to you."

"Last time," Annela fired back, "I said your presence on Stormwrack would materially injure your kin. You returned. Now your aunt is dead and your mother under criminal charge."

Parrish cleared his throat. "You cannot blame Sophie for Gale's death, Convenor, not when it was so long foretold and forestalled."

"Can't I?" She looked at him cannily and to Sophie's surprise, he looked abashed and turned away.

What's that about?

"Ohhkay. Material damage to kin. Beatrice got arrested, kinda my fault for coming back, true. But you're saying there was a . . . a prophecy? About Gale's death—"

"As for Beatrice's arrest," Parrish interrupted, "a citizen must answer for her own actions."

"What would you have had her do, Parrish?" Annela leaned back in her chair. "Raise Sophie on Low Bann?"

"Sophie stopped an invasion of my nation," Lais said, surprising everyone. "Tiladene owes her a favor, and the Convene does, too. It's not a stretch to say she preserved the Cessation of Hostilities."

"For how long? Without Gale to fight off the inevitable next assault on the Compact—"

Verena paled. She stood up suddenly, gave the faintest of bows, and stalked off.

Annela quirked her eyebrows at Sophie. "Are you going to ask what that's about, Kir Inquisitor?"

"Don't need to," Sophie said. "It's obvious. She screwed up one of her 'I'm the new Gale' spy assignments and now you're threatening to fire her.

In the process, she cost *Nightjar* the ship's medical officer and bosun—they didn't die, but they huffed off, I'm thinking."

Annela shot a look at Parrish.

"I told her nothing," he said.

"I'm right, aren't I?"

"We've been delivering Gale's bequests to a number of portside island nations," he said. "At one such stop, the bosun's family asked us to add in a sail to Zingoasis with some magical relics."

"The musician's skeleton, in the hold?"

If Parrish was surprised that she'd had a poke through the storage crates, it didn't show. Annela's glower deepened, and Sophie remembered, belatedly, that she'd meant to try buttering her up. "Yes," he said. "It was meant to be kept quiet, but Richler found out, and his nation made a counterclaim for the bones. Verena had already offended him, once, with a perhaps insensitive comment about advanced medicine in the outlands. He's a good man, from the—"

"She accused him of having reported the skeleton's presence aboard. Then she suggested divvying up the bones like a pools win," Annela interrupted.

Was there something there she didn't want me to know? Parrish had been about to say something about Richler; suddenly her cousin had switched from censorship to storytelling.

A decent theory. Test it? "Parrish, you were saying something about Richler?"

"Ah—"

"Then, having by now upset both crew members," Annela continued, "Verena tried to convince them not to pass her offensive suggestion on to their home governments. The bequest's in court now; there'll be a duel over it. I'll be smoothing the choppy seas forever." Annela turned a pinch of bannock over in her fingers. "How you worked out as much as you did—"

"I believe this proves that denying Sophie access to books and her recording equipment is a pointless exercise," Parrish said. "In fact, if she were busy measuring the pull of the tides at the equinox or similar ephemera—"

"Ephemera!" Sophie objected.

"She's more interested in the natural world than she is in politics," he said, and now he was looking right at her. Still trying to tell her something? "If we returned her equipment and allowed her to focus—"

Annela said, "I will not further empower someone who is already a menace."

"What if I could talk Cly into dropping the charges against Beatrice altogether? Is that . . . legally possible? Parrish?"

He stroked his jaw. "Perhaps under the 'no harm done' provisions of the Judicial Code. There'd need to be a ritual exchange of sword blows."

"You believe you can do this because you don't know the man," Annela said. "Cly Banning is a reptile, Sophie. You're neither sufficiently well placed to hold his interest for long nor experienced enough to handle him."

"That's the difference between you and me," Sophie said, stung. "I wouldn't *handle*. I'd ask."

A snort. "Naivete won't help you, either."

"Right. And it's not *naive* to expect Verena to need time to learn all the nuances of her new job." With that, she threw her napkin down, emphatically didn't bow, and went after her sister.

She stepped out onto *Constitution*'s deck, into the moonlight. The seas were slate under its pale-bone glow, and remarkably still but for the wakes of the various ships. The lanterns of the Fleet were strung out across the seacraft to their rear. Off *Constitution*'s bow, the Fleet's monster flagship, *Temperance*, hulked its way through the water, leaving a track of churned-up foam behind it.

There was no sign of Verena.

"Kir Sophie Hansa?" One of the uniformed messengers, a boy of perhaps nine, held out an envelope.

"Shouldn't you be in bed?"

"Very droll, Kir," the kid said, with an attitude that said he'd heard that one before.

She expected to find the note was from Cly or Beatrice, but it was scrawled in an almost childish hand. Westerbarge, *midnight*, it said. *Corsetta di Gatto, Tibbon's Wash.*

She took one last good look around.

"What the hell." It was time to get out into the city unassisted. She stomped up to the hang glider deck and showed a taxi pilot her note.

"*Westerbarge* has no landing platform," he said. "I can drop you on a ferry."

"Fine."

The taxikites were flying rickshaws. She sat in an open cab—the pilot gave her something that wasn't quite a bear pelt to keep her warm. Sophie pulled two hairs from the pelt and tucked them into her questions journal. Her thoughts turned to the sanguarium in the market. All those blood samples, there for the buying, if only she could find a way to get them analyzed . . .

I won't further empower a menace, Annela had said. Perhaps it was perversity, but Sophie rather liked the idea of being a menace.

Funny that she didn't threaten to magically wipe my memory again. . . .

Climbing into the apparatus of the glider, the pilot angled the kite straight at the sky. They rose into the air as smoothly as if a cable had lifted them. When they were about two hundred meters above the Fleet he threw his legs back, with a faint jerk that reverberated through the whole of the craft, and extended the glider's wings outward. A moment later, they were circling.

No updrafts at this time of day, Sophie thought. Indeed, they weren't gaining altitude—rather, they were moving in ever-widening circles, losing height with every revolution.

Air rushed through her hair, mellow and warm, and she leaned forward to take in as much of the Fleet as she could, lanternlights marking ship positions. In the dark they lined up like self-contained city blocks, islands of human activity ordered across the black of the sea.

When they were well aft of *Gatehouse*, deep in the civilian block, the kite made a bank and curve, bleeding away the last of its altitude and all of its speed. The pilot kicked himself upright, creating wind resistance through the whole frame of the kite, and came to a controlled stop on a platform on a ship the size of a biggish tugboat.

"This is the night ferry, Kir," he said. "Four stops, maybe five, and you'll be at *Westerbarge*. Be sure to tell the purser where you want to go. That'll be fivecoin."

Sophie had made a point of watching the vendors make change in the mall that afternoon—she handed over the nickel confidently. "Is there a charge for the ferry?"

"Public service, Kir," he said, and began racking the kite for takeoff.

She made it to *Westerbarge* about ten minutes late for her scheduled rendezvous with Corsetta. It was part of a dive-y looking little block of cabins, all serving drinks, with seating in the middle. A bar, in other words. Raucous, beer-drinking-crowd sounds emanated from every deck.

The crowd seemed friendly enough. Sophie packed her little trove of coins away, where they would be hard to steal, and touched her can of bear spray for reassurance. Then she went looking for the girl.

She found her at a card table, with a decent pile of coin in front of her, a fawning dog trying to climb its way into her lap, and a beer in her hand.

When she saw Sophie, she announced to the group, "I'm over." There was some amiable grumbling as she pulled her stake off the table, but she pushed one coin back—"For the next round"—and they appeared mollified.

To Sophie she said, "Buy you an ale?"

"I just had a massive meal," Sophie said. "Thanks anyway."

Corsetta led the way out to a relatively quiet table on the rail. "You didn't bring the whole Judiciary with you. My thanks for that."

"For all I know they're hot on my tail," Sophie said. "What do you want?"

"My snow vulture," she said. "I charmed her, and she needs me."

And you need the credit for taming her, don't you? "I saw her today. She's unhappy."

Corsetta nodded and handed over a heavily scrawled slip of paper. "Claim of ownership, and a note saying I relinquish no rights."

Even the fifteen-year-olds talk like lawyers here.

She glanced at the document: it was better crafted than the short note Corsetta had sent her. She'd had someone write it on her behalf, Sophie supposed.

"How is this going to help? The bird can't read."

Corsetta handed over a strip of what looked like goat hide. "This bears my scent—it should reassure her that I'm alive. I'd have gone to her in person, but I assume the market is lousy with Watch."

"Why give this up?" Sophie asked, holding up the strip of leather.

"I have to back up my claim. I can't marry Rashad if the bird will not lay."

"Because that's the Queen's quest?"

"Favor. It's the way of our people."

Sophie said, "Have you contacted your boyfriend?"

Corsetta shook her head. "I have to get home to him. I can't think, I can't eat, I can't sleep. . . ."

You can evade arrest, play cards, and drink beer pretty well, though. "This guy of yours. How old is he?"

She glowed. "Just past the first blossom of youth, Kir, with skin of porcelain and a wit so keen! He makes that pretty sea captain of yours seem old and dim."

"Stop. Not my captain. Rashad is your age, then?"

"He writes poetry—"

"I thought his family owned a fishing fleet."

"The alchemical union of our souls has expanded us, allowing us to rise beyond the tethers of birth and family. As an outlander, you can't be expected to understand."

Alchemy, huh? "No, 'course not. I'm just a lumbering cynic from the wilds."

"Do you not believe in true love? In the perfect fusion of matched souls?" This came out loud, in a tone so horrified the girl might have been asking if Sophie drowned bunnies for fun.

"Fusion?" Parrish had just stepped into the bar, looking first concerned and then, as he took them in, relieved. Should Sophie warn her?

"Name your soul's base metal, Kir! I can help you. There will be a natural match for it out there—your true catalyst! You'll never find it if you don't look."

"Is this like astronomy? Water signs should try to date earth signs, that kind of thing?"

"Ah, you do understand a little." She spoke with an emphasis that suggested she'd drunk several pints already. "It's a law of the universe that we must seek to complete ourselves."

"That's *not* a law of the universe." She couldn't help herself; this greeting-card picture of romance annoyed her all the more now that Corsetta was throwing scientific terms into the mix. "It's a very comforting idea, but—"

"No, no. *Listen.* Think of magnetite and lodestone," Corsetta said. She clasped her hands, mimicking magnetic forces.

"That's not an argument."

"When I return and claim the Queen's favor, I will get permission to marry Rashad," Corsetta said, her tone insistent. "We'll sail in Rashad's crabbing dory, to the Scattering Isles. There we will catch bauble fish and earn shells. I'll gaze upon his face as he sits on the deck and makes up verses."

Which of you is going to fish, in that case? "But in the meantime, you want me to deliver this note and the leather to . . ."

"To the Judiciary. It will show that I'm the one who tamed the bird. Montaro has claimed otherwise. He wants my favor! This proves she is mine, does it not?"

"I have no idea," Sophie said. "I'm no Fleet lawyer."

"I can't afford to fall into court over this. I must get home."

"Yeah. About that. Nobody's buying that this is just about your boyfriend. The bird, the brother throwing you overboard, the fact that you were out by that derelict—their crew's missing, you know. Presumed lost?"

"You are entirely too full of wonderment, Kir. It's an acidic property of the soul."

"Honestly, Corsetta, the nature of whatever scam you've got on right now may be the least interesting mystery I've stumbled over since I got here."

"Will you give my notes to the Judiciary?"

"I'm probably supposed to arrest you."

"You're outlandish, aren't you? Of no nation, No Oath, not sworn to Fleet law?"

I'm bound by Annela's whims, if nothing else. Parrish had been sidling closer, easing his way between the obstacle course of drinkers. "The thing is—"

Corsetta saw something in Sophie's face. She leapt up, but the captain was already close enough to make flight pointless.

He took her by the arm, gently. "Make no trouble, Kir. We can say you surrendered."

"Never!" The kid turned her big wounded eyes on Sophie.

In a movie, this would turn into a brawl, Sophie thought. Corsetta would incite her poker buddies to intervene on her behalf, and things would degenerate into bottles smashing on heads and a tinkling player-piano sound track.

But Corsetta simply said to Parrish, "You are interfering with true love, Kir. I suppose you don't believe in it, either."

Parrish gave Sophie a surprised glance.

"I believe," he said, "that facing your accusers is the obvious way out of your difficulties."

"I *need* to go home." For just a moment, she looked very young and wholly desperate. Then she mastered herself. "Bad luck to you both, Kirs. Love will avenge herself."

"Flinging curses is poor form," he told her.

"What do you expect?" Corsetta told him, bitterly. "I'm just a goat-herd."

They caught a ferry to *Gatehouse,* left her there with the Watch, and went on to *Nightjar.*

"True love's gonna get you," Sophie said, making a joke of it.

"Corsetta is very young," Parrish replied. His expression was closed, guarded.

"Curses like that don't work, do they?"

"As with anything, my name would be required for a curse."

"She's pretty devious. Maybe she slipped it off *Nightjar.*"

"My middle name is lost—even I don't know it."

"Oh, I'd forgotten that."

He frowned. "I didn't know you knew."

Why does this feel awkward? "Did you by any chance find Verena?"

"She went to *Breadbasket* to see her mother." He shook his head. "Your mother, that is."

Beatrice. Stuck under house arrest, with no idea there was a scheme afoot to bail her. "There's something about this that you aren't telling me, isn't there?"

"My orders are very specific," he said. "And recently, bracingly, reclar-ified."

"Meaning yes."

"There's nothing you couldn't work out for yourself, if you directed your attention to the matter."

"Directed my . . ." She remembered what he'd said at dinner. "Politics, not nature. I will work it out, whatever it is."

He nodded, agreeing, somehow very sober.

"What happens with you guys while I'm off with Cly?"

"Unknown. Annela is unlikely to offer Verena a proper assignment. We may be at loose ends until there's a package to be taken to Erstwhile."

"She couldn't interest herself in this whole Tibbon's Wash situation, could she?"

"Verena?" Parrish gave her a considering look.

"Come on. Corsetta talks the big talk about being base to the poet boy's catalyst, but there's a reason she wants to get home before the brother does. She's desperate. Plus, we don't know yet who healed her or why she was aboard that derelict."

He said, "You don't lend any credence to her feelings?"

"That romantic stuff plays better in stories than in real life, doesn't it? Come on, she's fifteen? Once the hormone rush abates a little, they'll both move on."

"Is that so?"

"That girl's got bigger ambitions than some crab boat can hold."

"So if she's ambitious—"

"Ambitious and a liar. Definitely playing us, probably playing the elder brother, possibly even playing her alleged one true love."

"Then she's incapable of love? Or unworthy?"

"Oh, she can feel whatever she likes. They both can. That doesn't make them pair-bonded for life, whatever they may think now."

"I see," he said, words clipped.

She decided to ignore the tone. "Anyway, in what world does a family of fishers care if one of the farmgirls takes a useless young dreamer off their hands?"

"Tibbon's Wash is a stratified kingdom from the port side of the government," he said. "The Queen's favor allows people to attempt to earn boons from the crown. It builds in a little flexibility."

"A safety valve," she said. "I got that much."

He didn't look as though he knew what that meant. "They've been unfortunately stuck for a number of years. Nobody's been able to bring in a quiescent snow vulture. The appointed quest proved too difficult; there haven't been any boons for over a decade."

"Bad luck for them. But Gale used to do this, didn't she? Just decide to poke her nose into things? She didn't always wait for Annela to give her orders."

"I'll suggest to Verena that 'we poke into it,' as you say," he said. "Thank you, Sophie. It's kind of you to think of her."

CHAPTER 6

Some of the biggest ships in the civilian quarter of the Fleet were jammed from bilge to gunwales with law offices, and Mensalom Bimisi had a suite of cabins within one such enormous sailing ship in the civilian quarter.

He was a slow-moving Tiladene man, mushroom pale, with bedroom eyes and an odd, drawling Fleet accent. He laid the terms of the deal out for Sophie in pokey, exhausting detail.

The gist was that Cly would perform an unspecified "personal service" for Sophie (nowhere in the forty pages of "why" and "wherefore" did he admit to having influence over Beatrice's bail process) and Sophie, in return, would accompany him to Sylvanna. She would tour his lowlands estate, register at the birth office, present herself to the head of his family and—apparently this was key—attend some big summer festival at the Spellscrip Institute.

Neither of them was obliged to do anything after that. Cly could, if he wished, make her his heir. Sylvanna would, as a matter of course, automatically issue her a birth certificate.

It seemed crazy that she needed what was practically an international treaty just to go visit her birth father's home. But despite Cly's being a judge, it was obvious the Verdanii side of the family simply didn't trust him.

"At some point in this process, after you're documented Sylvanner, Kir Banning could give you an additional name," Mensalom said.

"A Sylvanner name?"

"As I understand it, yours has fallen into common knowing. Properly altering your identity would protect you from malicious enchantment."

"Okay, good." Her thoughts skipped over the memory of the two men she'd seen being killed by inscription.

Mensalom gave such an impression of overall sleepiness that she was tempted to assume he wasn't all that good at what he did, but she'd seen the looks on both Annela and Cly's faces when he'd been named as her lawyer in the action. At the very least, he had a fearsome reputation.

The lawyer glanced at a timepiece on his desk. "Your father should be here by now. Is there anything you'd like to discuss before I invite him in to review the amendments and sign the documents?"

She shook her head and her birth father swept in, kissed the spot atop her head, threw Mensalom a halfhearted bow, then draped himself in a chair.

"Is this it?" He picked the document off the table and began skimming, just looking for the places where Mensalom had tweaked the original text.

"Did you see you may bring companions?" Cly asked.

Sophie nodded. "I'd ask Bram, but he's you-know-where."

"Your half-sister?"

"She has business." *And she'd be obliged to cramp my research style.*

"Do you remember that cadet from graduation? She came in second in the Slosh?"

"Zita?"

"You have an excellent memory. She will be aboard *Sawtooth;* she's about your sister's age. Since you're too old for a governess and too well schooled to bother with a tutor, I have also engaged a memorician."

"I don't know what that is," Sophie said, and saw Mensalom's eyebrows quirk upward in surprise.

"He reads," Cly said. "And has perfect recall."

"A walking library, in other words?" She almost clapped.

"His shelf's a little empty at the moment, but you can stack him." Cly beamed. "Is there anything else you need? Any possessions you wish transferred to my ship?"

"*Nightjar*'s got my diving kit," she said. "Annela's confiscated my cameras and all our instruments, mine and Bram's. I don't expect you to perform miracles, but—"

"Watch me." Cly handed over a card embossed with the Judiciary seal. "If you need anything else, charge it to *Sawtooth*."

"An allowance, huh?"

"Traveling expenses," Mensalom said. "Provided for in the agreement."

"Right, right. I did listen, sorry."

"Sign here," he said, offering her a pen. "Kir Sophie, all my best. Your Honor, I'll have these read to the contracts registrar this afternoon."

To her surprise, Lais was lounging in the outer parlor when she and Cly emerged with their respective copies of the signed documents.

The two men exchanged perfunctory bows.

"How's your head?" Cly said. Lais had been badly injured six months ago in an assassination attempt. Like Corsetta, he was alive only because someone had written an inscription to magically restore him.

"Works about as well as it did before," Lais said. "I only use it to reckon racing odds, in any case."

"You underrate yourself," Cly said. "You've done my daughter a service here, in Bimisi."

"Mensalom? He only takes clients who interest him," Lais said. "Sophie's merits on that score have nothing to do with me."

"True enough. Well, I'm sure you have good-byes. Sophie, will you be all right if I leave you?"

"Of course," she said.

"*Sawtooth* awaits your pleasure." With that, Cly left.

"How'd you like Mensalom?" Lais asked.

"He's sharp," she said. "So. Verena and I left you to fend for yourself the other night, when we stormed out."

"It was all to the good. Convenor Gracechild is a *thoroughly* charming hostess."

She looked at him askance. "Does that mean what I think it does?"

"Unless you lack imagination. Verdanii matriarchs like a bit of young chaw. Didn't you know? It's one of that nation's more attractive qualities, as far as I'm concerned. Far outweighs the storied merits of their beer."

"Annela's got to be—"

"She's intelligent, self-aware, powerful. . . ." He waggled his eyebrows. "Physically fit—"

"Stop. That's way too much info."

"Now, Sophie, it's not as though she's actually an elder to you. You've met a handful of times. And I know you're not a prude."

"Still!"

"And you're done with me, aren't you?"

"Totally," she said, more coldly than she intended.

It was silly to be hurt. They'd hooked up for a week, six months ago, and she'd rejected him last time they were together because . . . well, she'd begun to think maybe Parrish . . .

She shook that thought away. At least Lais hadn't slept with Verena.

Yet. That I know of. "You want my mother's contact information while you're at it?"

"Pish? A married fraud artist? Not my style."

Now she was hurt and insulted. And embarrassed, somehow, that she cared at all. She tried to laugh, and it stuck in her throat. "Sorry, Lais. I don't mean to freak out. I mean, I was warned that you're from the Island of the Anywhere, Anytime, Anyone."

"Tsk. We're sluts, true, but none of us is—and certainly I'm not—undiscriminating."

Okay, now he was offended.

"I just didn't think—"

"You're from a conservative culture." He bowed. "Perhaps they'll make a Sylvanner of you after all. Fair winds, Sophie."

"Thanks. And for, you know . . ." She gestured back at Mensalom's inner door, but Lais was already gone, striding away, offering her one last look at his well-muscled leather-clad backside before disappearing through a hatch on the starboard side of the ship.

Way to go, Sofe.

"Come on," she muttered. "If nothing else, shouldn't he be bragging about his conquests? I mean, she's a congresswoman."

In for a penny, in for a pound. She went back to *Nightjar,* seeking out Verena.

Her sister was in the cabin that had once belonged to Gale, pacing it from the look of things, and reading a bunch of dispatches about Tibbon's Wash, snow vultures, and joint ventures at sea. "You about ready for your big adventure?" From her tone, Verena was looking forward to having the ship—or possibly Parrish—to herself again.

"Yeah," Sophie said, "But I want something."

"What a surprise."

"You must have a stash of the magical two-ply message paper—if only so you can keep your father up to date on what's happening to Beatrice."

Verena tensed but did not deny it.

"I want a few sheets—no, I want ten sheets—and I want their . . . counterparts?"

"Otherply."

"I want them sent to Bram."

Verena pulled at her ponytail, thinking.

"Come on. It'll save you going back and forth just to tell him I haven't drowned. My mom is freaking out every bit as bad as your dad, and presumably he knows what's happening to Beatrice, that she's safe. My parents don't have the slightest idea where I am."

With a sigh, Verena opened a locked cabinet and drew out a roll of paper. She sliced twelve pages with an obsidian knife. On the first she wrote, *Dad, please send the following pages to:*

She added the street address of the Dwarf House. "What's his zip code?"

Sophie recited it. Verena added it to the note, then started numbering blank pages, one through eleven.

"One page for you?" Sophie asked.

"Yes." Verena handed over page one. "Want to write him a starter message?"

Sophie took the pen and started in the very top corner. BRAM—ALL OK SO FAR. GOING TO SYLVANNA WITH CB. REPLY BELOW, WRITE SMALL. LOVE SOFE.

"Okay?" Verena said.

"Yeah. Thanks."

"Here's a couple sheets from me, so you can stay in touch with *Nightjar.*" She handed them over. "You think there's a conspiracy afoot with Corsetta?"

"Hopefully not another outbreak-of-war conspiracy, but something crimey is up there. She and the cat were aboard that derelict. It doesn't mean she was involved with disappearing its crew, but—"

"You haven't already figured it out? You're not sending me off to keep me busy or gather two last clues on your behalf so you can sweep in with the answer at the end, like Sherlock Holmes?"

"What?" Sophie was a little stung.

"Are you?"

"I have no idea what's going on with Corsetta," Sophie said. "But she stinks of scam. I saw you're having . . . you know, job issues. I thought, since Annela's coming down on you, maybe there's a win there."

Verena kept frowning.

"Okay! If it helps, I won't say a single thing more about it. Do it all yourself. If Corsetta comes to me and spills the beans, even, my lips will be sealed."

"Yeah, right." That almost got a smile.

Sophie put her nose in the air and tried to sound snooty. "As it happens, Kir, I have plenty of other questions to keep me busy."

"A whole notebook full. I noticed." A chuckle. "Okay, I'll hold you to that. Though, with the way my luck's been going, the Cessation will depend on that kid and I'll only figure it out when she's burned Tibbon's Wash to the ground." Verena closed the paper box, her expression broody.

Sophie found herself blurting, "And, listen, maybe we should talk about something else. Someone, I mean."

"There's nothing to say." Verena shook her head so fiercely that her ponytail whipped into a momentary blur. "Come on, I'll escort you to His Honor's ship."

CHAPTER 7

Sawtooth was a caravel, square-rigged and immense. It was crewed, or so it appeared, by kids in their teens and twenties, all in new-looking Fleet uniforms.

Her Judiciary flag was flying, as were the Fleet colors and the two-toned green flag of Sylvanna, a clear symbolic representation of verdant hills.

Cly was waiting as she came aboard. He was dressed down, in breeches and a white shirt, with a comparatively narrow rapier—it seemed to be made made from bamboo—slung at his hip. He looked like he was about to bound onto a stage and start declaiming *Hamlet*.

"Welcome!" he said, wrapping an arm around her. "It's good to have you back."

Sophie surprised herself by planting a kiss on his cheek. "Thanks."

Beside Cly was a teenage girl Sophie recognized from the night of Fleet graduation. "Kir Zita, right?"

"Tenner Zita," She smiled to show there was no accusation or anger in the correction. "It's my rank."

"And Krispos, our memorician," Cly said.

Krispos had a full-on Moses beard, bushy gray follicles so dense they seemed to be growing from his neck and chest as well as his chin. He was clad in a scarlet robe, newly purchased from the look of it, but his belt was worn and had several new notches. His skin was a bit slack: Sophie would have bet he'd been heavier at some point than he was now. His feet were bare. The left had the look of having been gnawed by something; neither foot had any nails.

Zita, meanwhile, was long of limb, hazel-eyed, and had the compact musculature of an Olympic gymnast. She was studying Cly's particular brand of lawyering, which meant court cases that ended in formal duels.

Sophie looked beyond them to take in the ship, whose decks were strangely quiet. "Last time I was here, the whole ship was given over to combat classes."

"I've got six sword fighters aboard, including Zita," Cly said. "The grapplers and boxers are training with an assistant, aboard another craft, while I am on leave. May I present my captain, Lena Beck? Captain, my daughter, Sophie Hansa."

Beck was maybe fifty, a stocky and intense-looking woman with jet-black skin, wiry salt-and-pepper hair, and a gold tattoo, a pattern of interlocking spirals, that ran up her neck in a choker.

"Beck was busy with other duties or you'd have met her the last time you were here. We're childhood friends."

Beck wore elbow-length calfskin gloves, though it was a warm day. One of them, the left, was cinched tight at the wrist and inflated around her hand like a balloon. As Sophie's gaze lingered there, she twitched a look at Cly, got the faintest of nods in reply, and removed the glove.

Her hand was gone from the mid-forearm—an amputation, and an old one from the look of the scar. Stubs of her radius and ulna extended about a centimeter beyond the skin.

Around the remains of Beck's wristbones there was more tattoo in gold, but this was in spellscrip. A spectral hand extended beyond the truncated pieces of real bone. It was three-dimensional but colored in photo reverse, its bones glowing palely through the shape of flesh and fingers like a hologram of an X-ray image.

Sophie looked up at Beck, who seemed untroubled by having exposed her . . . prosthetic? "May I?"

"Of course." She extended the spectral hand and Sophie clasped it in a handshake. The hand felt solid but where it met Sophie's skin there was a tingling, as of millipede legs. The nails had the same photo-reverse whiteness. Sophie turned it, palm upward, so she could have a better look. The palm was lined as anyone's would be; the creases in its surface were the deep gray of ash.

"Normal function and strength?"

Another hesitation, before Beck said: "A little stronger."

"The hand. You lost it?"

"Childhood leech infection," she confirmed. "The old Springtime spellscribe saved my life but not the limb." She pulled the glove back over the ghostly hand. "Do you fight, Ch—Kir?"

Sophie shook her head.

"You might care to learn while you're here," she said. "Those prying eyes'll get you taken for a spy."

"Not aboard *Sawtooth,* they won't," Cly said.

Beck bowed, at once acknowledging his point and extricating herself from the conversation. "I'd like to get under way."

"I've got all I need." He beamed at Sophie. "And you, my dear?"

"If I don't have it, it isn't coming," she said. "Any chance you got my cameras out of Annela?"

A smug expression crossed Cly's face. "Come with me."

He led her belowdecks, Krispos and Zita following, down to a corridor with officer cabins.

"Your quarters are there, child," Cly said, indicating a hatch. "Here, across the hall."

He ushered her into a cabin that smelled of new white paint and Sophie saw . . .

"Is this a laboratory?" She wasn't entirely sure. There were counters fixed to the bulkheads and at a good height for lab work. The whitewash gave the room a sterile look. But the equipment, if it was equipment . . .

There was a rack filled with colored candles that looked like a giant's crayon box. There was a boa of bird feathers in every size and hue, hung beside a pair of rattles. There were calipers—they'd be useful—next to a box of finger paints. A little cushion and a bowl of polished quartz crystals sat beside a case filled with worms, a ratty Goth rag doll straight out of Tim Burton, and a series of nested cups—measures.

Great, there's an astrology chart.

"I couldn't quite be made to understand which branch of the sciences might be your particular specialty," Cly said, as Sophie tried to look pleased. "These are a few basics for temperamentalism, aetherism, sympathism—"

"It would help to know your bent," Krispos put in. "I should like to read texts most of use to you."

"Books? There are books here?"

Krispos looked offended. "I shall do the reading."

"You may find Kir Sophie a bit unorthodox," Cly said.

"Don't worry, Krispos—if there are books here, we'll fill your head."

"But your specialty?" Cly said again.

"Ah," Sophie said. "I'll have to figure out what they call it here. I'm a biologist by training, but I've been boning up on my chemistry and physics. Atomic—"

Krispos looked horrified. "Not an atomist, surely?"

"Of course not," Cly said before she could answer. "That would be terrible."

Worse than being a nosy, prying spy? Off Cly's warning glance she said, weakly, "No, of course not. No atomism."

"Child—I'm sorry, *Sophie.* The laboratory is a work space, that's all. Clear out whatever you don't need. My feelings won't be hurt if you have the colored candles packed away."

Atomism is bad, hmmm? She had spotted a promising cabinet; opening its wooden doors, she found it was indeed, and blessedly, full of books.

Next to the cabinet was her trunk.

She cracked it open with a glad cry. Her DSLR camera was atop the pile, the digital video recorder next to it. Bram's massive surveying gadget was there, along with flasks, denatured alcohol, slides.

I wonder what they'll think if I ask for a microscope?

"I'll let you get settled," Cly said. "Krispos is at your disposal at any time, day or night. Zita has duties aboard ship and must practice her swordcraft, but otherwise she's available to you, too. I'd like you to see my tailor, so we can fit you with one or two Sylvanner garments. Would you wish a valet or hairdresser?"

"Seriously not."

"I had somehow doubted it. May I show you your cabin?"

"Sure!"

He conducted her back across the corridor to a decent-size berth, perhaps twice as big as her guest closet on *Nightjar*. Her clothes were already stowed in the wardrobe. There were five little netted bundles on her bunk.

"What are these?"

"Traditional wayfaring presents," he said. "One each from Annela Gracechild, your half-sister, Verena, that man Parrish, his first mate, and the Tiladene, Lais Dariach."

She picked one up and untied the ribbon, unwrapping a scrap of colored silk. Its contents recalled a Christmas stocking: a collection of goodies. There was a twist of lemon candies, some tobacco, two little waxed packets of loose tea, a hoop made of shell—she'd seen sailors wearing necklaces of the things—and a sachet of spices, rock salt with dried basil, in one case, dill and grated citrus peel in another. By the time she'd examined everything in it, the combination of scents was overpowering; she found a linen handkerchief and wrapped the tobacco in one and the spices in another.

One of the smoke packs had a distinctly skunky smell.

"Is something wrong, Sophie?"

"No. I just . . . I think Lais gave me pot as a going-away gift," she said. "Cannabis?"

"Ah," Cly said, clearly not getting the point.

"At home, marijuana's illegal."

"I'm surprised. It's such a versatile crop."

"Yes. Well. It's weird, getting a baggie of it in front of a judge."

"Oh! It's not an offense here," Cly said, taking the packet and giving it a sniff. "I don't use it. Dull's one's fighting edge."

"Right." That was a whole other avenue of investigation, she thought. Did they have coca here? Opium? Was anything illegal? She knew all the islands were allowed to do as they pleased within their twenty-five-mile limits: everything must be permitted somewhere. Parrish had mentioned a substance once: maddenflur?

Add it to the question book, Sofe.

Cly gestured at the arrangement of packets. "There's a casual trade in the bits and pieces you don't want. Spice packs are traditionally given to the ship's cook. A sort of offering of thanks."

"Okay."

He fingered the packet of marijuana. "The Tiladene owes you a debt. It's appropriate for him to send an offering of friendship."

"Friendship, absolutely!" she agreed with too much enthusiasm. "Nothing odd there at all!"

Okay, way to go. She could feel her cheeks getting hot. *If Cly didn't know about your shipboard fling with Lais, he does now.*

And he was putting it together, she could see it. The brightness had gone out of his face—there was a second where he was utterly blank and unreadable, as if there was nothing there. Then a flicker of something . . . anger?

Finally he settled into an expression that might have been watchful, quizzical. Like that of a cat that had whiffed its paw through a candle-flame.

Definitely not amused.

For all I know, Sylvanner men skewer people who screw their daughters. I should shut up, change the subject, let the moment pass. . . .

But when had that ever happened? "Okay, look. The thing about Lais. He's nice; we get along. He's a scientist at heart, which makes him my type."

"Your type of what?"

Don't say lover, don't say lover. . . . "I was warned about Tiladenes being poly. They hook up and move on, right? No big deal. And he *has* moved on, to Annela, apparently, which I do have to say kind of blows my mind—crap, now I'm gossiping."

"Then . . ." Cly struggled, visibly, to put it delicately. "In the outlands are you all . . . was the word you just used 'poly'? You behave like Tiladenes?"

"We behave like everything, Cly—straight, gay, monogamous, serially monogamous, polygamous. We have celibate priests and adultery and casual sex. And so do you! Don't pretend. You aren't going to try to tell me people don't cheat and bed-hop and generally behave like primates here."

He glitched again, processing.

At least we've drifted a little from "My daughter had sex with the cover model from Hot Horse Racers Weekly."

It was a damned good reminder that she knew sweet toot about Sylvanners, even though she was thinking of becoming one. Somehow every time she started to dig into what the country was like, something came up.

Or someone changed the subject.

Tonio had been about to say something at one point, and Verena shut him right down. . . .

And Parrish, not so subtly trying to remind her that politics mattered here, that she shouldn't just focus on ecosystem stuff.

"I know your people aren't keen on divorce," she began.

"A Tiladene? Did you even think, Sophie, how your parents would feel?"

"Okay, hold up. My *parents* have no clue what a Tiladene is, and they know full well that I'm not a nun."

"I don't know 'nun.'"

"Celibate. I'm not celibate." She gave that a second to sink in, steeling herself against embarrassment—it wasn't as bad as having this same conversation with her dad at home would be. "And you told me Sylvanna wasn't one of those places where women had to creep around with their heads bowed and their legs together."

"That isn't quite what I said," he replied. "But I can assure you I'd be just as—"

"Horrified? Scandalized?"

"—disturbed by this news were you my son."

"Seriously? So if I was male and I'd screwed Lais, we'd be having the same conversation?"

"Don't be coarse. But yes."

"Why? What's the rule? No sex outside marriage, for men and women alike?"

"For boys and girls alike."

"I'm not a girl. I'm twenty-five."

"One isn't an adult until one is married."

"What, even if you're a fifty-year-old bachelor?"

"Indeed," he said, and there was a note of bitterness in his voice.

"An unmarried person is a kid?" She saw it suddenly. "This is why you can't stop calling me child. This is why the contract I signed goes on and endlessly on about my status on Sylvanna being as 'a guest with the rights of a sovereign foreign adult.'"

Cly was shaking his head. "This is Beatrice's fault. If you'd been properly raised—"

"Oh no, you don't. I was raised just fine by the standards of the United States of America. I am, in fact, totally grown up. And who I have sex with is none of your business."

He threw up his hands, gave her one last balked look, and vanished down the hall.

"Oh, that was fun."

She closed the door, pulling out her sheets of magic paper. Bram had written one line under hers: WHY DIDN'T V TELL US THEY HAD TEXTING? XOB

She hunted up a pencil. V'S ORDERED TO LIMIT RESEARCH/EXPLORATION. HOW'S THAT GOING?

She thought a second, then wrote: MAKING RANDOM PROGRESS ON VARIOUS FRONTS.

WHAT'VE YOU LEARNED?

Map coordinates, they'd agreed, should be their first priority. 0 LATITUDE STORMWRACK LOCATED IN MOSCASIPAY, VERDANII. ALMOST EXACTLY WHERE SASKATCHEWAN CANADA IS. I'M BOUND FOR SYLVANNA (ROUGHLY TENNESSEE) WITH CLY.

She paused. Should she mention seeing Lais? Or all this stuff about Sylvanna and children and Cly assuming she was a virgin? Did it matter?

No, she decided. Better to save the magic paper. She signed off: XOSOFE.

They might warn her about being an overcurious spy here, but they wouldn't actively stop her from finding out everything she could about Sylvanna. It was time to take a good look at the books and equipment in that laboratory.

CHAPTER 8

Sawtooth was Cly's private sailing vessel, but he had some kind of complicated agreement with the Fleet whereby he leased it to them for training purposes and they provided his crew.

On Earth a couple hundred years ago, he'd have been a titular admiral, giving the orders while leaving Captain Beck to run the ship.

Normally training meant getting judges ready for dueling out-of-court settlements for Stormwrack's thousands of unresolved lawsuits. Right now, as he'd said, he'd packed off most of the fighters. The reason he had a boat full of teens was because they were practicing their seacraft. The officers herding the kids around were Sophie's age; everyone else was younger.

Since they were teaching anyway, Beck was happy to let her join a watch, to practice hauling sails and belaying lines. It gave her a chance to sharpen her archaic sailing skills and to learn the proprietary language of sailing used within the Fleet.

The memorician, Krispos, was essentially a searchable text archive. By a tragic mischance, he had spent most of his life on an island nation, Volos, serving as the backup repository of the entire creative output of a colony of budding poets. At this point in his career he should have had a head filled with useful knowledge, facts he could hire out. Instead, he was carrying reams of verse written in an obscure, rarely spoken language.

The poets had gone broke. He'd been bouncing from job to job ever since. Sophie got the idea that the scars on his foot had something to do with one particularly bad bounce. Now he was starting over.

She and he went through the books Cly had bought her and she started him with an overview of all the so-called scientific disciplines. Pretty soon she had confirmed her suspicions about the state of science on Storm-wrack: it was a mess. The Fleet had approved a number of practices that were mixes of fact and superstition.

Temperamentalism, for example, ascribed moods and qualities to a variety of substances—wax, iron, water, you name it—based on the temperatures at which they froze, liquefied, and boiled. Take copper: in the books, it was described as the element of vanity. Steel was made by condensing "the murderous principles of iron." The book had a chapter devoted to a lengthy argument between two scholars about whether the devilish substance known as petroleum did exist. If it did, one of them argued, it had such a noxious effect that it blighted the life of anyone who had ever found or used any, thus leaving that person unable to report the find.

Facts were leavened in with the magical thinking, which made it all the more interesting. The temperamentalism book contained an excellent chart of temperatures, allowing her to confirm that the boiling point of water was the same here as it was at home, and that the Stormwrackers understood that this changed with altitude (though this property was ascribed to the frivolous temperament of a fluid).

It was within temperamentalism that she found Corsetta's argument, stated as fact, that the magnetic qualities of lodestone showed that everyone had a single true love.

Then there was aetherism, a mishmash of superstitious beliefs about measurable densities of a particular type of spiritual energy, "frizion." According to the text, frizion increased with landmass and was dispersed by oceanic activity. The gist allowed practitioners to assume that bigger nations had more spiritual heft than smaller ones—it was a veiled rationalization for ethnocentrism. Aetherism also warned that the bigger the landmass, the more spooks, spirits, and other "manifestations" it might have.

"Consider the Butcher's Baste, for example," Krispos said, referring to a passage of water between Sylvanna and their near neighbor Haversham. "It's haunted by ghosts and hazards. If it wasn't properly tended by a well-paid detachment of aetherists, it might be unpassable."

"What ghosts?"

"A Havershamite seamstress and her ill-fated lover," Krispos said. "He was a butcher, from Sylvanna. Her family killed him in some horrible fashion."

Stormwrackers used aetherism as a basis for weather prediction and to explain the underpinning of spells that affected the weather. Along the way, it had tripped over some of the principles of chaos theory. That book also contained intriguing observations about magical backlash: when someone used an inscription to create a rainstorm in one part of the world, the authors noted, there was an unpredictable reaction elsewhere. Every action produced an equal but opposite reaction.

So they said, anyway. The evidence in that particular passage was haphazardly documented and, at best, anecdotal.

The discipline that packed the most common sense per square inch of printed text wasn't considered high science at all—it was seacraft. Sailors understood barometric pressure and inertia and celestial navigation. They could do a reasonable amount of trigonometry if fog or cloud made it impossible to chart their course by other means. A sailing master could calculate the volume of a ship's hold.

They also practiced something called interval navigation in hazard-filled waters. This seemed to amount to using precise velocity calculations and timed intervals to slalom one's way through a precisely charted passage when fog or simple darkness rendered sailors blind.

"Why is sailing 'low craft'?"

Krispos shrugged. He was more like a database than a fellow scholar. If he hadn't read something, he wouldn't speculate. He had no opinions of his own.

It was Zita who offered an answer. "It's primarily mechanical—so it smacks of atomism and mummery."

"And what's the problem with atomism, exactly?"

"Atomism is what destroyed the outlands, isn't it?" Zita said, offering this—like so much in the books—as a certainty. "Tapping into wells of noxious ichor, unleashing monstrous entities?"

Sophie laughed. "Since when are the outlands destroyed?"

Krispos took this as a search request: "In the final days of the Wasting, the seas climbed ever higher, devouring the land, attempting to drown the finery spawn."

"Which were?"

"Spawn of the finery?" he said, shrugging.

"Great. Very helpful." *Maybe it means rich people?*

He continued: "Panicked survivors rained mummer fire on each other, scorching all that remained. Creatures of the land drowned or starved. Birds burned in the air. Those in the seas saw their very shells and bones dissolve. Where there had been plenty, there was shortage, hunger, and want."

"Is there any more about the shells and bones?"

Krispos shook his head.

It's the Noah's Ark legend again, Sophie thought. On their last visit, Bram had begun digging into old tales about a great flood to see if they could find clues as to why Stormwrack's landmasses were so different from those of home when the moon, constellations, and boiling point of water were all the same.

"That's just a story," Zita said, earning a glare from Krispos. "We have no idea what the outlands are like. Obviously."

"You're being polite." Sophie's attention had been snagged by the parallel between the dissolving shell reference, in the memorician's story, and real-world acidification of the ocean. At home, rising carbon levels in the seas were making life ever less tenable for anything with a calcium exoskeleton.

But climate change and rising seas couldn't wipe the Rocky Mountains off the map, let alone all of Asia.

Zita sat up suddenly. "We're changing course."

They found Cly and Captain Beck up on deck, spyglasses trained on a sail so far away that it was a mere dot on the horizon. "Ah, Sophie—we were just about to send for you. Is that the ship you sighted when you were on *Nightjar*?"

Her camera's telephoto was a better glass than either of theirs: she zoomed in, then nodded. "Looks similar. I can make out the curve of that spherical wheel of theirs."

"The raider that's been sinking portside ships in Northwater?" Zita said. "You saw it?"

"Raise the mainsail," Beck ordered. "Pursuit course."

"I'm afraid we'll have to delay our homecoming, girls," Cly said as his young crew leapt to obey. "We are still a Judiciary vessel."

"You gotta do what you gotta do, right?" Sophie said.

"I believe I just said so."

"Never mind, Cly—it's an expression," Sophie said.

"Ah, I see. How long until we catch them, Lena?"

"Before nightfall, hopefully. After dark it would be easier to lose us."

"Don't give them cause to try too hard, mmm?"

"Deploy convex," Beck ordered. The ship shivered and a haze of steam rose before her in a curved curtain. The water was perfectly clear— glassine—and curved to bend light around *Sawtooth* in a way that would present a smaller image of the ship.

"Magic?" Sophie said. "The ship has magic?"

Cly nodded. "It's a parlor trick. As they look back, they'll see us maintaining our distance."

"Even as we catch up?"

"Exactly."

This explained how *Sawtooth* had crept up on *Nightjar* six months ago.

"Objects in mirror are closer than they appear," Sophie murmured.

"Ah, you're familiar with the principle."

Yeah, and I actually understand it, she thought, somewhat grumpily.

This was why they didn't trifle with proof and mistook science for a matter of opinion. When you could bend the rules of physics, it was only too natural to assume that the nature of the universe was malleable.

"I was rude last night." Cly interrupted her ruminations. "I hope you'll forgive me."

She nodded, unwilling to get into talking about sex or Lais again.

"Is Krispos working out?" He led her to a low table where he could keep an eye on the sail and indicated that one of the servants should bring tea. "Aiding with your investigations?"

It was a peace offering and she was happy to take it. "All of the schools of 'science' I've looked into so far seem to be built around a couple of reasonable observations, but they're wrapped in . . . do you know what I mean if I say superstition?"

He nodded.

"As far as I can tell, people here figure the nature of the world is a matter of opinion. If you're an aetherist, gravity works one way; if you do fluidics, then we're bound to the earth by sticky invisible strings. You pick and choose."

"Many of the nations have an approved state science," Cly said. "One that conforms well with their religious beliefs or their proprietary spells."

"That's insane. Science isn't a matter of opinion. I don't understand yet how magic fits into the rules, but something's either true or it isn't."

"I think you'll find any number of learned people who'd disagree," he said. "No, don't get offended. I'm not one such. I believe in immutable truths, and I've been pondering your chosen profession, daughter, ever since I learned of it."

She felt a sting, an interior desire to harden herself. *Here's where he'll tell me it's trivial or frivolous.*

"I think you have it in you to revolutionize the way we practice law within the Fleet," he said. "Your improvised interrogation of the doctor during your testimonial to the Convene, last time you were here—"

Sophie had realized the gathering—of most of the international government, as it turned out—was gearing up to accuse her of lying, fraud, and possibly even murder. To defend herself, she'd obliged a doctor to point out a few basic details about the body of a murdered man.

"That was just a bit of forensics, Cly. Not exactly my area, but not rocket science, either, if you know a little biology and chemistry."

"*Forehhhn sik,*" he said, rolling it on his tongue with satisfaction. "Yes. This is an Anglay word?"

"'Forensic.'"

"It will do nicely as the name for a branch of study. If forensic study could gain acceptance within the court system, it could become a sanctioned branch of knowledge within the Judiciary. That'd give temperamentalism a good stab to the left lung, wouldn't it?" His wolfish grin widened.

Sophie stared at her birth father in open-mouthed astonishment. "You want me to—"

"To compose or compile a reliable body of work that can be applied to court cases here in the Fleet, to call it forensic, to train adherents."

"It's not a religion."

"Yes, yes." An infuriating, dismissive flick of his fingers. "The point, child, is you could pursue your investigations into the nature of the world in a way that would substantially benefit the Fleet of Nations. This, in turn, should spill the wind from your cousin Annela's passion to contain and silence you. If you're usefully employed, Sylvanner, and sworn to serve the Fleet, there's no reason for her to bind your sails."

"Cly—"

"Are you all right?"

"This is . . . it's pretty much a job offer."

"Yes, indeed."

"A huge job offer." *Stormwrack CSI,* she thought, and she couldn't quite keep back a giggle.

"What kind of parent would I be if I didn't have an eye to your future?"

Her mind began to crank through possible approaches. "I thought you weren't going to take me seriously."

"It's a habitual pattern of thought with you."

"Thanks a lot, Cly."

"I speak as I observe. Someone's done you a disservice, no doubt by consistently underrating you."

"Okay! And when I want psychoanalysis . . ."

She paused because he was mouthing the word "psychoanalysis" with a look of delight at the sound. It was endearing, taking the sting out of his observation.

Parrish does that, too, she thought, grooves on unfamiliar words.

Inventing forensics from the ground up. Challenging a whole world's backward approach to science. A license to freely study Stormwrack, figuring out where it had come from and whether it represented some kind of threat to home. It was a dizzying prospect.

"What do you think?"

She reined in her imagination, considering the practicalities. "A lot of what I know of forensics—the theory, I mean—is basic science. There's lots of chemistry involved. I could learn to apply some of it pretty fast."

"And the practice?"

"Well, I've watched a lot of cop shows."

He gave her a polite smile, clearly unsure what that meant.

"At home relying on televised info, on stories, would be disastrous, but as we're getting started—we're inventing the procedures from whole cloth, right? We'd need rules about chain of evidence to ensure that somebody responsible had custody of experiments or samples or whatever."

"A sworn keeper of exhibits?"

"Yes. And specialists, carefully trained, to work in . . ." What would they need? Not so much fiber analysis or tire tracks but fingerprinting, for sure. "It would all have to work in an oceangoing city. And there are the technological limitations. No DNA sequencing here."

"Is psychoanalysis another science?"

"Sort of." She wasn't getting into hard versus squishy science with him today.

Cly was beaming. "Already hard at work, I see."

"You've given me a lot to think about."

"Excellent!"

"I'm pondering where to start."

"With court cases, presumably." The tea tray came and he began to pour. "I've asked Krispos to read up on a half-dozen hard lumps that have been crammed in the gizzard of the court system for years. Cases that could potentially hinge on matters of fact."

"As opposed to what?"

"Testimony. Opinion. Combat."

"Can you do that as a judge? Involve yourself?"

"Normally, no. I have a personal stake in these." He seemed pleased that she'd thought of it. "I'm already banned from involving myself officially. The irony is that means I'm permitted to influence them."

"Does Krispos have the hard copies?" Playing Q-and-A with the memorician was useful only once she knew what she was looking for.

"Of course. They're about animals and plants; I knew that much of your specialty, anyway. Sylvanna's rather plagued by such suits."

So there's a big potential benefit to you, back home, if you get me established in the court system. "I'll look at them right away," she said, rising.

He toasted her with his teacup and she found her way down to the hold. Krispos was murmuring over one of the transcripts; she picked up another, one he'd already read, and pretended to ignore his glower as she left with it.

Then, before heading back up, she ducked into her cabin, writing a quick note on the messageply: CLY IS SUGGESTING I START UP A STORM-WRACK CSI UNIT IN FLEET.

She was putting the page away when text appeared, so neatly lettered it might have been machine printed: *To do what?*

Sophie scratched out: REVERSE-ENGINEER FORENSICS, TRAIN EXPERT WITNESSES, PUT HARD EVIDENCE BEFORE PERSONAL TESTIMONY, THAT KIND OF THING.

She was putting the page away when more text appeared: HOW DOES THAT GET YOU BACK OUT TO DOING PRIMARY RESEARCH? OR FIGURING OUT WHAT/WHEN STORMWRACK IS, NOT TO MENTION WHETHER HOME'S GONNA GO KABLOOEY?

Sophie: JOB = SALARY + PERMISSION TO SAIL PLACES/STUDY THINGS WITHOUT GETTING STOMPED BY GOVERNMENT OR ACCUSED OF SPYING.

Bram: YOU'VE BEEN ACCUSED OF SPYING????

Sophie: NO.

NOT YET, ANYWAY. She added: THINK: IF WE HAVE HELP GATHERING HARD INFO RE STORMWRACK, IT'LL HELP US INVESTIGATE THE LINK BETWEEN HERE AND HOME. BETTER THAN GRABBING WHATEVER FACTS SLIDE PAST US.

Bram: YOU'D HAVE MINIONS?

Sophie: WOULD HAVE TO, I THINK.

Bram: THAT WOULD HELP. THIS IS COOL, SOFE—CONGRATS.

Sophie drew a little happy face on the sheet of magical paper: C GAVE ME CASE FILES. I'LL UPDATE YOU SOON.

Bram: KTHXBAI.

She laid a hand on the page: the illusion of texting made home and her brother seem very close by. Then, when no new words appeared, she picked up her transcript and headed back for the ladder up to the main deck.

CHAPTER 9

There was something like cheating in the way they spent the next few hours creeping up on the little sailing ship, using the illusion provided by the convex to keep it from realizing they were closing the gap. It was like watching a cat hunt an unsuspecting bird, the slow predatory creep upon an entirely helpless target.

Still, these people were suspected of killing the crews of half a dozen ships.

As the chase stretched, Captain Beck busied herself with preparing to board and search the target, talking the teenage sailors through a maneuver that would bring the ship into a sweep alongside the other craft. *Sawtooth* had two older cannoneers, taciturn men as muscled as *Nightjar*'s Krezzo, tasked with firing at the ship once they were within range.

Cly, meanwhile, drilled his half-dozen young duelists on boarding tactics.

If either Cly or Beck was concerned about taking on a ship that was allegedly full of murderers, using a crew of young recruits, it didn't show. *Sawtooth* was massive compared to the ship they were pursuing; she had numbers on her side, even if those numbers were largely inexperienced.

Zita was up drilling with the other duelists, so there was nobody but Krispos to talk to Sophie. Together they made a study of their target—she was maybe twenty feet long, with patched, greasy-looking sails. Looking through her telephoto as they got closer, Sophie counted six crew. Unless there was someone below, there were only four guys and two women aboard, all busily engaged in catching every breath of wind. They might not know *Sawtooth* was closing on them, but they wanted to leave her behind.

The ship was riding high in the water—whatever she had been stealing from the ships she'd sunk, she wasn't carrying any heavy cargo at the moment, Sophie deduced. The crew looked weary, unhealthy, even starved. If these were pirates, they weren't successful ones.

Why were they raiding ships at all? And how?

Violence again, she thought. Parrish had said life in the Fleet was safe, but here she was on the periphery of another fight.

It's not as though anyone expects me to participate. The thought wasn't as reassuring as she would have hoped; from time to time, she found herself checking her pocket for her key ring and the little canister of bear spray.

As the hours crawled by, the skinny captain got visibly edgy about his failure to lose *Sawtooth*. He and one of the others had an argument, gesturing over a bundle on deck. The crewman protested, furiously . . . right up until the captain smacked him. Shoulders sagging, he took out a long knife, opened the sacking, and cut out—

"Oh God, that's a heart, a human heart." Her gorge rose even as she took the shot.

Cly said, "Are you certain?"

She nodded and showed him the frame.

"How soon can we close?" he asked Beck.

"Not long," the captain said, considering it. "That's their lives, then."

"What?" Sophie said.

"Using human remains in an inscription is a capital crime, unless the subjects volunteered for use," Cly explained.

"How do you know they're using the heart for magic?"

"Why else would they be mutilating a body? They plan to work an intention against us."

"You mean the heart will be some kind of battle thing?"

"Attack or defense, yes."

"Why are they running if they can sink ships?"

"Their first two victims were barely bigger than bumboats, and the captain of *Drifter*, the derelict you found, was known to be a drunkard," Cly said. "She'll show her teeth, all right—she's desperate. We'll knock them out, no fear."

"I don't know that I am afraid," Sophie replied.

"Nobody thinks you're a coward," Cly said. "You keep your head in a crisis."

With that, he returned to his duelists.

Feeling nettled, Sophie continued to scan the boat. Small ship, small crew, no booty to speak of—well, they could be stealing something light but valuable, like diamonds—and they had a spellscribe.

What had the targeted ships been carrying?

"They're making for the islet," cried a crewman from the crow's nest.

The other ship wasn't just making for the peaked scrap of land, it was all but running itself aground on its shores.

"Ah." Beck grinned. "Hoping to abandon ship and vanish into the forest? Why not? We're hours behind, aren't we?"

"Send them into a panic," Cly said, with perceptible satisfaction. "Drop convex."

The shimmer surrounding Sawtooth turned to steam; the bow of the ship sliced through. Sophie felt a warm kiss of sauna against her cheeks.

Shouts of consternation arose from the small crew of the bandit. They threw themselves into furious action. The captain ran the length of the deck, scattering something grainy into the water. The ship itself began to thump, as if it were a drum. The rhythm was a pulse: *ba-dum, ba-dum*. Fist-size bubbles the bright green color of algae rose from the ocean around the ship, thousands of them. They pulsed, ever so slightly, in time to the beat as they drifted toward *Sawtooth*.

"Does anyone recognize this intention?" Beck asked.

A chorus of "No, Captain!"

She looked to Cly, who shook his head.

"Finish this before the foam accumulates," he said.

Beck nodded. "Cannons one and two, fire!"

The cannoneers had been forming sandspheres; by now, they each had a tidy stockpile. Sophie was reminded, again, of kids building up to a snowball fight. The taller of the two hurled blasts of fire at the ship's mainmast. One found its mark, exploding the wood to matchsticks. The other cannoneer punched two tidy holes in the hull, right at the point where her hull met the waterline.

She began to take water.

The *ba-dum, ba-dum* got faster; the greenish bubbles foamed like a pot aboil. The two ships were now perhaps fifty meters apart.

"Surrender and prepare to be boarded." Beck's words boomed out over the water.

"What do you think?" Zita had come up on deck next to Sophie. She held a flat, wide sword—would that be a cutlass?—whose blade appeared to be made of a wafer of inscribed bone or tusk.

"Looks like a last stand to me," Sophie said.

The water around the sinking ship began to heave. Figures belched up from it: human shaped, white in color, with no features except bloodred eyes. Were they made of sea salt? They looked a little like department store mannequins.

"Salt frights!" someone shouted.

One of the "frights" wedged itself into the gap where *Sawtooth*'s cannon had holed the hull. Its face stared out from the patch like a carved mask on a wall. Its mouth yawned open and, with convulsions that looked very much like it was vomiting, it began to heave salt water back into the ocean.

A pump?

"That's a heavy intention for such a small vessel to bear," Cly observed, as the rest of the salt frights began to follow the drifting array of greenish, pulsing bubbles toward *Sawtooth*. "The frights are defending the ship."

"Why bother?" Zita said. "They can't know we're understaffed. Scripped or no, six starved sailors can't hope to take on *Sawtooth*."

"They're dead for using the heart, right?" Sophie said. She was shooting pictures even as she spoke, taking frame after frame of the figures. "And for killing those other ships' crews?"

"And frightening, too. All capital crimes."

"What have they got to lose?"

"Run out the plank and prepare to board," Beck ordered. Two of the cadets had raised a hatch next to the rail; instead of a way into the bowels of the ship, it had concealed a trampoline, stretched hide covered in dense, bright-red spellscrip.

"Steady, cannon one," Cly said. "Bailor, bring me crossbows. One heavy, one light."

One of the crew scrambled to comply.

"Zita, you know this weapon, don't you?"

"At this range, Your Honor—"

"Come, give it a try," he said. "You're spoiled for targets."

The girl slipped up beside him, taking up the smaller bow and straining to load it.

"There," Cly said, picking one of the approaching salt figures. "For the eye."

Zita swallowed, drew on the golem, and sent a bolt wide.

"Keep trying," he said. "The rest of you, ready with blades."

With that, he raised his own bow and took a long, slow breath. Ignoring the salt creatures, he sent a bolt directly into the throat of the bandit ship's captain.

Sophie let out a shocked yelp as the captain of the other ship went down, thrown backward by the force of the bolt, dead so instantly he didn't even twitch as he fell.

"Surrender yourselves," Cly called to the other ship as its surviving crew—who looked young, suddenly, young and aghast and terrified—dove for cover. One tried to thin herself behind the smoking stub that was all that remained of the mainmast. One dove below. A third ducked behind a water barrel.

A blast of fire behind them made everyone jump.

It was the cannoneer up in the *Sawtooth* crow's nest. Greenish bubbles had adhered to his skin, coating him in a slick foam. He had fired a blast straight down, barely missing the trampoline. The wood deck erupted into flames.

"Fire on deck!" Beck said. "Port watch, put out that fire!"

Cly lowered his bow, making a tutting noise deep in his throat. "Sophie, can you see what that spellscribe is up to now?"

She raised the camera again. "No."

Cly caught the other cannoneer's eye and flicked a finger at the boy hiding behind the barrel. He lobbed a stone at the barrier, shattering the wood, which began to smolder and burn.

By now Zita had got a couple crossbow bolts into the salt creatures scrabbling at the edge of *Sawtooth*. They leaked when punctured, as if they were contained in sacks. A few of the bubbles had gathered on her wrists and forearms.

The young man flung himself out from under the remains of the barrel, running for cover, and Cly shot him neatly in the chest with a crossbow bolt.

"I won't give you another chance," Cly said reloading. His voice carried over the crackle of fire behind them. "Be reasonable. You're outmatched."

The other cannoneer punctuated this with a twin blast to the deck, which hurled another of the bandits into the water.

That was when Zita turned on her heel, swinging her sword at Sophie.

Definitely a cutlass, she thought, as she let herself fall backward. The blade whisked overhead and then Cly was there, parrying with the crossbow, the blade meeting wood with a dull thunk.

Sophie scrambled backward, trying to take in the whole deck at once. The seaweed bubbles that had been blowing up over the *Sawtooth* decks seemed to be concentrating on this part of the ship.

Whatever the reason, they were thickening around them like a fist. Many of the recruits had bubble-shaped splashes on their flesh; they looked disoriented, and a few had begun to brawl.

Not gas, Sophie thought. It's absorbed through the skin.

There were no bubbles on her yet.

I'm not a threat. They're massing on the people with weapons.

She had a sudden vision of Cly dicing his way through the ranks of confused teenagers.

She'd been wearing a fleece jacket when she came up on deck. She took a second to grab it, fighting her way into the sleeves and pulling the drawstrings of the hood tight over her face, covering as much skin as possible. The crossbow bolts had fallen to the deck and she scooped up a pair of them.

"Zita," Cly ordered. "Stand down. Stand down immediately!"

The first of the salt mannequins was pulling itself up onto the fighting deck.

Nobody aboard *Sawtooth* had died yet, as far as Sophie could tell. The kid officers were brawling with each other. Cly had flung Zita across the sword-fighting ring, depriving her of her blade in the process. Now he decapitated two of the monsters with a great, salt-spraying swing of his arm. He was gripping the rail with his free hand, looking white-knuckled and a little wild-eyed. Green bubbles were breaking against him, one after another.

"Stay back, child."

"You have to get it off your skin," she said, pointing to the residue.

"Understood." Instead, he stabbed another salty boarder.

If he recovers, we'll probably be okay. There aren't that many of them. If he doesn't . . . well, he's a killing machine. All these cadets.

Taking a deep breath, Sophie bolted toward the trampoline.

She ran a straight line toward the smaller ship—*commit, commit, commit!*—and jumped, thinking about where she wanted to land. On the deck, next to that hemispheric steering wheel.

"Flex your knees . . . ," but the landing was as gentle as if she'd been in an elevator.

The foam of bubbles rising from the seas around the small ship changed direction suddenly, making for her.

Spells are textual, she reminded herself. Destroy the text, destroy the spell.

She hit the deck running, skirting two cannon-blasted bodies, eyes open for spellscrip. "Text, text, text," she was muttering under her breath.

Instead, she saw a human heart.

It was mounted within a coral structure that appeared to be the ship's wheel, a dome-shaped growth, bone white in color. Portions of it had been sanded smooth and the writing was there, deep within, protected by sharp edges and spiny growths. The heart was nestled in a carved-out chamber near the top, its arteries connected to outcroppings in the coral structure, and pumping. It was covered in slick green slime—algae, Sophie thought.

She drove one of the crossbow bolts into it—not cleanly, or even with special force, but the ungainly move was nevertheless enough to pierce one of the ventricles.

The timbers of the small ship groaned—screamed, really—as if giant hands were bending them. It jolted and they listed to port. She heard a series of crystalline pops and wasn't sure if that was the green bubbles or the salt monsters.

Someone grabbed her from behind.

She kicked at the guy, a little feebly. It was all a bit like her self-defense class, suddenly, except that the guy wasn't padded. He wasn't playing, either, though his intent seemed more desperate than murderous.

She tried to swing him into the coral, failed, and fumbled for her bear spray. Could she shoot him without giving herself a blast in the face?

"No!" she said. "No, no!" Her instructor would be so proud.

The man tightened his grip as the judder of the trampoline rang through the air.

Suddenly Cly was aboard. He landed beside the mainmast and cut a bloody furrow into the midsection of the surprised bandit there. He whirled as she fell, found another, kicked him flat to the deck, then stabbed him in the chest.

Then he addressed himself to the guy still grabbing for purchase at Sophie's hoodie.

"Take," he said, "your hands off my daughter."

The man let her go as if she were hot, turning chalk white and putting his hands in the air. He had a bloody nose.

The captain of the ship hit him, she remembered.

Cly held out a hand to Sophie, helping her up, and then retrieved a handkerchief from the deck, cleaning red blood and algae bubbles from his blade.

He looked at the guy with an air of pleasant anticipation.

"He's surrendered," Sophie said. Her voice was shaking. "Cly, he's given up."

The man backed up to the rail. Cly strolled after him, bringing the point of the cutlass up to his chest, then coming in close, wrapping his hand around the thin neck and beginning to squeeze.

"Cly, stop! What's wrong with you? He surrendered!" She grabbed for his arm, which was iron.

He turned, regarding her as if from far away. The expression—or lack of one—on his face raised the hairs on her neck.

They froze there, the three of them, the bandit thrashing and gasping, Cly looking at her like a scientist staring down a microscope, Sophie bone-chilled and realizing: Oh! Oh! This is what the Verdanii wouldn't say.

Except her birth mother *had* tried to tell her: *What if you'd found Cly,* Beatrice had said, *and his title was Lord High Executioner? What if he was the guy who pressed the button on the gas chamber?*

"Please," Sophie said. "Don't kill him. Please, Cly."

He opened his hand and let the man fall. "As you wish, daughter. Kir, consider yourself impressed to the Judiciary."

The man gasped at her feet.

Cly surveyed the scene then, both ships smoldering, four bodies on the deck in spreading pools of blood and a fifth in the water, and the clusters of salt dissolving in the sea. He smiled very slightly.

"You saved us, Sophie." He put his arm out but she slipped out of reach.

"Don't." She was seriously considering whether she might throw up.

"You're shaken; it's understandable. We'll get you back aboard *Sawtooth.*"

"Thank you," she said.

Before he could say more, she began a slow circuit of the deck, putting what space she could between them.

It wasn't much. The ship was small, barely twenty feet long, and quarters were cramped. A sheet of sail hung over an improvised hammock, hinting that there wasn't room below for even a crew of six to sleep comfortably. There was a pair of shallow bowls beneath a bench, one empty but for a dessicated twist of what looked like sardine, the other with a residual ring of mineral on the bottom. A water dish, but one that had fallen out of use.

The hemisphere of coral at the center of the ship did indeed seem to serve as its wheel: it was mounted on a tilting plate and had two smooth branches that allowed one to steer it to and fro. Within the center of the blood-spattered branches was the ship's full name, *Rettegrad Salla*

Incannis. Magical lettering was laid down in lines of seeds that had been stuck into place. Sophie remembered kindergarden art projects: writing her name in glue and then scattering glitter overtop.

She scratched off a small sample: they might have been anything, these small dots, but they reminded her of poppy seeds.

She could feel Cly's eyes on her. She pocketed the sample of coral and seed and moved on.

Near the stern of the ship were two wooden folding chairs, ratty and heavily used but otherwise no different from beach chairs she'd find at home. Next to one of these she found a sack of short, somewhat coarse hair and a spinner. The individual strands were multicolored: gray, brown, white, even apricot. Together they made a muddy gray-brown yarn with the bristly texture of coarse wool.

She fingered the bag, letting herself think about it, letting the process of consideration calm her, as far as that was possible. Her mind offered up random conclusions: *cats are rare, the bandit captain hit our prisoner, this whole ship was built to make . . . salt frights, they called them.*

By now Captain Beck had put two boats in the water, crewed by teens who were rowing mightily. Eager to survey the scene of their victory?

Cly, meanwhile, had searched his prisoner—coming up with a jar of poppy seeds and an awl—and bound his hands. "Is this your brainchild, spellscribe? Are you a frightmaker?"

He shook his head violently.

"Your life's already forfeit, if we prove banditry. There's no harm in admitting it."

"No. The ship makes the frights, when properly . . ." He swallowed. "Primed."

"With a human heart, mmm?"

"Please," he said. "I didn't inscribe the ship."

"Tell me your name. Are you of Haversham?"

"Nobody, Kir, of no nation whatever."

"It's Your Honor, not Kir. Well, someone will claim you."

Sophie raised the hatch, peering below. The little ship was taking water, though slowly. The crew had come close enough to the islet that the ship was all but resting on the bottom; she could feel the occasional wave raising and shifting them, then the bump as they touched down again. Sunlight shot through the blasted-out hole where the magical cannonfire had struck it. The gap was big enough, possibly, for a small person to escape through.

Had any of them gotten away? If so, there was no sign of them. She wasn't about to suggest that Cly hunt them down.

The hold—the portion of it that wasn't underwater—was as small and cramped as she had guessed.

She perched on the ladder and raked her fingers through the rising water, almost catching her extended hand on a fishhook before retrieving a random selection of items: a straw hat, carved wooden utensils, a safety float, and a pair of small crates. There was a long wooden bar with a beaded string affixed to it, but she let that float away.

By now, the rowboats must have arrived. She heard Cly say, "Return Sophie and the prisoner to *Sawtooth.*"

She stepped back out onto the deck. He had pried open one of the crates, revealing a bowl of amber pieces and a collection of small speckled eggs, packed in straw.

"Bring back a carpenter. I want the wheel taken aboard," Cly added. "The Spellscrip Institute will want a look at it. We'll tow whatever's left out to open water and scuttle her."

"Yes, Your Honor," chorused the kids.

"Are you ready to go, Sophie?"

She nodded and swung a leg over the listing rail, landing easily and then holding up her hands to help maneuver the bound man into the boat. They were going to end up staring at each other all the way back.

Is he glad I saved him from Cly? she wondered. Or would he have rather just died?

"May I help row?" she asked, and one of the sailors handed her an oar and let her shift into position.

"On my count. One, two, pull!"

They rowed. The prisoner, if you could call him that, sat shivering with his head down.

Soon enough she was climbing a rope ladder dropped from *Sawtooth*'s main deck, taking Beck's spectral hand and letting her raise her the last few steps.

"You saved us considerable trouble and injury," Beck said warmly. "Thank you, child."

"Not a child," Sophie told her wearily. She headed down to her cabin, taking a seat at the little writing desk. There was a not-a-text from Bram, English words cribbed in a tight, handwritten font, on the writing paper: HOW'S IT GOING WITH THE PATER?

Her eyes filled with tears and she picked up the pen. With a shaking hand, she wrote: I THINK CLY'S A SOCIOPATH.

CHAPTER 10

Bram didn't answer.

Sophie spent a couple minutes below, crying out the tension from the fight and then taking a stab at meditating. But with the ship damaged and a crew of teens aboard, it didn't feel right to just hide. Besides, her mind was too full for the confines of her cabin.

Drying her eyes, she headed back topside.

The prisoner was gone, presumably locked up somewhere. The fire caused by the dropped cannonball was long since out and a couple young carpenters were prying out the boards that had been burned.

Across the water, older cadets were crawling over the beached ship, going through the crates and completing the search Sophie had begun.

A thread of doubt assailed her. Perhaps Cly had been enraged by the bandits' cruelty.

Sociopathy's pretty rare, she told herself. Everything happened so fast, and the guy had grabbed me.

Instead of obsessing, she found the second mate. "What can I do?"

"We heard you're a medic."

"I know a little first aid. I brought . . . I have pills. Outlander medicine."

The mate shrugged. "Check in with the doctor on deck three."

"Aye, aye." Apparently they didn't say that here—he looked at her blankly and pointed the way.

The infirmary occupied a large area belowdecks, more or less directly

below her laboratory. It was a lavish allocation of space, but it made sense—
Sawtooth was, after all, a fighting gym at sea. There was one doctor and
three patients down there. The unconscious cannoneer was in a half-
seated position, bound to a yoke with his arms behind him. Beside him
were two young crew members.

The doctor glanced her way as she came in. He was stitching a long gash
in the boy's leg.

"I'm Sophie," she said. "They thought you might need help?"

"Sent my nurse home to Tiladene for a rest when His Honor went on
leave," he said. "Kir Waller here, she's took badly to the bandits' spell."

"Okay." The girl was sitting quietly enough on a bench. Her breath was
labored, and when Sophie turned to her, she raised her chin for inspec-
tion. Her neck was covered in bright red angry-looking hives . . . and in
scratches.

"The green bubbles hit you here?"

"Yes, Kir."

"Looks to me like she's allergic, not that I know anything," Sophie said
to the doctor. "Do you . . . have that here? Immunology?"

"Told you, she took badly," he replied, impatient. "Likely the spell uses
maddenflur. We'll have to test."

"I didn't bring antihistamines. Oh, wait, that's not true. . . ." There was
a blister pack of cold and sinus something in her bag, wasn't there? That
might help a bit.

"Maddenflur thorns," the doctor said. "The blue pottery jug in that cabinet. No, that one. Take it out."

He didn't want her for her first aid skills; he just needed an extra pair
of hands. Relieved, Sophie did as he asked. The glaze on the jug was clev-
erly done and had a symbol in black, a skull not very different from that
on a poison warning at home.

"Take out a thorn, just one."

She fumbled to do it. They were tiny, curved like cats' claws. "Okay."

The kid being stitched up cried out a little and the surgeon spoke to
him softly, in a language she didn't recognize. "Did Kir Waller break any
of her weals?"

Sophie looked at the scratches on the girl's forearms. "Oh yeah."

"Press the point of the thorn against the raw flesh."

"I'm all right," the girl protested. "It's not maddenflur sensitivity."

"Easy does it." Sophie did as the doctor instructed. It was an awkward operation, balancing the thread of plant against the scraped spot. The effect wasn't quite instantaneous, but it was fast enough: within thirty seconds, that part of the girl's arm had whitened and she was wheezing harder. Also crying.

"I'm making her worse," Sophie said.

"Hold my thread," the doctor said.

They switched places, Sophie finding herself going from laying her hand on the girl's wrist to pinching two strips of gashed flesh together and hanging on to a needle.

"Hold it tight," he advised.

Any germs the girl had, the boy's got them now.

The doctor hadn't washed his hands, either.

He eased the wheezing girl into a reclining position—she was sniffling—and gave her what looked like a smallish lollypop. Then he dug out a thick, greasy-looking salve and spread it on her, covering the entire affected area on her chest and arms, and a good chunk of other real estate besides.

"Thank you," he said, taking back his stitching. Sophie slipped out her hand sanitizer and scrubbed to her elbows.

"She'll be okay?"

"Maddenflur sensitivity is serious business," he murmured. "She's finished as a duelist. She'll have to take a job within the bureaucracy."

"But she'll live?"

"Yes." He finished with the boy, went and pried up the cannoneer's eyelids and thought a bit before going rooting in the cabinets of sealed jars. "Kir Sophie, in the hold aft there are a few of my trunks. I'm looking for a wooden case marked 'For Skull Fracture.'"

"The text is in Fleet?"

"And Sylvanner. Would you fetch it, please?"

"Sure."

"Take that lantern."

She obeyed, headed down the corridor, counting hatches. She bumped against the bulkhead on the way, as the ship made a sharp course correction.

Guess they got the mainsail back up, she thought. And then, with a shudder: If we're moving, Cly's aboard again.

She forced herself to focus on clambering down, one-handed, to the hold on a fixed wooden flight of steep and narrow steps.

The storage hold was for more than just doctor stuff: there were about a hundred labeled cabinets containing weapons—swords of various lengths, pikes, clubs. There were a handful of punching bags and practice dummies in neat piles on the floor and a clothing rack of leather armor.

Most of the weapons were made of wood, treated with that iridescent glaze that made them metal-strong and sharp.

Beyond the gym equipment, in a cabinet walled in silk, was a woman.

At first glance, she startled Sophie—it was like coming upon a person lurking in a corner. Then she realized it was a ship's figurehead, carved from a woody substance she didn't recognize.

The carving was intricate and lifelike: the woman looked to be thirty-five, with smile lines just starting to set in around her eyes. She was clad in real clothes, a loose, silky dress of the type that looked so good in classical carvings. Her feet didn't disappear into the post welded to her back. Rather, she dangled, showing a hint of a sandal beneath the hem of the skirt. One of her hands held a serrated blade.

Before Sophie could turn away, she flickered. Light filled her eyes and spread across her face and down her throat. The shape of her breasts and hips glowed through the fabric of the dress.

She looked down at Sophie with an expression of friendly, thoroughgoing delight. "Who might you be, child?"

Gee, that's not a complicated question. "I'm Sophie."

"Sailor or duelist?"

"Videographer. Scientist. Who are you?"

"I am Eugenia Merrin Sawtooth, face and spirit of this vessel." She held out the hand not holding a weapon. "You resemble Clydon! Can it be he has some kin at last?"

"Uh, yes. His daughter."

Eugenia's smile brightened. "I'd no idea."

"Neither did he."

The figurehead did a complicated wriggle with her shoulder blades and dropped off the beam of wood supporting her. She put one cool hand on Sophie's shoulder. "What brings you to the hold?"

"Skull fracture." She explained about the cannoneer.

"Surgical supplies are here." Eugenia made her way to the back of the hold and opened a pair of trunks.

"I have so much I want to ask you," Sophie said. "What are you doing in the hold, for one thing, and what are you?" And was she happy and how did the glow work and, most of all, what did she know about Cly?

"Return to your patient," the woman said, stretching. "I'm not going anywhere."

A talking figurehead who seemed to know at least something of Cly's history. Feeling pleased, Sophie brought the skull fracture box back to the medical officer. It was itself a skull, broken into pieces and wired together again so that the spaces between each piece left room enough for the medical officer to slide it over the injured canonneer's head, like a cap. The calvaria and eye sockets lay over his face in a piece. The doctor tucked a leech underneath the forehead before covering the patient with a blanket.

"When the skull is struck hard, there can be blood," he explained, "in and around the brain."

"I think we call that a subdural hematoma."

"Fancy language won't heal a bruised brain, Kir. The cap aligns the broken bones and the leech draws out the bleeding. It—the skull—was the head of a healer who set such injuries."

Sophie nodded. "I've seen another magic skull, actually—a lantern. And there's a lawsuit brewing over a musician's bones."

"Relic craft," he said. He was monitoring his patient's pulse now. "Very common."

"I don't know the term."

"One uses the remains of someone who has died to preserve and exploit the magical intentions laid upon them in life. You've been inscribed so you speak Fleet, yes?"

"Yes."

"After your death, your tongue might be used to translate your native language to Fleet."

"Just what I always wanted—an afterlife as a disembodied tongue."

"You should make specific mention of it in your will. It's how many magical objects are fashioned: our boarding trampolines are made from acrobats' sinews." He surveyed the infirmary, then rummaged in a drawer, coming up with a sack containing about six lemons. "If you'll watch over the patients for twenty minutes or so, I have business elsewhere."

"No problem."

She took out her camera as soon as he was gone, taking shots of the medical lab and in particular the labels on all his concoctions. She lingered over the locked cabinet with the maddenflur products, then leafed through an anatomy text. Next to that was a treatise on common fighting injuries and a stack of pamphlets about treating scribed people with other than human characteristics—bird bones, lizard skin, you name it.

The problem with being somewhere where everything is unknown and cool is you can never narrow down your field of inquiry enough to learn anything in depth, she thought. Getting to understand Stormwrack would take years. Possibly decades.

The question returned: Was she ready to spend that much time here?

Having no answer, she contented herself with gathering information, taking photo after photo of the pamphlets about magical alterations.

After the doctor returned and dismissed her, she checked in again with the second mate. "You may resume being a guest, Kir," he said. "The crew is grateful for your assistance."

"What's Cly up to?"

"Reporting the action, I believe. His Honor is hoping we can rendez-vous with someone who will take Kir Lidman back to Fleet."

"Kir who?"

"Your prisoner."

"Mine, is he?" She returned to her cabin to check the messageply—no answer from Bram yet—and then poked her nose in the lab. Krispos had apparently been there the whole time, engrossed in a book titled *Intersections of Aura and Temperament*.

"You read those lawsuits Cly mentioned, didn't you?"

He brightened. "Indeed. I've read the transcripts for all five cases. The first—"

"You put the other transcripts away?"

He looked a little crestfallen but opened a cupboard, revealing the encyclopedia-size sheaves of paper.

She swapped in the transcript she'd taken, opening the next. As with the other, its first chapter was an overview. She skimmed it while the memorician huffed and sighed.

"I'm sorry, Krispos," she said. "I appreciate what you do, and you're going to be really helpful. It's just my custom to flip through things."

"Yes, all right, I understand." His tone was sulky.

"It's an outlander thing."

"I understand." Definitely sulking.

Sophie kept skimming until she'd looked at them all.

"Cly says he has a personal tie to these cases."

"They affect his lands, friends, or near neighbors."

"Which one's dearest to his heart, do you think?"

He nudged the oldest of the case files, a dispute with Sylvanna's near neighbor, Haversham. The government of Sylvanna alleged that Haversham had deliberately infected their lowlands with a species of invasive vine that, from its description, sounded much like kudzu.

Haversham's defense was that the passage between the two nations, the Butcher's Baste, was too heavily guarded to allow saboteurs.

"Hard to prove if the trail's been cold for twenty-five years, don't you think?" Sophie set it aside.

The next two were suits filed against Sylvanna's national spell research institute. One claimed they had propagated a turtle species native to another island; the second, that they'd exploited some kind of honeybee, in violation of Fleet treaties. The last two were straightforward accusations of theft or maybe industrial espionage: they claimed the institute had flat-out stolen newly developed spells and rushed them through the Fleet certification process—which sounded like a patent office—even though the spells weren't theirs to certify.

She could feel the weight of Krispos's attention as she flipped.

"This Sylvanner Spellscrip Institute gets sued a lot," she hazarded, which was more a comment than a request for information.

"The honeybee case references sixty other actions in progress against them as of Maille last year."

"Sixty accusations, huh? What are the odds they're entirely innocent?"

"I'd need a treatise on odds-making to answer that," he replied.

She poked the pile of doorstop-thick transcripts. "Cly thinks these cases could be winnable—there could be hard evidence to prove them."

"Yes?"

"That argues Sylvanna's in the right, as far as he knows."

The memorician squinted, apparently trying to work out whether she was asking him something. His eye wandered to his book on auras.

Sophie picked up the turtle case. "The first question would be whether the turtles from Grimreef really are the same species as those on Sylvanna."

Krispos perked up. "That was agreed by both parties in a hearing six years ago. Physical characteristics were found by the court to be identical—"

"External characteristics only? Or did they dissect?"

He mouthed the word "dissect" with apparent discomfort. "The presiding judge looked at a specimen from each beach."

Sophie could just see it: a judge with two turtles, flipping them over and concluding, "Gosh, they look the same to me!"

Of course they wouldn't consult a taxonomist. If they even have such a thing.

"The auras of the specimen turtles were examined by a prominent aetherian. Most tellingly, spellscribes were able to use the shells of both species as mixing bowls for the specialized armoring intention used on quarry workers."

"A hearing like that, is it something they could revisit?"

She could almost hear Bram chuckling. *What are you going to do, Sofe, run the turtles' DNA?*

"I haven't read the Fleet Code of Law, Kir."

"No." That was Cly, appearing suddenly, in that catlike way he had, lounging against the hatch of Sophie's lab. "The courts are busy enough as it is without requestioning established certainties."

"Certainties," she said.

"Physical examination is a flimsy standard of proof—you're right about that. But the two shells produced the same magical outcome. That is conclusive."

I'll have to find out if that's true. She added a note to her book of questions.

"You're looking at the Turtle Beach file, then? Not the throttlevine?"

"Just browsing." She searched his face. She wasn't a psychologist or psychiatrist—her certainty, an hour ago, that Cly might be sociopathic was eroding. He had always seemed emotional enough: he was all hugs and smiles, and there was that needle-sharp sense of humor.

Maybe I watch too much crime TV.

Stop guessing. Test him.

"How's the survivor from the other ship?"

"Survivor? The man who laid hands on you?"

"The term's fair if the others are all dead, isn't it? Lidman, I think he's called?"

Instead of taking the bait, he said, "Did Sophie tell you she saved us from military embarrassment at the hands of a six-man sloop, Krispos?"

"Indeed, Kir?"

Cly had not crossed the threshold of the lab. "May I come in?"

Seriously, waiting to come into my space? Good boundaries.

"Of course."

He perched on a bench. "She charged our plank as confidently as if she'd taken the Fleet boarding exam. Landed right beside their spellscribe and knocked out their primary offensive inscription. You've the makings of a warrior, girl."

"Cly—"

"Yes, yes, the prisoner. His teeth are loose in his head and he's got scurvy. Doctor's feeding him lemon juice. Looked minded to hang himself, so he's bound."

"Did you figure out what they were up to?"

"It appears to be petty banditry." Cly opened a hand, revealing a spiney pink whirl of calcium, coiled like a corkscrew at its base and then straightening to a point. "Curling anemone," he said. "Most valuable thing we found aboard, though there was a sizeable amount of powdered madden-flur sap and a cache of the petals. The seeds, too—you found those."

"Maddenflur's an opiate, am I right?" Parrish had mentioned it once, and Sophie had gotten a good look at it in the infirmary; the plant was thorny, but the flowers, seeds, and pods were reminiscent of opium poppies. "Painkiller, addictive."

"Yes."

"What's with the anemone spike?" She took it, examining it closely.

"They also have various benign and recreational uses."

"Another drug?"

"It seems likely that the ship *Incannis* most lately sank was transporting spell components and medical contraband."

"So . . . we have bandits sinking smugglers?"

"A little side business for their captains. Shady, but common enough. Nothing to warrant murdering their crews."

"Nobody deserves to be executed," she agreed, remembering the bandits' captain falling with the crossbow bolt in his throat.

"It's an all-around-terrible business," Cly said, tone sober. "But—the turtles?"

She decided to go with him on the change of subject. "Well, the other island in the suit—"

"Grimreef," Krispos and Cly said simultaneously.

"Grimreef accuses the Sylvanner Spellscrip Institute of transplanting them to this one beach—basically, sneaking a bunch of turtle eggs from Grimreef to Sylvanna. The idea is once the turtles hatched there, that's where they'd return to lay. They say this happened about eighty years ago?"

"Yes."

"There won't be any evidence of the theft left, unless of course there's documentation, a paper trail."

Cly grinned. "I was rather hoping you'd prove we *didn't* do it."

"Truth's truth, Cly. Aren't you a judge or something?"

"Quite right." He bowed from the neck. "I believe I can guarantee there's no paper track to find."

Which doesn't mean they didn't do it. "I have some ideas about ways to start documenting the animal behavior patterns. It'll cost your institute guys or . . . does someone own the beach?"

"Yes, it's privately held."

"Well, it'll cost some money and might take a few years to build up good data, but—"

That pish-posh flick of the hand. "No matter. The case would be in court for another decade, at this rate. You see what a boon your forensic practices might be?"

Is that sincerity or flattery?

"Now—I wondered if you'd consent to having that conversation with the tailor I brought. I'd like you dressed as a Sylvanner when we arrive. But . . ." He inclined his head.

Sophie glanced at her clothes. There were green blotches on her hoodie where the maddenflur bubbles had popped, blood on her jeans from helping with the gashed sailor's leg, and a long smear of something sooty.

"My clothes are too filthy to go see about my clothes?"

He laughed. "Put that way, it seems silly."

"I'll clean up."

She crossed the corridor, going into her cabin, and checked her messageply. Bram had not wasted words. OMG, SOCIOPATH? NEED SYMPTOMS? SHALLOW EMOTIONS, LYING, NEVER ADMITS TO BEING WRONG, TRIES TO CONTROL PEOPLE, WANTS ADMIRATION, CHARMING, MANIPULATIVE. SOFE, RU GONNA BE OKAY?

She scrawled back: COULD BE OVERREACTING. CLY'S NO DANGER TO ME.

"I have salt monsters and bandits with scurvy for that," she muttered.

Verena had written, too, finally: talked to Lovergirl's captain, Montaro from fishing vessel *Waveplay*. He's sticking to story that Corsetta tried to steal their cash box. He tried to have her locked up so she couldn't talk to anybody. Something hinky there.

Sophie's eye fell on the satchel of animal hair—tabby cat hair, the same color as that of the cat they'd pulled off the derelict—and the spinner she'd taken from the bandit ship. She had promised Verena she'd stay out of the investigation of Corsetta. How would her sister feel if she learned Sophie had stumbled over a connection to *Waveplay,* way out here and far away?

Think about the little schemer later. She washed her hands, changed the green-splattered shirt, and accompanied Cly to his cabin, which turned out to be a full suite of rooms, including an office and a parlor.

The tailor waiting there might have been the oldest person aboard ship. He was a spidery black man with white hair and a sleepy air. Measuring tapes dangled around his neck, and a pincushion—the needles were bone and quill rather than steel—was bound to the back of his left wrist. He didn't speak Fleet.

"You travel with a tailor?" she asked.

"I hired him for this cruise," Cly said. "I've seen your outlander clothes."

"They've barely raised an eyebrow in Fleet."

"Fleet personnel are used to interacting with a cultural hodgepodge and to being polite about it. The Autumn City is less cosmopolitan. It's better if you blend in."

The tailor had tacked together a half-dozen outfits for Sophie, the first of which reminded her of a British riding habit—short breeches and a vest.

"We call this a sporting suit," Cly said. "For outdoor activity. See, it leaves the arms free for swordplay or riding—well, try it on. You may change back there."

She stepped behind a screen. "Tell me about Sylvanna."

"With pleasure. What do you wish to know?"

"Anything," she said. "I meant to look it up in Gale's big index of nations, but her books had been taken off *Nightjar,* and the crew was . . ." She stopped short of complaining about how Verena and Parrish had been ordered to block her explorations at every turn; somehow, it felt disloyal. "I never managed to get to it."

"Other things were more interesting than your homeland, perhaps."

"It's not that I'm not curious."

"No, but given the choice between looking at a new bird or studying humanity, you seem more inclined to the natural world."

"There's a lot to absorb here, Cly. A lot of shiny and only so many hours in the day."

Manipulative, she thought, remembering Bram's sociopathy symptoms. See how fast he got you on the defensive?

"True enough. Let's see: Sylvanna is the third largest of the great nations, as measured by land area. Only Verdanii and Zamaduccia are larger. The name means 'land of abundance.' The nation in its current political form was established by Merkady Iblis Brightburing, our first president. She—"

"A woman?"

"Ha. I thought you'd appreciate that."

She finished buttoning the breeches and vest: they seemed perfectly fitted and very comfortable. She stepped out and tried swinging her arms, then did a knee bend. "You really could do sports in these."

Cly had one big hand over his mouth. "Oh. Child."

His voice was tight.

Okay, if he's faking emotions, he's damned good at it. Her own feelings surged.

"Hey," she said. "It's okay."

"When I think of you as a girl, how you would have looked running a pony cart on the great lawn of Low Bann, with a nurse trailing after you. Winning achievement pins at school . . ."

"I'm here now. Just chill, okay?"

"Here for how long?"

She was saved from answering when the tailor, impatient with waiting, shoved her arms up so they were out at her sides. The back of his pincushion rolled over the underside of her forearm, prickling.

"Forgive me," Cly said. "It's an unfair question, I know that. You have a life in the outlands, a brother . . ."

And parents, she thought guiltily. "Yeah."

He let out a long breath. "Go try on the dinner gown. I promise to control myself."

What was she going to do? Move to Stormwrack, vanish from her family's lives, give up her friends? For the first time, she wondered if she might have been better off not knowing about any of this.

The dinner gown came to just below the knee. It had a flared skirt and a cowl neck; it was comfortable enough, but somehow it reminded her of the 1970s.

Disco isn't dead; it just came to Stormwrack.

It was made of a thin, silky fabric, green in color, so sheer it was nearly weightless. The tailor frowned at it as she stepped out from behind the screen, twitching the cowl over her chest—she'd been showing a bit of cleavage. He absolutely glowered at her bra.

"That's not coming off," she said, and he promptly put a stitch in the cowl to hold it demurely shut over her chest.

Am I really going to move to a world without spandex? She could feel a giggle building.

Cly was true to his word—he'd stopped being emo, or faking it, perhaps. As she attempted a twirl, he nodded. "You look lovely, my dear."

The tailor muttered something.

"He says you're built like a mermaid."

"Swimmer's shoulders," she said.

"Indeed," Cly replied. "I think perhaps . . . two more sporting sets, then, and a second dress in what color?"

"I look good in deep blue," she said.

"That chestnut hair," he said. "Beatrice does, too."

He spoke to the tailor and dismissed him, then picked a wooden box off the desk.

"What's this?"

"A gift."

"Cly, you don't have to keep giving me presents."

"Sylvanner parents believe in giving their children everything they want," he said. "I'm well behind."

She fingered the box. "What if what I wanted was for Beatrice to be off the hook?"

"She should be home soon."

"On bail. She's going on trial for fraud, isn't she?"

"She behaved with criminality and malice."

"Ever hear the phrase 'no harm, no foul,' Cly?"

"I was excluded from most of your childhood," he said. "I call that great harm."

"What about 'forgive and forget'?"

A blaze of fury in his face, unmitigated rage, and that emotion she did entirely believe. And then it winked out, like candleflame being snuffed. "Open this gift and I'll consider it."

She fumbled the latch.

"I realize the lab and the memorician are probably more to your taste. Clothes and fancy balls and visiting other estates . . . I've no idea if that holds any appeal."

"It seems a little old-fashioned, but I'm game to try if you are." She opened the box. Inside was a jade necklace, intricately carved with images of braided leaves.

"Allow me." He opened the clasp, slipping it around her throat. It was a snug fit. "There. Brings out your eyes, I think."

Accepting it felt odd, like sneaking something past her parents. "It's lovely. Thank you."

"Sit." He gestured at a chair and as soon as her butt hit the seat, a steward appeared with a silver tray containing coffee. "Let me try again to tell you about Sylvanna, shall I?"

"That'd be good. Let's start with this whole thing where unmarried people are children."

He poured a steaming cup and nudged it over. "It's been a problem for me. My parents never reconciled themselves to the divorce. The day Beatrice left me, they moved my possessions back into the nursery."

"Harsh!"

"They tried for a time to find me someone new, but . . . well, maybe if I'd been home more."

"You arrange marriages on Sylvanna?"

"Sometimes. All this occurred during my early days at the Advocacy, when I was very much at home in the Fleet. I know what it is, Sophie, to be pulled in two directions."

Manipulative. She swallowed.

"My estate, Low Bann, is in the lowlands, on the northeast coast in the Autumn District, quite near the Butcher's Baste. Much of the land in that area is swampy; we hunt alligator and a big fish called saltsander there, and harvest figs and wild redplum from the preserve. I have some land under cultivation. Hemp and tobacco mostly. We also raise nightshades."

"Hemp, huh?"

"Sylvanna does trade in rope. It's not as fine as Ualtar's, but we make do. And hemp's crucial to binding spells. Tobacco's a popular smoking herb, and you can kill crop pests with it. There's a poison—"

"Nicotine." She nodded.

"When I was a child, I would sometimes elude my tutors and attempt to make a big circuit of the estate. They usually caught me at the boat launch. I was often restless, and there was something about pacing out the boundaries of Low Bann that I found . . . calming."

"Is there a High Bann?"

"Yes. In Winter District. It's held by distant relations, but there's no real family connection there."

"You make it all sound very landed gentry. Country estates, agriculture, hunting, fishing, riding." As she said this, she felt a hint of disquiet. Tobacco plantations, she thought. "What about cities?"

"Ah!" He leaped up, opening a chest and bringing out a huge leather-bound folio that turned out to be full of watercolor paintings. Cracking it open, he laid a picture in her lap.

It was a city viewed from a height. Its structures were largely made of red brick. A cluster of towers maybe five stories high marked the downtown core. The cityscape lacked steeples or domes. Its most prominent features were a marble turret and the double spike of a clock tower. East of that was a high ridge with what looked like giant marbles scattered across it.

"This is Autumn City," Cly said, "capital of the harvest province, nearest city to Low Bann. The complex on the hill, with the round structures, is Autumn's Spellscrip Institute."

"This is an aerial view," she said.

"You're familiar with hot air balloons?"

"Yes."

"The artist sketched the city from above."

She laid a finger on the clock tower.

"The county government," he said. "The nation is too populous to be managed by a single bureaucracy, you see. There are four districts, named for the seasons."

The bridges over the river showed a suggestion of horse-drawn carriages, and there were riverboats on the water. How many people lived there? A hundred thousand? Two?

She turned to the next picture in the folio, finding a painting of a stone-faced boy holding a dog that might have been a whippet. He had the blank expression one saw on devil-children on the posters of horror films. "Is this you?"

"Awful, isn't it?" Cly nodded. "Mother and I had a row over me sitting that day; she made an especially unflattering portrait as revenge."

"These are—my grandmother painted these?"

Cly thumbed to another picture, removing the blank expression from view. She didn't blame him. It was an unnerving image. "I thought you might be interested, since you make pictures, too, in your way."

"In my way," she echoed.

"You are stunningly easy to offend," he commented, which miffed her all the more.

The next picture showed a dock extending into a swamp. The path to the dock had been carved through foliage so dense it looked like a green tube, with a little skylight cut through it for light. The brush had been cleared around the dock itself to create a work area—there were two canoes tied up in the water and a third racked between two nearby trees. The close-cropped grass was decorated with sprays of red flowers and nodding Jack in the pulpit. A cleaning hut sat back from the water—a trio of dead rabbits, dressed but not yet skinned, sat on a low shelf beside its door.

"Is this the boat launch you mentioned? Where they'd catch you?"

"On my escape attempts, yes."

Her eye fell on a painted trunk of a dead tree at the edge of the clearing. It was covered in vine and familiar bursts of purple blooms.

"Throttlevine," Cly said. "You reviewed the case?"

"The brief, yes. Sylvanna thinks the . . . you call them Havers, right?"

"The people of Haversham? Yes, they're Havers."

"That the Havers deliberately introduced the vine to your ecosystem. It does look like kudzu."

"The case was part of the reason I joined the Judiciary."

"The infestations are on Low Bann. On your estate? That's why you're recused from the case?"

"Exactly. It's all over the lowlands." He nodded. "Under control, for the most part, but ineradicable."

"Controlled how?"

"In the Autumn District, at last count, we had corps of four hundred transformed slaves—"

Sophie got to her feet so fast she didn't even feel her grandmother's watercolors spilling off her lap onto the floor.

CHAPTER 11

She didn't try to explain herself; there was no explaining, and so she just ran, out of the cabin, still clad in the super-thin green seventies dress and the jade necklace. She blew past the captain, Beck, and then froze.

Cly would just follow her to her cabin.

The talking masthead, she thought, and made her way below.

Eugenia was arranged on her post, a dangling angel. She reminded Sophie of a play she'd seen: *Peter Pan*, Wendy hovering from the fly loft on barely visible cables.

"Are you a slave, too?" Sophie demanded, but Eugenia remained wood.

She sank to the floor, hugged her knees, and started to bawl. "Oh, Bram, I've been so stupid."

She'd known some of the island nations kept slaves; the Piracy smuggled them, and the theocracy she'd tangled with last time, Ualtar, kept people in bondage. But it wasn't allowed in Fleet, nobody ever talked about it, and she'd assumed . . . what?

That it was the minor countries, the ones that used that phrase, what was it?

We're no great nation, that was it.

Sylvanna was big and rich and she'd figured it was kind of corporate, what with all the big talk of the Spellscrip Institute and its accomplishments. And once again she'd gotten all wrapped up in vegetation and swamp ecosystems and turtles.

Asking the wrong questions.

She thought of Tonio, trying to say something and getting hushed. And Parrish, every time he'd said something about one nation or another. This country, from the port side, he'd kept saying. That one, to starboard. Euphemisms for slave and free.

To hell with obeying orders. He should have just said!

A hand on her shoulder—Eugenia.

"What is it, child?"

"Not—a—child," Sophie managed to blurt out between sobs, and then she cried the harder.

"I feel uneasy," Eugenia said, when she began to calm. "I wish my crew were aboard. Cly and his training cruises . . . the cadets yank me around so."

"You're the ship?" Sophie sniffled. "Does it hurt where the deck caught fire?"

"Like a healing wound now. Itches. Tell me, Sophie, what's wrong?"

She shook her head. "I just realized something about . . ." She paused. Eugenia was probably a charter member of the Cly Banning fan club. "I don't think I can become Sylvanner after all."

"You're from one of the free nations."

She nodded. "Parrish was trying to tell me. They must have ordered him not to, Verena and Annela and Beatrice; they must have known I'd missed it."

"Beatrice Feliachild Banning would *never* have agreed to deceive you about that."

"You know her? My birth mother?"

"She had many a good weep right where you're sitting, in the later days with Cly. And once, more recently."

"When Cly hauled her off to face charges."

Eugenia nodded.

"How could she do it? How could she marry someone who keeps four hundred slaves in his personal swamp?"

"It's a difficult situation." The carved woman tiptoed over to a barrel, one of a bunch lashed to a low shelf. It contained some kind of wood oil. She ran it up and down her arms like lotion, working it into her body until she glowed, lavishing extra attention on her toes.

"Issle Morta doesn't have slaves, does it?" Sophie asked.

"Which one is that?"

"The monks who care for the dead. They used to be pirates."

"Oh, flailers. Yes, but they use the slavery clauses in a rather peculiar way—to protect kidnap victims. Why?"

She colored. "No reason."

Eugenia finished working the oil into her limbs and said, "Come. I know something that used to cheer Beatrice."

"I'm not sure I want to be cheered." But, despite everything, curiosity stirred. Beatrice had, so far, seemed entirely bad tempered. What could put a dent in that much sour?

Being married to a slave-owning, sociopathic, court-appointed killer might make me pissy, too.

Eugenia pulled a sheet off of a huge draped object. It looked like a double-wide harp, two strung frames like a butterfly's wings, with a low platform between them.

"Nice," Sophie said.

"Come, play with me."

"I don't know beans about the harp. I play guitar, but—"

"Don't worry, I'll do the tough work."

"Won't someone hear?"

"Do you think your father doesn't know exactly where you are?"

Sophie's spirits sank. Of course he did. "Okay. Show me what to do."

Eugenia led her to the harp and stepped onto the platform, holding out a hand. Sophie joined her. They stood almost back to back, and she could easily imagine what a sight it would make in a grand hall. Two musicians, prettily dressed, framed by the spreading wings of the harp.

The wood of its frame was darker than Eugenia's; it had gold filigree in flowered patterns.

"Pick a note, any note."

Sophie plucked a string, sending a low, humming note through the boards of the hold.

Eugenia chose two of her own, strumming, and the note became a chord, ringing sweetly to the rafters.

The harps are tuned so they'll play chords, she thought. She chose another string, then a third. Eugenia counterbalanced them, filling the cargo hold with music, a not-quite-tune in no style Sophie could pin down. It had the random quality of improvisational jazz, but the harp's sound was reminiscent of Celtic music, and the flow of the notes was a bit pendular. A dance, perhaps?

Once she had the hang of it, Eugenia fell into a pattern of six notes, over and over, two sets of triplets. *Thrum thrum THRUM, thrum tum TUM.*

"Can you sustain this?" she asked.

"One two THREE two two THREE." Sophie nodded. "No problem."

Eugenia cut loose, hands flying over the harp's strings, filling the chamber and presumably the whole of the ship with a hearty, soaring melody. It was triumphal, fit for the Queen marching into Westminster Abbey at the head of a conquering army. She threw back her head and let out a high soprano cry, bright wordless notes that raised the hair on the back of Sophie's neck.

One two THREE two two THREE. She kept her attention focused entirely on the pattern of strings and the rhythm.

It stilled her mind, even as it scoured her—her whirling feelings fell into order. There was the music itself, a feeling, pushing through her, making her bigger, opening her soul. It clarified the terrible realization: Cly was pretty much an alien form of life. She took one steady glance at the possibility of reconciling herself to a Sylvanna that kept slaves and found certainty.

I could never, I will never.

One two three two two three. As the song wound to a sudden, gentle close, she found herself easing into a sort of chilly sangfroid, a sense of resolution.

Eugenia lay a hand on her shoulder. "I would be very grateful, Sophie, if you told Beatrice how happy I was to see her again."

She hugged the figurehead, encountering wood instead of flesh, and felt a harrowing loneliness. "That was incredible. Thank you."

A genial smile. "My timbers are easier now."

"Mine, too." It was true.

She helped Eugenia drape the harp under its sheet and then peeked out of the hatch, half-expecting Cly to be out there, waiting to pounce. But the corridor was empty. He wasn't lurking on the passenger deck, either, or in her cabin.

She sat at the writing desk and started with Verena writing:

HE'S A SLAVER??? ZOMG, DEAL'S OFF. COME GET ME.

And then one to Bram. I'M NOT OKAY, AS IT TURNS OUT. NOT OKAY AT ALL. COMING HOME AS SOON AS I CAN GET VERENA TO FETCH ME. AT LEAST THE PARENTS WON'T HAVE TO STRESS OUT ANYMORE.

CHAPTER 12

She was surprised when Cly stayed out of her way for the remainder of the day, and all of the next one, too. She ate with Zita and and spent her hours in the lab, dissecting a rat that had turned up in the hold, and on the little portside deck, looking for things to film and longing to see *Nightjar*'s sail.

Krispos didn't seem to notice anything was amiss—he sat in his accustomed place in her lab, reading and answering questions about more of the bogus sciences, sympathism and alchemy.

To keep her mind occupied, she turned to the turtle migration lawsuit. Cly had brought a number of turtle shells aboard, from the species in question, and they seemed normal enough in terms of their makeup and texture.

By day's end, she'd written out two possible paths to pursue on the turtle case. One would require some research; the other was a reasonable experimental protocol for proving whether what Grimreef alleged was true—that the turtles returned to whatever beach they hatched on.

Zita turned up that second afternoon. "We're a day out from Sylvanna."

"I'm *not* setting foot—" Sophie checked herself. This wasn't Zita's fault.

The girl lifted the corners of her mouth in a smile that didn't reach her eyes. "His Honor asked me to beg you for an audience."

"Beg, huh?"

"He's terribly upset," she said, and now she was the one stopping herself from saying more.

What am I gonna do, avoid him forever?

She went back to her cabin and checked her notes. Bram's reply had been: SOFE, IT WILL BE OKAY. TELL ME HOW I CAN HELP.

She missed him.

Verena had been less generous: MOM CAN'T GO HOME IF YOU BREAK CONTRACT.

So that was why Verena had bought in. She'd known Sophie wouldn't go with Cly if she knew the truth about Sylvanna.

Wouldn't I do the same, if it was Mom?

Maybe, but that didn't stop her from replying: YOU SHOULDN'T HAVE LIED. ARE YOU COMING FOR ME? PLEASE PLEASE PLEASE COME GET ME!

Stomach churning, she read her contract again. Then she stomped off across the hall to her so-called lab, where Krispos and Zita were holed up, not exactly hovering. She handed the contract to Krispos, who absorbed all forty pages in about fifteen minutes flat.

He handed it back. "I'm no lawyer, but the language seems clear enough."

"So if I refuse to get off *Sawtooth* when we dock . . ."

"His Honor is no longer obliged to perform the unspecified favor mentioned in clauses four, six, and paragraph—"

"Right. He won't let Beatrice have her bail. Are there any loopholes? Penalties I missed?" She felt a surge of remorse as she said it. Basically, she was saying, *Screw Beatrice, what about me?*

Beatrice. If she hadn't whisked me off to San Francisco, I might even now own people. I might be okay with owning people.

The wave of revulsion was so great her knees buckled. Zita put out a hand to steady her.

"It's a simple pact," Krispos said.

"Forty pages of simple."

He waited, no doubt hoping she'd ask an actual question.

"My take on it is the minimum I have to do is spend a couple nights in his house and review this birth registration he's filed. And here: it says, 'consent to be introduced to first circle of Autumn District.' Do you know what that means?"

He shook his head. "I'm not Sylvanner, Kir."

"Zita?"

"I think it means meeting his neighbors. Isn't there a festival you're supposed to go to? You'll have to ask His Honor."

Subtle hint there. She went back into her cabin and glanced at the messageply again. ARE YOU COMING FOR ME? remained unanswered.

Come on, Parrish, she thought.

"Fine, I'll talk to Cly." She went up to the fighting deck to find him.

He was dueling with Captain Beck, the two of them dripping with sweat as they circled and hacked at each other with every appearance of deadly intent. Beck's spectral hand was extended behind her for balance, ungloved, the bones showing through as always, and she was surprisingly light on her feet for someone who seemed so solid, so rooted to the deck of the ship.

The two of them were moving fast, and the clash of magically treated blades made a terrible racket. Each stroke beat against Sophie's nerves, which were already strung tight after a night without sleep.

She turned her back on them, staring out across the sea, willing *Nightjar* to appear. But it didn't work that way, did it? They'd been talking to people from Tibbon's Wash, trying to find out what was up with Corsetta and the bird she'd tamed. Even if Verena was at all tempted to help Sophie out of the jam she'd gotten herself into, they'd be a week away, maybe more.

The fight behind her stopped abruptly. She turned to see Beck with her blade at Cly's throat and an unhappy expression on her face.

"*Hes,* Lena." He inclined his head, conceding graciously, and the two shook hands. As Beck walked away, she gave Sophie a scowl whose meaning was clear enough: *Stop being a histrionic princess!*

When they were alone, or as alone as anyone could be on the busy main deck of a big ship, Cly said, "You didn't know Sylvanna was one of the bonded nations."

She shook her head, not trusting herself to speak.

"If I point out that my nationality is an accident of birth—"

"You're going to make excuses for owning people?"

He favored her with an expression she couldn't read. It wasn't penitent or defensive, merely watchful.

Shallow emotions, Bram had said.

"What would you have me do, Sophie? Sell them?"

"Sell? Oh my—"

"I have been in this trap before," he said suddenly. "Grappling with someone who could not, would not be pleased, who seemed to imagine I could simply wave my hand and change the world, who otherwise was determined to be miserable and make me so."

"I'm not out to make you miserable!"

"No?" Bitterness there.

"But slave ownership is pretty much a deal breaker."

"Pretty much?"

"I'm not going to sail around Stormwrack letting people think I'm okay with owning people."

He sheathed the sword. "I suppose there's no injustice in the outlands. This paradise you come from . . ." He mastered himself. "Forgive me—I slept poorly."

"Cly, I don't want to hurt you. I am sorry. This whole . . . mess, it's my fault. If I'd learned more about Sylvanna, I'd never have got your hopes up."

"You're generous to say so. Were you kept from learning more?"

"Even if I was, it's my fault for not trying harder. Parrish encouraged me to notice. I'm supposed to be observant."

"Fairly spoken. For my part, I should have ensured that you knew." He gritted the words out. "Will you honor our contract at least?"

No, she thought. "I've got a day to think about it?"

A curt nod. He looked so closed off, so armored against rejection, and she remembered the first time she'd seen him, aglow with delight at the mere fact of her existence. That bright smile, that first hug . . .

Could this really be him manipulating her? Or was he hurting, as anyone would be? Her heart went out to him.

"What can I do? Tell me, ch—Sophie."

"Tell me some things."

"Such as?"

She thought of Parrish, trying to hint at it. He'd kept talking about the two factions within the government: the port side and starboard side. She thought back to her appearance at the Convenor, six months before. "It's half, isn't it? Half the nations. Not some lunatic fringe like Ualtar and the Piracy."

"Yes, half the nations of the Fleet are bonded."

"Tell me," she said, forcing herself to walk over to the table where they'd taken coffee the day before. "I'm ready to listen."

Over the course of the next hour, she drew a picture of the Fleet's constitutional history from him.

When the Fleet had been a mere dozen ships, chasing bandits around the Nine Seas, he told her, the free nations had been willing to hold their noses and ally with anyone willing to go up against the Piracy. As it got bigger and their leadership started laying the foundation for what eventually became the international government, the issue of slavery had been a sticking point.

By then, Cly said, a number of the smallest and most vulnerable of the free nations had all but beggared themselves to join the peacekeeping force. They'd built ships they could ill afford, contributed sailors who should have been home fishing or farming. Those destitute countries had pushed hard for a compromise. It wasn't merely a matter of losing valuable goods and personnel on the oceans, not for the lesser nations. In many cases, stopping the raids meant their very survival.

Sophie believed him. The first nation she'd seen upon coming to Stormwrack, Stele Island, had consisted of a few little fishing villages clinging to the side of an inhospitable rock. A raid on a place like that could reduce the number of healthy, able fishers below the level where a village could feed itself, dooming the survivors to slow death by starvation.

The first thing they'd told her about themselves had been: "We keep our place in the Fleet."

After the pirates were cowed, all the seagoing nations had convened and written up a constitution. Article One had stated that every nation was sovereign and could make its own laws on its own soil and within its territorial waters.

Making the transport of slaves outside of those waters illegal had come next. It hadn't been a hard sell. Abducting and transporting people was the backbone of the Piracy's economy. Even the slavers agreed they had to be stopped. So there was a human dignity and right-to-freedom clause.

Finally, each country also got a concession—a single provision of the Fleet Compact that didn't apply to them.

"So the constitution says there's no slavery, but the bonded nations use the territorial sovereignty and their concessions to ignore the right to freedom and dignity?"

Cly nodded. "It was an ingenious suggestion. The free nations were getting a gift, and they knew it. The portside governments had to exclude Article Two, but those to starboard got to pick whatever concession benefited them most. It made the whole Compact easier to swallow. In reference to any given sticking point, negotiators could say: "Don't like it? Let that be your concession.""

They'd built their entire government on a loophole.

No wonder everyone spends so much time bashing things out in court, Sophie thought.

The history discussion sanded the edge off the tension between them, though Sophie continued to watch for *Nightjar*. It was easier than looking at Cly.

By now they were passing ships bound out toward the Fleet and other places from Sylvanna. One came alongside to deliver a bundle of mail. When it was sorted, a cadet sailor approached. "Mail, Kir." He handed Cly several sealed envelopes.

"Thank you, Jonno." Cly looked at the pages and bowed to Sophie. "We can talk later?"

She nodded and he strode off.

"One for you, Kir." The boy held out one last little billet.

The letter was from Beatrice.

Sophie, it began, in English.

"No 'dearest child' here," she muttered.

> *I've just learned how my cousin Annela has roped you into this scheme to get me off of Breadbasket. I suppose I ought to thank you (and I do want to go home) but I want you to know this wasn't my idea. If they'd told me, I'd never have agreed.*
>
> *Since you're at sea with Clydon now, I will say that you're not in danger. You don't need to be afraid of your father, and if*

you're with him, you shouldn't need to fear anyone else. But he wants something from you, Sophie, and whatever it is, it won't be good.

Break your agreement with him, if you can. Don't worry about me. I know everyone's whining about ugliness in the Convene and a scandal over this whole mess, but Clydon needs to be divorced, more badly than I do. He'll concede in time.

There it was. Sophie was off the hook if she told Cly to stuff it.

This will blow over in time. Besides, anything you do in a well-intended attempt to help is likely to make things worse.
Beatrice Vanko.

"Thanks a lot," Sophie said.

Strangely, the letter made her more determined, rather than less, to help her birth mother.

"Land to port!" one of the kids shouted then, and she got her first sight of Sylvanna.

It was an emerald glimmer on the horizon, dotted with the barely visible glints of lighthouses, pinpoints of radiance that would brighten as the sun went down. Sophie could just make out a denser cluster of lamps rising from the coastline. The city Autumn?

The sea between them was full of ships.

"That's the Butcher's Baste," said Zita, as Sophie turned to ask. "Sylvanna and Haversham lie within each other's territorial limit."

Sophie busied herself with taking footage. "Looks like they're keeping a close eye on each other."

"A well-lit border keeps nobody awake, the expression goes."

The telephoto helped separate the two islands from each other, revealing the stretch of water that separated them. A big, wind-sanded tower of rock jutted up at the entrance of the Baste. "I'm guessing the lights help prevent shipwrecks, too."

"It's a dangerous passage. Mad currents, shallows, lots of rocks, and, they say, ghosts and monsters."

"The star-crossed butcher and his dressmaker girlfriend, I remember."

"The most gifted sailors in Fleet are sometimes challenged to race its intervals. Racing the Baste, we call it." Zita said this in a tone that suggested this particular form of attempted suicide was on her bucket list of life goals. "We'll reach the Autumn port before dawn. What are you going to do?"

Sophie looked at the letter from Beatrice, then at the rack of swords gleaming on deck, the marked-out boundaries of the duelists' circle.

Cly wants something from me. What?

Believe me when I say I want to go home, Beatrice had said.

She thought again: if not for her birth mother hauling her off to California, she'd own a swamp and the people in it. Even now Beatrice would rather remain under arrest than see Sophie compromise herself.

"I've come this far," she said. "It'd be wrong to turn my back."

CHAPTER 13

The buildings of Autumn City were made of brick, just as they were in the painting she'd been shown, but Cly's mother hadn't captured the touches that made the city autumnal—the street lamps were carved in the shape of gourds, and the road cobbles were patterned to evoke interlocked red and gold leaves. All the public art was concerned, thematically, with aging—the statues depicted people at the point where midlife started to cede to old age. There were waning moons everywhere and the planters were filled with species that had lots of red chlorophyll. Everywhere she looked, she saw huge arrangements of dried flowers—red and gold petals, sunflowers.

Sophie almost balked when she got her first glimpse of a slave, an ordinary-looking woman bound on some kind of business, only recognizable as such because of her wrist manacles.

But Sophie was committed. She'd finish out the trip and get Beatrice off the hook—entirely off the hook, if she could—before going back to San Francisco.

Verena had answered her with a short note:

> Sophie: I'm really sorry. I stupidly told Annela you'd never go for
> a sail to a slave nation, so she explicitly forbid us to mention it.
> She figured once you signed a contract, you'd feel obliged. I was in
> trouble anyway—I guess I was too chicken to defy her.
>   We're en route. Parrish says a few days if winds are fair.
>   Just FYI, the whole Fleet is in a lather: the Verdanii Allmother

tried to nudge the courts into letting Mom go and Sylvanna's allies made a big stink about Verdanii entitlement and miscarriages of justice. Things are supertense. If there's any way you could spend a few days on the island humoring His Honor, I'd be grateful. Thanks, V.

Bram was briefer: WHAT'S GOING ON?

As they disembarked, Sophie was clad in her outlander outfit—as Cly put it, and to his obvious displeasure—jeans and a T-shirt. She was determined not to be taken for a landholder, as it was euphemistically called.

He was dressed more or less as usual, in what she was beginning to think of as his Shakespeare suit—breeches, peasant shirt, rapier—but he'd donned a white sash marked with several broaches.

"I've hired us a carriage," Cly said, with a light emphasis on the word "hired." Sophie looked over the driver anyway, checking for manacles. He had ringworm and colored his hair, which was graying, but he also had a money belt under his shirt and smooth, unadorned wrists.

"Where are the others?"

"Krispos and Zita will meet us at Low Bann," Cly said. "You and I must go to the birth registry with Beatrice's warranty of marital fidelity."

She clambered into the carriage, which left her facing him.

"Why did you change your mind?"

She read him a rough translation of Beatrice's letter.

He sniffed. "One might wish she'd expressed a little affection for you."

"She's honest."

A quirked eyebrow. "Compared to whom?"

"Is she right? Is there something you want?"

"Your mother doesn't know me as well as she claims," Cly said. "I wish to become acquainted with you."

"I think I'm going home after this," Sophie said.

"To the outlands? What about your studies? The position I've offered you?"

What indeed? Loss gnawed at her. She hadn't even managed a single research dive. "I'll have to give up on that."

"All because Sylvanna is bonded?" he growled, looking out the window.

"It's a big deal, Cly."

"I suppose I'll follow you to the outlands, then."

She couldn't help smiling. "What a can of worms that would be."

"Come, teach me a few words of Anglay."

"What words?" *Out of my way, peasant, or I'll cut you?*

He shrugged and they fell silent until they'd reached a columned building whose window screens were painted with autumn leaves. Despite the decorations, it had a decidedly institutional air. Cly helped her down from the carriage before a slave could offer and then opened the door to the building, too.

Once inside, he strode up to the receptionist, exchanging a few quick words with her in Sylvanner. The woman made a gesture toward a side room that appeared to be a parlor—at least, it had tables, lamps, and books.

It was fairly packed with bored-looking Sylvanners.

Books, thought Sophie. Part of her was smarting from having told Cly she was packing up her toys and going home.

Cly glanced at the waiting room, shook his head curtly, uttered a speech that included a few Fleet phrases: "—still on Maple Lane?" and "—await your pleasure."

Then, with a bow and a "Come, Sophie," he swept back into the street.

"We're not doing the birth registry after all?" she asked.

"The registrar can find us," he said. "I see no reason to sit in a dingy administrative parlor waiting on the convenience of a minor bureaucrat."

He ushered her down a lane lined with peach trees, heavy with green-gold underripe fruit, and then up onto the porch of a big building whose open door exhaled the scent of baking bread and fresh-brewed tea. Striding past the hostess, he chose a beautifully positioned table that offered a view of the town square and the registry.

"Sit," he said, taking the other chair.

Sophie wasn't about to turn down the chance to have a good look at Autumn City. She took in the square, the winding paths paved in interlocked stones, and then at the homes. They had the spread and columns of big Georgian courthouses—she was reminded of the White House—but the columns themselves weren't stone as far as she could tell, but looked instead to be some kind of wide-bore bamboo plant.

Judging from the size of the downtown core and the density of the people, she guessed that the city had, perhaps, a population of a hundred thousand. They were dressed for the most part in a unisex version of the sports jumper Cly had had made for her—the pants that came to just below the knee, the loose shirt beneath a vest with open arms.

Everyone but the youngest children and the slaves wore a sash like the one Cly had put on himself.

Social coding, Sophie guessed. Cly's sash was white, but most of those worn by the adults were black. Kids and young adults wore crimson. The sashes were adorned with ladder-like arrangements of stick pins with emblems on them.

The first pin, atop each black sash, resting more or less where the collarbone would be, usually depicted two hands clasped together. Cly's, on the white, was an open hand. The second, in most cases, showed a stylized house. Cly didn't have that one.

So a quick look at a person's chest tells you who they are, whether they're . . . married, maybe? And a slaveowner. What's the symbol for that—a boot on a neck?

There were a dozen or so young couples, all but one of them heterosexual, parading about. They had flowers—real, perishable ones—pinned to their red sashes. They were being accorded an elaborate, almost ritual respect, and served first at the cafés.

"Betrothed," Cly explained as a pair came in and claimed a tray of tea that had been headed toward the two of them. The waiter shot Cly an apologetic look and got the hand flick in reply as he rushed off to get another.

"All these couples are engaged?"

"It's the season."

"Pardon?"

"Midsummer is when families solidify unions. These children"—flick at the tea poachers—"have been accorded an opportunity to practice the privileges and responsibilities of adulthood until they actually wed."

"That's right, you said marriages were arranged."

"Usually. It's quite the celebration. Houses merge, favored slaves are freed, there's gift-giving and music. The festivals . . ." As he spoke, he removed two new sashes from his case—one black, one red, and got to his feet. A slender woman with a burgeoning leather case was rushing across the table to them.

"Kir Banning," she said, bowing, and then came a rush of words, some of which Sophie caught: "waiting," "honored," "paperwork."

Overlapping vocabulary. The Sylvanner language must have been the basis for Fleet, or related to it.

"My daughter speaks only Fleet," said Cly.

"Forgive me," she said more slowly. "I am Munschler from the Registrations Office. It is . . . Zophie?"

Sophie nodded.

"I have your Assertions and Rights of Claim."

"Sit," Cly ordered. Soon he and the woman were deep in the bureaucratic tangle. They seemed to require little from her.

Sophie stared out the window, taking in the betrothed couples, a bricklayer mortaring a low wall, a small flock of ordinary-looking brown pigeons circling the skies above one of the older buildings.

Her gaze fell on a perfectly coiffed woman with a patched dress and a white sash topped by an empty-hand pin, just like Cly's. A widow? She was standing beside a stone bench, selling oranges from a basket to the passersby. Most of the people heading past avoided her gaze, as they would that of a panhandler at home. One snarky-looking betrothed boy demanded an orange from her and did not pay.

Munschler coughed, drawing her attention back to the table. "Know you anything that would oppose the idea that this man is your father?"

Sophie shook her head. "He and Beatrice were married."

"Are married," Cly corrected. "Beatrice broke contract and thereby annulled our divorce."

"You know of no other contenders, then, child? Nobody has claimed to be your father?"

This world seriously needs DNA testing. "I only just met them."

"Sophie was fostered in the outlands," Cly explained.

"The assertion is a formality," Munschler assured her, sliding a page across the table. "We need know only that nobody has told you of a competing claim."

She thought of her dad briefly, of his tight brows and railing about imprecision and lazy thinking. "Nobody else has ever said they were my birth father."

"Good, then, sign it." Munschler dove back into her paperwork.

A minute later, a white-gloved girl with manacles clamped around her wrists brought a paper-wrapped packet to the table and set it before Sophie.

"What's this?"

"Just a treat. It's traditional," Cly said.

A treat for the child, brought by a slave, she thought. It smelled like pork and was wrapped in a heavy-looking pastry.

Fling it away? No, the orange lady looked hungry. Sophie walked out to the street, offering it to her.

The woman reached out to take it, then drew back as if her fingers had been burned.

"It's okay," Sophie said. She could feel as much as see the people turning, all around the square, to watch. She'd committed a social transgression of some kind. But hey—what the hell. She was a big old outlander, right? Or at best a child. "Take it. Have a bit of protein."

The woman bowed. "Thank you, Kir."

She returned to the teahouse, to Cly and Munschler. The bureaucrat had turned a bright pink and was talking a bit loudly. Pretending not to have noticed anything? Cly was eyeing Sophie as if she were a horse with a thrown shoe.

The orange lady took an indelicately large bite of the bun, then another. She paused to sell an orange to an old man who gave her a bright coin. As he walked away, he shot a glare at the teahouse. He was followed by a betrothed couple who insisted on paying her for two oranges. Then another came.

Apparently Sylvanners didn't appreciate it when you offered their beggars a bite to eat.

Over the course of the next ten minutes all the people in the square quietly bought the woman's basket down to nothing. There was an odd tension to the ritual. They'd let her eat a few bites of the pork bun. Then a few of them would pay her—overpay, from the size of the coins—for an orange.

An air of disapproval built up, thicker than the considerable humidity within the square. When she'd finished her bun and the basket was empty, the last sodden orange sold, the uniformed man who bought it spoke a few words in the woman's ear.

What had he said? *You're out of oranges, so push on?* The woman shambled away, shoulders heaving a little. A competitor rushed to occupy her piece of shade.

"Sophie." Cly rapped on the table. "Perhaps if you're finished shaming all of Autumn, you'd care to witness your certification of birth."

Munschler held out an official-looking page. "Ah. Sign here."

Sophie looked it over. It was in Sylvanner. "All this says is I'm your daughter? I'm not agreeing to buy a bridge or join a convent?"

"Convent?"

"Never mind." She signed it and the bureaucrat scuttled off, leaving the table in humid silence.

"I gave a hungry woman a bun. What's the big deal?"

"It was an act of kindness," Cly said, with apparent reluctance. "Will this happen every time one of the bonded hands you something to eat?"

"Pretty much, yeah. Or when they treat me like a six-year-old."

He simmered across the table at her, but she held his gaze, refusing to be stared down.

Finally he summoned a waiter. "Have my carriage sent after the widow," he said. "Tell the driver to help her harvest another basket of oranges and take her wherever she'd like to go. Buy her some eggs while you're at it."

With that, he began transferring some but not all of his pins from the white sash to the black one he'd taken from his bag.

"I suppose I should explain about these," he said.

"It's not that hard to work out," Sophie replied. "They signify social status. Anyone can tell, at a glance, who you are and where you fit within the pecking order."

"I suppose you know why I'm switching colors, then."

"Your status has changed because you've got a kid. Your . . . divorce from Beatrice screwed something up, back in the day. You said your parents considered you a child? Moved you back into the nursery?"

"Indeed. I was little better than that widow. Now I'm a father," he said. "Black sash. Automatically adult."

"So it's better for a Sylvanner to have a child than not? A kid can offset the social disadvantage of being divorced and childless."

"Widowed and childless, yes. My situation has ever been exceptional."

"And the pins' specific meanings?" She didn't much feel like talking, but silence, she sensed, might be worse.

"Clasped hands—wedded. Sailing vessel—bound to Fleet. Peach blossom—parent. Crossed swords—duelist." His clipped tone showed he wasn't feeling all that impressed with her, either. "House—head of household."

"You didn't have that one on your white sash."

"Childless, unmarried adults are rarely considered fit to administer an estate. My awful cousin Fren has been running Low Bann. Let's go demote her, shall we?"

"Gee, that sounds fun."

"We'll be riding now."

"Horses?"

"What else?" he said. "You've obliged me to give the carriage away for the afternoon."

"Whatever," Sophie said, suspecting she sounded like the child she kept insisting she wasn't, but unable to rise, entirely, above the tension.

She hadn't ridden all that much in the grand scheme of things, though as a kid she'd been to camp once or twice. They'd probably give her a little-girl horse so her legs would dangle. At least she could shoot pictures in the open air rather than through some smeary volcanic-glass carriage window.

"Here's yours." Cly handed her a black sash with a single pin, adorned with a piece of white quartz cut in facets. It reminded her a little of a crystal doorknob.

"What's this one mean?"

"Foreign adult, as per the contract."

"Thanks." She put it on.

Getting horses consisted of walking to the stables and demanding them. As seemed to be his wont, Cly strolled past the first mounts offered without even looking, instead selecting a pair of massive black horses who looked like they might be Percherons. He had them loaded with flasks of water, appropriated a pair of linen sun hats, told the stable keeper to charge it all to Low Bann, and led her out to a paddock while they were saddled.

Sylvanner saddles were more British in style than Western—no pommel—but the bridle, reins, and stirrups all served the usual functions. Sophie's mount, Ballado, was a huge step up and wide across. Once she was astride him, she took him in a circle, once and then twice around the paddock. The groom watched attentively, then nodded.

"All right?" Cly asked. It clearly hadn't occurred to him that she might not ride.

She checked her seat, then arranged her cameras so they were within easy reach. "Yes."

"Let's go." He gave his mount the barest of nudges and they clopped out into the city.

They set out on the main road with its interlocking-leaf pattern, then veered into a residential neighborhood. The residents seemed affluent at first, at least to judge by the stand-alone houses and their trappings, but over time the houses shrank, the yards got smaller, and the trimmings fell into disrepair. Their doors bore wooden equivalents to the status sashes. Covered strips of varnished wood hung diagonally above the doors, pegged with the various symbols—the hands, the homes.

Who you are matters terribly here, Sophie concluded.

As they left the town behind and moved along the orchards, there was plenty to observe and to film. Fields of familiar crops—apricot, plum, peach, nectarine, apple, and pear—alternated with some that were unmistakably new. She saw big cherries, so purple they might have been blue, and a red-skinned citrus she'd seen, on Erinth, when she visited before.

Half a dozen canines, too small and dark-furred to be coyotes, followed them for half a mile or so as they moved past the boundary of the city. Less because they thought they could take down a horse and rider, Sophie thought, than because they had nothing better to do.

Out of the city, it was even hotter. The air felt wet, like someone's breath on the back of her neck.

She looked ahead at the figure of Cly, riding and self-contained. *No di-*

vorce on this island, so they labeled him a childless widower. That's obviously not good, if that old lady's any example. Now he's got a kid, he's better off.

Cly's original sash hadn't had head of household on it. Sophie had signed her birth certificate and now Cly had been bumped up his family's chain of precedence. They were on their way to dislodge a cousin, he'd said. Someone else who'd been running the family home.

Beatrice thinks he wants something. Maybe it's just control over his estate? It would be worth it to figure it out, since she was here anyway.

There was a profusion of red birds, each as small as her thumb, in a bush near the road. Some had blue eyes, the others gray. The former would be one sex, the gray the other.

She reined in, steadied Ballado, and shot thirty seconds of video. They seemed fearless, and as she continued to observe, she saw a gray snake, the same color as the tree trunk, winding up the branch hoping to catch one.

She zoomed in, forgetting everything. The snake was perhaps eighteen inches long. Against the ash-colored trunk of the bush, it was very nearly invisible. It glided up, edging closer to the branches where the birds were hopping to and fro. Patiently, it folded itself to strike.

Sophie lost herself in the shot, zooming in on the snake and the branch, that little bird landing platform in the frame. The horse moved under her. "Shush shush," she told him absently.

A bird dropped to the branch. The snake snapped out, jaws extended. There was a miss, a red blur, and all the little spoonfuls of red feather burst from the bush at once, peeping madly as they shot past Sophie. The snake opened and shut its cotton-candy mouth once or twice—Sophie almost imagined it smacking its lips—and then stretched itself out to wait for their return.

"Missed, did he?" Cly had reined in beside her.

"The predator can't always win, can it? I don't know this species."

"Soot viper," he said. "They're drawn to cooling campfires sometimes. These orchards are fenced against them."

"They're poisonous?"

He nodded.

"He's not advertising. No red and black markings."

"Why would such a creature make itself conspicuous?" Cly asked.

"To warn off predators."

"Dust vipers are less hunted than hunting."

"Sneaks, in other words."

"Nothing wrong with a well-laid ambush in the cause of supper." He sidestepped his horse closer to the bush, lashing out with a hunting knife she hadn't known he was carrying and beheading it with a swift whisk of his arm.

"Hey!" Sophie objected. "Was that necessary?"

The pieces had landed at the base of the tree.

Killing animals, she thought. Sign of sociopathy?

"They kill fruit pickers. The suffering the bites cause is terrible. There must be a break in the snake fencing; we'll watch for it."

Sophie reined Ballado, leapt down, and picked up the snake's body pieces. Farmers killed pests, that was the way of things. And Cly claimed he was protecting others.

"What are you doing?" She felt almost dissected by the gaze he'd turned on her: it was like being scanned for something.

"No reason to let a perfectly good sample go to waste." She wrapped it in a handkerchief, tucking it into one of the saddlebags.

At her answer, he seemed to relax. Sophie raised her eyebrows in a silent question.

"I'm relieved," he said. "I'd wondered how far your soft-heartedness might extend."

She was astounded. Here she'd been wondering if he had the emotional makeup of a serial killer, and he was simultaneously trying to figure out . . . what? If she was some kind of total vegan pacifist? "Killing a pest that might hurt a fruit picker, or even performing a dissection . . . it's a little different from chopping up an unarmed bandit who's surrendering, don't you think?"

It took a moment before he answered with a mild, "Just so."

Then he turned his horse, riding away in silence.

Sophie remounted and followed, leaving the little red birds to reclaim their bush in safety.

CHAPTER 14

Low Bann was about a ninety-minute ride, or it would have been if Sophie hadn't stopped twice more to take shots of unfamiliar species—a tree in one case and a peculiar, green-toned millipede.

Cly's childhood home was built into a hillside that rose up from marshy saltwater flats and extended beyond them in every direction. Up on the terraces of the hill was an orchard filled with bluish cherry plants and nearly ripe plums and fences lined with honeysuckle.

The countryside was alive with bees—the trellises were crawling with workers in pursuit of pollen. Apiaries hunched along a fence near a biggish bird coop.

As they rode up to the house, two slaves opened the double doors and a quartet of richly dressed redheads emerged, almost mincing to stay within the shadow of parasols upheld by still more slaves clustered around them. They were led by a woman of about thirty-five years; behind her were a man the same age and two children who looked to be fifteen, the latter nearly identical except that one was a girl and the other a boy.

"So it's true," the man breathed. He had a squarish, fireplug build and the pins on his sash seemed to indicate he'd been assigned, at one time, to the Fleet. "Beatrice has returned from the outlands."

The woman snorted. "That's not Beatrice. It's a child."

"My child, as it happens. Kir Sophie Hansa." Cly swung down from the horse, utterly in control of himself and wearing the sharkiest of his grins.

"Sophie, my cousin Fenn and her husband, Ilden. Their twins, Mirelda and Mervin."

Sophie slid off her horse and gave her best approximation of Parrish's little bow. Then she turned back to her mount. A slave was already leading it and Cly's horse away.

Her father caught her arm before she could go after them. "Stay. Nobody bonded will lift a finger to do anything more for you. My word on it."

She remembered Parrish suddenly, telling her parents that she'd be safe here. Saying "my word," in English, while her father tried to place his accent.

Okay, I can do this.

"Hi, everyone," she said, edging away from the group before one of the entourage could put a parasol over her.

Fenn was studying the two of them minutely. She didn't have much of a poker face—whatever she saw made her furious. With teeth gritted, she said, "Welcome home, cousins."

"How long will you be here?" asked the man. His hostility was tempered with resignation. "You must have cases to adjudicate."

"*Neneh,* I'm on leave from the Judiciary." Cly ambled across the porch, ignoring—or enjoying—their rising distress as he unpinned the head of household icon from Fenn's sash. He tucked it into his pocket. She flushed red and her eyes flicked to his sword. "I might stay a day, or a month, or forever."

"The country life—you?" The man barked laughter.

I wonder how long they're planning to sit out here fencing? Sophie considered following the horses to the stables after all—she should rub down her own mount.

The Sylvanners' weird shaming of the widow rose, unbidden, in her mind. If she did some slave's job, would the slave be punished?

Cly wouldn't dare, she thought. *He's been holding his temper all this time because . . . why? What's he want from me? Is it this?*

Deciding to give the awkward family scene five more minutes, she turned her attention to the kids.

Up close, they were less perfectly identical: Mervin was more muscular, and Mirelda had a milk-pale complexion and a faint whistle in her breath. Asthma? Caused by anxiety, or was it the undoubtedly high pollen count? She was standing too straight, as though she was uncomfortable. Sophie looked for a cause. There—her feet were all but popping out of the petite and pointy white shoes they'd been jammed into.

Looks like they'd fit her mother.

Mirelda's coils of hair were perfect, nothing out of place. All this was a big show for Cly's arrival. He must have sent a message ahead to announce himself; or maybe Fenn had spies in town.

There was a yellow stain on the boy's hand. *A smoker? Kid, you're fifteen*—but once Sophie saw it, there was no denying that his overall fidgety air looked remarkably like he was having a nicotine fit.

He caught Sophie's eye and raised his brows, making a face: *Isn't this all so dumb?*

Sophie replied with a quick, noncommittal smile.

Cly had caught the exchange. "Where are my manners? Come in, all of you."

With a grand gesture, he ushered everyone inside, as though he'd been here all along and the rest of them had just showed up for Thanksgiving. Deftly taking the door, he swung it wide, murmuring a few words to the manacled woman who'd been holding it.

The slaves folded their parasols and made themselves scarce.

"Dear Sophie," he continued, "I don't mean to involve you in the dull business of auditing the household books. Would you wish to explore the estate with your cousins?"

She nodded and he said, "Children, show Sophie the grounds."

With that, their elders vanished deeper into the house.

It was a relief to be away from Cly for a while. Sophie smiled at the girl and gestured at her shoes. "Do you want to get those off?"

The girl grimaced. "I can barely walk."

"You don't even have to tour me around the grounds, if you don't want."

The boy sighed. "Come on, Mirrie. You know we better do as he says."

The girl slipped out of the white shoes with a sigh of relief, picking them up and disappearing inside. The boy loosened his collar, rolled up his cuffs, and fished in his pockets for the makings of a cigarette. "So, Kir, you're Verdanii?" His Fleet was decent, his accent faint.

Sophie shook her head. She'd renounced any claim on Verdanii citizenship when she first came here. It was that or basically steal Verena's life out from under her. "They tell me I'm an outlander."

"Marvelous! Is it true what they say about the outlands?"

"What do they say?"

"Petrodemons hunt the unwary by night, roaring, with glowing lamps for eyes."

"Petrodemons, huh? And what, exactly, would they be?"

"They breathe fire and choking blackness—"

Mervin was interrupted by his sister's return; she had a pair of boots and was looking around in confusion.

"Where's Betta?"

Mervin said something in Sylvanner, in an undertone and fast. Mirelda snapped Sophie a glance and struggled into her boots. It was apparent that she usually had help.

"Come on," Sophie said, after she'd laced them up. "Let's have a look at the joint."

Neither of them seemed inclined to lead, so she headed off the veranda, into the full sun and the sauna of midsummer. She picked a direction, heading out along the boundary of the orchard, picking a leaf or two off every plant she came across, tucking them into one of her notebooks. They followed a fence that ran parallel to the estate's driveway, climbing a low hill.

"How much of this is Low Bann?"

"All you see," Mirelda huffed, "and more besides."

So Cly's family had more land than the three of them could wander in a short stretch of time.

They reached a long hedge of flowered bushes—a lagerstroemia variant, Sophie thought, as she took a leaf and a blossom. They'd be deliberately cultivating them within a convenient distance of the apiaries. Behind the hedge, hidden from the house, was the bird coop she'd spotted. It was occupied by a dozen ordinary chickens and one smallish ostrich.

"Want to pet her?" Mervin suggested. He had lit his smoke and appeared to be enjoying the amble. Mirelda looked as though she couldn't believe she'd made it this far. "Her feathers are very soft."

His sister shot him a look, sideways.

"You first," Sophie said, and Mervin's smirk widened. "Yeah. Thought so."

"She'd have left you your fingers," he said, with a lazy grin that probably disarmed people all the time.

Sophie took a few photos of the ostrich and continued on.

Nothing she saw over the course of the next hour did anything to convince her that Mervin was anything other than a mean-spirited little thug. Mirelda, she wasn't so sure about—she was unused to walking and kept hinting they should just go back to the house.

The air was hot and thick and there were marvels at every step: potter wasps and sawflies, and more sun-burnished, half-ripe peaches and nectarines. She saw a huge leopard frog for all of an instant before it shot off its log and into the shelter of the nearest puddle of water.

Sophie made her way down past the built-up area the house occupied to a boardwalk that led to the increasingly lush swamp.

Mirelda balked. "I think we've gone plenty far."

"Go back to the house . . . it's fine."

An anguished look. "Mervin."

"Come on, Mirrie, it'll be fun. Cly told us to entertain Cousin Zophie."

He means maybe Cousin Zophie will get herself scared by an alligator, Sophie thought.

"Seriously, Mirelda, you don't have to come."

"Look!" The girl pointed, tone falsely bright. "It's the Autumn spellscribe!"

Two vehicles were rolling up the drive. One was Cly's carriage, laden with trunks, and—she assumed—carrying Krispos and Zita.

Behind it was something that looked less like a wagon and more like a rolling teacup, chariot-size and orange in color, horseless, with a whirling base that glowed even in the midday sunlight.

"They haven't seen us," Mervin said. "We can vanish into the swamp."

Sophie considered. It was only two hundred meters. But if Zita was in Cly's wagon, maybe she could trade the twins in for better company . . .

not to mention getting Mirelda out of what she clearly saw as a forced march.

She probably got blisters from wearing Fenn's shoes.

"Let's go say hello."

The vehicles stopped as soon as the driver saw them. Zita disembarked, wearing the same foreigner's sash Sophie wore—black fabric, white glass bauble—and an expression of sheer amazement. Her surprise doubled when Sophie bounded up and hugged her.

Krispos peered out at her from inside the carriage. He'd had his nose in a book, naturally. "Well met, Kir Sophie."

"Hi, Krispos." To Zita she said, "I'm going to say hello to some scribe, then I'm headed off exploring. Want to come?"

Zita grinned. Aboard ship, she'd never quite shed her air of military discipline, but now she seemed more relaxed, a bit like a college student on vacation. "I could use a decent walk on land."

Mervin didn't look as though he had much idea what to do with himself amid this sudden crowd. He hung to the rear, recalculating.

Mirelda, all smiles, led a spindle-limbed woman, with ink-smudged hands and a slight limp, toward them. "Cousin Sophie," she said formally, "this is Autumn of the Spell."

Sophie matched Zita's bow and said, "My friend, Cadet Judge Zita."

Zita shot her a second surprised look and Sophie suppressed a smirk. *Of course I've picked up some Fleet etiquette.*

Autumn returned their bow.

There was an air of expectation that suggested to Sophie that it fell to her to push the conversation along. She tried: "So, what brings you to Low Bann?"

"I come often to visit." She gave Mirelda a warm smile, and Sophie saw a gap in her teeth, likewise marked with ink.

She chews her pen.

"Mirelda hopes to join the institute once she's married."

"Nice," Sophie said, liking the girl better for having a vocation.

"Shame she's dumber than a Haver," Mervin muttered, too softly for Autumn to hear. Mirelda heard, though: a shock ran through her, making her curls bounce.

"We're off to explore the swamp," Sophie said. "Maybe, Mirelda, you'd like to go with Autumn here? There's space in Cly's carriage. Is there a library in the house? You'd really help me out if you got Krispos reading indexes, directories, anything that offers an overview of local politics or science."

"I'll find him something." Mirelda scrambled aboard with her head raised, though she was blinking back tears. Krispos patted her hand.

Sophie looked at Mervin.

"Oh," he said. "I'll stick with you."

"Suddenly not so sure you're invited."

"Stop me," he said, sauntering back toward the swamp.

Autumn gave them a resigned shrug, then climbed back into her fabulous teacup, whirring up the drive. The wagon followed; Zita and Sophie started for the boardwalk.

"Cousins of yours, the girl said," Zita said.

"Evil troll child, in Merv's case. He's hoping I'll see a spider and faint dead away."

"I studied with a fellow like that."

"It's good to see you."

Zita's eyes—they were amber, almost as yellow as a wolf's—got wide. Sophie remembered, suddenly, that she was gay. "Not that I'm flirting."

"Understood." An easier smile. "Your Fleet cutter has been sighted en route here."

"*Nightjar*?"

"They'll make port in a few days if—"

"If winds be fair?" The thought of getting back to *Nightjar* was like seeing the sun after weeks of cold and rain. "What a relief. I've done the birth registry, I've seen Low Bann. Now all that's left on that damn contract I signed is surviving this summer ball and seeing the Spellscrip Institute. Then I'm out of here."

"I'm sorry it didn't work out," Zita said, more formally.

That's right, she worships Cly.

"Sorry," Sophie said. "You're in an awkward position with all this."

Zita waved off the expression of concern as if it were a harmless insect. It was a gesture Sophie recognized—she'd picked it up from Cly.

The boardwalk led through a trimmed corridor of branches, carefully hedged and netted—because of the poisonous vipers, Sophie would have bet—and then out over a riparian strip leading to a circular, mirror-smooth pond. The grass ceded to muck under the boards, then to actual puddles pierced at the edges by needle-thin reeds. The water was alive with clouds of insects. No mosquitos, thankfully, but there were plenty of dragon-flies darting about. The air thrummed with frogsong. Water skimmers swirled over the surface of the pond in packs, like kids skating. Sophie spotted a toad that was extinct in the wild at home and felt that ache again, that sense of having to choose between two lives.

She should be moving through this swamp a few square feet at a time, inventorying wildlife species, taking pictures and samples.

She thought of an otter-built raft she'd seen six month earlier, out in the ocean. Just one of who knew how many wonders waiting to be dis-covered.

The trees here were of a broadleaf species; their trunks were the same ash-colored hue as a bush she'd spotted on the road. Here at the trailhead, where the boardwalk skirted the lake, the trees were widely spaced. Man-aged, Sophie suspected. The leaf litter on the land side of the boardwalk was thick, wet, and sludgy. But some of the puddles in the muck around the lake—a few dozen of the hundreds visible from this vantage point— had been cleared of refuse. In each of these puddles one green leaf sat, centered in the shallow water, bowed upward like a little umbrella.

Sophie bent, carefully fishing up a sodden stick, discarding it and then finding a dry one.

"Want my sword?" Zita said.

"This'll do." Using the stick, she lifted one of the umbrella leaves. It had been floored in a delicate web that held the water as she raised it. A dark green shape, eight-legged, many-eyed, stared back at her.

She raised the whole thing, setting it on the boardwalk, and took out her camera.

"The structure of the web makes both a floor and a float," Sophie said, setting the camera, too, on the boardwalk floor and crouching down un-til she was almost on her belly to take the shots. "It sits below the surface of the water and the bugs skate in."

"So, a spider?"

"Want to see?"

Zita smiled and bent to peer inside.

Mervin had vanished beyond the lake, into the deeper swamp. Now he returned at the mouth of the next cut-in corridor of vegetation. "Are you coming, Kirs?"

"Are we?"

"Much as I'd like to show up the little troll, we don't have provisions for a good hike," Sophie said.

"I'm sure His Honor didn't mean for us to disappear for hours."

"Plenty to see right here." She offered Zita a look at the camera, got an incurious head shake in return, and replaced the spider within its puddle. Then she took a closer look at the lake's edge. The water looked to be maybe eighteen inches in depth—she pushed her stick down. It resisted when she pulled it back. "Spongy, you see? Not sandy."

"Who's a coward now?" Mervin shouted.

"Look," Sophie said. She had the camera trained on the water—a school of green minnows was passing through. One blundered into a spider trap that had drifted out into the open water. The leaf rocked wildly.

Rather than try to take on a fish, the spider cut the strands of its floor loose. The leaf sprung free; the minnow shot back toward its school.

Patiently, the spider began to rebuild its home.

"Any interest in this?" Zita had found a fire salamander on a nearby leaf. It blinked at them, unconcerned.

Sophie grinned at the amphibian. "He's lovely."

She could do this forever: sit in an abundant ecosystem, near water, and just take it in.

Rustling across the lake drew her attention next.

Her first reaction to the figures was excitement, a bursting, exuberant *Oh!*

And then it was *Fauns, wow, fauns!*

And then realization, like being plunged into ice water: *Oh.*

If you couldn't see their legs, the three slaves did look a little like mythical Greek fauns. Stubs of horn protruded from their foreheads, and their faces were elongated into goatlike muzzles, with sharp, small, close-set teeth, optimized for cropping and grinding. But their limbs were ropey, their toes long rather than hooved, the better to climb and grip the vines and tree branches.

Goats atop, apes below, she thought.

They made their way around the edge of a pool, taking care not to wade, half-climbing the trees to keep their legs out of the water.

They clambered onto a big tree choked with the throttlevine Cly had mentioned, the kudzu variant. Methodically, they began stripping off the bark and munching. Dull brown manacles encircled their wrists.

Sophie shot a look at Zita, who was trying to master her own expression of horror.

"Oddities," she whispered. "I had heard there was a problem with their swamps, that they'd transformed."

"Hundreds," Sophie said. "Cly told me there were hundreds."

Zita's lips moved . . . in prayer? She tried to look away from the three malformed people, perched in a tree and eating a knotty vine of, probably, limited nutritional value, but her eyes were drawn back.

"You've never seen a slave before, either," Sophie said.

"I'm of the Tall. But . . ." She meant she was from one of the free nations, Tallon, one of the few Sophie had seen with her own eyes. She seemed to be forcing the words out. "The Fleet of Nations respects the concessions of all its member states."

Pah. You're as freaked out as I am. "I'm sorry," Sophie said. "I know you're pretty keen on Cly. As a mentor, I mean."

This time, Zita did manage to gather herself. "He's a man of the Fleet. Truly, Sophie, it's not the same. You must see—"

"This is his land, Zita. He *owns* them."

Without discussing it, they walked further, rounding the curve where Mervin had been lurking, taking themselves out of sight of the tree and its occupants.

"I'm being hypocritical, aren't I?" The words came bursting from her. "Letting Cly shoo the household servants out of sight, telling myself I'll do some minimal socializing and get Beatrice out of jail and run off without getting my hands dirty. But it's all around—landowners didn't build this boardwalk I'm walking on, or tend that fabulous horse I rode here from the dock."

"Sophie?"

"I just. Don't. Understand." She felt like some kind of lady with the vapors, breaking down in tears here in the wilds.

Zita had a glance down the next corridor for Mervin and then said, quietly, "Before the Compact was signed, a little over a hundred years ago, the Piracy had free rein to prey on the lesser nations. They'd sail someplace weak, like Redcap Island, and scoop up whole villages. They'd kill as they pleased and carry prisoners back through the archipelagos of the Bonded Isles, selling them at market. The free nations made attempts, now and then, to stop them, but . . ."

"In time they started to form up in a larger fleet. Even the bonded nations could see value in stopping the raids on their shipping and their cargo vessels. The pirates place great value on reputation—whenever one of them was trying to make a name, often as not they'd kidnap someone rich from a great nation and subject them to horrors before ransoming them."

Horrors. Bram had been grabbed by pirates. They'd used a needle to force a pearl under his thumbnail.

"It's what happened here—they grabbed an estate holder and her seamstress and tortured them to death in the Butcher's Baste. It's why Sylvanna and the Verdanii agreed to commission the building of *Temperance*."

"Why are you telling me this?"

"You want to understand, don't you?"

She rubbed at her eyes and nodded.

Zita continued, "When the preeminent nations from both sides agreed to stop the Piracy, others joined up fast. Sylvanna convinced their sister nations on the port side that the only way to truly stop the raiders was to outlaw the transport of slaves. My gran says the free nations told themselves that without shipping, without new . . ."

"Bodies? Raw materials?"

Zita didn't argue with her word choice. "They were naive. Some thought that over time, conscience would take hold among the slavers. Others believed that if the raids on lesser nations stopped, the bonded nations would start running out of slaves. But breeding and smuggling . . . and even under Fleet law, if you commit a serious crime, you can choose bondage over execution. So there are as many bonded as ever."

Sophie stared at her dully. "You buy their goods. Ualtar . . . Tallon buys their spidersilk rope for shipbuilding spells."

"What would you have the free do, Sophie?" Zita spoke gently. "The Fleet shields the lesser nations. The Convene has spent a century trying to come to an agreement on slavery that would alter the balance and satisfy everyone, but each side has their concessions and nobody's giving them up."

"You could help people escape."

"There are many who do so. Why do you think the Butcher's Baste is so heavily defended?"

"And encourage rebellions?"

"Of course. But who do you think gets killed when there's an uprising?"

"The slaves." Sophie sighed. "Naturally."

"My gran says it'll come to war, maybe soon. That the free and the bonded can't ignore their differences forever, and the Cessation will break." Zita looked up suddenly. "What was that?"

"That" had been a cry of sorts, a quiet one.

Sophie leaped to her feet and trotted back the fifty or so feet to look at the vine-choked tree. The three slaves were thirty feet up its trunk now. They were looking farther into the swamp—the noise hadn't come from them.

Farther down the trail, Sophie thought, doing a one-eighty and hauling ass into the corridor.

Zita had already gone that way, along the boardwalk, and as Sophie sprinted along after her, she heard a splash and another cry.

It was Mervin—he was a few feet out into the water, flailing and apparently panicked.

"Zita, no!" Sophie shouted, but the other girl had sheathed her sword and reached out to the boy.

He caught her outstretched hand on the first try . . . and pulled.

Zita went down, into the muck, with a huge splash.

Slapping, this kid needs a slapping, what was the point of that? Little jerk I knew he was a nasty little jerk. . . . Sophie sprinted out to the spot on the boardwalk.

Mervin was still trying it on, seeing if he could get her, too. "Cousin! We're stuck!"

"You deserve sticking," Sophie told him. Zita had surfaced, sputtering. She was uninjured—the water wasn't deep—but for some reason she was going shock white.

Sophie knelt on the boardwalk, anchoring herself, and held out the stick she'd been using to probe the mud. Zita seized it gratefully, steadying herself as she mushed back to the walkway. It wasn't far and the water wasn't deep—she shouldn't have needed much help, despite the sucking mud. But she was paler with every breath and by the time Sophie hitched her up onto the boards, she was shivering.

"Aren't you going to help me, cousin?"

"Drown if you're gonna," Sophie told Mervin, yanking up the sleeve of Zita's blouse. Her arm was covered in inch-long leeches the color of flame.

She peeked under her shirt. There were hundreds of them.

Mervin looked startled. "So many . . ." He stopped screwing around and waded out of the water, hefting himself onto the boardwalk.

"Sophie?" Zita was looking drowsy.

"I bet you kept your smokes dry, didn't you?" Sophie snapped.

Mervin nodded. A few leeches dropped off his throat, apparently disliking the taste of him. "I didn't know there was a nest."

"Light two cigarettes." She unbuttoned Zita's shirt entirely and snapped her fingers as the kid dug out two hand-rolled somethings and a friction lighter and lit them.

"You burn her, I'll run you through with her sword," Sophie said, hoping she sounded convincingly violent. She took the smoke and began killing the leeches on Zita's abdomen, touching the cherry of the cigarette to one creature after another.

Mervin, to his credit, didn't hesitate to follow suit. The two of them worked feverishly for about five minutes, filling the air with the smell of tobacco and scorched escargot before rolling Zita over and starting on her back.

"Mine's done," Mervin said.

"Reload." Sophie unbuckled Zita's belt.

"They won't have gotten past that. Check her ankles."

He was right, fortunately enough. Zita's belt was tight and her pants were tucked in at the boot.

"Help me get her over my shoulders. Then run ahead. Get help," Sophie said.

"I doubt I'll find anyone. Cousin Clydon told the bonded to stay out of your way, remember?"

"You'd better find help," Sophie said, heaving Zita up. "She's one of Cly's favorites. Can you say the same?"

It was like firing him from a cannon: Mervin pounded off down the boardwalk as she began to make her own way back, a step at a time, with Zita in a fireman's carry. The girl was slender but solid enough; Sophie was an athlete, but Zita was a dense bar of muscle, just about more than she could carry, and the air was thick.

One foot at a time.

She could feel Zita's pulse wherever their skin met, in her belly, against her shoulder.

Could've been worse. Swamp's gotta have alligators.

Breathe, breathe. Did she just go limp? "You with me? Zita?"

No answer.

She'd made it just about to the edge of the boardwalk when a party from the house met her—Mervin, his sister, the spellscribe, Autumn, and six burly-looking guys with wrist bangles holding a sheet. Sophie rolled Zita onto the sheet and they trotted her over to the nearest shade tree, a big pear.

Cly and the other adults were headed down from the big house. Cly took in the situation, leveled a look at Mervin that made the boy shrivel, and knelt beside Zita.

She hadn't regained consciousness.

"She gonna die?" Sophie asked, between gulps of breath.

Autumn flicked a look at Cly. "Is she?"

"No," he said. "As her mentor, I have her middle name in my keeping."

"We can save her, then. Mirelda, you'll assist me."

"Sophie, stay with her," Cly said, and then without bothering to see if she was going to obey, switched to Sylvanner and addressed a string of words to Mervin in that low growl of his.

Whatever he'd said, it went through Merv and his parents like a jolt of electricity.

"Come, girls," Autumn said, laying Zita's hand in Sophie's and somehow signaling to the six men that they should start toiling up the hill to the house.

"What'd he say?" Sophie whispered to Mirelda.

"Merv's to be punished," she said.

"Malicious little troll. Punished how? Whipped?"

Mirelda shook her head. "He's not a—"

"Not now, children," Autumn said. They had arrived in a conservatory of sorts, with windows made from panes of Erinthian lava glass and a large shelf of potted herbs in its brightest corner. Cabinets of books and scrolls lined the walls, alternating with shelves of powders kept in jars.

A mosquito net hung over the middle of the room, draped in a dainty tent over a wide writing table. Two others hung from the ceiling, limp as shrouds.

"Put her there," Autumn ordered the men carrying Zita, who laid her down, sheet and all, on the floor. They arranged the mosquito nets around her.

"Mirelda, is there a leech kit already made?"

"No, but we have everything."

"I'll want some of the leeches."

Mirelda promptly went to one of the cabinets, fetching out a small wooden bowl and a paddle.

"Use whitestone," Autumn corrected, not unkindly, and Mirelda made the switch. She slipped inside the netting around Zita and—to Sophie's surprise—without quailing went looking for a leech that Sophie and Mervin hadn't yet scorched.

"Check her head," Sophie advised. Mirelda immediately came upon one of the gastropods, blood-gorged and entangled in Zita's hair. A second, behind her ear, was even bigger. She transferred them both to the bowl.

Cly emerged from another part of the house with a scrap of paper. He handed it to Autumn. "Zita's name."

"Anything I should know about?" the spellscribe asked.

"She had her teeth straightened when she was nine."

"She can bear a major intention, then."

"She's a duelist," Cly said. "She's young yet for such a heavy load."

Autumn was looking at scrolls now, examining each. "If it was just the blood loss, we might transfuse, but leech sickness, with a foreigner . . ."

"We will transfuse. Just prevent the infection. And speaking of which, Mervin has forfeited his immunity to the creatures."

"The family spells are there." Autumn gestured at a cabinet she'd opened earlier.

"I'll find it." Sophie hopped up, trying to look nonchalant, and opened the cupboard. There were envelopes and rolled scrolls and sealed boxes, all wrapped in one way or another.

She had imagined they would be labeled—and they were, but not in Fleet. There were spells for Mirelda and Mervin, for Fenn and her husband, even one for Beatrice, written on an ivory parasol. Cly, too—a thick accordion of a spell, sealed with wax. One word on that label did look familiar: TEMPERAMENT, it said.

"Find it?" Cly purred.

Sophie held out two scrolls with Mervin's name on them.

He plucked one from her grasp. "Do you wish to come downstairs?"

"If Autumn doesn't mind, I'd like to stay."

"For Zita or to observe?"

"Um, both." She felt herself coloring. "If it's okay."

"Autumn doesn't notice anything when she's working," Mirelda said. "We could play a double-harp."

Cly tapped at her camera. "Don't enpicture Zita's full name. It's the key to enchanting her."

"I remember."

With that, he stalked away.

Sophie watched him go, then looked around the room. Autumn and Mirelda were focused on Zita.

On impulse, she transferred the spell with Cly's name on it to an unlocked drawer, farther down within the cabinet, before relocking the cabinet securely and then taking a position where she could film the inscription process.

Autumn had laid out a series of herbs and begun grinding them between two black and white flecked pieces of granite. Mirelda was watching from a quiet corner, alert for orders, like a nurse assisting a surgeon.

Sophie joined her, turning on her camera and taking footage of Zita—the leech marks, the burned leeches. Then she made a quick turn around Autumn, who was examining a pristine-looking pair of ostrich feathers, seeming to weigh which would best suit her purposes. She did indeed seem oblivious to Sophie and the camera.

"The spell itself will be written on calfskin," Mirelda murmured as she returned. "What is that object, cousin?"

Sophie answered as Parrish had taught her. "Atomist gadgetry from the outlands."

"Oh." Mirelda lost interest, as most people did, but she sounded a little disappointed.

"So . . ." Sophie switched into interview mode. "You know a lot about scribing?"

A mix of pride and shame crossed the teen's face. "Mervin's right—I don't deserve to be taught. I'd be a waste of resources; I don't have the makings of a scribe."

"Autumn seems to think differently."

She shook her head. "There are many ways to be of use to the institute. I'll be an assistant."

It seemed harsh to deny her the chance. "But you understand the principles?"

Autumn was mixing the ink now. Her expression was serene.

Much of what Mirelda told her next was stuff she had already seen in action: you had to know the subject's whole name, you had to write just the right words on the right material, using the ingredients precisely defined by the spell's precedents and nature. They called it laying an intention on someone. Intentions had weight and one could only bear so much.

"That's why Autumn wanted to know what else Zita had done to her."

Mirelda nodded.

"Cly's going to tear up Mervin's immunity to leeches . . . so he won't be impervious anymore."

"He was a sickly child," Mirelda said. "Mother had it done, just in case. He shouldn't get leech sickness from the spell's reversion."

"If he does, will he die?"

"No. He's stronger now, and he eats swamp food. It's really just foreigners who die, those who get lots of bites." She gestured at Zita, whose wounds were already looking festery. "I'd be surprised if he so much as fevers up. May I ask *you* a question, Cousin?"

Sophie made a go-ahead gesture.

"Beatrice is Verdanii. A Feliachild."

"Yep."

"Not you?"

"I repudiated Verdanii citizenship." *And now I'm blowing off Sylvanna.*

"The Feliachilds are said to be one of the ancient branches of the Allmother's line."

"Um. Maybe?"

"The nine families, then, they're a myth?"

Gently she said, "Mirelda, all I know about the Verdanii is they're in what used to be the grain belt and their culture is institutionally biased in favor of women. I haven't a clue what you're talking about."

Mirelda paused. "The nine families are said to practice an older form of magic. Wordless, irreversible, beyond inscription—and each family has its own knack."

"That's news to me." But she thought of Aunt Gale, fumbling that odd-looking brass watch just before the first time Sophie found herself in Stormwrack.

Or Verena, with her pewter clock.

There's the way she always takes us from and to clocks—the great tower on Erinth, the grandfather clock at Beatrice's San Francisco home, the one in Gale's old cabin on Nightjar. . . .

"You *do* know something."

She'd promised not to tell anyone here about Earth. "Is this something you're thinking you could learn? Since you've less aptitude for . . ." She indicated Autumn, who was busily scribbling.

"Would it be possible?" Hope bloomed on the girl's face. "I'd heard abilities ran in families, through the Allmother's blood tree. Mother to daughter. Isn't that why Arpere permitted Cly's marriage in the first place?"

"Is it indeed?" Her thoughts raced. *Mother to daughter, inherited magic—this is part of why everyone was so hung up on my being Gale's heir, and it's why they're so freaked out about me learning too much. What if they're afraid they can't keep me out of Stormwrack?*

This could be why Annela jumped on the chance to have me repudiate Verdanii. And why she kept threatening me with magical amnesia.

"Sophie?"

"Sorry, Mirelda. Thinking hard. I wish I had answers for you."

And Cly. If what Mirelda just said is true . . . could he have chosen Beatrice because of her family connections?

She moved to get Zita back into the shot. The festery, red look of her weals was washing out as Autumn worked on inscribing the calfskin; they were pursing shut, like little mouths, becoming mere wrinkles on her flesh that, in their turn, also vanished.

Autumn set down her pen. "Mirelda, go see if your uncle has summoned a blood donor."

The girl bowed and left.

Sophie was still humming with that sense of discovery, of pieces snapping together. She thought of Gale's watch, tucked away on a shelf at Bram's place.

Magical amnesia, she reminded herself. She would have to tread carefully.

Cly appeared in the doorway with a big, soft-looking fellow in tow. He gestured, and the man knelt beside Zita, chafing her wrists and the insides of her elbow. Then he laid the flat of his enormous hand against her chest.

Sophie leapt up, bringing the camera as close as she could. The man's palm had darkened, the skin mottling to a wine-colored blush, and she could see an impression of red wetness in the join between his flesh and Zita's, as if it was soaked there.

"Want a look?" The man raised his palm carefully, about an inch above her skin. Rivulets of blood, thin as twigs, were twisting against Zita's flesh.

There were no visible breaks in his skin or hers, but Zita's color was returning.

"How do you know your blood type is compatible?"

"It's the family business," he replied. "My mother's mother's mother was a giver, and my father's going back six generations. I have papers from my nation, Gittamot. We provide givers to all of Stormwrack."

"So you know you can donate, and you only marry people who are also donors?"

"Only bear children with them."

"But you don't actually know how many blood types there are, or—"

"There are two. Giver and not."

"There's more than two," Sophie said. But if all the givers were type O negative, they could donate to anyone, whether they were A, B, or AB, positive or negative.

"We follow strict sanguinistic procedures. Here."

He extended his free hand, pointing at her with his index finger. She filmed it as a little whirl of blood extended outward from the tip.

Sophie held out her hand, palm up, in the video frame. "No guts, no glory."

"Marvelous sentiment," Cly murmured.

"Small pinch," said the donor. She felt it, as the blood spout made contact, a quick painful jab. The little thread whirled around on her palm, which pinkened. She could just feel a sense of increased pressure there. Then the donor closed that fist, withdrawing the spout.

There wasn't a mark on her palm.

"That's incredible!"

"I thank you, Kir." He turned to Zita, whose color had about returned to normal. "She's out of danger. And ready for a proper bed, I think."

"Sophie," Cly said. She climbed to her feet and let him draw her off to a corner.

"First, you deserve multiple apologies for my awful family."

"You're not responsible for Mervin's actions."

"I am, actually, in law. But what I wish to say is thank you. For helping Zita. You acted quickly. I so admire your cool head."

She couldn't quite crush a swell of pride. "No problem."

"I also wondered if you might like to meet someone more . . . compatible with your inclinations."

"Meaning?"

"Some faint proof that some of my countrymen aren't . . . how did you put it? Malicious trolls?"

"You overheard that?"

"It had the inestimable ring of truth."

Note to self: keep lips buttoned, she thought.

Then she heard Bram's voice: *Yeah, Ducks, when have you ever managed that?*

"Mirelda seems like an okay person," she said.

He gave her a look that seemed to say: *Who?*

"There's a fellow who's interested in your thoughts on the turtles. I recognize it's been a long day. . . ."

It had been, hadn't it? Perhaps more for him than her: he looked tired and strained.

And, maybe, more likely to slip up? She hadn't seen any behavior that absolutely argued that he was or wasn't sociopathic.

If she and Cly were away, Fenn and her family could lick their wounds in private for a while.

"Should I change?" she said. "One of those sporty outfits?"

He nodded. "That would be very . . . yes. Thank you. I'll show you to your room."

Her room looked out over the apiaries and the hillside, a view terminating in the green jewel of a swamp. There was no lava glass here: the screen was made of a silk so sheer it was almost transparent. The breeze shivered the strands. The bed was covered in a russet, leaf-shaped blanket and the walls held more of her grandmother's oil paintings. It had an odd atmosphere: not quite tense or impersonal, but somehow far from cozy.

"I'll be out in a second," she said.

"At your leisure," he replied, shutting the door.

Sophie pulled off her swamp- and sweat-soaked T-shirt and then opened her trunk, digging out her messageply sheets from Bram and Verena.

Verena: ARRIVING SYLVANNA TOMORROW. CAN YOU HOLD IT TOGETHER FOR ONE MORE DAY?

Bram: WITH VERENA, COMING TO FIND YOU. DIDN'T SAY ANYTHING TO THE PARENTS.

She stared at Bram's message in mixed delight—she missed him!—and consternation. Last time he'd been on Stormwrack he'd gotten kidnapped; the pirates had hurt him.

They formed the Fleet to stop that kind of thing, Zita had said. Held their noses over the slavery so they could stop the raids and torture.

A tap at her door. "Sophie? Should we bring your memorician?"

"No. You and I need to talk, Cly." She yanked open her bag, found a protein bar, devoured it, and pocketed another.

"We can send Krispos ahead if you think we'll need him."

"I should be okay. Let him read."

Bram, coming back to Stormwrack. She inhaled, fighting the whirl of her emotions: excitement, joy, relief, and more than a little fear. What if he got kidnapped again, or hurt? Or killed?

Well, the answer was to get herself and him back home, pronto. If she didn't come to Stormwrack, neither would he. If he didn't come, they'd both be safe.

Because that was the answer, wasn't it? It was all very well to maunder on about the cost to herself of living, even part-time, in this other world, but she couldn't keep risking Bram's life.

She would have to give it up somehow.

Which meant, suddenly, she had a pile of things to sort out. She grabbed the turtle case file and her own notes, changed hastily, and ran a brush through her hair.

Okay. Agenda item one—see what Cly knew about the Verdanii succession and spellcasting. Item two—the Turtle Beach guy. Item three—finish seeing Sylvanna, free Beatrice, then hook up with Parrish and Bram and Verena.

Finally, get herself and her brother the hell out of here before she ran out of K bars.

Could she do all that in a few days? She'd have to try.

"Sophie?"

"Ready," she called, running out.

CHAPTER **15**

The horses were waiting at the gate, and the groom didn't quite have enough time to vanish before she spotted him. He had an arm amputated just below the elbow, but Sophie managed to catch an image of him with her camera.

She climbed aboard Ballado.

The estate, otherwise, seemed deserted.

"So, daughter? You must have some ulterior motive for enduring my slaver company."

"That's a little dramatic, don't you think?"

"Am I wrong?"

She sighed. "What did the government tell you, exactly, about Erstwhile?"

Cly nodded, as if her question confirmed something important. "You were raised in an advanced atomist culture. Your air chokes on burnt fuel and your natural legacy dies, species by species. Your devices are driven by caged oddities inscribed with petroleum, you have used up vast troves of iron, and your society lies on the edge of unimaginable desperation."

Nothing like leading with the bad news. She fought the urge to break in with a defense of Earth, or a list of all the good things, amazing things, that technological civilization had accomplished.

"There are billions of you, a number my mind can hardly encompass, many of whom own nothing more than hunger, and the rest equipped with weapons more potent than the steel musket John Coine brought back."

"The pistol he almost shot you with?"

"Just so."

"That's the official story? It's like they don't want you to visit."

"The Fleet government is terrified that when your nations fall, your people will flee here. Your billions," Cly said. "But that was hardly the most remarkable thing I was told. People believe the outlands are a place one sails to. But Annela tells me they are a time, a long-ago—"

"She specifically said the past? Not, say, an alternate dimension?"

"That would be one of your fine atomist distinctions," he said. "Beyond my understanding. What I do know is they can only be accessed by wild Verdanii magic."

"Except when pirates go there buying guns and grenades."

"Ah." There was no mistaking that smile. It was pride. "I wondered if you'd see the crux of the issue."

"Tell me."

Cly petted his horse. "The Verdanii believed the Feliachild ability to eraglide . . . eraglide?"

"Like they'd tell me."

"Tsk. That the Feliachild ability was the only way to and from Erstwhile. That they form a natural choke point, a defense against the outlander hoards and their mighty devices of death. The only gateway. But if this is so, one of their kin brought those pirates to your city, Sanfrah—"

"San Francisco."

"So either there is a traitor Feliachild—an unpalatable prospect unless it happens to be you—"

"Me? It's not me!"

"—or they don't possess this monopoly they imagine. In either case, the idea that people of Coine's quality might transit to the land of muskets and grenades . . . it was grenades?"

"Grenades," she affirmed. "And rocket launchers and F16's and weaponized anthrax and mustard gas—"

"Oh," he said, with no emotion at all, "that's easily made here. Alchemists have the formula."

Well! There's one big tick mark in the "yes, he's a sociopath" column.

He broke off quickly. "Good afternoon, Kir Erminne. May I present my child, Kir Sophie Hansa?"

CHAPTER 16

Rees Erminne was one of those people she couldn't help liking. Tanned, blocky of body and ever-so-slightly ill-kempt, with patched trousers, leech-scarred hands, and an unhurried, friendly air, he exuded a slow-moving calm that put Sophie in mind of a koala bear. He adored his horse. He listened to Sophie with care—and not only because his Fleetspeak was only just passable. It was apparent, as they all continued to ride toward the beach, that he knew every inch of wild land within this corner of Autumn District.

According to his status sash, he was legally a child, though he had to be in his late twenties.

As he led Cly and Sophie down the trail to Turtle Beach, Rees explained about the dispute with Grimreef over whether the turtles had been artificially introduced to Sylvanna.

Sophie had already read this in the court documents: Grimreef insisted the turtles always returned to the beach where they had hatched to lay their eggs. The Sylvanners, meanwhile, said the animals went to and fro between the two beaches.

"It's all rather 'Does not, does too!'" Erminne acknowledged. "Like many of these affairs: hard to prove and not quite worth dueling over."

"Sylvanna seems to have a fair number of those," Sophie said.

"The Spellscrip Institute is aggressive in pursuing new inscriptions. It leads them down legally complex paths. I'd be grateful for any solution you may propose."

Sophie handed him one of the turtle shells Cly had given her, pointing out the notches she'd cut into its cervical scute. "You can make marks safely here and here, without hurting the animal."

Erminne fingered the shell with interest. "And then?"

"The rest is basic observation and recording. Form a team. Some from Sylvanna, some from Grimreef, maybe a court observer or some other neutral party?" It all seemed straightforward, obvious, but Rees was spellbound, listening as though the idea were revolutionary. "You start notching the Sylvanna turtles when they return to the beach, after they lay. You notch a number of the hatchlings, too, when they emerge every spring. Do the same, using different markings, on Grimreef."

"Oh! One notch for Turtle Beach in Sylvanna, two for Goldensands in Grimreef, that sort of thing?"

Sophie nodded. "At that point, it simply becomes a matter of observation and bookkeeping. Each year when they arrive on the beach, you do a count and mark a few more animals."

Erminne thought it through and then nodded. "We'd have to hurry to organize it for this year. The lay is soon."

"As a secondary strategy we—I mean *you*—could also try relocating a clutch of eggs to a new beach," Sophie said. "If the Grimreefers are right, you'll be able to establish them elsewhere."

"They're not!" He feigned affront, puffing out his chest. It was a bit adorable.

"It's not a good idea to go introducing new animals into other microclimates anyway. But if Sylvanna's in the right, the babies hatched on Turtle Beach will turn up on Grimreef . . . how long does it take them to mature?"

"I wouldn't know. How does one work out such things, as a . . . was it a Fornsich?"

"Forensic. It means—"

"Forensic practitioner," Cly interrupted. "The science of proof in court."

Guess we've got that branded, then. Call the trademark office!

They were on the beach now, having ridden out of the marshy lowlands and up an outcropping of stone that extended a long finger into the ocean. The water caressed a wide strip of coarse-grained sand, reddish in color, rather like crushed brick, she thought. Stubby breakers of the red rock had been arranged about fifty feet out into the shallows, forming a dotted line around the beach.

Beyond them, she could see the shallow expanse of water that separated Sylvanna from Haversham. A stout-looking, armored ship patrolled in the distance. The passage was broken by craggy islets and piles of boulders that looked man-made, a hazardous obstacle course guarded by fast-looking warships.

Turning in a circle, she looked up and down the spit of land, spying a platform just up the rise with a view of the Butcher's Baste. Guard tower? A lighthouse? Probably both.

"The turtles don't need much help, but this calms the waters a little," Erminne explained, drawing her attention back to the circle of wave-breakers at the beach's edge. "Sometimes it can keep the late autumn storms from laying waste to a whole year's hatchlings. The institute will send apprentices to rake the sand in about two weeks. Makes it easier for them to dig."

"The beach is entirely managed?"

"Yes."

It made sense, if the turtles were a precious resource. She asked a bunch of questions: How many turtles did the institute harvest each year, and what kind of predation did the young turtles face? How precisely could they predict the dates for migration to the beach and for hatching?

By way of answering the last, Rees took her to the base of the guard tower. A large rock there had dates of past migrations scratched into its surface. A scrap of repurposed sail canvas hung above this. It was a poster, and chalked on it were gambling odds on two-hour periods over a four-night window due to start in a few weeks.

"You run a betting pool on when the migration will begin?"

"Don't laugh," Rees said. "It's one of my primary sources of income."

She took a photograph of the rock and the poster. "So . . . you think the third day?" She tried converting the information to normal dates from the Fleet calendar. About a month, then—mid-August.

By then I'll be home. "Do you use the land for anything else?"

"Spring picnics," Erminne said, his fondness for the place obvious in his smile.

While they talked, Cly had dismounted, rolled up his trouser legs and shed his boots, and waded into the shallows with a foxy expression on his face and a net in his hand. He made a few scoops at something—once she even saw it, a slick gray shape leaping out of the net's embrace—but came up empty.

"If this works, you'll have done the institute and my family a great favor," Erminne said.

I'm always doing science favors for people here, she thought. It was a pleasing idea, in its way. "Your family?"

"My great-great-grandfather painted this beach, over a century ago, turtles and all. The pictures have been locked up in court for decades— the Grimreefers say we forged them, but nobody can prove it."

She remembered seeing this in the documents. "Cly says my grandmother painted."

"It's a common pastime among the idle landowners," he said, and suddenly his tone was a little careful. Excluding himself from that category, somehow? He certainly didn't have the pampered look of Cly's cousins; looking at him, it was obvious he worked hard at something.

So he's land rich but otherwise poor—which is probably why he's not married. Turtle gambling must not yield that much income.

"I'll be interested to hear how the case turns out," she said.

"I'll write you," he replied. "Care of His Honor, as is proper."

That torn feeling again. *What am I going to do?*

She couldn't stay, she told herself. Bram coming after her was the last straw. She couldn't let her obsession with Stormwrack deprive their parents of both children.

"Have you made any progress with the throttlevine infestation? I know that must be as dear to your heart as to—" Erminne broke off, clearly noting that Sophie had stiffened. Cly turned his back, taking a futile swipe at the fish he was pursuing. "I've said something amiss."

"Sophie and I have been grappling with our cultural differences," Cly said, his voice carrying over the water. "No harm done."

Sophie was trying to swallow. The image of those altered goat-people in the marsh had seized her imagination again, and she was flailing in a sea of guilt. To feel regret of any kind for a backward asshole place where one person could do that to another . . .

She made herself speak. "It's okay, Kir Erminne. You couldn't know."

She unshipped her camera and took footage of the beach, walking off in the direction of the water, examining shells and a feather, coral in color, that had fallen on a dry patch of sand. She stared at the sea, longing for the comfort and clarity afforded by a good swim.

All this time here and I've barely been in the water.

Just then Cly folded his net, wrung out the water, and came in. "Shall we?"

They waited as he rolled down his pants legs, then mounted up and headed back.

She was starting to feel the effects of a day spent on horseback, an ache in her thighs and knees.

"This is my path." Erminne reached over and seized her hand. "We will see you, won't we, at the festival? If you're to save my grandfather's paintings and restore the honor of our family beach, I wish to introduce you to my mother."

"I've given my word that I'll go," she said, dully.

It wasn't quite the answer he was expecting, but he rallied. "Tomorrow, then." He flourished without bowing, turned his horse, bent to kiss its neck and speak a few words in its ear. It was only too happy to break into a canter, no doubt in the direction of its bed and the rest of its herd.

By contrast their mounts, hers and Cly's, were deeply unimpressed when they took the road to Low Bann rather than turning toward town.

They rode in crushing silence for a while, and then Cly reined in near one of the citrus plants, an obvious volunteer tree, and began loading that net of his with red fruit.

"Cly—"

"It's wild," he said, holding out one of the fruit. "I must keep you fed, mustn't I?"

Part of her wanted to be stubborn, to tell him that all economic and ecological systems were bound and connected, that for all she knew someone else was counting on this tree. But, in the end, she held out a hand, accepting the fruit.

He's trying so damned hard. Was he just playing her?

"Wouldn't do to get scurvy," she said. *Peace offering.*

"No," he agreed. "You must eat at least a few bites at the festival or you'll offend our hosts."

"Must I?"

"I'm not honoring our agreement if you make a scene," he said.

"Beatrice—"

"Beatrice can rot," he said, wearily.

"I'll do the minimum."

Handing her the net full of fruits, he rode on.

This was unbearable. As always, she couldn't leave a silence alone. "Tell me about the throttlevine."

"You read the case logs."

"What's it to you? Erminne suggested it's important to you. Personal. How?"

He eyed her, lizardlike. Weighing whether it was worth it? "All right. Some you'll have gleaned from the brief?"

"Some."

Throttlevine was native to Haversham, the island northwest of Sylvanna. They lay nestled against each other, like yin and yang on the map, and Haversham was a free nation.

"We fought many bloody wars before the Cessation." Cly told her that Sylvanna had been the early loser, subjugated for many years to its neighbor. Then in a relatively short space of time, it had liberated itself and gotten wealthy. Once the scales tipped, Sylvanna repaid Haversham in blood, raiding her coasts and taking her people into bondage.

"When people talk of war breaking out between the port and starboard sides of Stormwrack, they look to the two of us, snarling at each other across the Butcher's Baste, and feel nervous. We are," he said, "the logical tearing point for the Fleet Constitution."

"Sylvanna got wealthy," Sophie said. "How did that come about?"

It had been one of those crucial intersections of necessity, good leadership, and the right resources: Sylvanna had been struck by a tobacco blight,

Cly said, and her government had taken a risk, going deep into debt so it could attract spellscribes to the island, soliciting anyone who might be able to cure the big cash crop. The institute had been the result; the cluster of researchers had in time managed to find a way to inscribe a tobacco field that resisted the blight. Along the way, they developed an inscription that made transforms who could find castaways from wrecks, then a spell to help maddenflur addicts. Next came an inscription that increased the reach of lighthouses.

The scribes, many of them foreigners, had a network of international contacts: the institute began forming agreements with some of the smaller islands to lock down acquisition of crucial supplies.

"Suddenly you had spells as well as tobacco for sale."

"Exactly. And because there'd been a shortage, tobacco itself had become expensive."

At least a handful of those early brilliant researchers had come from the island next door, tempted away from Haversham by promises of unlimited resources for study and a pampered lifestyle.

As Sylvanna prospered, her ships became a tempting target to raiders. The country directed some of its new wealth into building up its navy, but few nations could stand against a determined assault. The institute was in danger of having its growing intellectual treasury stolen.

"It was around then that the Verdanii and the Tall put to sea with a few of their allies, looking to put a dent in the raiding traffic. They sent out an open invitation—expecting, you understand, that their allies would join them and the rest of us would decline. But our president sent *Excelsior*."

The history lesson was intriguing. Sophie peeled another of the red fruits and, forgetting herself, offered Cly a segment. He took it with a smile.

"The story goes that it was Stormwrack's quietest uproar. Uproar here in our Citizens' Hall—what was Bellina thinking, allying herself with children of the Allmother?"

"Another woman leader?"

"You're giving me a bad impression of your home nation," he said. "I am not sure, had we been led by a man, that the Verdanii wouldn't have found some excuse to leave *Excelsior* out of the convoy. But the Allmother of Verdanii liked Bellina, and the institute had just developed cannoneers—you remember our cannoneer, of course."

Sophie nodded. "*Nightjar* has one, too."

"*Excelsior* put to sea with forty cannoneers."

"So you had the big guns."

"Our other option for self-preservation would have been to take the cannoneers to the bandit fleets."

"Join the Piracy?"

He shook himself. "Haversham had been covertly supporting the bandits. They had no more idea of Sylvanna joining the Fleet than anyone else—and they were furious. They made a clumsy attempt to assassinate Bellina, to see if we could be drawn into a local war. This made them look bad in the eyes of the community coalescing asea. Then they joined the Fleet themselves, to agitate against expanding it any further, before more nations like Sylvanna—"

"Slave nations, you mean?"

"Yes, before more slavers could join. But the winds were driving it all forward: the Piracy was defeated in the Raiders War, the Compact was written, and the Cessation of Hostilities began.

"By then, the bitterness between Sylvanna and Haversham was set. In peace, it has festered."

They have such a romantic way with words here. Homesickness spiked through her. *Dad would love it.*

Cly continued his tale: The first attempt to undercut Sylvanna's position as a great nation had been in a resurgent form of the tobacco blight. Spies managed to get their hands on the inscriptions for the protected fields in Springland and destroyed them; the blight broke out, and then there had been an infestation of beetles. But the Haversham operatives got themselves caught and were tortured until they confessed.

Tortured. Sophie swallowed.

"There was an international outcry. The new government, terrified the Fleet might break apart underfoot, leveed a fine on Haversham. It was an outlandish sum, but by the time they realized that, all they could do was encourage our government to collect it gently."

Forgive the debt, in other words. "I bet that worked great."

"No," Cly said, missing or electing to miss the sarcasm. "So the Havers decided to be subtler."

Thirty years passed. Then Sylvanna had a trio of exceptionally promising presidents who'd gotten into office and then—almost certainly due to inscription—become emotionally unstable. There'd been an economic disaster, but no evidence that proved Haversham was involved.

"I'm taking rather a long time to get round to the point, aren't I?" Cly said.

"Where else are we going to go?" Sophie said. "Besides, I came here to learn about you, to learn about your culture and Stormwrack."

He didn't comment on the fact that everything she'd seen so far had created a gulf between them.

The throttlevine had first been seen in the swamps not far from Low Bann, when Cly was a boy. Nobody'd thought much of it at first; the stuff grew all over Haversham, and the ecosystems were similar—it was only twenty miles away, after all. They'd burned it and shrugged it off . . . the first time. And the second.

But a decade went by, and the infestations kept resurfacing. Everyone became sure Haversham was responsible, yet nobody could figure out how they were doing it.

"You said it's how you came to the Judiciary?"

Cly nodded. "I have two qualities one seeks in a Judiciary duelist—fighting spirit and a fondness for reading and writing. There were some prominent Havers in the courts; our government wanted volunteers to write the entrance exam. The hope was that some of the highly placed Havers would know about the sabotage. Having failed to surpass us economically or to gain the upper hand through dirty tricks, their leaders concentrated some resources on permeating the Fleet bureaucracy."

"An arms race within the civil service."

"A competition, at any rate. It's a fruitless investment of energy, all this hatred."

Was that real regret? Or him trying to play her? "So you don't feel it? You don't share the animosity?"

Cly shook his head. "Killing Havers on the dueling deck is no more and no less satisfying than killing anyone else."

Which was a little hair-raising, as observations went, and didn't answer anything.

The trail narrowed, pressed on either side by densely overgrown bamboo, then widening again just beyond a ramshackle gate, as the untended overgrowth gave way to groomed hedges of the same species.

"This is the edge of Low Bann," Cly said. "We're home."

CHAPTER 17

That night they had an interminable dinner with Cly's cousins. Sophie's relatives ate beef, greens, and roasted pears, all harvested and prepared by the bonded. She ate a protein bar, two of the red citrus fruits, and a selection of berries Cly had obliged Mervin to go and collect for her.

"There's a Verdanii embassy here," he told her. "By breakfast I'll have arranged to buy some grains from them. Mervin will pick them up."

If her cousin resented being turned into an errand boy, he knew better than to complain. He was a little pale and stank of smoke but otherwise there was no sign that having his leech inscription torn up had materially damaged him.

After she finally got away from the table, Sophie smoothed out her two messageply sheets, one from Verena and one from Bram, looking for their latest answers to her notes.

Verena had nothing new to say.

The Bram page had *Hang in there* again, along with some other stuff; they were keeping the books out of his hands, too, but he'd calculated the difference between a Fleet mile and an Imperial one (a Fleet mile came to 3,502 feet, it turned out, though of course they didn't measure things in feet or inches either). He'd confirmed their observation about the length of the days and "borrowed" a calendar from Sweet—the Stormwrack calendar had ten thirty-six-day months and a three- to four-day "new year's interval." They manually adjusted the start of their new year to midnight on the winter solstice. It was a big annual ritual, as it happened, on Verdanii—the setting of the World Clock.

SUMMER IS WHEN EVERYONE ON SYLVANNA GETS ENGAGED, she wrote, following up with things she'd seen during the day: nothing heavy, just enough to let him see she was well. Saving paper was less urgent now that he was on his way.

She sat down with the notebooks she'd bought, paging through the one she was beginning to think of as her book of questions, thinking about all the things she wanted to investigate here in Stormwrack. The other book was pristine, devoid of answers or anything else of use.

"I'm leaving and I'm not coming back," she whispered to the pages, to all the scrawled notes, all the mysteries and unknowns. Then, despite her resolution, she turned to a blank page in the questions book and added more mysteries to the list.

Feeling jangly and disconsolate, she took out her video camera, running through the footage gathered so far: the red birds and the soot viper, the twins and the tour through the swamp, and Zita's accident.

Not an accident, she thought.

She watched Autumn Spell working to save Zita, a tiny digital record of the inscription process.

The video was a reminder of that spell with Cly's name on it, and the word that might, in Fleet, have meant "temperament."

TEMPERAMENT, she wrote in her notebook. EMOTIONAL TEMPERAMENT? TIED TO SOCIOPATHY?

It doesn't matter," she whispered. "I'm one party away from being done here."

How much could she learn in a day?

Nothing, if she just sat around.

She dragged her jeans off the floor and wriggled into them, tiptoeing out into the hall.

The house was quiet.

This was foolhardy. Cly had to be a light sleeper.

She made her way up to the inscription room without waking anyone.

At first glance, the cabinet full of inscriptions appeared to have vanished. Sophie circled the room, navigating by the dim moonlight shining through the windows. Then she pulled out her camera, lit up the screen, and looked again.

It was sitting there when we came in, she thought. In front of the wall with the big tapestry.

Could it be that easy? She tiptoed across the floor, pulled the tapestry aside, and found the cabinet tucked into an alcove.

The padlock was back in place. She opened the unlocked drawer beneath, flipping through its contents, and finding the thick envelope she'd seen before: CLY—*TEMPERAMENTE FEL MEDDIA*.

Breaking the wax seal, she opened the envelope carefully, finding within a stiff card—made of paper, as far as she could tell—bent accordion style. The spellscrip on it glimmered—all spellscrip seemed to glimmer—as she laid it on the floor.

The magical text was beyond her ability to read, but if she could find a friendly spellscribe, she might find someone to translate it.

"Temperament." Is it even the same word in Fleet and Sylvanner? And, if it is, does it follow that someone made Cly sociopathic? It'd be handy, if they were trying to make a killer judge.

She shuddered, remembering that scowling, horror-movie portrait of her birth father as a boy.

She focused on the card and filmed every word except the top line, where Cly's full name (his middle name looked like it might be Iblis) could be found.

I bet name stealing's a big ol' crime here.

Having finished the recording, she looked at the spell directly.

What was interesting about the text on this one was it was sealed between the paper and some kind of clear wax. It shifted and moved beneath; in fact, it looked more like water than ink, clear, still wet, with a smattering of little seeds or particles within.

It's a long document—hopefully that means the whole magical alphabet's in here.

Returning it, she closed the cabinet and draped the tapestry over it. Then she turned her attention to the still-open book Autumn had referenced when writing the spell for Zita. The instructions were written in Fleet and read like an extremely detailed recipe:

> *... inscribe text on the flesh of a calf, stillborn in the month of Maiia and the first born by its mother. Ink to use portion of blood from the leeches themselves, a drop of fine whiskey not under five years aged ...*

And so on. She filmed a thirty-page sample of the book. It had spells for managing beehive infestations, something for taming and training alligators. It had instructions for creating something called a follow-box whose ingredient list was much like the package she'd bought, back in the Fleet, containing the passenger-pigeon skin. There was even a boutique section: perm your hair, straighten your hair, brighten your eyes. She flipped through the whole thing, took a shot of the title—*Common Spells of the Autumn District*—and looked for the transformation spell that had turned those slaves into oddities.

Nothing; this book, at least, had no slavery-related spells.

She flipped back to the leech cure and put the book back where she found it. Then, creeping downstairs, she went to sit with Zita for a couple of hours, using the dark and quiet to order her thoughts. This Highsummer festival was the last hoop she would have to jump. Beatrice could get her bail. As for whether she got convicted or successfully divorced Cly, that was out of Sophie's hands now.

Or was it? There was this throttlevine case. Cly was clearly invested. Maybe he would still go for the upsell if she learned something that would help with that.

Wait, stop! I have to get home. I have to stop luring Bram here.

She remembered, six months earlier, diving the floating conglomeration of wreckage and driftwood, constructed by a species of otter, and the diversity of life that raft had drawn—fish, weeds, sea worms, barnacles below the water, and plants, bugs, and birds above.

And what about this whole wild Verdanii magic thing? If Sophie could learn to transfer back and forth between the worlds as Verena did, she wouldn't necessarily need government permission to go diving.

It was a defiant thought, but it lacked conviction. Was she really going to sneak in and out of Stormwrack illegally? Even if she did, how would she hire a ship to take her out to the otters?

She'd burned her chance at Verdanii citizenship without a thought . . .

. . . and against Cly's advice, she remembered, a bit ruefully.

And now she couldn't become Sylvanner.

Give it up, give it up, give it, oh, can I, I can't I can't I can't. There has to be a way. Maybe—

But it was late. Instead of offering up a tidy solution to her bizarre immigration woes, her mind served up an image of Parrish, half a dream, in that bomber jacket of Bram's, smelling of leather.

She shook the image away.

Annela Gracechild's the key, she thought. She's the one handing out travel permits and ordering Verena to keep my nose out of the world's business. Maybe Parrish can tell me how to—no, Verena, maybe Verena can help.

It wouldn't hurt to ask Parrish, too.

Okay, if all she could do was default to thinking about Parrish, then she needed to turn in. She made her way back to the bedroom. Just as she got there, she heard the main doors of the house closing. Someone coming in? Going out?

She hurried into her room and peered through the silk window, checking the yard. Nobody. From the position of the moon, which was one day short of full, it was late. Two, maybe, or three o'clock.

She stood stock still, listening for footsteps.

They came. Confident, quiet, neither stomping nor tiptoeing. Mervin scuttled, and Mirelda dragged her feet. The steps came right to her door, paused.

One of the adults, then. Cly?

Checking on me? She flashed on memories of her father, peering in through a crack in the bedroom door at night, making sure she was still breathing. Emotion tightened her chest.

She hadn't gotten into this for weird worlds and magic and otters who farmed, after all—she'd just wanted, in the beginning, to understand who'd made her. To lay eyes on her birth parents. To be able to say: This is where I came from.

If he cracks the door, he's gonna see me standing here, fully dressed, eyes wide open. He'll wonder what I've been up to.

So? What's he doing out at this hour?

God, I hope he didn't go out to hunter-gather me an alligator or something.

Oh no, now I'm gonna laugh.

A creak—the steps resuming. Cly, if it was Cly, went upstairs.

She buried her face in her leaf-shaped pillow, giggled until her ears were ringing, and then pulled off her pants and climbed into bed.

One more day, she thought. Do a little dance, fake a little nice, get the hell out and sail somewhere sane.

If Nightjar *docks in the morning, maybe Parrish can come to the festival.*

OMG, Sophie, forget Parrish!

It went like that for what felt like another hour before the cicadas finally drove her mind off the one track and into sleep.

She woke early and had a long stretch in the cool of the morning. It would be another hot day.

Throwing on her last clean pair of jeans and a T-shirt, she went and tapped on Zita's door. She called through, "How are you feeling?"

"Better, thank you. His Honor didn't kill the boy, did he?"

"You are joking, right?" Sophie's blood ran cold all the same.

"Of course."

She shuddered. "Mervin was sulking his way through dinner last night. And you are a good person for caring."

"Maybe I just want to bloody his nose myself." Zita stuck her head out into the hall, grinning. She had a towel wrapped around her and was covered in soap. "I'm out of water. Can you—"

"No problem." Sophie took the offered pitcher. It was glazed red clay and weighed a ton. She went downstairs. There'd be a pump in the kitchen, wherever that was. . . .

"Probably near the dining room," she murmured. There'd been a little door behind Fenn's chair. Sure enough, there was a drab, low-ceilinged hallway there that led into a world of restaurant smells. Baking bread and cooking eggs—her mouth watered.

The hall ended in a room where six women were engaged in various stages of making what looked like a mountain of pastries, all wearing the not-quite-ornamental shackle on their left wrists. They had been engaged in conversation but when Sophie came in, they fell silent.

Sophie gave them an awkward smile and took one step toward the sink, but a gazelle of a woman stepped in front of her, whisking the pitcher out of her hand and handing it off to one of the others, who took it and began working the pump.

Don't look away. Don't refuse to see this. Sophie examined each of them in turn, meeting their solid, determinedly placid gazes. They were neither well fed nor emaciated; they had the muscles and calloused hands of people who worked hard, extremely hard—like Rees Erminne, she thought— and the eldest of them was about forty. Their skin colors varied—there was a pale, freckled blonde, whose nose and eyes were so red she must either have a cold or been crying, a woman with olive skin, and a black woman, too. No bruises on them, but their clothes were concealing. If they had whip marks on their backs . . .

She swallowed.

"I've been wanting to talk to . . ." she forced herself to finish the sentence ". . . some of the bonded. Hello."

"Neyza dinn Fleetspak." The woman slapped the jug into her hand with a slosh of cold water and a bright, pleasant expression.

"But—"

"Neyza dinn Fleetspak!"

"Okay. Thank you," Sophie said, and retreated.

She crossed the dining room and then froze in the foyer—Cly was there, speaking in Sylvanner. *"Pej battro tard, con nyu annit—"*

He broke off—the woman he was addressing had seen her.

Sophie pushed through the door.

Her father was standing with a tall, auburn-haired matron who wore a white widow's sash.

"Ah, Sophie. I thought perhaps one of the young cousins was—well, no matter. Child, may I present Kir Erminne?"

Another Erminne. She tried to bow without spilling the pitcher. "Pleased."

The woman quirked her brows, amused. "What are you doing?" Her tone was kind, and she wasn't fazed by Sophie's outlander clothes, either, which won her points.

"Oh—my friend. *Our.* Zita, she needed water."

"Erminne is Rees's mother," Cly said. "We won't keep you, but I hope we'll all have a chance to talk tonight."

"It was lovely to meet you," Rees's mother said. "Don't let us keep you from your friend."

Dismissed. "Thanks," she said, mulling as she walked up to Zita's room.

Zita opened the door, still wrapped up, and took the the pitcher gratefully. "I'll be down soon."

Sophie went looking for Krispos. "Did you read that Sylvanner Fleet phrasebook?"

"I'm halfway through." He held it up.

She recalled Cly's words: "*Pej battro . . .*"

"*Battro* is 'betrothal' . . ." He flipped ahead. "*Pej* is 'late.' Late betrothal."

"*Nyu annit?*"

" 'Soon year'?" He frowned. " 'Later in the year'?"

"One or the other?"

He shrugged. "All I'm learning is vocabulary."

"Okay. Thanks."

Betrothal. He's talking betrothal with Rees's mom.

She began to hyperventilate. Was Cly thinking of marrying her off?

CHAPTER 18

She retreated to her room, staring around blankly until it occurred to her that she could pack, and then went into a frenzy of shoving things into her bags, getting everything stowed so she could make her escape.

He wouldn't, would he? I must have misunderstood.

It tracked with him hauling her out to meet Rees yesterday. Wait—she had picked the turtle case herself.

Maybe all of the lawsuits he'd given her were connected to eligible young men.

She had everything packed and repacked, the bed made, and she'd even dusted by the time Mirelda and Zita showed up, carrying a disco-era ball gown, in rich brown silk, in a paper-wrapped package.

Zita was in full dress uniform, sword and all, and her foreigner's sash had a new pin—a carved impression of a woman's face, bound with red ribbon.

"His Honor recalled that I'm inclined to women," she said, when she saw Sophie looking at it. "I told him I don't mind dancing with whoever asks, but—"

"But he got you a lesbian badge of honor anyway?"

"It was thoughtful of him, wasn't it?" As always, there was that little bit of a pitch there: *Take it easy on Cly, Zophie, Cly rocks.* He'd picked her a nice friend who just happened to be head of the Team Cly cheerleading squad. If that wasn't manipulative, what was?

"You look very dashing," Sophie replied.

Mirelda's dress was a more shapeless version of Sophie's, also brown, with white gloves and shoes to match her little-girl sash. The pair of them helped Sophie into the ball gown. Zita cast a covetous eye over Sophie's bra.

Did I really think I wanted to move to a world with Age of Sail technology?

Since her hair was short and curly anyway, all they did with it was give her a wreath of orange daisy-like flowers—osteopurnum or something like it.

The foreigner's sash with its one adornment hung like a beauty contestant's sash across her chest. Mirelda gathered the slack at her hip clumsily, pulling it into something like a rose.

"Your papers," she said. The Bram pages on her desk were filling with text.

SOFE, WE HAVE DOCKED IN AUTUMN CITY AND PARRISH IS ARRANGING FOR A CARRIAGE. CLY SENT INVITES TO US ALL FOR THE BASH; THE IMPLICATION IS THE DRIVER WILL TAKE US TO YOU, WHEREVER YOU ARE. UNLESS YOU WANT TO MAKE A BREAK FOR IT . . . :)

Emoticons, she thought. So cute.

NO, she scrawled, also in English. IF I CAN JUST GET THROUGH TONIGHT, BEATRICE GETS HER BAIL.

"Powder?" Mirelda said. She was holding out a pot of pinkish . . . blush?

"What's that for?"

"You're quite tan. It's not genteel."

"No powder, then."

"You have an answer," Zita said.

She glanced at the reply from Bram. WHAT ARE THE CHANCES OF THAT? ME GETTING THROUGH? Sophie wrote. DIMINISHING.

New handwriting—Verena. She imagined them together in *Nightjar's* galley, bent over a page. SOPHIE, BEHAVE.

TRYING, OMG, I SWEAR, TRYING.

Mirelda took a swipe at her with the blush.

Sophie gently pushed her hands away. "Listen, I'm not gonna pass for a genteel Sylvanner anything. Or a woman of the Fleet, for that matter."

"No," they agreed, Zita with humor, Mirelda with a touch of anxiety.

"If Cly doesn't like the image I present, he can park me in a dark corner."

"Nonsense." Cly's voice came through the door, followed by a knock.

"Come on in," Sophie said, opening it herself.

Zita's dress uniform was snazzy. Cly's was just shy of outrageous. The Sylvanner sash was twinned with something that must be judicial—they wound around each other in a braid, ornamented with medallions and ribbons. His red cape, which had gold epaulets, was so impeccably brushed that it glowed.

Like Zita, he wore a sword, a wide-bladed, sharp-looking saber made of stonewood.

"I find no fault with the way you look," he said.

Faint praise, Sophie thought, wondering suddenly if she and her father would get along.

"You look like the king of something," she said.

"You're too kind."

She folded her texting papers and tucked them into her questions notebook—and saw Cly noting that she'd packed as she did.

"Girls, please wait for us on the porch," he said, and Zita and Mirelda made themselves scarce.

"So," she asked. "What's the program tonight?"

He held up two new stickpins. "This is a sage designation. It represents intellectual achievement. Your . . . Master's degree, you called it?" It looked vaguely like a protractor. "The second is a nonspecific indicator of dietary restrictions. You may continue your hunger strike after all, if you choose."

"Thanks," she said.

"The program, as you say, is merely to mingle. This is Autumn District in the height of the summer festival—it's not our time, so we celebrate the ascendancy of the people in the next district. We laud the summerborn and the nearly grown."

"And other than that it's walk around, chitchat over canapés, listen to the band, try not to get wasted."

"Children don't drink at functions."

"Not a child, remember?"

"See if you can manage to get through this evening without acting like one."

They glared at each other over the pins until he handed them over and stalked out without giving her a chance to ask if he was selling her in marital bondage to Rees Erminne.

Which was ridiculous, or even paranoid, because he wasn't. Reassurance would have been nice, but it wasn't necessary.

Ask him now, she told herself, following him out. But he'd vanished deeper into the house.

Mirelda was calling her. "Our carriage is here!"

The object pulling up to the gate, horse-drawn, of course, had to be a low wagon, but it was decked out like a parade float. A flowing fabric cover, pink and ruffled, concealed a little ramp up to the wagon in back. A half-dozen dressed-up Sylvanners and a mandolin player were already aboard.

"Let's go," Mirelda said, tugging Sophie along. Mervin and his parents were making their way toward the float.

Sophie balked. "Just us?"

"Cousin Clydon and Tenner Zita ride on the Fleet display."

One last hoop to jump. Sophie thought of her bags, packed and ready to go so that all anyone . . . any *slave* would have to do was haul the stuff onto whatever ride brought her back to *Nightjar.*

The thought of the ship worked its usual magic; she felt her spirits lifting. "Okay, let's do this."

They rushed down Low Bann's long drive and—Mirelda took her hand—up to the float. It smelled of roses and the horses pulling it were a creamy white color. Lippizaners? Sophie wondered: Could a show breed have survived, if the two worlds were somehow the same?

Annela had told Cly that Stormwrack was a future version of Erstwhile. Which implied something would happen to turn her world into this one.

Then she was on a platform with Cousin Fenn and her family. There were six or so neighbors from someplace called Low Frake.

"This is Clydon's daughter," Cousin Fenn told them. "The outlander."

"But Verdanii?" one of them asked.

"No," Sophie said. "Total savage."

Okay, Sofe, you promised to try for Beatrice's sake.

What do I owe Beatrice again? I'm doing this for Verena.

Not to impress a certain someone else?

Shut up, random voice.

The float was part of a real parade—as they rode east, toward Turtle Beach and Erminne's estate, the slaves came out to line the road and quietly wave at the landowners, who were throwing small coins to them.

They passed three of the women whom Sophie had encountered in the kitchen on the way to get Zita her water. The blonde who'd been crying was there, staring defiantly. She locked eyes with Mirelda.

Sophie felt curiosity stir. Then she saw kids, eight of them, little ones with tiny bangles on their wrists, and she forgot everything except *I'm going to be sick.*

"Sit," Fenn said, pushing her toward a bench. "Breathe."

Sophie raised her head and glowered.

"I know our ways must seem—"

"I'm so totally sure you don't want to finish that sentence," Sophie said.

"Beatrice felt as you did," Fenn said. "I think she loved Cly sincerely enough until they came home."

She imagined Beatrice in the middle of one of her epic freak-outs, shrieking about the slaves. Somehow it seemed perfectly appropriate.

Fenn shrugged. "Well, we're on Erminne land now. They're radicals."

"They don't—?"

"Erminne's father freed them all on his marrying day—it's an old custom. The estate's gone to ruin since. Why do you think they need their art collection so badly?"

"Radicals. Abolitionists?"

"Sophie, you must see that if you pull your father in that direction, it will ruin us all."

"Like Cly would ever consider ditching his vine-munching goat transforms, let alone whoever dumps his chamberpot."

"Does he care if we're reduced to poverty? He lives asea—he's got a Fleet pension. And any alliance with the Erminne . . . well, Fralienne would insist." She brightened. "But you've got a point. As long as the lowlands are infested with throttlevine, the government would forbid his divesting."

"You're serious." Sophie gaped at Fenn. "You think he's gonna set up an engagement, and then . . . no more slaves on Low Bann?"

He had asked: *What would you have me do?*

"There are many reasons why expanding Low Bann eastward would be beneficial, I grant you. The Erminne estate is a desirable property."

"But not without an unpaid workforce, am I right?"

"Precisely." A puzzled half smile from Fenn.

"So he marries me to Rees Erminne and frees all the people on Low Bann and throws your lives into upheaval . . . for what? So I can get along with him? Could he want my approval that badly? He can't think getting me hitched is the way."

Fenn had listened to all of this with a tiny frown. Now she said, "Your approval would hardly be an issue. Our young do as they're told or they're scripped to obey."

Sophie drew a long, slow breath, stunned. She'd expected Fenn to agree with her, to say an arranged marriage was impossible.

"He knows your name, does he not?"

"No." Sophie's voice was small. "Cly's not stupid. Anyway, he wants me to be—"

"To be what? Half Feliachild? Potentially useful, I'd agree, if you hadn't thrown that bit of your heritage on the midden. A *temperamente* spell wouldn't damage your outlander education, if that's what he's looking to exploit. If you were bound to Rees he could leave him here, charged, I suppose, with running both estates into poverty. He could take you and—"

She remembered Beatrice's letter: *He wants something, and it won't be good.*

"He wouldn't," she said again. There was something she'd missed here.

"There's nothing he wouldn't do. Getting his way is what he does. Convince him an alliance won't work, Sophie. Failing that, convince the Erminnes." With that, Fenn stepped back to the edge of the float, drawing a confused-looking Mirelda with her.

Sophie reached for the calm she felt on dives or when climbing, when things went wrong. That focus that made the difference between getting everyone back safe or coming home broken . . . or not at all.

Nothing. Her mind churned. *Bram, you'd better get here quick.*

They'd arrived at the Erminne estate, and Rees and his mother were climbing aboard the float now. Their house did look ramshackle. Wet climate, constant maintenance, Sophie thought. The roof was patched; the paving stones were uneven.

"It's nice to see you again," Rees said. He'd combed his hair; the outfit he wore, unlike the one she'd seen earlier, was in good shape—minimally worn, without visible repairs.

She shook her head, trying to provide a polite answer but too freaked out to muster any courtesy. He took the hint, moving to the edge of the float. He and his mother had coins to throw but there was nobody lining this stretch of road.

Curiosity, ever the traitor, stirred. What was it like to be an abolitionist here?

She took a close look at Fralienne Erminne. She looked about thirty-five—which must be affected by magic, Sophie supposed. Curl your hair, straighten your hair, hide a few wrinkles. This evening, as this morning, she was heavily powdered.

Tanning's not genteel, she remembered.

She wore gloves, as Mirelda did, but they were longer, and as Sophie watched she saw Fralienne tug at them, fiddling.

She imitated the motion subconsciously, thinking, If her skin's dry—if she works, if she's calloused, then the fabric of the gloves might snag on the dry bits of skin.

She was fitter than Fenn—she had real shoulders and gave no impression of softness. Unlike her son, who emanated a sort of smart but pleasant harmlessness, she was visibly worn.

They rode past two more "normal" estates and the others went back to flinging coins at the slaves who lined the roads, Fenn and some of the others casting disapproving glances at the small copper coins tossed by the Erminnes. All they can afford, Sophie deduced.

Starting up a series of switchbacks, they merged into a longer line of floats, all flower-covered and impressively ornate. There were fake, petal-clad trees, a giant, nesting flamingo, a sperm whale, a representation of the setting sun, and more than one sailing vessel.

Aboard the floats were more families, women dressed in flared skirts and fitted tops, all wearing the colors of fall leaves and harvest. The floats bearing betrothed couples were the most elaborate, the engaged kids themselves all dressed in summer green and garlands of flowers.

As the floats converged, the musicians aboard began playing the same song, a gentle thing Sophie might have characterized as a reel. People bobbed in time and clapped. Everyone seemed in good spirits.

They reached the top of the hill, a flattened mountaintop, the sort of thing the ancients would have used as the base for a series of temples. Instead Sophie saw low-slung brick structures, two and three stories high, each of them windowless and round as globes, lying like marbles on a green that was, effectively, a botanical garden and a zoo—trails wound between the buildings, garden beds, and habitats for various animals.

The central building of the Spellscrip Institute was the biggest sphere of the bunch, and its brickwork glittered with hints of shine, silvery black in color, that Sophie suspected was hematite.

Autumn Spell was standing atop this, clad in what looked like a gold and red body stocking, with long swirls of scarf flowing around her, borne on invisible breezes. She looked down at Sophie; their eyes met and her mouth moved.

"Welcome, honored guest." The words sounded in her ear as if Autumn were standing right beside her.

"Thank you," Sophie managed.

A uniformed slave was waiting to hand her down to the green, but Rees Erminne strode up suddenly, offering his arm. "There's a corner around the rear gate where the bonded don't serve," he said. "We pariahs socialize there. Will you come?"

She weighed the options unhappily and decided she might as well. She could have a tactful word with him about Cly's plan.

If in fact there is a plan . . .

Fenn confirmed it. How much proof do you need?

Uncertainty assailed her. Cly hadn't known her long, but he couldn't possibly think she'd consent to marry some guy she'd known for a day.

She was working herself up for nothing.

The young are scripped to obey.

Cly said "betrothal" and Fenn confirmed it.

He's not that dumb, he's not. He's socially agile.

"Thanks," she said, choosing Erminne over the butler. Mirelda startled and rushed to follow, making a quick detour to grab a couple sandwiches for herself off a silver tray.

All the spellscribes were turned out as Autumn was, clad in tight leotards and surrounded by the scarves that preserved their modesty. The air was filled with the scent of cooking stews and something that reminded Sophie of chili. "This must be a good climate for growing peppers," she said, randomly, and Erminne nodded. Five seconds later they rounded a curve in the trail—all the trails were curved, there were no corners here at all, as far as she could see—and there was a pepper garden, enclosed by a low brick wall, containing about ten different species: jalapeños, sweet peppers, bananas, habaneros, and two varieties she didn't recognize.

She felt Rees chuckle against her at the coincidence.

Okay, I'm not going to freak out. We're not getting married, we're not. Cly isn't planning anything. Observe, she told herself. Whatever you do, don't say the wrong thing. Beatrice's freedom is almost in the bag.

"How do you get into the buildings?"

"Much of the institute is underground," he said. "The entrances to the study spheres are beneath them."

"It's incredible." She'd always been a sucker for monument-scale art. Mom and Dad had taken them to the Valley of the Kings and she'd bawled, for sheer joy, when she saw the Great Pyramid. Her father had almost panicked, she'd cried so hard. "I don't know about practical."

"The institute was constructed in the first days of real Sylvanner wealth; we were showing off."

"Conspicuous consumption."

He shrugged. "They have a certain irresistible charm. And the scribes say it's restful to draft spells in them. Contemplative, you know. Good acoustics."

"I can see why Mirelda would want to work here."

"Each of the institutes is a marvel. One day you'll have a chance to see Winter District's," he said. "Your father has ties there."

She shook her head. "I don't see myself coming back to Sylvanna after this is over."

"No?"

"*Ever,*" she said, underlining it just in case.

If her assertion was bad news, he kept it to himself.

As they walked, people raised their glasses to them. Erminne responded with an upraised hand and a smile. Another turn brought them to the brick-fenced edge of a perfectly round pool that abutted the edge of one of the smaller, bungalow-size spheres.

"Alligators," he said. "Do you have them in the outlands?"

She nodded, nevertheless peering over. The alligator in question seemed morphologically identical to those she'd seen in Florida; there was no reason to assume there were any differences at all.

A betrothed couple—two boys, as it happened—walked by, hand in hand. They were a little puffed out, like roosters, proud to be adults. They were also maybe fifteen. Erminne's eye lingered on their sashes.

Ten years older than them, and Rees isn't married—not an adult, she thought. Because he's an abolitionist? And his mom's a widow, which has to be troublesome, too.

This is a stupid, stupid society.

"Sophie," he said, "there's an urgent matter I must discuss with you before you leave."

Her anxiety spiked. "Now?"

He shook his head. "At the giraffes."

"You have giraffes?"

They rounded another sphere, this one seated in a pond and made entirely of ice, a great circular piece with chill wafting off it, covered in condensation and carved with the images of fish and mermaids. Streams of iced water drizzled off the mermaids' outstretched fingers—Erminne took a cup from a nearby tree and filled them each a drink.

Little kids frolicked in the shadows around it, squealing when the chilly streams touched them. A shadowy figure moved within the sphere.

"The icemaker," Erminne explained. "An important profession in this climate."

"They'd be scribed, I guess. Transformed."

"To drive the heat out of things, yes," he said. "It's a complicated spell—has to be written in the depth of a cold night, in total darkness. The transforms have been known to die of exposure. Taking the cold to the marrow, it's called."

She thought of Bram's superhero comics, one of his first rebellions against Dad and the canon of English literature. One of those had an ice-maker mutant, didn't it? *X-Factor?*

She indicated the glinting, condensation-covered fish. "Do the icemakers sculpt?"

"They make blocks for sculptors. Our most prominent ice shaper, here in Autumn, is married to this maker. It's a great partnership, as all marriages should be."

"While we're on the topic—"

"Ah, here we are," he said.

"Here" was next to a giraffe enclosure, a paddock with three lemon-colored giraffes with garlands of flowers around their necks. The grove around them was planted with acacia and, on this side of the fence, was a convex flower garden, patches of red, yellow, and orange blooms. A table of meats, fruits, and vegetables had been set out next to a bonfire. The idea, obviously, was to skewer yourself a shish kebab and DIY your dinner on the campfire.

All right. It was time to stop freaking out and find out what was going on. She followed Erminne's lead in spearing a bunch of fruit and meat and let herself be led to the fire. The meat went into the flame with a sizzle. Lamb, she thought, from the smell.

"Cly's cousin, Fenn, said something about your estates adjoining each other."

He nodded. "Turtle Beach is barely beyond the boundary of His Honor's—"

"She seems to think the two of them—your mother and my—"

"Your Honor!"

It was a warning. Cly was gliding toward them with Fralienne Erminne, arriving at her elbow before they could discuss matters further. "Finish up," he said. "The feast is beginning. You're all at the Fleet table."

"My meat's too rare," Sophie said.

"It's what you get for presuming to cook. The two of you are getting along?"

"Why are you asking that?"

Cly gave her a quick, innocent look she didn't buy at all. "You've been deducing things again, haven't you?"

Holy crap, he was smiling.

"I haven't deduced anything. Fenn is all over telling me what you're up to. She's scared you're going to bankrupt her, and—"

The flick. "Oh, Fenn."

"Don't pish posh me. Are you seriously considering—" She couldn't say it, just gestured at Erminne and Fralienne.

"Not this year, obviously."

"Not this *year*?"

"What's going on?" Erminne said. "Mother?"

"You're not in on it, Rees?" Sophie said. "You just said we had to talk."

"About the turtles," Erminne said. "What are *you* talking about?"

"Child—" Fralienne began.

"Oh, you are unbelievable, Cly."

"I thought you'd be happy," Cly said.

"How could you possibly believe that?"

Her voice had risen, and people drifted closer. *This is the gossip gold mine of the year, I bet.*

"Your lamb is burning."

She pulled the skewer out of the fire, blowing on it furiously.

"It's true, Rees," Fralienne said. "His Honor and I have been discussing whether next year, come betrothal time, we might entwine Low Bann with our estate."

"Really?" he said. And then it seemed to sink in. "Oh. Sophie, before you—I think you've—"

"Did he tell you I'm promiscuous?" She said it loudly, and the whole garden fell silent. You'd think she'd dropped a bomb at their sexually conservative feet.

"Sophie!" Erminne said. "Please."

She was turning bright red, and her voice was shaking, but why stop now? "No, seriously. We outlander girls? We get around. Practically the first thing I did when I got here was find myself a Tiladene guy. Lais is his name, horse breeder, quite the stallion himself, actually." By now, she had that feeling of having climbed way out onto a branch that wouldn't hold her weight.

Commit, commit, commit.

"Of course, I haven't seen Lais in weeks. But maybe you'd like a go—"

She turned, panned the crowd, got a look at Cly's expression of frozen horror—

That's an emotion, right? Tick in the "not a sociopath" column.

—and, behind him, she saw Bram, Verena, and Garland Parrish.

A shocked laugh broke from her—she covered her mouth. "I'm gonna go hug my brother now," she announced, starting for Bram with as much dignity as she had left.

Cly seized her arm as she passed. "Our agreement was that you wouldn't embarrass me."

"Yeah? What agreement did I sign that says I get to be sold into frigging marriage?"

"Fralienne and I were discussing the possibility of marrying *each other*," he growled.

"What?"

He gave her a little shove in her brother's direction. "Tell your mother to enjoy incarceration."

Oh. Sophie's knees buckled and she stumbled past Parrish. *Why did they have to bring Parrish?*

Bram caught her.

"Well done, Ducks. That was classic."

"You're laughing, you bastard."

"So are you."

"At least I didn't use the word 'slut.'"

"That would've been over the top," he said. "Let's get you out of here before they stick you in a convent, okay?"

They began the incredibly long walk of shame, out of the Spellscrip Institute, down from the ridge's lofty heights to the port below.

CHAPTER 19

Nightjar's sails always had just a hint of pearliness to them, a shine like the inside of an oyster's shell, and in the setting sun of a warm Sylvanna evening, they looked like an oil painting about the romance of the sea. Sophie couldn't help smiling at her first sight of her; she was, she realized, almost hungry to be aboard again.

Sylvanner parade floats were making their way uphill to the Spellscrip Institute as she and the others headed down, moving against the flow of traffic.

She buttonholed Bram as her walking companion, switching to English—it was a relief, after weeks of hearing only Fleetspeak and Sylvanner. Verena and Parrish seemed only too happy to stroll on ahead of them. "So. Catch me up. Why'd you decide to come?"

"Are you kidding? After you said Cly might be sociopathic? Is he, by the way?"

"Jury's still out."

"Well, thinking you were off alone with a remorseless killer was more than I could take."

"I'd have done the same."

"Convincing Verena that you and Cly would come to loggerheads and pooch Beatrice's bail after she concealed the slavery thing wasn't hard—"

"Funny thing, that's just what happened." She fought back the guilt. Cly would hang on to Low Bann now—Sophie signing the birth certificate was enough for that. But Beatrice was back at square one, and it was all her fault.

"Has it occurred to you that he's maybe been looking for an excuse? He could have told you what was up. People here . . . sometimes it seems they're bent on hiding their cards. Setting you up to fail."

"Someone set me up to fail, all right, but it wasn't him. His cousin saw me jumping to conclusions. She decided to tell me all my paranoid fantasies were justified."

Bram frowned. "Why would anyone do that?"

"Revenge, I'm pretty sure. She lost position, her son got into serious trouble with Cly. When I started to freak out she took the chance to stir up trouble." She told him about Mervin's prank on Zita and its fallout.

By now they had arrived at the port. Parrish and Verena broke out of the hush-voiced consultation that had occupied them since they left the festival; then Parrish went on ahead, without a word, to charter a ferry out to *Nightjar,* leaving the three of them to wait for Sophie's trunks to arrive from Low Bann.

Verena looked miserable. "Annela's going to have me decapitated."

"We'll try something else," Sophie said.

"Like what?"

"We'll give Cly another reason to take his claws out of Beatrice."

"Such as?"

"He's a big shot within the Fleet," she said slowly, turning over everything she had learned. "And he loves that. But his position here on Sylvanna is shaky. If we learned something that endangered his reputation as the mighty duelist-advocate, maybe he'd do another deal just to keep from losing everything."

Verena's eyes stuttered to *Nightjar.* "I don't know if we can get Parrish to agree to extortion."

"Can't you just order him?" When she'd thought she was Gale's heir, she'd bossed him around all the time.

"No. It turns out Gale left him the ship but asked him to keep sailing me around. He and I have to agree on a course of action."

"Oh."

"It's nice—it's good that she did. I don't want to be his employer."

"Fair enough. But he and Gale used to bribe and blackmail . . . what, warlords? Didn't they?"

"Warlords? Is this an episode of *Xena*?" Bram muttered.

"They did that for the peace, not for personal gain. And I don't think they went actively digging for dirt."

Sophie wondered if that was true or if Verena had Parrish up on a pedestal. "Okay. So we tell him there's some hope Cly actually misstepped in his career, and . . . oh! What if we say we're looking into why he married Beatrice? If it was for false pretenses or something, maybe we can throw the whole marriage contract into question. We can get that lawyer, Mensalom, to look at it and talk to some people who knew him then."

Verena weighed it. "Annela should be willing to choke up the original contract documents. And if there's a way to annul the marriage to Cly, then Beatrice isn't a bigamist. But they must have examined this all those years ago, when she got pregnant."

"Sofe," Bram said. "You've joined team Dad is bad now? He *wasn't* trying to marry you off, remember?"

She felt something stick in her throat. "It's possible he . . . I think maybe he screws his slaves."

His eyes widened. "Okay. Dad *is* bad. I am so on board. But, jeez, Sofe, are you sure?"

"No. What was I gonna do, ask? Anyway, Beatrice is still in this crazy legal tangle and I have to try sorting it out."

"It's gone beyond a tangle. Sylvanna's Convenor has been telling every journalist who'll listen how hard done by their illustrious judge has been." Verena threw a rock into the sea. "After a lifetime of putting the Fleet first, poor Cly's on a spike, expected to rise above while irresponsible Verdanii witches turn his stolen daughter against him."

"Great." No wonder Verena looked miserable. First her mom got jailed, then she had job trouble, and now there was a sprawling family crisis in the news.

"We'll look into the early days of Beatrice and Cly. If we find anything we can use, that's when we'll worry about any scruples Parrish may have." She found herself feeling unaccountably happy. "It's gonna be okay, guys. The three of us are unstoppable."

"Mmm," Verena grunted.

The harbor was all but deserted; everyone was at festival parties. A few patrol types watched the docks, protecting them from nothing more hazardous than a scattering of opportunistic gulls and the occasional stray dog.

An hour passed, then another.

Finally her bags arrived. There was more luggage than she'd expected: Cly had apparently sent a big trunk. She cracked it open: all the pseudo-science texts and the accounts of the five legal disputes were in there.

Poor Krispos, she thought, fingering the throttlevine case. I wonder what Cly will do with him?

By then, Parrish had summoned a harbor ferry and porters to carry them to *Nightjar*.

They trooped aboard. Sophie saw Tonio give Parrish an inquiring glance and get a minuscule head shake in return. "Raise anchor," Parrish told him. "We're Fleet bound."

Sophie's last sight of Sylvanna was the hill that housed the Autumn District Spellscrip Institute. The party was reaching a pitch as the sun went down, and a great glowing image was taking shape over the rise; fireworks enhanced by enchantment forming a single tall tree, green-leaved as befitted the height of summer.

The course *Nightjar* set from Sylvanna was north-northeast; the Fleet was sailing toward them and they expected to rendezvous within days. Tonio was the one who sketched out their route across the map of Northwater; Parrish seemed to be avoiding her.

Sophie told Bram everything she'd seen on Sylvanna, starting with wildlife species and agricultural practices. She told him about Erminne and his abolitionist family, Turtle Beach and the methodology for the experiment she'd suggested to help sort out that case.

She told him about the time at sea with Cly, the attack by, or on, the bandits, and the one man, Kir Lidman, whom they'd managed to save amid the chaos.

"What happened to him?"

"Sent to await trial at the Fleet, I think," she replied. "They wouldn't let me talk to him. Said he was depressed."

She told him about Low Bann and the awful cousins and the swamp, throttlevine, and slaves, and Zita's accident. She started to tell him about the Spellscrip Institute before ending with: "Well, you were there."

"Just for the big finish."

Bram caught her up on the San Francisco headlines and the state of their parents. They did a bunch of math—recalculated the circumference of the world, which was the same as Earth's, no surprise—and worked on figuring out Stormwrack's axial tilt. Bram thought it might be a hair steeper than their own twenty-two-to-twenty-four-degree norm, but to be sure, he wanted more astronomical data.

Sophie borrowed an old pot from the cook and had a go at calculating the salinity of Northwater, coming up with a rough reckoning that it was below the 3.5 percent typical of the Atlantic and Pacific.

"That may suggest there's more water in the world overall." Bram was becoming more comfortable at sea—less nauseated, except when it got really choppy. To her surprise, he didn't seem homesick. In fact, he was apparently reveling in having hours on end to spend running his enormous brain around the question of how Erstwhile and Stormwrack connected. "Might fit with a comet strike."

"What if millions of years have passed?"

"There wouldn't be people anymore."

"There shouldn't be," she said, not unhappily. "But millions of years fits better with the variations in the animal species. Time for evolution, right?"

"If we theorize that there are two separate worlds and they evolved in a similar direction, the question becomes: When did the divergence occur?"

"It had to be after the evolution of modern humankind."

"What do you mean?" Bram said.

"Remember the Convene?" Sophie said. "The people we saw when the government gathered? There were recognizable racial types: people who looked Chinese, African, North European. Parrish could pass for South

Asian, and Tonio's got all these Italian qualities. Erinthian even shares some words with Italian."

"So speaking very generally, the two Earths might have been very similar until the evolution of cultures and languages, like Italian."

"And German. We'll need a linguist to pin down specifics, but Fleetspeak and the Sylvanner language both have a Germanic sound to them."

"Then there's Noah's Ark," Bram reminded her. Several of the islands had stories about a time of fire and flood, when humankind took shelter in a life pod or some kind of ark. The stories varied from nation to nation: sometimes the refuge was a boat, a seed pod, a submarine. People and animals took shelter in caves or eggs. In one tale with shades of the Jonah myth, they were eaten by a big fish and then spat out, a few at a time, on the various islands.

They were trying to fit a theory around it when, a day out from Fleet, a message came from Annela.

"'Well, girls,'" Verena read, "'We have heard that His Honor is displeased and that Sophie is in breach of contract. If you were going to make things worse, I would rather you had not bothered at all.'"

"Yeah, right," Sophie said. "Send me off to Sylvanna without telling me they're bonded, then blame me when I act—"

"A bit like Beatrice?" Bram said. She poked him—hard.

Verena waited, pointedly, until they subsided. "'The Allmother is threatening to pull *Breadbasket* from the Fleet for a month. This is a major protest, and the Convene is very tense. If there is anything you might yet do to mollify Clydon Banning, I beg you to set aside your pride and petition him for mercy.'"

Sophie groaned. "I knew I was overreacting. Knew he wasn't crazy enough to betroth me. If I'd just kept my mouth shut—"

"Don't do that, Sofe," Bram said. "Does it say anything else, Verena?"

She scanned the page and then handed it over. "Just that Corsetta has escaped from the Watch again."

"How is that your problem?" Sophie said.

"I made it my problem when I started poking into it," Verena said. She didn't add "at your suggestion."

"If there's anything I can—"

"You said you'd stay out of the Corsetta thing," she said, her tone sharp. "I'll go up to *Constitution* and talk to Annela about seeing Mom's marriage papers. Maybe you and Parrish should go on to *Pastoral*?"

"Uh . . . sure. What's that?"

"A residential block for retired and semi-retired Fleet bureaucrats. You want the skinny on why Cly and Beatrice got married? That's a great place to start."

Before she quite knew how it had happened, Sophie found herself on a ferry, approaching the retirement home, with Parrish seated across from her.

He had spoken to her perhaps three times on the sail from Sylvanna, all perfectly correct stuff. "Pass the peas," that kind of thing. He wasn't sulking or rude, but somehow he was managing to hold her at a distance, to roll away from her in a little bubble of remoteness.

She tried to hold her peace—she needed to practice, obviously—but could only keep her lips locked until they were transferring to the ship itself. "What's the plan here?"

Parrish replied, "You want information regarding your parents' courtship and the early days of His Honor's career. We'll talk to the people who were running the Fleet at the time. This ship is a storehouse of such knowledge."

Without another word he toured her through a sunroom, eventually conveying her to a chair and then settling in for a long jaw with a couple of elderly card players, all of them jabbering in some tongue Sophie didn't speak.

While he talked, she took a good look at the operation. The retirement home seemed to run on cooperative lines, with younger, semi-retired residents doing a lot of the caregiving for the eldest bureaucrats. There were a few nurses and medics around, though fewer than she would have guessed. Nobody seemed senile . . .

. . . they maybe inscribe against that.

Maybe she could learn something else, while Parrish chased the gossip. She flagged down a passing elder. "Is there a spellscribe aboard?"

"Deck four, Kir, portside."

She found her way down and tapped on a door painted with the medical cross and a few letters of spellscrip.

"Come in." The room's sole occupant was a bald and somehow childlike woman, sitting at a long desk, reading a book written in spellscrip.

"Hi," Sophie said. "I'm wondering if you can tell me the purpose of an inscription I saw not long ago."

The woman smiled. "I can try."

Sophie unshipped her camera, found the shot of the scrip—*Clydon, temperament*—and enlarged it so it was as readable as possible.

"What is this device?"

"I'm from the outlands," she said. "Sorry about the text being so small."

"I can make it out." The scribe looked at the image, lips moving slightly, then handed it back. "It's a tempering spell for a child."

"What does that mean?"

"On some nations, it's believed that certain childish tendencies are . . . aberrant. Excessive emotionalism, for example, or inclination to the same sex."

Sophie let herself entertain, briefly, the idea that Cly might have been born gay.

"A tempering inscription is meant to make them more mindful or obedient, especially toward tutors and teachers. The inscription can be beneficial if the student can't settle to their studies."

Magical Ritalin, in other words, thought Sophie.

"I can't say I agree much with the philosophy," the scribe went on. "Children are entitled to a certain amount of exuberance. But in this case—"

"What about it?"

"It's meant to instill fear in a child who has been setting fires."

Whoa.

"Thank you." Disturbed, she headed back up to the lounging deck.

Parrish was waiting. "I know who we need to talk to. He's an old Judiciary clerk."

"Here on *Pastoral*?"

He nodded. "Apparently he naps in the mornings. But I've asked if we can lunch with him. What would you like to do in the meantime?"

Fires.

She couldn't think about that now. "Clear the air?"

"I beg your pardon?"

"You've been giving me the cold shoulder since Sylvanna."

She waited for him to deny it. Instead, he let out a long breath. "On the island where I was born, Sophie, there was a monk who sewed cloaks. He tended the goats, spun the wool, and dyed it. He wove the cloth into long, almost shapeless outer garments. They were warm and practical and hard to tell from one another—the monks used to have to mark the collars."

Animal hair, Sophie thought, remembering the satchel of hair she'd picked up on the bandit ship.

"One day when I was about eleven, just before I left for the Fleet, a corpse was brought into the harbor. The monks, you probably recall, care for those who are slain by magic—someone has to watch over them, until the spell reverts and they rejoin the living."

She nodded.

"It was a woman; she'd been important, widely beloved. There was a great search for the inscription that had killed her, and she would be receiving visitors. The island expected a lengthy procession of guests on her behalf. It was decided that our service to this woman would include a receiving room. We built a bier in the village of Lamentation, and Brother Sparrow was told to weave her a shroud."

"The shapeless-cloak guy," she said, to show she was following.

Parrish's expression was faraway. "He dyed the wool a soft green, like shoots of new grass, shot through with beads made of shell, tight whirls of caramel brown and copper highlights. They wrapped her in it like a child abed and fanned out her hair around it. She looked . . . it made her look quite at rest. It was a beautiful garment.

"Afterward, I looked at those shapeless cloaks, and when eventually I asked Brother Sparrow about them, he told me, 'It's important to know the difference between a tool and an ornament, boy.'"

"And this is supposed to have what to do with you annoying—sorry, I mean avoiding"—*oh, this isn't going badly at all*—"me?"

He gestured back at *Nightjar's* pearly sails. "The ship, and we who sail it. We're means to your ends."

"That's so not true! I'd set up house on *Nightjar* tomorrow if I could. I love—" She didn't quite know why her throat was tightened. She forced the words out. "You came for me. You came, and you brought Bram, and I know it's your boat. You don't have to mind Verena, so . . ."

"Having asked you to help with Beatrice's situation, and having allowed you to walk into the situation unknowing, we could hardly abandon you when you ran into trouble."

"So you only came for me because it was the right thing to do?"

"You're upset."

"You've upset me."

"I apologize for any distress I may have caused."

"You're not avoiding me because you're a tool, Parrish."

"On a ship the size of *Nightjar*, I could hardly avoid—"

"Even if you wanted to?"

"I have no wish," he said, "to exclude myself from your company."

She could hear her voice rising. "Then why are you?"

"Doing your duty doesn't always mean simply following orders."

"Duty and honor." She felt as though she were outside herself, watching as for no particular reason Sophie tried to pick an argument. What was wrong with her? "You came for me because it was your duty?"

He pulled himself upright, still as a statue, and looked into her eyes. "Are you planning to ask why Bram came for you?"

"Bram knew I'd stick my foot in my mouth first chance I got. Bram loves me—" She ran dry for a second. "Deflecting much? Why do you keep telling me why you came for me when what I'm asking is why you're hiding now?"

"I sail," he said, "where I believe I'm needed."

"I need some air." She climbed up blindly, looking for an outer deck, and leaned against the ship's mainmast, which was sticky with the lubricant that allowed the hoops of the mainsail to rise and lower easily. At home it would be machine grease; here, it had a pine scent. The seas were choppy and the Fleet was sailing on a brisk easterly wind. The hang gliders that taxied people between ships had stopped flying. She imagined them safely stowed in their berths.

Most of the ships—the ones not propelled by magic, that is—had all but one sail reefed and tightly bound.

It was a minute or so before Parrish followed her.

"I'm sorry," Sophie said, before he could speak. "Everything that happened on Sylvanna, it's left me a little raw. Ignore me."

"Never." He reached out, carefully, and laid a hand on her arm. "Sophie, I—" Then he frowned over her shoulder.

"What?"

"Tonio's raised a signal cone." He indicated a triangle, rising against the sail, hung point down. "It means there's a—what's your word?— situation aboard *Nightjar*."

"Do we need to go back?" He'd had a hand on her shoulder; she'd turned to look at the ship, and his arm had curved around her. His skin was distractingly warm.

"Not if it's just one; it means it's under control. It's an alert."

"He's giving you a heads-up."

He nodded.

"Just what we needed. A situation."

They watched for another minute, in case a second cone rose up on the sail. But none did, and then the shipboard bell rang.

"Lunchtime," Parrish said, pulling free. "Shall we?"

It was obvious at a glance that the old court clerk was another transform—he smelled oniony and was covered in what looked like onionskin paper. Toothless, with knobby joints, he had two steaming mugs on the go. One was full of beery-smelling tea; the other of a thick creamed soup, orange in color.

He set himself up at a table for three in the corner of the dining room and took obvious pleasure in ordering them a full spread, a meal that could be chewed. Beetroot salad, roasted cuttlefish, a dark rye bread. He insisted on pouring them each a cup of his tea, too—it smelled darkly of barley and old boot, but the flavor was nutty and distinctly bracing.

"So you're the new Sturma, are you?" he said, when he'd had a delicate sip of his soup and they'd tucked in. He spoke slowly; without teeth, his diction was a little soft, but he was comprehensible enough.

"I'm who?"

"Kir Hansa is Sturma Feliachild's niece," Parrish inserted, before Sophie could tell the guy no, she wasn't planning to grow up to be a super-spy at sea. "She is also the natural child of His Honor the Duelist-Advocate."

"Little Kir's all the news," he said. He pinched her chin, squinting. "Ye don't dress as a Sylvanner."

"Thank heaven for small mercies," Sophie grunted. "I grew up abroad."

"Outlander, then?"

"We're interested in His Honor's early days in the Judiciary," Parrish continued.

A keen-eyed glance. "Scandal-mongering? You?"

"Not at all," Parrish said.

"Totally," Sophie said. "Lay on the dirt."

The old fellow laughed. Leaning back in his chair, he rolled up a sleeve, exposing a pale, fibrous, multilayered arm. He pressed his soup spoon against the forearm, a gesture disturbingly reminiscent of drawing a blade down his wrist. As he pushed, though, text flashed to the surface, dense black handwritten letters, layered one over the other, as if he were made of rolls of superthin paper. The text moved and shifted, now visible, now not, all too fast to make out words. But eventually he grunted, "Thought so," and pinched himself. A winding strip of paper-skin came up, tearing off neatly, leaving moist glistening paper and an onion stench in its wake.

He set the torn-off strip on the center of the table.

Hamish Cordero. Born Junnaio 4, y. 32 of the Cessation. Died Fusto 33, y. 474.

"I'm not saying this is the chink in His Honor's armor. Honestly, girl, that'd be you. But it's the only time in his career he veered toward scandal."

"Who was Cordero?"

"Someone your father killed, long ago."

Killed. And as a kid he set fires.

"Tell us," Parrish said.

"Eat, eat and I will."

Sophie put a beet in her mouth, chewing woodenly.

"Clydon Banning came to the Fleet already something of an oddity. The

Sylvanner kids who join us are married, always married. They have pe-culiar ideas regarding maturity there."

"Do they ever!" Sophie agreed.

"He got top marks as a cadet, in book learning and martial prowess, wrote the law specialization as soon as he was allowed to declare, and graduated tops. He won the Slosh at his graduation. Like you, Parrish."

"Winners all round," Sophie muttered.

"There was no question but that he'd go to the Judiciary. He sued for custody of *Sawtooth*. There was a bit of a fluff over that—her masthead is a fright who babbles her full name to anyone who'll listen, so there were plenty wanted her sunk—but he got her and began training. He passed his writtens early, and then it was all fighting—he was waiting for his first official duel.

"The duelist-advocate in those days was a constipated old cod from Haversham, Fae Marks by name, and having to mentor a rising star from Sylvanna . . . oh, it jammed up her egg tubes. She set young Cly on the duel-ing roster obscenely early, hoping, it's thought, he'd misstep. Or, better yet, get himself wounded."

"No joy?"

"Soils don't stick to Cly Banning," the oldster said cannily. "You'll want to remember that when you go digging."

"What happened?"

"Marks had miscalculated: Banning won every fight she threw at him—some just by his scruff, but still. Every debate, too. And then one of her middle-ranked judges got herself fatally speared by a ringer the pirates slipped in on a duel. Ol' Fae was suddenly looking at having to promote a twenty-year-old child up the ladder.

"Oh, the politics were thick as that chowder! Since their two nations don't get on, Marks couldn't just pass him over without looking very bad indeed. She tried the 'he's not an adult at home' angle, and that's when he pulled Beatrice Feliachild out of his pocket.

"Up until then, all this had been a wee brewpot of a problem within the Judiciary, no matter for gossip. But then the marriage! Sylvanner and a Verdanii, and a Feliachild at that! A future matriarch of one of the nine families, high in the line to be Allmother, and they said she wanted to study magic at Sylvanna's institute. Suddenly this was no quiet little power wrangle over whether Clydon Banning had a future on the dueling deck. Everyone in Fleet was watching. Poor little BeeBee Feliachild had never had so much attention."

"And?" Parrish said.

"Marks contrived a last round of hurdles for young Banning to jump—a series of fights. It was a final attempt to wound him so badly he'd end up battling a desk."

"Trying to clip his wings, we'd say," Sophie said.

"Yes indeed. She set her chief dueling trainer on him."

"Hamish Cordero?" Parrish was leaning forward, caught up in the story despite himself.

A nod. "Hamish was Havershamite, too, like Fae; he and Her Honor Marks were close as littermates. And he'd got into trouble—gossip had it he was involved in some scheme against the Sylvanner Spellscrip Institute.

"Those two islands, they scrap back and forth. Well, you know . . ."

"Right," Sophie said. Cly had told her some of this, hadn't he? "Is this about the throttlevine? It keeps coming back to the throttlevine. He said it was why he joined the Judiciary."

Or did his family just send him to Fleet because he set fires and liked to fight? Were they afraid of what he'd become if he stayed home?

"Did he indeed?" The old man was checking the densely printed text on the back of his hand. "Cordero challenged the moment the case was filed. Before he could be compelled to answer questions or swear his innocence, you understand. It would be a real fight. Most people who challenge the Court, they lose. And Cordero was the Court."

"But he lost?" That was Parrish. It wasn't really a question.

"His Honor—the current His Honor—gave him plenty of chances to surrender. Wounded him in three places, never fatally. It was quite the risk to take. Even hurt, Cordero was a lethally dangerous man. Unbeaten, and big as a battleship." Letters glimmered on the old bureaucrat's onion-skin flesh.

"You saw the fight?"

"Everyone went. *Martial's* viewing deck was jammed so tight the crowd was just about knocking each other pregnant. We were standing in their blood. Cordero was cut a-wrist, a deep one in the leg, and there was a delicate little slash above his eye. Banning had just missed having his throat cut—his shirt was in tatters—and he'd got his guts pricked. They were both so fine and terrible. It's what war must have been like."

"Yeah, 'cause war's so romantic and fabulous," Sophie said.

Parrish put a hand on hers, a not-so-subtle cue to shut up. Their lunch companion cackled, and Parrish pulled away abruptly.

"Cordero was weakening. He was elder and had bled more, and by then he knew he was the slower. Banning, unbelievable as it seems, had kept a rug thrown over how very talented he was at swordplay. All those fights he'd barely won—he'd been toying with his food. Her Honor the Duelist-Advocate had underestimated him.

"So Cordero threw himself at Banning. His sword was a blur. He couldn't see out of the bloodied eye, and he was roaring.

"'Dirty lickspittle slaver!' I can hear him bellowing it even now." The onionskin man's expression said he was far away. "He was a huge fellow, a bull to Banning's stallion, and he'd clearly decided to put all the *viva* he had left into overbearing him, hammering through his defenses, making him afraid and then chopping through his sword, and cloth and skin, to his bone. Live or die, Cordero wouldn't concede."

"He backed Banning to the very edge of the dueling deck. I saw your father consider—I think he truly regretted it. But live or die? He had to choose. He stepped sideways, fast, so fast—and sliced his blade across Cordero's neck.

"The old bull died right there. The thud, as he hit the deck . . . he was just meat. Already gone."

The old clerk took a long, delicate sip of his pureed soup and dabbed his lips.

"Why was any of this scandalous?" Sophie asked.

"Court etiquette. Banning should have refused to fight. The disagreement touched upon his family lands."

"It's why he came to the Judiciary," Sophie repeated. "The throttlevine case. He said it brought him into the law."

"Well, Her Honor Fae Marks had dropped anchor on herself. She assigned the fight. Banning should have recused, but when he didn't, she declined to disqualify him. Responsibility gravitates upwards."

"It was obvious she'd hoped he'd die?" Parrish asked.

"Everyone wanted that troublesome little Sylvanner dead: the duelists, his Verdanii in-laws, maybe even his own kin on Low Bann. Instead he hopped about three rungs up the Judiciary promotion ladder. Four, really, after Marks retired in disgrace."

"Did Cordero have family?" Parrish asked.

"Wife and son, yes. They're aboard *Blister*. Now—" His eyes brightened. "Coin for coin, Kirs. You're the Verdanii's niece, but . . . not of the All-mother, I understand?"

Sophie entertained him for the remainder of the meal with an edited version of what had happened when she'd first come to Stormwrack. The old man was a bit bloodthirsty, for all he was made of paper—he grilled her extensively for every detail of the inscription deaths of the two pirates who'd attacked her six months ago, and then about the mezmer attack on Gale. She was acutely conscious of Parrish at her side as she answered the clerk's questions about Parrish's good friend's murder.

He sipped barley tea and acted perfectly calm . . . at least, he did until the old man said, "Sturma's murder was always foretold, was it not so?"

"Foretold? Are you kidding?" She couldn't quite keep from snorting.

Parrish had overslurped and burned himself. "Yes," he said, with obvious reluctance. "Gale's eventual death by homicide was predicted on the day of her birth."

"Why would anyone do that?" Sophie said.

"You'd have to ask the Allmother," Parrish said, and she could feel, suddenly, an ache blowing off him like a strong wind.

The bureaucrat cackled. "She's as odd as they say, then? You've met her?"

"Excuse me." Parrish got up, bowed, and walked away. His face had locked into grief: she remembered the expression from just after Gale died.

Sophie shrugged apologetically. "They were close."

"Lost a few of those myself. All you do, you get this old, is lose friends. It's all right, girl. Go after your man. Visit me some other time. I'm due another nap anyway."

"He's not my—" But the old fellow was creaking to his feet, taking both his tea and his soup cup with him as he shuffled off.

Left alone at the table, Sophie took a second to gather her thoughts.

Predestination. Is there anything they don't believe here?

Was it possible? Was she going to have to give credence to every crazy fairy tale thing she'd ever heard?

No. She brightened. *They believe in aetherism and astrology and phrenology and voodoo, too. So Gale's murder was foretold. It's just a coincidence that it came true. Or self-fulfilling prophecy—what if they planned for her to be a spy from day one?*

Buoyed by this idea, she set about getting back to *Nightjar*.

CHAPTER 20

The rising weather wasn't a storm yet, just a patch of choppy sea, heavy winds, and miserable, chilly rain. They were silent on the ferry ride back to *Nightjar,* Parrish locked in his own thoughts or maybe just freshly grieving Gale, with the scab ripped off.

Sophie had all but forgotten that Tonio had hung a "situation" signal from the topsail.

When they climbed aboard, though, he was waiting. "It's *ginagina* sunburn. Corsetta."

"She's here? Didn't someone tell us they'd caught her again?"

"She persuaded her guard to bring her." He pointed at a massive, uniformed Fleet sailor.

"What does she want with us?"

"She won't tell me." Tonio spread his hands in an extravagant gesture. "A mere ship's mate? Never!"

"Verena?" Parrish said.

"She's thrown in the towel. She said to wait for the . . . I think she called you a 'brain trust,' Sophie."

"Are you sure she didn't mean Bram?"

Tonio shook his head. "Bram's over there holding his belly, poor man."

"I'll talk to her," Parrish said.

Bram was aft, wrapped in rain gear, fighting nausea by taking huge gulps of air. Sophie put her arms around him and just leaned.

"What's going on with Verena?" he asked, quietly, as Sophie's sister emerged from belowdecks and conferred with Parrish.

"She's not Gale."

"Someone expects her to be?"

"Her? Annela?" Sophie shrugged. "I think we can deduce that the Verdanii are insanely hard on their daughters."

The rocking motion of the ship was invigorating. Bram got queasy; she had always thrived on having a little physical discomfort. Something to push against, she'd sometimes thought. Her parents had made the mistake of taking them camping once, when she was little. She'd begged and begged them to take her again.

She hadn't understood that they all hated it. Dad making fires and cutting wood and trying to find ample light so he could lose himself in the Romantic poets. Mom cooking canned spaghetti on the campfire. Being out in the sound of wind rushing through leaves, the babble of water in a river—Sophie had been the only one to thrive in that environment.

My poor bookish folks, she thought, grinning fondly and feeling simultaneously homesick.

The air was surprisingly warm, considering how far north they were. The wind was cool but had no real bite, and the occasional spatters of raindrops were barely below lukewarm. It was still summer, she thought, for a while yet.

Sweet brought blankets and coffee and they sat comfortably, watching the seas.

Tonio was on hand with a crew on the sails, ready to adjust their course if the wind changed. All the sailing ships of the Fleet were similarly livened, decks at the ready with snugly dressed sailors poised for any shift in the weather. As it continued to darken, fog crept up from the surface of the water.

The Fleet disappeared into curtains of mist—one minute they were at the heart of the great floating city, the next they might have been in the middle of nowhere, unremarked and alone.

Bram's expression tightened. Sophie guessed he was trying to calculate how many of the Fleet's hundreds of ships might collide in the murk.

Before she could come up with a reassurance, there was a rush of noise, reminiscent of chirping crickets. A whirl of glowing motes drifted back from the fore of the Fleet. Some clung to the rigging and sail of *Nightjar,* outlining the ship in little winking lights. Others passed to the rear, lighting up the ships nearest them.

The lights put her in mind of stars. "If we had a nice accurate shot of the night sky, and an astronomer, we could calculate how many years have passed between 2015 and now."

"Easier if you're right and it has been millions of years," Bram said. "If the stars have had time to move significant distances."

"My theory is it has been millions," she said. "Divergence in animal species—evolution takes time, even under pressure."

"They could have been magically altered."

"Maybe. But magic depends on animals and plants: inks from one species, writing surfaces from another. We'll have to check it out, but I'm thinking if you need a perfect pink tree frog from the Isle of Bambo for a given spell, you can't use magic to create the frog and then use it to do the spell. It's recursive."

"Millions of years doesn't explain why there are still modern humans," he said.

"Maybe that's where the magic comes in. Or the Noah's Ark legends aren't about people waiting out the disaster in flood shelters. Maybe they fled to the future."

She saw him mulling it over.

"It's easier for one species to be the exception, especially if that species is us."

They had no way of knowing if this was their world or a parallel maybe-future, but if it was the same, they knew that time travel existed.

So . . . a disaster, at home, within the next five thousand or at most ten thousand years. If there was time to evacuate, that meant either it unfolded slowly or they saw it coming.

"It wouldn't be flash-bang gone," Bram said. "And they'd have to know Stormwrack existed."

"Ha. That's what I was thinking."

They shared a grin.

"You know, Cly said the government is afraid that we'll have a disaster and try to evacuate here. But he meant—when he talked about the disaster, he sounded like he meant climate change stuff."

Bram was looking less green.

"An archaeologist would help," she said. "If people just cropped up here, after centuries of being extinct, there'd be evidence. Stuff to find."

"But where to dig?"

She flipped through her notes. "Verdanii. Biggest landmass, and the matriarchs apparently took it over from some ancient civilization that practiced an older form of magic."

"You're not allowed on Verdanii." When she'd repudiated citizenship, she'd agreed to stay away.

"So? I'm also not an archaeologist. We'd have to get one. Or train one."

Bram shifted on the bench. "It might not be our world anyway. More likely a parallel."

"Couldn't parallel worlds suffer parallel disasters?"

"Good point," he said. "But if we're talking about a ten-thousand-year window on whatever it is—that's huge."

"Right," she said. "So it's not like doom's gonna befall Erstwhile tomorrow. Right?"

"Let's change the subject before we freak ourselves out," Bram said.

"To what?"

Her brother's gaze wandered over the deck to Parrish, who was just emerging from below. The dimple in Bram's cheek appeared, then vanished; he was fighting a smile.

"No." Sophie said.

"Sophie and Garland, sitting in a tree, Kay-Eye-Ess-Ess—"

"I will throw you overboard, Bramwell," she said.

He subsided with a squelched interior chuckle—she felt it, his ribs to hers.

"I think he believes in predestination," she said, breaking her own declared resolution not to discuss Parrish.

Bram made a dismissive noise. "They also believe that if you're born during the first hours of daylight, you'll have a more pleasant disposition."

Parrish crossed the deck to where they sat.

"How's it going with Verena and Corsetta?" Sophie asked.

"Verena interviewed a number of people while you were gone," he said. "The Tibbsians, you remember, have been trying to acquire snow vulture eggs. Part of the trick of . . . what did you call it? Bird whispering?"

Sophie nodded.

"Part of the trick is, essentially, convincing the bird to give up a certain number of eggs in exchange for having the rest of her chicks reared in a protected environment. Corsetta says she'd done so and the bird was laying when she was thrown overboard. The captain of *Waveplay*, Montaro, says there were no eggs, that Corsetta tried to rob the crew and fled."

"Do we buy that?" Sophie said.

"We believe she's sincerely fond of the boy, Rashad, back on Tibbon's Wash. We believe she's fearful that he'll come to harm if she doesn't return home. As for who's in the wrong in this conflict with Rashad's brother or who healed her when she was dying . . ." He shook his head.

"The Tibbs government has thrown its support behind Rashad's brother and is requesting that he be freed to return home. There's something neither party will tell us."

She squinted at Parrish. "Did you really get rid of Gale's encyclopedia of all the island nations?"

He raised his nose. "It's easily replaced."

She let the pieces of the puzzle churn for a second, trying to fit them together.

Bram murmured, "Verena needs the win here, remember?"

Right. She had promised to keep her mouth shut and let Verena work on it all.

She looked up at Parrish. He had been dampened by the rain, and a thread was dangling from his coat sleeve. One of his cuffs' buttons was loose. She tugged it before it could fall, handing it to him. His skin was warm.

"Thank you, Sophie," he said gravely.

She was suddenly, acutely aware of Bram, sitting there observing, drawing silly conclusions and gathering ammo for another round of teasing. There was no reason to help him, was there?

"No problem," she said lightly, going belowdecks and tapping on Verena's hatch.

Her sister was sitting on Gale's old bunk, toying with her sword and glowering at a practice dummy. Her nose was red.

I forget she's a teenager. Sophie poked her head through the hatch. "Can I come in?"

"I suppose you've got it all solved already," she said, then blushed. "Sorry. I mean . . . I don't know."

Sophie looked around the room. She hadn't gotten a good look at the cabin when it was Gale's, but her sense was that it was more spartan now. At length, she spotted an ordinary deck of cards on a shelf and picked it up, joining Verena on the bed.

"My dad . . ." She refrained from specifying, *not Cly.* "He's big on English literature—not a jock, not all that science-y. For kids he got me and Baby Einstein up there. He used to sit us down with our schoolwork, really tough stuff, and we'd ask him to help. I would, more often than Bram. And he'd say, 'I don't have the answers. You want the answers, you make it happen. Find the answers.'"

"Sink or swim. He'd make a good Verdanii."

"In the last few weeks I've upgraded my definition of jerky dad behavior."

"We warned you about Cly," Verena grunted.

Sophie fished through the deck. It wasn't just ordinary—it had come from home. The box had a Las Vegas casino name on it. Setting it aside, she fished for the queen and king of hearts. "Corsetta and Rashad, obviously." Then the joker. "Rashad's brother, Montaro. What are the other pieces?"

Verena took the deck. "King of clubs—the Tibbs government. And—crazy eight of diamonds—the snow vulture."

"Eights are wild, I like it."

Digging in her pocket, she came up with some of the hard Sylvanner nuts Cly had forced Mervin to harvest for her. "Ships: here's *Waveplay,* Montaro's ship."

"And the derelict boat . . ."

"We need something for the cat," Sophie added.

"The cat?"

"They're valuable, right?" Sophie laid a gnarled nut among the cards. "You have the answer, Verena."

A flash of something . . . anger? despair? "So, what? Your dad would lay out the problem and leave you to flail?"

"No," Sophie said. "No leaving."

"I've been over and over this. You're the great observer. You solve it."

Sophie shook her head. Her father, at this point, would have said, *Quit if you want to.*

Verena sighed. "Here's what I know. Tibbon's Wash is all uptight about who's who and all their social rules, but anyone can get a favor from their queen by winning whatever challenge they've got going. Their last snow vulture stopped laying about fifteen years ago and now that's the challenge. But they're hard to catch. They need someone with a gift, an affinity. So they've had this . . . plug, I guess, in their social safety valve."

Sophie said, "Enter Corsetta—"

"Who schemes and scams. She's good at escapes, possibly inscribed for it. Can she pick locks? We don't know. But she works in Montaro's household as a goatherd. They want to send her vulture hunting, but she's such a handful. Nobody trusts her."

"And who wants a goatherd getting the big prize, am I right?"

Verena picked up the king. "I think they threw young Rashad into her path."

"Seducing the scammer?"

Verena nodded. "The *Waveplay* crew and the Tibbsians I met with in Fleet all say the same thing about the guy. He's young, he's cute, he's maybe not so bright, but he's a big hit with the girls. What if elder brother Montaro set the two of them on a collision course?"

"To what end?"

"If it was me, I'd tell younger brother to get Corsetta's name."

"Oh," Sophie said. "So they can inscribe her? That's kind of evil, isn't it?"

"She falls for the cute boy and agrees to go after the bird . . . then something goes wrong."

"For who?"

"For big brother. He doesn't know it at first. He gets his vulture, waits until she lays an egg, throws Corsetta overboard, and makes for the Fleet."

"There's his big score," Sophie said. "Corsetta's gone, and he gets the prize from the Queen."

"But she survives . . . why heal her?"

Sophie kept her mouth shut. *You can do this,* she thought.

Verena lashed her sword, jumping to her feet and spearing her practice dummy. "Okay. So he gets to the Fleet with the vulture, home-free, tries to sell it for a pot of money. But the bird's moping without Corsetta. Next there's a message from home; Rashad fell for the girl, Rashad's suicidal."

"So, what? Put him on suicide watch, right? That's what I don't get."

"Oh!"

Dropping the sword on the bed, Verena strode out of the cabin and over to Corsetta's cabin. She unlocked and threw open the hatch. "It isn't a suicide pact at all, is it? It's a spell. You die, he dies? He dies, you die? As you got worse, out there in the sun, Rashad started to sicken. You're effectively holding him hostage; they had to heal you."

Corsetta leapt to her feet. "Without each other, life has no meaning! We're meant to . . . the longer you keep us apart . . ." She dissolved into tears.

Verena looked to Sophie. *Faking?* she mouthed.

Sophie shrugged and then made a little jabbing gesture, as if she were fencing. *You can do this.*

Verena all but squared off against the kid. "They say there was no egg."

"There was, I swear!"

"Why not sell it? It was worth a bundle. And they're trying to keep you here, in Fleet, far away from their precious son."

"I'm not good enough for them."

"They don't want you going home," Verena said. "Don't want you claiming the Queen's favor, but it's not just that, is it?"

Sophie fisted her hands against the urge to pile in.

"There's something else. Something they're afraid you'll tell."

"There's no secret," Corsetta said. "You're on the wrong course. My beloved's family hates me!"

"What secret could only matter at home?"

"Nothing!" Corsetta said. "Please, Kirs, take me to my beloved."

Verena circled, her eyes glazed as if she were far away. "Oh," she said. "I see, I totally see. I do have all the info."

Corsetta paled. "Kir."

"It's not that whatever you two are hiding doesn't matter in Fleet. It's that neither of you can reveal it *in Fleet* without being arrested. Whichever of you gets home first, inside that cozy sovereign limit where the Watch can't arrest you . . ."

By now the girl was all but shock white.

Verena sat. She was ramrod straight, so tense, and Sophie was struck by her and Corsetta's youth. They should be acting out cop and criminal in a school play. But this was a real interrogation.

"Look," Verena said. "My aunt was a big deal in the Watch. I'm cousin to Annela Gracechild. I'm new at this, I know, but I can tell them right now that you and Montaro are in a race to get home. We know you were aboard the derelict ship, the first victim of those raiders."

A single fat tear rolled down Corsetta's cheek.

"They helped us," she whispered.

"What?"

"We met the raiders, the crew sailing *Incannis*. They had just attacked that ship, maybe a day before. They were on their way back, and they were waiting to offload their cargo."

"The crew had fought—the ship was damaged. They had a drape over her name but we saw it: *Incannis*. I saw it. We should have run, sent a message. But Montaro talked to her captain. I overheard—"

"You overheard?" Verena said skeptically.

"You were aboard," Sophie said suddenly. "You took it into your head to steal the raiders' cat."

Verena looked at her.

"I meant to tell you," she said. "They had cat stuff—dishes for food, toys—but it hadn't been used for weeks. Banana came from the raiders' ship."

"He was a gift for Rashad." Corsetta's lip curled. "For his fishing boat."

"So you went to bag Banana and ended up eavesdropping on Montaro?"

She nodded. "They gave us—him—something. A cask. Money, I assumed, or goods. And they told us where to find the derelict. It helps, when you're trying to tame a snow vulture. It needs somewhere to land. But I think—"

"Yes?" Verena said.

"I think Montaro meant to meet them all along. I think—it's death, isn't it? Aiding and abetting banditry? And if I'm executed, Rashad dies, too."

"Did you find out what was in the cask?"

Corsetta reached into her voluminous dreadlocks and produced a smooth piece of amber with a single grain of something about the size of a chunk of black pepper within it.

"How big a cask?"

Corsetta held out her hands, miming a box about the size of a French loaf.

"So if you got home, would you have turned Montaro in? Or just black-mailed him to leave you alone?"

Corsetta looked down, expression miserable. "I have to get back to Rashad, Kirs."

"Okay," Verena said. "Sit tight, Corsetta. I'll see what I can do for you."

The girl nodded, looking wrung out. As they closed the hatch and locked it again, they could hear her sobbing into a pillow.

Sophie asked: "What kind of spells does amber go into?"

"There's a range." Verena was lost in thought. "I need to talk to Annela."

"Hey," Sophie said. "You got a confession out of the little schemer!"

Verena flushed and almost smiled. For a second Sophie thought she might even reach out for a hug. Then she ducked her head before striding away.

CHAPTER 21

By dawn, the fog was thick as curtains but the Fleet carried on, twinkling in the murk, the sailors occasionally calling out halloos to each other to reassure themselves that everyone was where they should be. The taxikites were grounded, but small ferries plied a careful trade between the big ships, appearing out of nowhere to take on passengers, then gliding off out of sight.

Verena took one to *Constitution* before breakfast. "I sent a message to a reporter friend of Gale's," she said to Sophie before she left. "Maybe she'll know about this duel between Hamish Cordero and your father."

"Okay. Thank you, Verena."

Her sister shifted from foot to foot for a second, looking as though she wanted to say something more, then abruptly turned and transferred to the ferry.

Sophie stood at the rail, watching the small boat disappear into the murk. It seemed ludicrous that so much responsibility should be dumped on Verena's shoulders. Okay, people were considered adults here at an earlier age—and she jumped on anyone who tried to treat her like a kid.

She heard herself telling Cly: *Don't call me "child."*

Okay, but there was a difference between seventeen and twenty-five.

And just now, that guilty expression on her face: like a kid who'd been caught joyriding or maybe drinking . . .

"What are you doing?" Parrish said.

"Verena said she'd asked someone to come help with the . . . with learning about Cly and Cordero."

His eyebrows rose: this was clearly news to him. "It may take a while for anyone to arrive in this fog."

"We'll just do some science, then, while we wait."

He nodded, not bothering to make a pretense of stopping her. "I'll be aft; we're mending some of the old sails today."

Bram had drawn out another world map, this one sized to match the framed version in Sweet's cabin, and in much the same style. He laid it out now with a sheet of tissue paper over it.

"That's not magic paper, is it?"

He shook his head. "Tonio took me to that market you mentioned."

She'd borrowed a little bit of resinous gum from the galley; using it, they tacked the pages down. With the two layers fixed to each other, they found Moscasipay on Verdanii and drew a longitudinal line through it. "Zero. World Clock."

"And mid–North America. Saskatchewan." He began to sketch latitudinal lines: the Arctic Circle, the 49th parallel, and eyeballed the eastern and western boundaries of North America.

They spent an hour comparing the two—figuring out that cities like New York and Washington, DC, were underwater, if they had existed here at all.

Stormwrack had so little landmass; the archipelagos looked minuscule when set against the continents of home.

Sophie ran a hand over the biggest of the landless waterways. "Asia's basically gone." The island furthest east within what should be Europe was about where the Dardanelles would be.

"We can calculate the total landmass above water. And if we identify a high point—I was hoping Everest, but . . . anyway, we'll be able to calculate the amount of water on the planet now."

"The ocean rise." She looked over the map, looking for mountains she knew.

"Mont Blanc should be around here." She tapped the map not far from Erinth. "Or . . . look! There are a bunch of islands in the Pacific Northwest. Mount Rainier's here. We could use that."

"Or Hood."

"Rainier's, what . . . fourteen thousand feet?"

"If it hasn't gone the way of Mount Saint Helens." He poked an archipelago northeast of the Pacific islands. "So these were the Rockies?"

"Maybe." She nodded. "You still thinking a comet strike did this?"

"There's nothing yet to rule it out," Bram said. "A comet would bring in more water, pulverizing the landscape."

"Wipe out Asia?"

He paused. Asia was so big, and the Himalayas being gone—it was unthinkable. "Multiple comet strikes?"

"How does anything survive that?"

"We gather evidence. We find out."

They shared a grin.

"Evidence of comets," she said. "What would that be?"

"We need real maps of the islands. Detailed topography. There could be evidence of impacts, craters."

"And you say we can calculate the global volume of water?"

"Yeah."

She chewed that over. "Gravity would increase, right, if the comets brought in mass?"

"Possibly. If we had a scale and something with a fixed weight—"

"My tanks," she said. "They probably have scales aboard—we just have to figure out the units and how to convert back to pounds or kilograms."

They were hard at work when a private ferry hailed them. Inside was an extraordinary-looking woman: seven feet tall, with caramel skin and a veritable lion's mane for hair.

She swaggered aboard *Nightjar,* exchanging a few words in Erinthian with Tonio. She took Parrish's arm—he had a strange, strangled look on his face—and snuggled in before nodding to Bram and Sophie.

"Langda Pyke," she said, before Parrish could introduce them. "From the journal *Foghorn.*"

"Hi," Sophie said.

"Verena didn't tell us you were coming," Parrish said.

"She's a dear girl, isn't she? But you . . . is it Zophie?"

"Sophie," she corrected.

"Rumor has it you're looking to blackmail His Honor the Duelist-Advocate. No, don't look shocked—I'd never print something so scandalous. Even if the censors would allow it, which they wouldn't, I'd lose my sources in the Judiciary."

"Great." She was . . . glossy, that was the word, and her grip on Parrish had a proprietary air that Sophie didn't care for. "Why help us?"

"What woman can say no to an old flame?"

Parrish stood a little straighter, attempting to disentangle himself from her clutches and failing. Sophie felt her jaw set.

Which was silly. He was allowed to have exes, and she had no particular claim on him anyway.

Is this who I am now? Little Miss Jealous Person? Snapped at Lais about Annela, and now I'm all bristly just because Parrish has former lovers? Tall, exotic, gorgeous, pushy former lovers—

"I wanted a look at you," Langda was saying. "If you're going to be the breaking of the Fleet—"

"I'm not!"

"You, boy, get me a brew. Don't care what, as long as it's hot."

Rather than tell her he wasn't part of the crew, Bram ambled off toward the galley.

"This way," Parrish said, leading her out of the damp. "Our current line of inquiry concerns Hamish Cordero."

Pyke stretched like a cat, waving her luxurious hair as she took a seat, "Ah, Cordero. Old fool. He could have surrendered to Banning. Instead, he all but forced your father to kill him."

Which takes us back to the throttlevine, Sophie thought, but gives us nothing.

"Oh, relax, little Kir, I'm not done. Two days before the duel, there was a murder. An atomist constructor, a Sylvanner who'd defected. He was scripped to death. He'd been on Haversham for years. He defected right before the throttlevine started taking root on Low Bann. And he was living in Cordero's family home."

"Cordero and a Sylvanna defector?" That was Bram, coming back laden with a big tray of steaming mugs. He set them down and sat beside Sophie.

"Delicious, don't you think? The unofficial story is this: Cordero let the atomist, a gentleman named Highfelling, stay at his home, where he somehow created or facilitated the throttlevine infestation. Years later, the Bannings sent their pet boy-killer—no offense, Kir Sophie—to Fleet to join the duelists and see what he could learn. When he got close to exposing Cordero's involvement, his co-conspirators killed the atomist."

"Why scrip him to death? Why not use some other means of assassination?" Parrish asked.

"Highfelling saw it coming—he'd fled and gone into hiding. Magic was the only way to get to him." She all but purred the words. "Are you still ticklish, Garland?"

"I assume so." He had recovered from the surprise of her arrival, Sophie deduced—the question didn't faze him. "You were saying?"

"Cordero, when he was caught, threw himself into an all-or-nothing duel with Banning. He couldn't win, so he committed suicide by combat."

Sophie said, "How does any of this help us?"

"Ah, because I know a secret. The scrip that killed the atomist turned up about six years ago. It's with his body, the case evidence, and all his portable goods." Pyke was examining Parrish, gauging the effect of her words. When nobody replied, she added, "Perhaps, as I hear you're outlanders—"

"We understand what you're saying," Bram said. "People who get magicked to death end up in the care of the monks on Issle Morta."

With the monks who'd raised Parrish, in other words.

If the scroll or whatever—it was sure to be written on dead-yak dung or something equally appalling, Sophie thought—was on Issle Morta, they could tear it up. They could make the Sylvanner live again.

The idea of it, of resurrecting someone—and he'd been dead how many decades?

Pyke was watching Parrish with the canny gaze of a hunter. "How long has it been since you were home?"

He spoke with that perfection of diction that, Sophie was beginning to realize, accompanied discomfort. "Gale Feliachild and I were there ten years ago."

Sophie wasn't one to let a tense silence run long or at all. "So, Miss Pyke, you write for a newspaper?"

"Kir Pyke. And we say 'newsheet' or 'journal.'"

"How does that work? You have folks out on boats delivering the sheets at dawn, in rain, snow, sleet—" She'd started chattering to draw the reporter's attention, but now she considered it, that was ridiculous. "I'd have seen papers. Besides, none of these ships would waste space on a press or use up that much pulp."

"I don't know that word, 'press.'" Pyke leaned back in her chair. "Our crier memorizes the master copy. People draw the information in a variety of ways."

Sophie trolled her memories. "Lights blinking in Morse code, maybe. And I've seen people listening to shells."

"Eraseable slates," Bram said. "Tonio's got a tray covered in fine-grained sand."

"You're sharp, Kirs." Pyke was grinning. "May I also play at guessing?"

"Guess at what?"

"Your Fleet—someone impressed it on you, didn't they? There's no way your accent would be *Constitution*-perfect if you grew up outlandish. You'd sound like . . ." She inclined her head at Bram.

"Yes, it was a spell," Sophie said. "On Stele Island."

She cocked a brow at Sophie.

"We're taking turns?" Sophie said. "What is this, Ping-Pong?"

"If you've run out of observations . . ." A shake of the lion's mane, and a yawn.

"You're old," Sophie blurted.

"Excuse me?" Mock offense.

"Your boots are a more fashionable version of the ones I just saw on that retirement vessel, *Pastoral*. They're braced, for supporting weak ankles, balancing on shifting decks. Your face has a youthful appearance that puts you under thirty, but the skin on your hands is papery. I see your veins, and there's a scar. . . ."

Pyke stretched out her arms. "I may have gotten a bit of sun as a child."

"Maybe. You carry a fan, you're dressed in layers—so you can shed them in case of hot flashes? You addressed Tonio in Erinthian when you came aboard, and he replied, *Gennadonna*. I don't speak the language, but I know you say *ginagina* for a young lady. You replied in kind, so you've spent time on Erinth. And that's where you go when you want to get your age spots sanded away but you can't turn back the clock . . . if you can. Can't you just be younger?"

"Reversing one's age is a much heavier intention," Parrish said. "Most who try are broken under it."

Pyke surprised her by laughing. "I see why Convenor Gracechild thinks you're dangerous. If you can do this with so little experience of the civilized world, imagine what'll happen once you're well traveled? Just as well you're taking her off to the monkish corners, Garland."

"The chances of Sophie picking up no useful knowledge on a sail to Issle Morta," Parrish said, "would seem low."

"They're zero," Sophie said. "If you're gonna quote odds like Mr. Spock, get the math right."

"I don't know the math."

"Ask Bram."

"Don't drag me into this," Bram said.

"Garland, the two of you deserve each other," said Pyke. "Well, girl, I can't say I hate you, though I rather wish I did. Enjoy the boneyard."

"Thank you, Langda," Parrish said, helping her to her feet. Pyke held on to his arm right up until she disembarked, stepping back into her hired ship and vanishing into the fog.

They stood together, the three of them, until the silence was thoroughly awkward.

"Tibbon's Wash is roughly on the way to Issle Morta," Parrish said. "Were we to further investigate Corsetta's dispute, we could ask questions there."

"Verena's case, Verena's call." Sophie wondered if he was just trying to buy himself a few more days not being home. "How much of a delay?"

"Two days?"

"If winds are fair?"

"I always catch the fast wind west," he said, with a rueful expression.

"Well, that's neither here nor there." Tonio plopped down beside them with a sigh. "The cabin lock's been jimmied. That little scamp Corsetta's made off again."

CHAPTER 22

The Fleet's annual summer sail took a northerly route west, threading a route past chains of islands located where northern Canada should have been. After leisurely visits to a number of those nations, the ships would pause at Verdanii, taking on grain and vegetables before continuing west into what should have been the Pacific. Finally they'd sweep southeast, easing back along the other remnant of North America, a scythe of islands that curled outward and down from the location of the Pacific Northwest, east and south to Haversham and Sylvanna, and thence southward, dropping below the equator, through the latitudes Sophie couldn't help thinking of as Caribbean. As autumn continued and the days shortened, all the ships would sail in the direction of the remains of Africa.

By heading west and making straight for Issle Morta, Parrish proposed to outrace the Fleet's long arc of a route.

Verena came back with a grim *Do whatever it takes, just solve the Corsetta problem* from Annela. She took the news of Corsetta's escape philosophically. "If the Watch can't hang on to her, why should we try? If she stayed aboard, she'll surface when she's hungry." With a quick glance at Parrish's charts, she agreed to the plan.

She seemed lost in thought or perhaps morose. Sophie did nothing to jolly her out of her mood. She'd ambushed Parrish by sending his ex-girlfriend to *Nightjar* with no warning: she was actively messing with them. Try as she might to remind herself that Verena was just a kid, a love-struck kid, she couldn't shake a growing sense of annoyance.

Parrish, too, seemed withdrawn. He watched the seas, checked all the hatches, kept an alert watch on the crew.

The sea, as they sailed east, became a strange purplish blue, ultramarine edging to, at times, periwinkle. It held a stunning profusion of life. There were pods, hundreds strong, of dolphins to be seen every morning. The cook had crew out netting an unfamiliar and quite ugly fish they called saltsander.

The water foamed easily and smelled, to Sophie, of springtime.

It was a fast crossing—the winds did indeed seem obscenely coopera-tive. They were zooming along at a clip so quickly, Parrish rarely had to order up the mainsail. Had they bent every sheet, the ship might well have flown . . . until her masts cracked under the strain.

Corsetta had indeed stayed aboard. One day out from Tibbon's Wash, she tried to take over the ship.

There was no gunpowder aboard *Nightjar,* but the ship carried plenty of flammables. Parrish kept a supply of lantern oil, and she'd made her-self a wad of reeking, incendiary rags.

Bolting out onto the deck, she had thrown the rags atop a stack of dried, folded laundry. Then she waved a long flaming something that looked like a torch from the tomb of some old-time adventure movie. "I'll set the mainmast aflame," she shouted. "I've already started a fire in the hold!"

"This is suboptimal," Bram said. He and Sophie had been working on their map again, and he looked less afraid than inconvenienced.

Verena drew her sword, pacing forward deliberately until Corsetta was just beyond its reach. The girl did not back away.

"Take me home!" Corsetta demanded. "Or I'll burn this ship, crow's nest to keel."

Parrish's lips thinned. "Beal, Bram, go below. See if she's telling the truth about another fire."

Corsetta remained squared off against Verena as Bram descended. "Order your captain to bear us to Tibbs."

"It's his ship, not mine," Verena said.

"Then he should have a care not to lose it."

Sophie moved to follow Bram, but Parrish had her by the arm.

"Corsetta." Verena extended the rapier. "What are you going to do? Even if we lower a boat for you, you can't hope to outrun us, paddling."

"I'll take someone with me."

"We'll give you nothing," Parrish said. "No boat, no hostage, no ride to Tibbon's Wash. You can't hope to swim the limit—I've overlooked the currents here. All you'll achieve is to drown. Then your Rashad will die, too, will he not? Or perhaps you've misled us about how much that matters to you?"

Corsetta feinted, making as though to light her rags. Verena swung at her wrist and Corsetta darted aft.

Something hit the girl from above.

It was big and black and fast; it drove Corsetta down, out of view, behind the jib. The cat, Banana, streaked past, a tabby blur, scrabbling at the boards of the deck as it fled whatever-it-was. Corsetta's torch rolled astern.

Parrish scooped it gracefully off the deck, tossing it underhand to Sweet, who had been ready with a bucket.

Verena had leaped into whatever fray was developing up on the bow.

"It's all right," Parrish said to Sophie. "We're perfectly safe."

With that, he strode into the bow.

Corsetta and Verena were in a three-way wrangle with a winged man.

He didn't look in any sense angelic. His wings were white and tattered with use—*snow vulture, wings,* thought Sophie—and the egg they'd grown from was still stuck between his shoulder blades, a wet remnant of shell and yolk that smelled of rot. Plucked chicken flesh covered his skin from just below the neck to above his pectorals, and all of his musculature—his upper arms, shoulders, back, and chest—had been built up to cartoonish, Popeye levels.

The egg was fixed to his skin, as far as Sophie could see, by amber slivers jammed into his skin like pins.

Amber, she thought. They met up with the raiders to get amber.

He had a loose-skinned, almost starved look.

Had to lose mass to fly at all, and then to come . . . how far is it? We've been covering over a hundred miles a day. He's gotta be wrecked.

Parrish had apparently reached the same conclusion. He ducked a flapping wing with his usual grace, catching the man by the arm.

"That's quite enough, Kir!" It was a bellow. Sophie would never have guessed anyone could be so loud, much less someone so mild-mannered.

Everyone froze.

Parrish lifted the winged man as though he were a toy, raising him to his feet and giving him a little push starboard before helping Corsetta up. Her face was bleeding.

Verena, looking scalded, leaped to her feet before he could help her, too.

The man lunged, but Parrish caught him with a hand.

"This festering pussball of a goatherd has ravished my brother!"

So this was Montaro.

"Your brother wooed Corsetta at your suggestion, Kir," Parrish said. "What would you do? Drown her and him, too?"

A look of triumph crossed Montaro's face. "We know the scribe who knotted their life-threads."

"That does you no good if the inscription remains intact. Has your brother given it up?"

"I will have their fates unbound!"

Corsetta's lips skinned back from her teeth. "You would have me dead? Tear up the spell you used to heal me of wounds you inflicted?"

"I would have my brother detached from someone who risks herself at every *oksakkin* opportunity."

They slipped into Tibbsian, yelling.

"Maybe the boy should get a say," Sophie said, and silence fell.

Verena had been gearing up to say something. Now she shot Sophie a furious look. "Wasn't there a fire aboard?"

Crap. I was supposed to be staying out of this.

"My mistake." Sophie went below to see if she could help Bram.

He was just packing away an innocuous-looking pair of wooden boxes. "Crate of Tonio's wine, bunch of straw soaked with lantern oil, and another lantern set to catch it all. Cigarillo as a trigger. Beal's making sure there aren't any more. A fruit bat could have disassembled it."

"Good. Because you're not becoming the Stormwrack bomb squad."

"Like that's up to you."

"Bram—"

"Don't, Sofe." He spoke with surprising heat. "I have as much right as you to come here and risk my butt."

"I meant—"

"What? You get to research all this, and I stay in San Francisco in a nice padded room, reading up on your crumbs?"

What could she say? That she was afraid for him? That it was hard? That only she was allowed to take the risks that had been stressing their parents out for years?

I've been using Bram as an excuse, she thought, a reason why I have to go back to San Francisco. Maybe I just want to go home.

As she was standing there, open-mouthed, too shocked even to sputter, he broke into a grin. "You busy with that epiphany, Sofe, or you want to help me with this?"

"Um. I'll help." They cleared up the last of the oil-soaked straw in silence, putting it in an old flour sack.

Could I do that? Go home if Bram stayed? Be the padded-room kid? It was one of those questions that felt ridiculous in every way. She might as easily ask if she wanted to grow a duck's bill.

"Wanna go up?" Bram said.

"Yes, but aft. I think I've stuck my foot in it again."

He led the way to the rear of the ship, found a pitcher and some soap, and washed the oil off his hands. The two of them climbed the ladder back to the main deck. Sophie glanced up, into the ship's rigging, and then scanned the deck. No sign of Verena.

"What are you gonna do about this mess?" Bram asked.

"No clue. Everything hinges on getting Beatrice out of jail. Verena's goodwill, Annela's willingness to let me do research—"

"Beatrice herself thawing out?"

"Fat chance of that," she said.

Bram shrugged.

It was, more or less, true. The tangle of home versus Stormwrack hadn't gotten any looser—it was such a tight knot now she'd never pick it apart. She couldn't just be here and vanish on her parents. Yet the thought of going back to the real world forever felt heart-rippingly wrong.

"Can you love a place you barely know?"

"A place?" he said.

"This isn't just about Parrish."

"You can love anything, can't you? Why not a world?"

"I mean *love*. Corsetta's die-without-Rashad thing."

"That's hormones. What is she, fifteen?"

"Yeah," she said, unconvinced.

"The little animal whisperer and Verena are both sex smitten. You know as well as I that the idea of one true love is a media package."

"Love at first sight?" They'd had this conversation before . . . she could even supply his next line. "Your choice of mate will inevitably be made by powerful pre-programmed biological instincts."

"You're the biologist, tell me I'm wrong. You know we're driven to pair up. To cheat, too."

"I don't—"

But suddenly the hatch at their feet was opening again, and Bram interrupted. "Hey, Parrish."

The captain nodded, quite stiffly, Sophie thought.

He said, "Everything all right?"

"Corsetta's a better escape artist than a mad bomber," Bram said. "Her fire trap was barely smoldering. Someone would've found and doused it quickly enough."

Parrish nodded. "Verena's sent for the brother, Rashad."

A long silence spilled from that. To break it, Sophie said, "Do I hear thumping, down by the galley?"

Parrish put a hand on the rail, and something in his face made Sophie think about true love again. "We're rearranging some bulkheads below; *Nightjar*'s fore cabins convert to an arbitration space."

"If Verena finds a resolution here, will it keep Annela from firing her?"

"It will depend, I suppose, on the resolution."

"I guess she's still got the magic back-and-forth power. She can get to and fro between Erstwhile and Stormwrack."

"Would that keep the government from reducing her to just that—a letter carrier between worlds?" Bram asked.

Parrish refused to be drawn out—he just gave them a polite smile.

She didn't quite finish high school, did she? Once Gale died, she figured she was moving here, full-time. She's got nothing left at home; she'd have to finish out her senior year, start making friends.

She's spent all her life learning to fence and speak languages nobody on Earth knows. . . .

"What's a hormones?" Parrish asked suddenly. Changing the subject?

Bram smirked. "You're the biologist, Ducks."

"Don't call me Ducks." She gave Parrish a dry little lecture, starting with bees and the alarm pheromones they used to communicate, hoping to see his eyes glaze over. He hung on every word.

Jeez, you're adorable. The thought made her feel more flustered, not less.

Boring, Sofe, be boring. She was up to describing household traps that used gypsy moth hormones to lure them onto sticky paper, when a small ferry appeared, sailing from the direction of Tibbon's Wash. It bore three wildly well dressed figures.

Corsetta and Montaro both leaned on the rail, near the bridge, watching the ferry's approach.

"What's to keep Angelboy from flying off again?"

"Honor?" Parrish said.

If he chucked a fifteen-year-old girl off his ship, he wasn't likely to have any of that, Sophie thought.

Parrish may have read her face; he added, "The appearance of honor will matter, at this point."

In any case, Montaro looked exhausted. The spell that transformed him would have worked better on someone jockey-slender; the wings drooping from his shoulders were massive, but everything had its limits. If he wanted to remain an aerialist, he'd never eat a decent meal again.

There was a final, percussive cluster of bumps and sliding wood, and Verena appeared at the fore of the ship. Now, as the ferry reached them she crossed her arms over her chest, in imitation of a pose of Annela's. She was clad in what must be a traditional Verdanii tunic of flowing green silk. One of her fencing blades hung from a gold scabbard. Gale's Fleet badge dangled like a big flashy pendant at her throat.

The party from Tibbon's Wash consisted of three people: a man, a woman, and a teenage boy with cherub cheeks and thick gold curls. The latter, Sophie assumed, was Rashad.

There were introductions all around. The man was an envoy from the Queen, and the woman, it turned out, was the spellscribe who'd worked both the suicide pact on the young lovebirds and the cure for Corsetta's sun exposure.

Rashad reached for Corsetta. The Crown envoy blocked him, shooing him instead toward his brother. They settled for making eyes at each other.

"Does everyone here speak Fleet?" Verena said. There was a quaver in her voice.

Nods all around.

"Follow me, please."

They trooped down the ladder through the galley and found the two fore cabins, Verena's and Parrish's, transformed. The bulkhead between them had been pulled and packed, the bunks stowed. In their place was a conference room, formally arrayed, with a linen-covered table, pitchers of cold water, and, to Sophie's surprise, a tray of small baklava-like cakes. Red curtains imprinted with the Fleet insignia hung around the table, creating false walls that squared and enclosed the space (and hid Parrish's collection of souvenirs). Beal had donned a scribe's uniform and waited to take notes. All very official and tidy.

The formality of the surroundings had an immediate effect. The kids became drop-jawed serious. The envoy cast his eye around approvingly and took a seat midtable, gesturing for the spellscribe to stand behind him.

Montaro had to duck below the hatch to get his wings in and crouched on a low bench instead of a chair.

When everyone was settled, Verena uttered a long stream of formal-sounding Verdanii. Then she said, "We're here to consider events aboard a ship of Tibbon's Wash, *Waveplay,* five days after midsummer, in North-water."

"The Fleet has no interest here," the envoy said. "This is a local matter, a family feud."

So he's siding with Montaro, Sophie thought.

"The government's interest is, as always, justice. Kir Montaro stands accused of attempted murder in open waters."

The boy, Rashad, went a little bug-eyed at that.

Verena laid out the story: their discovery of Corsetta half-dead in Northwater, her various misadventures in Fleet, and the flurry of accusation and counteraccusation between both parties. She detangled, in detail, the bureaucratic moves that had thwarted Montaro's and Corsetta's respective attempts to flee back to Tibbs.

Verena declined to raise the issue that might have gotten them both executed: Corsetta's assertion that Montaro was in league with the bandits.

"The great rush to get here all comes down to you, Rashad," she concluded, gently as she could. "Your brother hopes you'll give up the inscription you made with Corsetta—the life-and-death pact. Corsetta needs you to admit your brother asked you to seduce her so she'd go on the sail with him."

The boy looked from his brother to his girlfriend, clearly torn. "What will happen to Montaro if—"

"We'll decide that today. He might go back to Fleet, for questioning about other matters."

"Other matters?" Rashad asked. He seemed bewildered.

If Montaro had been friends with the bandits, Sophie guessed the brother didn't know it. Montaro himself paled, becoming almost as white as his wings.

Verena looked to the envoy. "What's the penalty if he's tried at home?"

"Risking the life of a minor servant is hardly a crime," said the envoy. "Attempting to steal the Queen's favor, on the other hand . . ."

Now it was Rashad who looked stricken.

"Well. As an oddity, Montaro would have his uses. He might serve the Queen as a penance for his crime."

Montaro burst forth with a protest, in Tibbsian, clearly appealing to his brother. Corsetta shot Rashad an urgent *Shut up!* glance.

Oh, this is getting messy.

Sophie bit her lips to keep from offering her opinion, then looked to her brother. Bram was sitting back, listening to the flow of Fleetspeak and concentrating, pretty obviously, on catching what nuances he could of the argument.

Verena, too, was waiting, just taking it in. It'll fall to her, Sophie realized. She'll send Montaro home for one kind of punishment or haul him to Fleet for another. Judge and jury, with her cousin the Convenor coming down on her hard if she makes the wrong choice.

This was what you got in a court system with no standards of proof. Cly might be a slave-owning jerk wad, or worse, but he wasn't wrong about the system being hopelessly arbitrary.

Verena stood, drawing everyone's attention. "Rashad," she said, and she was doing her utmost to seem impressive. "This is not a situation which requires you to choose between your girlfriend—"

"My beloved!"

"—and your brother. Your loyalties are irrelevant. All we require from you is the truth."

The kid's breath hitched. Once. Twice. "Montaro asked me to get to know her."

The brother's wings drooped slightly. Corsetta made a small noise.

"He'd seen she had a way with wild things. The goats, of course, but birds, rabbits, cats. And—" Now he looked angry. "He thought at sea she'd grow to like him."

"But once I knew her, my feelings changed. Corsetta is the finest, most beautiful, the smartest—"

Devious, light-fingered . . . , Sophie thought.

The government envoy couldn't contain himself. "Silence, boy! You're embarrassing yourself. She's a goatherd."

"She's a goddess!"

The spellscribe was trying not to laugh.

Rashad went on, "I asked her to marry me, if we could get the Queen's permission. But we didn't trust Montaro—"

"Whose idea was it to have the life-binding done?"

"Mine," Corsetta inserted.

Something passed between them. "I needed assurances," she said. "It was me who didn't trust Montaro, not Rashad."

Getting their stories straight, right in front of us.

"This is why cops interview witnesses separately at home," Sophie muttered to Bram.

The envoy looked from one to the other. "At any point, Rashad, did your brother reveal an intention to betray Corsetta, once the snow vulture was secured?"

Rashad squirmed.

Oh! The little poet boy was in on the plan to kill her, at least at first. And Corsetta, poor Corsetta, she had guessed it. She was covering for him.

"Just the truth, Kir," Verena repeated.

"He knew nothing!" Corsetta protested. "The spell was my idea."

The kid let out a long breath. "Only one person can claim the Queen's favor. If Corsetta did not return, Montaro could claim the prize."

"That's premeditated murder," Bram said.

The envoy, hearing Bram's accent, raised his eyebrows. Before he could ask who the wacky foreign observers were, though, Rashad went on: "We sought the life-binding as protection. And I told Montaro. I told him, if she doesn't return, I will die."

Everyone looked to the tattered figure of Montaro, crouched miserably on his bench. He barked, laughing in a way that sounded painful. "I thought he was being poetic."

"So they did tell him," Bram whispered. "He just didn't listen to little brother. Tsk."

Sophie elbowed him in the ribs.

The envoy looked with distaste at all three of them. "The goatherd would appear to be relatively blameless. There is no doubt that she cozzled the bird, or that it has chosen her as its protector. The Queen's favor and the proceeds of sale will go to her."

Eyes huge, Rashad asked, "And Montaro?"

"If he goes to the Fleet, he'll be prosecuted for trying to murder Corsetta," Verena said. "If he goes home—"

"Charged with stealing the Queen's favor," the envoy confirmed.

Rashad leapt to his feet, clutching his heart. "Brother! The truth has condemned you!"

All that's missing is a 'Zounds!' Sophie looked at Bram, which was a mistake . . . he was repeating what Rashad had said, translating, and any second now they were both going to lose it to a fit of the giggles.

"I know what we can do!" Corsetta reached for Rashad and the envoy slapped her hand, hard. She ignored him, twining their fingers. "We can ask for clemency for Montaro. As our favor. He won't face execution. You said he can go in service to the Crown if the Queen forgives him?"

"Without her favor, you can't wed," the envoy said. Then he brightened, probably realizing that he liked Montaro and was against the wedding anyway.

"Does this mean you've forgiven me?" Rashad blinked tears off his cherub cheeks and wrapped his arms around Corsetta.

Jeez, stop, where did they get this guy?

Bram broke eye contact with her. He was staring at the ugly, wounded, chicken-skin flesh of Montaro's collarbones, using it to fight off the attack of inappropriate funnies.

The envoy pried the kids apart before they could start working on their firstborn. He repeated, "Without the Queen's favor, you can't wed."

Corsetta twinkled at him. "Well, there's always the next challenge, isn't there? In the meantime, Rashad won't be the first landowner to keep a goat slut in his barn."

Slut in the barn. The phrase speared Sophie's ballooning urge to laugh, all at once. She thought of Cly, coming back to Low Bann, late at night, and her stomach did an uneasy flip and roll as she remembered the slave, crying in the kitchen the next morning. The little slave kids on the parade route . . .

It's not proof, not proof, I could be wrong about him, I was wrong, so wrong about him arranging a betrothal. . . .

The envoy gritted his teeth, making a gristling sound that brought Sophie back to the present. "Clemency for Montaro depends on the Fleet waiving its right to try him for attempted murder asea. We remain beyond Tibbon's wash's territorial limit."

All eyes turned to Verena.

We should ask him about the bandits, Sophie thought, and that got her thinking about Cly again, about how he'd shot the bandit captain in the throat, about how all of that ship's crew would be dead, if not for the fluke of her having gotten between him and the last guy.

There's a connection there, something I haven't seen yet.

"Verena—" she began.

Her sister made a furious *Shut up!* gesture and spoke, loudly: "If I take Montaro back to Fleet, you kids can use the royal favor to get married. He might as easily be a messenger there."

"I won't testify against him," Corsetta said.

"Nor I," said Rashad.

"How would the attempted murder be proved?" Corsetta said.

Verena replied, "Is this truly what you want, Corsetta?"

"I must sail my soul's wind." The girl nodded. "Montaro is my beloved's family, and this is a Tibbs matter."

Verena let out a long sigh. "Fine. Go, all of you."

The envoy turned to the spellscribe. "Take them above, and for Lady's sake, keep them separated." When they were gone, he turned to Verena. "She's trouble, that one. You sure you don't want her back? She must have broken a few laws in Fleet."

"None Montaro didn't break, too."

"What a shame. Well, you've done us a favor. I'll be sure to send my appreciation to . . . Convener Gracechild?"

Verena blinked. "Thanks. I'll—can I see you to your ferry?"

"With pleasure." He bowed impressively and they, too, vanished out between the velvet curtains. That left Sophie and her brother alone with Parrish, who hadn't said a word the whole time.

"Is there a . . . 'pheromone' for forgiving your enemies?" Parrish murmured. "Corsetta showed extraordinary generosity in sparing Montaro."

"Or she's being practical," Sophie said. "How long will Rashad keep up the 'oh my love, my only love' riff if she gets his brother hanged?"

"Keep up the . . . riff?"

"They're kids," Bram agreed. "They've got decades to get tired of each other."

"I thought you valued the evidence of your own eyes."

"You saw true love, did you?" Bram said. He gave them another of his snotty-brat looks and sauntered out.

Oh. No way was she staying to discuss the nature of romantic love with Parrish. She scrambled after Bram.

They found Verena on deck, still in her green wrap, waving good-bye to the delegation.

"Hey!" Sophie said. "You did it!"

"Mostly," Verena replied. For no reason Sophie could see, she was looking stung.

"Come on, give yourself the win. True love, clean living, and you."

"Did I ask for a cheerleader?"

"Verena—"

"Why can't you just go home?"

Sophie's mouth fell open as she strode away, all but tangling with Parrish as he climbed the ladder from the galley.

It was Tonio who broke the silence. "Set course for Issle Morta? Captain?"

"Yes," Parrish said, in a tone so colorless the word might as well have been typed on the clouds rather than spoken aloud.

CHAPTER 23

"'Dearest Sophie,'" Sophie read to Bram. "'I have been much occupied with thoughts of our recent time together, what went wrong and how matters between us might be amended.

"'I think you know I had no idea of your being ignorant of the fact that Sylvanna is a bonded nation. Had I realized, I would have told you. It is the way of us, in fleet, to talk around the subject, always. I suppose I should have guessed, rather than choosing to believe you had reconciled yourself to it, as your mother attempted to do.'"

"Subtle dig there," said Bram. "Beatrice was okay with it."

"'As for the misunderstanding regarding Rees Erminne and his mother, I assure you I am not one to throw a child into marriage with someone they've known but an hour.'"

"Given that he's a lawyer, I feel I should say this doesn't mean he wouldn't throw you into some other marriage, if he could."

"Or maybe we're being unfair."

"What else does he say?"

She read on: "'You ask what it would take for me to intercede with the Court on behalf of Beatrice. You use the phrase "let her go," though I assure you it's not so simple.

"'I continue to see no reason why I, as the party defrauded, denied my parental rights and now facing a socially complex divorce, with a daughter who would under other circumstances have been proud heiress of Low Bann, should attempt to make things easier for the author of my misery.

"'Beatrice has set her sails; let her ride the winds.

"'Ever your loving father, Clydon Banning.'" With that, she handed the page over, as though she thought Bram would see something in it she hadn't. Bram read it, slowly, familiarizing himself with the spelling and grammar of the Fleet words.

"You didn't ask if he was sleeping with the slaves?"

"In a letter?" She shook her head. "I chickened out. I don't have any decent evidence, and after how badly I misjudged the betrothal thing . . ."

He nodded, reaching the end, and folding it. "There's no admission of fault in this. Sociopaths don't."

She nodded, agreeing but not entirely sure what to do with the bundle of issues that was Cly. He'd been a fire-setter as a child and the Bannings had magically tempered him. Killing was part of his day job. Even if she had no proof that he forced his slaves to sleep with him, just thinking about that filled her with rage and despair.

And they were his, weren't they? His responsibility?

If so, by extension they were hers, too. She thought again of the goat-people, of that stomach-turning moment when she realized they weren't fauns.

Despite everything, part of her hungered to believe in the Cly who'd seemed so vibrantly alive. The delight he seemed to take in everything, his excitement when he'd learned of her existence. Even the hurt he'd expressed when he'd talked about trying—and failing—to make Beatrice happy.

Did that make her a bad person?

"Was it all just an act? Could he really be so awful?"

Her brother rolled his head side to side. "Pretty seamless act, if it is. Hey—totally other topic—there's Mount Rainier."

It was a transparent offer to move on to less painful terrain, and she was only too happy to take it. She turned, taking in the familiar cone, a dark blue shape etched on a fog-gray horizon, less a sighting of land than an implication of one.

Over the next few hours, the mountain and the rest of Issle Morta came into focus. The clouds at its peak separated, revealing a flatter top. Even here, it dominated the landscape. Rainier's slopes were clad in green and blue, the cedar-spruce-dogwood-and-fog palette of the Pacific Northwest.

"It's smoking," Bram said as they approached. "It's active."

Sophie glanced at him carefully. There'd been an active volcano in Erinth, too, and he'd been less than thrilled to be near it.

"It seems apparent that Stormwrack's a lot more active, geologically, than Erstwhile."

Bram nodded agreement.

As the day wore on, they saw the approach to the island had been made into an obstacle course: massive stone skulls, not quite human, with exaggerated canines, rose from the surface of the water. Barnacles encircled their high waterline, and each had a single redwood tree planted within the bowl of its stone head. The cawing from above and the lime below indicated there was an enormous murder of crows living within the canopy of the artificial forest.

Parrish took the helm himself as they approached, wheeling them between the skulls on an apparently random route. He had a stopwatch out and was timing the gaps between skulls as they traveled; his face was set.

"What's he doing?" Bram asked.

"It's called interval navigation," Tonio said. "A lot of islands built hazards, before the Cessation, into their vulnerable shore approaches. They salted them with shallows and shipwreckers. These"—he waved at the skulls—"date back to when Issle Morta was part of the Piracy. If you know the waters well enough and you fix your speed, you can time your passage of any landmark and then steer into the harbor blind, or in fog, just by counting."

Sophie was filming the skulls themselves. "They look like cat skulls."

"Specters," Tonio said, just as they broke out of the hazard and into open water, a small port facing a drab village, walled, consisting of cedar A-frames built up around a square whose centerpiece was a long, square pit. A sculptural representation of an open grave?

"The town is called Lamentation," Tonio murmured.

"How very consistent they are with their branding," Bram said, an edge in his voice. When they were last in Stormwrack, he had been grabbed by the Isle of Gold, taken hostage. Golders tortured their hostages as a matter of course. But Cly had intervened, arranging for them to hand Bram over to Issle Morta until Sophie paid the ransom.

Holding hostages, acting as go-betweens was one of the things the monks of Issle Morta did. They ensured that kidnap victims weren't hurt or killed . . . but if a ransom deal with the kidnappers went south, honor forced them to use their own particular twist on legal slavery to keep the hostage. Forever.

Bram had almost ended up spending his life in this desolate, backwater place.

She groped for his hand.

Tonio had changed out of his sailor's clothes into a plain brown cloak and boots.

Parrish frowned. "Tonio?"

"Believe it or not, Garland, I have business with the dead."

Lamentation was apparently where you moved if you wanted to live in grim seclusion, especially if you had a loved one in the monastery, someone you wanted to end up buried with, or someone who'd been scripped to death.

"No kids," Sophie observed quietly as they came ashore.

"There might be five or six," Parrish said. "But the residents tend to be widows and widowers. They come here later in life, when their children are grown. The forests have their hazards; this is no place for the young."

"Lamentation's where you come to be clinically depressed?" Bram said.

"Many Lamenters sail on after they've taken time to mourn. It's a good place for it. Quiet. And the brothers help."

Sophie thought about that. The idea of withdrawing from life until you were stronger, of just going somewhere where everyone understood and nobody expected much from you. Not having to try just to get through the days, to go back to work, whatever. "I can see how it'd be restful, or healing, or whatever. But I'd go nuts."

He gave her a closed look and she remembered, once again, that he'd been superclose to Gale and she'd only been gone . . . seven months now?

She turned away, examining the town, trying to think of something kinder to say. What came out was: "That guy looks ready to leave."

Parrish followed her gaze. There was a shockingly tall man standing on the dock. He was knobby-limbed and covered in bug bites. He also had a hole in his left calf big enough to see through.

"We're not a passenger ship, Sophie," Tonio said.

"Look at that cross on the pottery jug beside him," Sophie said. She had the advantage over them, because her camera's telephoto brought the man into view so much more clearly than their spyglasses. "The symbol on it means he's into medicine, doesn't it? And the herbs he's poking into that jug are willow leaves—he's making a painkiller."

Parrish took the camera from her and peered through. "A medic? What makes you think he wants to leave Lamentation?"

"Who wouldn't want to leave?" Bram said. Sophie elbowed him in the ribs.

"That spot where he's perched: he's dug out a little seat in the sand, sized for his body. It's his spot. And look at the placement."

Parrish nodded. "To maximize his view of incoming ships. He's watching people come in."

He considered it. Then: "I have to arrange for supplies before we go up to Ossuary. Would you talk to him, Tonio?"

"Of course, Garland."

They loaded up some baskets of salted fish and pickles before disembarking. Parrish hired donkeys in town: one to carry the provisions and another to bear blankets, bedrolls, and a sheaf of short, wicked-looking javelins that appeared to be carved from whalebone. The donkeys came with a handler, a spry man of about fifty, Hispanic in appearance and armed with a stout staff.

By the time he'd made the arrangements, Tonio had rejoined them. "Sophie's right—he's a medic," he said. "Name of Watts. He's gone aboard *Nightjar* to meet Banana. If that works out, he'll join us."

"Huh?" Bram said.

"He's from Ehrenmord," Tonio said.

"And again: huh?"

"Oh, they're cat worshipers. He's been stuck here waiting for a ship with a resident cat."

The morning passed quietly. Verena and Parrish led the procession, talking softly and urgently in Verdanii—they might, almost, have been arguing. Tonio had fallen into conversation with the donkey handler, and Bram was deploying his magnetometer.

That left Sophie free to film the forest and observe the ecosystem.

The trees and flowers were generally familiar: sword, liquorice, and maidenhair fern; salmonberry; wild rose; cattails and fireweed; and enough stinging nettle to keep everyone on their toes. The only birds seemed to be crows and a dusky variant of a Steller's jay, sharp-billed, with only a hint of blue about it.

This part of the world was lousy with bald eagles, at least at home, but there were none to be seen here.

Maybe they're scavenging on the shore, she thought. She saw a salamander, a garter snake. Parrish paused once on the trail and pointed out an opossum. His expression was hopeful.

She shook her head. "Seen it."

With a cheerful shrug, he returned to his confab with Verena.

The trail broke out into a marshy plain, fed from above by a stream, wet enough that someone had laid a road with stones the size of small cars above the level of the water. It led across to a continuation of the dirt path, eighty meters or so to the east.

Sophie gasped, catching Bram by the hand. There were primates wading in the murk.

For just a moment she thought she was seeing the goat transforms of Low Bann all over again, or something like them, but these were the real deal. They were gaunt and long of limb, with fur shaded in dull grays that would fade well into the hues of the forest, perfect camouflage. A white, papery pattern on their cheeks resembled lichens. Their faces had a roundness that reminded her of orangutans.

There were five individuals: a male, three females, and an adolescent, all perched on the edge of one of the boulders, munching on a massive growth of shelf fungus and slimy spike caps. Their eyes were big, black as glass and fringed with huge white lashes. The adolescent was eating with his feet, revealing long, flexible toes.

"We call them wood children," she heard Parrish say.

Sophie felt a shiver of recognition—they looked a little like the mezmers who'd been sent to kill Gale on Erinth. Had one of these creatures been used in a spell to transform a slave, just as Montaro had been transformed, with a vulture egg, into a boy harpy?

The alpha male gave a resigned-sounding hoot—*Oh, great, people,* it seemed to be saying—and heaved himself off the rock, goosing one of the females to send her up a nurse tree with their haul of mushrooms. The females went willingly—the juvenile had to be pinched hard.

Sophie caught it all on camera. *They're tailless. Another similarity to orangutans.*

Something—a ripple of water—sent the primates shooting up to the canopy.

Bram looked nervous. "Any idea what that was?"

"Bear, I hope." The donkey handler was philosophical. "Try not to worry, Kir."

"Gee, thanks."

"Look at it this way," Tonio said, "The whole island's essentially a cemetery. If something gets us, we're already buried."

He said it deadpan, and Sophie tried out a dutiful laugh. Bram turned back to his equipment with a grunt.

She felt that pang again. The two of them—what if they vanished? Would Parrish—or Verena, or someone—even go tell their parents they'd died?

Verena's here, too.

The primates began shrieking then, letting out a chorus of shrill *gah-gah-GAH!* sounds that ripped at the nerves. The donkeys moaned and picked up their pace. They had crossed the stone walk and were back on the trail by now, nearly to the next turn upward onto dry land and higher elevations.

A cat rose out of the water, maybe a foot from where the primates had been.

It was smaller than a mountain lion, which should have been reassuring. Dripping wet, too, which might have made it comical. It had that funny, reduced, wet-cat look, the fur plastered against its body and making it small.

Instead of making it cute or pathetic, though, the soaking emphasized the leanness of its lines, the alley-cat dangerousness of it. Its fur was dove gray and it had huge paws, the low-slung proportions of a puma, and elongated canines that came to points well below its upper lip. Its eyes were the color of flame.

"Stop recording." Parrish was, suddenly, beside her. He had four of the javelins in his hand. Sophie let the camera fall to its position at her side and accepted one of the double-pointed spears.

"Send the donkeys up first," he said, urging the handler to the fore of the party, so that the five of them—Parrish, Tonio, her and Bram and Verena—were arrayed on the trail facing the cat. Verena had her sword out; Tonio had produced a wicked-looking stiletto from somewhere.

"I thought you said cats weren't allowed on dry land!"

"It's native to the island." Parrish spoke loudly. He was flapping his coat, making himself look big. Sophie squeezed Bram between them and flapped, too.

"Go on," Parrish said to the beast. "Go!"

It rippled a lip at him, sneering feline contempt, but by now they were all flapping and stomping. It eased out of its hunting pose all at once, sitting on the wide, flat rock and washing a paw.

"Up the trail," Parrish said. "Go, Bram. Then Sophie."

They backed up until they were out of sight of the thing, then rushed to catch up to the drover, who'd waited half a kilometer up. "It'll be stalking us now," he said dolefully.

"We're a big party," Parrish said. "It knows we'll fight. And we're nearly to Ossuary."

Sophie felt calm descend as they continued to climb. She was listening to the sound of the wood, waiting for the crows to go silent, listening for footfalls—but the specter would be silent, she supposed.

She stayed close to Bram. Nothing's getting you, she thought.

He was thinking the same thing, probably: they were so eager to play protective sibling that twice they almost tripped over each other.

"Jeez," Bram whispered. "This was almost my postal code."

They were both a little strung out, as if after a caffeine binge, by the time they reached the monastery walls.

The walls were unexpectedly colorful—red and gold lacquered bamboo tiles, from the look of them, had been laid over the stone wall. They were carefully polished, but where tiles had fallen out, here and there, they had not been replaced. A relic of luxurious old days when the people of Issle Morta stole from others rather than serving the dead?

Despite its adornments, the wall was a substantial fortification, forming a stockade around a small village. The gate was wide open and unguarded.

"What's to keep kitty out?" Bram asked.

"Them," Parrish said, pointing. Another family of the primates, twenty strong, was lounging on the wall, jumping to and from an old guard tower. The wood children hooted as the party crossed the threshold, tossing down pine cones. Parrish caught one before it could bean a donkey. He got pelted for his trouble. A pine cone stuck in his hair.

The village at sea level, Lamentation, had been drab but ordinary enough. The villagers, though they'd mostly been fifty or older, had come in an even mix of genders. Here, Sophie and Verena were the only women.

"This is your hometown?"

Parrish looked around at the hovels and statues, and shrugged.

Ossuary was also, in fact, a cemetery. Stone monuments and crypts alternated with huts people were obviously living in; a monk emerged with a freshly laundered cloak and draped it on a line strung from a monument to his roof. Another was using a gravestone as a backrest as he . . . napped?

"There are a few empty shelters over there," the drover said.

"These two?" Parrish walked toward a pair of small cedar A-frames, peering in. "Hello?" he said in Fleet, and then, *"Seggin fra?"*

No reply. "We can sleep here."

The drover had already looped the donkeys' leads around a crudely carved representation of a robed man. He began unpacking the provisions, laying out the baskets of food they'd brought onto a crypt in the midst of the stockade. One monk promptly came and chose an orange from the pack; he took a second and threw it to the primates.

"What happens now?" Bram said. "We sit around until someone takes notice of us?"

Parrish shook his head. "We'll spend the night. The scripped dead are kept in a cave within the mountain, and we'll need permission tonight to revive Highfelling tomorrow. Most of the monks won't speak Fleet, I'm afraid. Many won't speak at all."

Bram was turning a slow circle. "Using the monuments of the dead for clotheslines doesn't seem very respectful."

"Those interred here inside the wall are the monks themselves. They . . . it's part of the practice. Their own deaths are as nothing to the suffering they—our people—caused in the past. So their remains don't deserve reverence. Some don't even opt for burial. They ask to be thrown outside the gates to rot."

Sophie scanned the mix of hovels and graves. It was a decent-size town; she'd have to get up above it to see it all. "Where's Tonio?"

"Pursuing his business," said the drover, sharply. "One dinna ask what the living might wish with the dead."

"We don't ask a lot of things here," she said. "Whether you have business with the dead, whether a nation's free or bonded—"

"Whether Spook Island is filled with big, man-eating cats," Bram muttered.

"What are ye, spies?"

Parrish looked at the bunch of them rolling out the bedrolls and blankets in the cabin. "Bram, Verena—would you mind setting up camp? The village is safe enough. The wood children will shout if there's a specter coming."

"And me?" Sophie said.

Verena flinched.

"There's something I want to show you," Parrish said.

Her half-sister turned away, clearly furious.

"Coming?"

"Where?"

"It's on the trail to Hell."

"Excuse me?"

"The capitol, but we're not going that far."

Sophie followed. "Your capitol is called Hell. Of course it is."

The two of them proceeded to what she thought of as the back wall of the monastery and she saw the gateway into the caves. It was covered by a double door, red in color, that reminded her of a barn. Parrish ignored this, leading her instead to a rickety-looking staircase that climbed to another trail, switchbacks rising high up the mountain.

It was a steep climb, one that, conveniently, left no breath for casual conversation. In time, it took them up to a cliff's edge so sharp and square and level it might have been cut by a diamond saw. She could see all the way to the village, the harbor far below.

Planted at three-meter intervals along the cliff's edge were poplar trees, straight of trunk and perhaps seventy-five feet tall. Their trunks were carved or otherwise shaped to form figures, humans, all with their bare feet planted squarely on the lip of the cliff. White roots dangled over the edge from their toes, bone-white and hairy as rats' tails. The woody arms exploded upward in bursts that might, in abstract art, have been hands, long thin branches like fingers reaching skyward.

The poplars were covered in leaves that, at first glance, reminded Sophie of peacock feathers—they had that false eye that many species used to deter predators.

She looked at the trees carefully, then turned to Garland. "More oddities?"

"Yes." He led her to the second-last in the line, a woman, whose wooden face gazed serenely out to sea. "People held here under the hostage concession sometimes opt to be altered in this fashion. They can look out at the world they've left behind . . . well, it's reckoned to be less painful than permanent homesickness. Or even constant boredom."

"I can see that, I guess," she said dubiously.

"This," he said, delicately, and then he cleared his throat and started again. "Sophie, this individual is my mother, Stronia Bel-Parrish."

Her jaw dropped a little. "Buhhh . . . you've brought me to meet your mom?"

He nodded.

What is going on with you today?

But the answer to that was obvious: he was essentially visiting a grave and yet the woman wasn't dead. No wonder he hated coming home. "Can she hear me? Do I say hi?"

"Stronia never learned to speak Fleet."

"So how do you say hello in Issle Morta?"

"Actually, it sounds about the same."

"Parrish."

"The most appropriate greeting would be *Vaspe denneh me maney.*"

"That sounds Russian."

He shrugged. "I don't know Russian."

She repeated the phrase and then looked at him: *What now?* He added a few phrases of his own, starting with "Zophie Hansa" and going on for a second longer. The accent definitely had a Russian sound. Gale's name figured in his monologue, too.

"Are you telling her Gale died?"

He gave her an odd half smile and seemed unable to speak. The tree's not-carved face did not move, but its branches shuddered in the wind, and the eyes on the leaves all seemed, suddenly, to be looking at her.

"Know what? I'm gonna give you guys a minute." She gestured at a thread of trail heading upward.

"Take a javelin," he said, and she did.

His mom's a tree. A dryad? Naiad? She wasn't up on her fairy tales. *I should've played more Dungeons and Dragons in college instead of volunteering to go shoot wildlife for every ethologist with a research grant and a boat.*

Once the transformed trees were out of sight, the trail she had chosen might have been any little strip of land in the Pacific Northwest. It led upward to another little shelf of rock, another viewpoint. This one had a tumbled plate of stone, much like those that led across the marsh, lying like a table on the land. She hitched herself up on it, as if it were an oversize bench, and set herself to watching the landscape.

From up here, the harbor, encircled as it was by land on one side and the skull planters with their redwood trees, looked like a lake. Shifting clouds of crows moved in the trees, giving the perimeter of the foliage a black, mobile border.

After about ten minutes, Parrish appeared, moving silently. Something in the bush caught his eye, and his hand darted out. He brought it to the table, laying it there. A white spider the size of his thumb tumbled onto the stone table.

"Crab spider. Blends in with the lichens," she said. "Nice specimen."

"You've seen it, then."

She nodded. "So . . ." She laid down a pause, but he didn't pick it up. "Your mother's a tree?"

He seemed to be considering where to start. "It's customary for all the island nations to send a certain number of children to the Fleet each year. Issle Morta, as you deduced, has a low birth rate. The monks generally buy and then free a number of willing adolescent slaves from the Isle of Fury. But my mother always intended me for the Fleet. And when I was gone . . ." He made a gesture, indicating the cliff below.

"You didn't know she was planning to get transformed?"

"In retrospect, I might have guessed." He let out a long sigh. "I wanted to go. The Fleet sounded magical. It was a chance to be . . . to live, to see the world."

"Why'd you quit?"

"I was expelled."

She remembered suddenly: Cly had said he'd been disgraced.

"I'm sorry."

"It was a long time ago. And it led to . . ." He gestured down at the harbor, at *Nightjar*. "All those years with Gale. I'm not sorry."

They sat in silence, looking out over the ocean, the clouds. It was deliciously quiet. The air was just verging on cool, and the sky was dotted with high cirrus clouds, spread like fish scales across the blue. The air smelled of cedar and ponderosa pine, and after weeks at sea it was nice to be somewhere so still and rooted.

"After matters with Beatrice resolve," he asked, "you'll return home?"

"I don't know. I feel so—I need to be here. But how do I give up everything? Plus I'm endangering Bram."

He nodded, indicating assent and understanding, and his total lack of a good answer.

You don't bullshit people, she thought, admiringly. It was a rare gift. Impulsively she reached over, taking his hand.

She'd meant just to squeeze it and let go—probably meant to, anyway—but his fingers turned in hers, intertwining, and a jolt went through her. She hadn't really thought this through, and now he was holding on.

And it wasn't as though she wanted to wrench free.

He introduced me to his mom. Took me home to Mother.

Parrish shifted so they were face-to-face and put out his free hand, fingers brushing her cheek. His gaze was so steady, it felt like a dissection.

Sophie's mind whirled through a dozen possible things to say and came up dry. That one hand continued its tour of her cheek, resting briefly under her chin, and when she didn't break away he curled his fingers back, brushing the nape of her neck and pausing there.

She shivered.

The space between them had closed; she didn't remember getting closer, didn't remember him moving but he was inches away now, and one totally unwelcome thought ran through her mind: *Bram, you little shit, you could've just said he liked me back, instead of teasing me about having a crush....*

And then Parrish was kissing her. It was unhurried, sweet, the contact laced with a strange abundance of gravitas. Just one long kiss, then he pulled back. To what? Check she was okay with it?

Okay? *Hey, let's brush that crab spider off the stone table and . . .*

"Sophie," he said.

She returned the kiss, with a lot less solemnity, then broke away. "Yes?"

"If you're amenable . . ."

"Yes?" I'm amenable, she thought. If anything, she was too amenable.

"I'd very much like to court you."

Court?

Don't laugh, don't laugh, he's sticking his neck out here. "If by 'court' you mean—"

A crashing off to their left interrupted her. Parrish had his javelin out and her behind him in a second.

The oldest ambulatory person Sophie had ever seen in her life came battering his way out of the deep bush, dressed in a tattered black robe and smelling of manure and woodsmoke. It smacked the javelin away and then slapped Parrish, hard, across the face.

"Garland!" It had a voice like a teakettle. "What are you doing? Unhand that female immediately, you lecher!"

CHAPTER 24

Parrish broke into that infectious, delighted smile. "Brother—"

"No!" Horrified, steam-whistle shriek. "I'm one of the nameless now. I have let the last shred of proud individuality. . . ." The stranger mimed releasing something to the wind. "Shame on you, mating here like Erinthians and your mother, what? Fifty meters away?

"This is a place of contemplation and penance, Garland. You of all people should know what happens when we give in to our base urges."

Brother No Name was clearly an extremist even by the monastery's standards, believing not only in no sex but no hygiene and, possibly, no food. Mortification of the flesh he left to the environment—under his ratty robe, Sophie could see that his pallid, leathery flesh was covered in scratches and bites.

Parrish seemed thrilled to find him alive, even though the monk switched from Issle Morta's language and began haranguing him in a piercing whistle.

The sermon went on for so long that Sophie began to doubt what had passed before. Had Parrish really kissed her? Maybe they were at a higher altitude than she thought. What could a person like Parrish possibly mean by 'courting'?

"Speak Fleet," Parrish begged.

"—*fes matalla* . . . sleep in a bed, do ye? Three meals a day?"

"I am very comfortable, yes."

"Now that Verdanii spy who enthralled you is finally gone to ash and story, you could return to the forest and repay your debt to the dead."

"The brother was opposed to my going to Fleet," Parrish explained, by way of including her.

"Only one who was. His mother, ol' Brother Cray, the boy himself, all mad to fling him to the sea. Look how that turned out. Sailing hither and yon, no home, all to keep that scandalous woman alive, and now you seem to have picked up a new one."

Here Sophie got a significant glance.

"Righting wrongs and saving lives, humph!"

"He shouldn't right wrongs?"

"Death finds us all, girl. That woman was doomed, double-doomed from birth."

"Meaning what? Why fight fate? Why rush it?"

"Exactly!" He beamed at her, snaggle-toothed. His breath was eye-wateringly rotten.

Parrish said, "I'm at peace with my current circumstances. My past actions, too."

"I won't have you rutting like a Redcap silverstag while you're home! Your word on it, Garland."

He didn't try to hide the smile. "I am sorry we offended you."

"That's no promise." The monk brightened. "Well, you stink of lust. I'd better stick around to stiffen your resolve. Are you Hell-bound?"

"No. Back to Ossuary."

He wriggled between them like a five-year-old, almost as light, bony as scythes and his robe greasy with filth. "Let's go."

Thus chaperoned, they marched back down the mountainside in near silence. At least one monk failed to hide an expression of dismay at the sight of the nameless brother. The old man promptly whistled at him.

As they stepped back within the confines of the monastery's wall, Sophie took a step toward the red door. But Parrish kept moving, widening his eyes meaningfully and steering toward the cabins where the others were waiting.

"Who's this?" Bram said as they approached the two A-frames. Tonio, she saw, had returned. He seemed sober, lost in thought.

"Found Garland copulating in the woods. On his mother's grave, no less!"

Verena looked as though she'd been slapped.

"Strictly speaking," Sophie said, "that's not—"

Parrish interrupted. "The brother has graciously agreed to join us for the evening. Tonio, may I ask if you concluded your business?"

"I did, Garland, thanks."

Did Parrish think Tonio was up to some mischief? What would that entail here? It was almost as elusive a concept, in this setting, as courting.

"Would you ask the monks for a washbasin and a fresh robe?" Tonio nodded and headed across the compound. Parrish continued, "Tomorrow we'll wrap up our visit here."

He was choosing his words with care.

Hiding our purpose? wondered Sophie.

"Bram, perhaps you can take your sister"—he emphasized their relationship, none too subtly, so the nameless monk couldn't rise up in ire at the prospect of Sophie going off out of his sight with a man—"and see if the two of you can arrange for us to have that conversation in the morning?"

"Why me?" Bram said, but Sophie hauled him up.

When they were out of earshot, she murmured, "I'm betting Brother No Name will disapprove of our waking the dead. Parrish seems to be hoping he won't find out why we're here."

"And since the guy's clamped on to him like a lamprey . . ."

"It falls to us to make the appointment. Exactly."

"Makes sense." He looked at her sidelong. "So. Sofe."

"Oh, don't, Bram."

"Rutting on Momma's grave?"

"It was a kiss! Also, he wants to court me."

"Once again you've found yourself on the cutting edge of the eighteenth century."

"Anyway, his mom's not dead, exactly. She's a transform."

"That makes all the difference in the world," he said gravely.

"I will make you eat that magnetometer." She led him to the barn doors she'd seen earlier, knocked until a monk peered out, and asked about the defector, Highfelling.

"We'll bring him up from the catacombs tonight," the monk said. "We must review any instructions left by his widow or offspring and the language of the inscription itself. It was a long time ago; I wasn't keeper then. What are your names?"

"Sophie and Bramwell Hansa." She realized that she knew someone else on the other side of that crimson door—a man from Isle of Gold, John Coine, who'd arranged Aunt Gale's death and then, later, sacrificed himself in a conspiracy to make it look like Sophie herself had been the guilty party. He'd be in there somewhere, dead. . . .

"Do they rot?" she asked.

The monk shook his head. "When they cease, putrefaction ceases, too."

"Hooray for that." Bram rolled that over. "The bacteria involved in the process of decay must die along with the subject of the spell."

"Or suspend, somehow. If they're not really dead."

"I don't know 'bacteria,' Kir," the monk said politely. "But I assure you that my charges aren't asleep. We'll have Highfelling prepared for a dawn rising." With that, he closed the door in their faces.

"Thanks," Sophie said to the closed portal. "Do you think we offended him?"

Bram shrugged, glancing back at the A-frames. "God, they're washing the old guy down. Let's *not* go help with that."

"Agreed." They walked instead toward the gate, taking a seat on a fallen log that may or may not have been a monument to a dead monk and watching the wood children. The primates were munching, contentedly from the look of them, on a haul of salmonberries and wild blueberries.

"I almost ended up living here," Bram said.

"I'd never have let that happen."

"I know," he said. Then, in a rush he said, "Sofe, it's okay to want things. You know that, right?"

"Are you talking about Parrish?"

"Parrish, sure. And a passport and the right to do research here. You don't have to try to pick the least of them and negotiate with the universe— 'hey, if I only want this and I give up the rest, can I have it?'"

"You're therapying me again."

"You're allowed to want things, that's all."

"I'm making Verena miserable. You're risking your life."

His tone sharpened. "I'm allowed to want things, too."

She thought about reminding him about their parents, then decided that a fight wasn't what she wanted right now.

"We can do the astronomy capture tonight," she said. "Set up the camera, shoot the night sky. Maybe one frame every five minutes? It's clear out and there won't be any light pollution. Depending what we get, we might be able to work out how many years it's been since the twenty-first century and whatever year this is."

Bram nodded. "How good will the images be?"

"It's not a telescope. But an astronomer could probably work with whatever we catch. Unless of course you want to make that your next doctorate."

"My next project is gonna have to be learning to read spellscrip," he said. "How else can we come to understand magic?"

"How are you going to accomplish that?"

"Not sure," he said. "If Annela comes to trust you, or we come up with some reason why the info would be useful, she'll relax."

"Worth a try." She nodded. "In the meantime, I shot a few pages of a spell book. We'll have to try to get the pictures home."

"I can probably memorize them, if I learn the alphabet. But I also brought a spare camera chip. I'll swallow the one you're loading, if I have to. Oh, and that box of stuff you bought with the dead homing pigeon is a spell kit."

"You took my bird corpse?" She wanted the passenger pigeon for comparison with the species that had become extinct, at home, in 1914.

"I'll get you another. Come on, they've got the monk washed and dressed. Night's coming; we should turn in."

Easier said than done. Bram, like their parents, was ever a reluctant camper. He settled into his bedroll and then commenced noisy fidgeting. The worst of it was he was trying to be quiet; but every time Sophie started to relax, he'd explode again.

Brother No Name had divided up their borrowed pair of shacks so that she was with both siblings, and Verena was managing to lie without moving against the wall of the A-frame, radiating rage and jealousy across the wood-beam floor.

Parrish told Verena he was taking me up there, she thought. Broke it to her that he was going to . . . ask me out, basically.

She hoped this was true; otherwise, Verena would have gotten the news when the eccentric monk said they were making love at Stronia Bel-Parrish's feet.

Next door, Tonio and Parrish were bunking with the monk. Or trying to—she heard the occasional rustling there, too, and once an aggrieved and piercing shout of "Watch your elbows, lad!"

Who wouldn't be attracted to Parrish, what with the face and the build and the lamb's-wool hair and the fact that he was the only person on this superstition-ridden world who was interested in provable facts rather than hocus-pocus?

Even if he did seem to believe in true love and, possibly, predestination.

He's not into Verena, he's just not. He's almost twice her age. She's a kid; she'll get past it.

This bit of rationalization didn't do a thing for the irrational guilt, the sense that she'd somehow wronged her newfound sister.

After everything, had she just come back to Stormwrack for Garland Parrish? Was all this desire to explore and angsting over citizenship and butting heads with Cly and trying to help Beatrice just some kind of extended subconscious agenda in getting close to a cute guy?

Supercute. And what the hell does "courting" mean?

In the other hut, someone—Tonio?—snored softly.

Sophie turned her head until she could see across the compound. The great gate was shut for the night, a precaution against specters (happily, serving the dead didn't mean providing easy prey for the big cats), and a small herd of goats had been corralled nearby to serve as additional warning, not to mention bait, if one got in. The grave markers and huts were barely outlined, velvety black on black. The moon was new, the sky so dark that, given the lack of light pollution, the only thing you could see with any accuracy at all was the stars.

They were scattered across the black, vivid constellations, some familiar. Stuff she had seen before—the triangle of Saturn, Spica, and Mars, the constellation Cassiopeia.

She could hear high-pitched chittering—bats, out on the hunt—and the rush of wind in the foliage. Some of the wood children hooted to each other. A monk was praying out there, too, soft bass voice singing cadences in a language she didn't understand, and something was snuffling out by one of the graves.

There was so much to discover here. She thought of walking away before she and Bram had unlocked the puzzle of Stormwrack and Erstwhile, how they were related.

Issues they weren't supposed to explore.

She caressed her book of questions, thinking about how Cly had said he'd follow her to the outlands.

Thought experiment: What if I stayed away, but Parrish came with me?

She imagined him living in San Francisco, sipping lattes and checking his e-mail on a smartphone, making his living as . . . what? An underwear model? Maybe he'd help her analyze reef footage.

Nope, that didn't scan at all.

There was plenty of science to do at home.

But magic had ruined that a little, hadn't it? Inscription was a game-changer. She didn't know how it worked, but it blew all their assumptions about the nature of reality to hell. If she wasn't allowed to tell anyone, it only increased her duty to research it. Her duty, and Bram's, too.

They still didn't know whether their world turned into this one or, if so, when catastrophe would strike.

You're allowed to want things, Bram had said.

Bram's breathing had lengthened at long last and Verena had stopped thrumming. Sophie should have been able to sleep.

First things first, she decided. She had to see through this tangle with Beatrice and Cly.

In the meantime, it won't hurt to ask Parrish what "courting" means.

It wasn't much of an answer; she wanted something easier, cleaner. But *muddle on* seemed to be all there was.

She must have dozed, skimming over the surface of sleep without dipping in, floating back into wakefulness. It was pitch black out now; the stars were gone, and something was tugging, ever so carefully, at the lace on one of her packs.

She had her dive light at the ready. Turning it on, she speared a raccoon in its beam. It had its paw wound into one of the nylon straps of her pack.

It gave her a saucy, unconcerned glance and waddled away.

Pregnant, Sophie noticed.

She slid out of her bedroll noiselessly, grabbing up her shoes and tiptoeing into the compound. The white light of the flash formed a dense cone with the raccoon at its edge. Fog had crept in, turning the air to soup.

She checked her camera—still tied in place, still shooting frames at regular intervals, battery fine. She left it, though the sky wasn't likely to clear before dawn.

You'd think in a holy place, some Obi Wan Kenobi type would materialize out of the fog and offer some cryptic but decipherable advice about sorting all this out.

Follow your heart, weigh your choices, today's the first day of the rest of your life, a woman's work is like a fish . . . no, that's something else.

Fluttering shadows drew her eye—then the beam of the light—to the crypt doors. A skinny, lurking figure in new robes was caught in her spotlight. Brother No Name: he shot her a vicious glare, shook the doors, then minced up the path to the heights of the mountain.

No more chaperone, she thought. If Parrish was awake, we could get on with some quality courting.

The memory of that one kiss rose, making her shiver a little, putting the lie to her pretense of lightheartedness.

She leaned against the A-frame, feeling churned up, waiting to see if he'd come out. Maybe he couldn't sleep, either. Maybe he'd turn up, sleepy, tousled and disaffected by this homecoming. Needing comfort.

Ha, she thought.

She took a seat on what passed for the porch and was still out there, half-dozing, more than a little horny, when the sky began to lighten, the monuments and shadows of the monks drawing colorless lines on the white cotton curtain of morning, as if even the colors of the waxing day were forbidden in this desolate place.

CHAPTER **25**

Tonio was first to arise the next day, maybe fifteen minutes after dawn broke. He sketched a wave and a friendly glance in Sophie's direction, then made his way into the fog, headed for the outhouse.

The monks sang as they emerged from their shacks, joining the lone voice who'd sung all night. The group of them built a low chord that was unmistakably a lament. Sophie was reminded of the Whos coming out of their homes at Christmas in the old Grinch cartoon, except of course that instead of cheery "wahoo and dahoo," this was all "woe, oh, ah."

Sustained musical chords built in complexity as more singers came out, adding mournful notes to the chill. The song rose, rolling through the encampment and the forest, cold and damp like the fog, and even the crows and wood children seemed to fall silent as the sound permeated everything.

The reverberations of sorrow drove the others out of their sleeping bags. Verena appeared, favoring her with a neutral "Good morning" and then balancing her leg, like a ballet dancer, on a crossbar of wood while brushing her hair, preparatory to binding it into the screamingly tight ponytail she favored.

"Can I borrow that after you're through?" Sophie said, just to break the silence.

"Sure." Short word, bitten off angrily.

I shouldn't say anything, Sophie thought, but what came out was "You know that monk overstated what Parrish and I—"

"It's none of my business," Verena said.

So much for rapprochement. The men appeared, one by one, Bram wide awake, as always, with no apparent need for a transition between deep sleep and full consciousness. Then Parrish, clad in his white shirt and a pair of Bram's bike shorts. His eyes found hers just as she was taking in his bed head. He barely smiled in response. She felt a schoolgirl flutter and then, a moment later, a deeper, more internal response.

Verena broke their gaze by walking between them, proffering the hairbrush. "Your turn."

Sophie took it. "Thanks."

"There anything else of mine that you want?"

"Ahhh." She felt herself coloring. "I think I'm good."

"Yes, you sure do." Verena didn't move, just stood there between her and Parrish.

Sophie ran the brush through her curls. "I need a haircut," she said, inanely, just to make a sound.

"Done?" Verena held her hand out pointedly.

Sophie returned the brush. "I appreciate it."

"Verena," Parrish said, and she turned, rapidly, teeth all but bared. "Might I?"

"Keep it." She shoved it blindly into his hand and took off.

Tonio bit his lip. "Someone should—"

"I'll go after her," Bram said. "Garland. Will they feed us?"

"Not in any way we're likely to appreciate."

"I have protein bars," Sophie said.

"Let's resurrect the saboteur, charm the truth out of him, and get going, shall we?" Tonio said.

"Agreed," Garland said.

"Where's your governess?"

Sophie laughed. "If you'd like Brother No Name to reappear, I'm sure all Parrish and I would have to do is step into one of the cabins together."

"He crept out, late," Parrish said. "He may find sleeping under a roof uncomfortable, after living in the wild."

They repacked their things. Bram returned with Verena, who threw them all a sullen "Sorry," and went inside to sort her bags.

The chorus was wrapping up the morning etude when the monk Sophie had spoken to yesterday, named Brother Piper, approached.

"Fortunate morning to you all," he said, breaking the somber mood with a great, beaming grin that suggested that, given the slightest encouragement, he'd hug them. "How was your night?"

His Fleet accent was different from Brother No Name's—he said *nicht* for "night." His arm bore scars from some terrible long-ago accident, hooks and drag marks that had left his hand twisted so it hung backward. He had holes in his ears, marks left by piercings, jewelry he no longer wore. Not a native, Sophie deduced—he'd come from another island.

He rapped on the red lacquered crypt doors and a white-robed monk pushed them wide, letting them into a stone atrium little bigger than a cloakroom and lit by torches. The room was bare, and its floor was carved with words in a hundred or more languages. Those she recognized seemed to be words and phrases of farewell: "good-bye," "safe journey," "good luck to you." At the end of this textual carpet was a path leading down into a narrow corridor, so steep that the wooden rungs or stoppers had been hung or affixed to the stone, making of it an amalgam of staircase, ladder, and path into blackness.

She could hear Bram breathing heavily, slowly, controlling his not-so-latent claustrophobia. It wasn't usually so bad, but . . . ah, he was drawing Verena's attention, obliging her to caretake a little.

Saint Bram, taking her mind off Parrish, Sophie thought. I don't deserve you.

The air coming up from the shaft was fresh, cold, and ever so slightly wet. Cave breath, she called it: the moisture that permeated systems that lay atop fast-moving underwater rivers.

"We've had the Sylvanner brought to an audience chamber," Brother Piper said. "Follow me."

Sophie raised her light and camera, capturing the text on the floor before stepping eagerly onto the incline. The stone underfoot was slick and the passage led down a good long way—about thirty vertical feet, she estimated—then ended in a shaft that might have been a train tunnel, lined on both sides by regular round chambers, each barely illuminated.

Brother Piper managed the incline nimbly, smiling encouragement up at the others before leading them along the corridor. It was punctuated by random boulders, above and below, and he'd utter a cheery "Watch your head!" or "Mind your toes" with about every third step.

They arrived in a space that was brighter by several orders of magnitude than the corridor, dominated by a pool on the floor that appeared to be filled with bioluminescent dinoflagellates in—Sophie dipped a finger for a taste—fresh water. The glow emanated upward, bouncing off a big silver bowl, newly shined, set into the ceiling. There were candles, too, set at one-foot intervals on a ledge that encircled the chamber.

Sophie took a slow circle of the room, recording everything, before homing in on the body.

Highfelling had been laid on a carved stone couch angled much like a recliner, with a chest strap to hold him in place. Under the belt, he was clad in a long white robe. Beside him was a low table with bamboo cups of cold water and a steaming urn of what smelled like rosehip tea.

He was unmistakably dead but, as advertised, he had not decayed; the smell in the air reminded Sophie of something in a butcher's shop, meat nearing its expiration date but not quite past it. . . .

Tonio took a position as far from the corpse as he could, quietly muttering what Sophie guessed was a prayer, in Erinthian.

Brother Piper rang a bell, held his hands over the dinoflagellate pool, then washed them in a nearby basin before holding them over the body. "It is no small thing to restore the murdered," he intoned. "Who would take responsibility for such a portentous choice?"

Before Sophie could respond, Verena said, "I am the interested party here."

"You will feed Wevvan Highfelling, clothe him, take him where he wishes to go? Answer his questions, hear his travails, seek his loved ones?"

"I will."

"You will face with him the censure of the living and the wrath of those who fear the lately dead?"

Verena did a decent impression of Annela's placid Verdanii smile. "I will."

"You'll want gloves," he said, handing her a long black set. Donning a pair of his own, he produced a thick length of felt, stitched with hair to a pair of what looked like human ribs, or what human ribs would look like if they had been straightened from their natural curve.

"The deceased, Wevvan Highfelling born of Sylvanna, rejected the nation of his birth and never took another. His resurrection is encumbered by no request or law. He has no surviving family and left no will. Does anyone stand in opposition to this fell deed?"

"Fell," Sophie thought. Now there's a word out of Tolkien.

"Speak now or forever hold your peace."

Bram whuffed softly at that, probably hiding a reaction to the misplaced wedding-ceremony language.

Brother Piper turned to Verena, nodding, and she yarded on the two rib bones, stretching the fabric between. Crimson words appeared on the fabric, neat embroidered stitches that pulled at the felt, resisting the pressure.

The shredding sound filled the room, a raspy tearing, as of ships' sails or machine belts. A stench of boiled blood and sour mash, cabbagey and rotten, gusted out from Verena's outstretched hands. Tonio gagged, quietly. The monk had a wet towel at the ready, and he grabbed at the remnants of the inscription, which were wet and suddenly stringy.

Like guts, Sophie thought randomly.

Sophie looked at Highfelling. He had been quiet as a waxwork figure, with that strange absence, almost fakeness, that the dead possessed.

Now he was breathing.

The corpse opened his eyes and began to cough. He accepted a glass of water from Brother Piper before falling back against his seat, looking from one of them to another.

Choking awfulness all but overcame her. She remembered being on a dive once with a student videographer whose oxygen supply had failed, and that *oh no, oh no, please stop this from happening* feeling. Then, and now, it was an almost physical sensation, like having a stomach full of fresh blood.

"Do you know where you are, Kir?" Piper asked. His face was drawn but his tone was kind.

"No . . . ," Highfelling began, but before he could say more a number of things happened, all at once.

"I stand opposed!" shrieked a teakettle falsetto that rang off the chamber walls. "There's no making peace with this!"

Parrish turned, saw *something,* and yanked both Sophie and Verena sideways, pressing them against the cave wall. Candle flame cooked her neck on one side; his breath warmed the skin on the other.

Something whisked past them.

A javelin caught Highfelling in the chest, piercing his heart.

"Uhhh!" His eyes bulged. Blood spread across his white robe.

The sense of awfulness broke, like thin glass. Suddenly Highfelling was a man, mortally wounded, suffering.

Sophie disentangled herself from Parrish, running to the stone chaise. "I'm sorry, I'm so sorry. We didn't mean to—"

"*Hes,* it's best," the man said, speaking in a thicker version of Cly's Fleet accent. "LoBanning?"

"Uh . . ." Did he mean was she a Banning? "Sort of."

"Seek my . . . plans."

A glugging exhalation, and he was dead. Again.

Leaving them with a profusely bleeding corpse and Brother No Name.

Brother Piper seized the monk by the scruff. "What have you done?"

"Sorry I'm late," he whistled. "Brother Stinking Stodgepot wouldn't let me into the crypt, so I had to climb up from the weasel hole where the water pours out the mountain."

CHAPTER 26

After the second murder of Highfelling, Brother Piper hauled Nameless out to the compound. By the time he returned, two younger monks had appeared and were already shrouding the body in a long, heavy wrap. They took the gory shreds of the spell that had killed him initially and the javelin that did the deed the second time.

"We're going to be arguing about his action for some weeks," Piper said. "I'm so sorry."

"What happened?" Bram demanded.

Piper said, "Resurrection is an issue of contention among the brothers. Brother Pict—the nameless brother, that is—tried to enter the crypt last night but was barred. There's disagreement there, too. Anyone who wishes to object to a resurrection should be given a chance."

"Why wasn't he?"

"The brother is . . . he's very holy. Devout. His commitment to the penitential duty of the island is extreme. But he's also . . ." He opened his hands. "Ahhh . . ."

"A pain in the ass?" Bram offered.

"We are men, flawed and petty like any," Brother Piper said. "The brother has become a thing of the forest; he comes and goes as he pleases. He offended the night keeper and was barred. Then, as he said, he found his own way into the tomb through the sewer."

"I bear some responsibility," Parrish said. "We tried to hide our purpose, but—"

"There are no secrets in a tomb," Piper said. "Kirs, are you all right? It's a troubling thing, to witness a revivification and then—"

"A murder?" Bram snapped.

From his expression, Piper didn't quite see it that way, but he spread his hands, acknowledging Bram's words.

Sophie was surprisingly unstirred by having seen Highfelling stabbed. The feeling of awfulness that accompanied his waking, tense and lurking wrong, had seemed to fill the room, choking and lethal as smoke. It was only when he'd been fatally wounded that she'd felt able to approach, much less speak to him.

But now they were back to square one with Cly.

Or were they? "He had things, didn't he?" she said. "Someone . . . Langda said the evidence from his murder was here."

"Yes. I'll have his possessions brought," Brother Piper said. He vanished immediately into the crypt and, about fifteen minutes later, four younger men came in bearing a quartet of heavy trunks with smashed locks.

"*Seggin bale,*" Parrish said to them, in a tone that hinted that this was monkish for "thank you."

They stared at each other over the trunks. Then Bram yanked at the nearest lid. Its stonewood hinges crumbled and the lid came off in his hand.

Sophie pried hers open more carefully. It contained a bundle of letters, all in Fleet. She browsed them, finding correspondence among the Haversham Crime Office, The Fleet Judiciary, and Brother Piper's predecessor, the managing brother of the crypt here in Ossuary.

She read one page aloud: " 'He died suddenly, falling to his knees in the garden in his hiding place on Zingoasis, bending backwards in an impossible fashion.' "

"Like John Coine," Bram murmured.

"Yeah," she said, remembering. Two captured prisoners gasping, helpless, eyes bulging. Twin death rattles . . .

"Sofe?"

She returned her attention to the letter: "Highfelling died about a week after Cly's duel with Cordero. The Judiciary had named him as a possible witness in the ongoing dispute with Haversham."

"The throttlevine thing," Bram said.

She picked through the next batch of pages. "The next is just delivery arrangements, getting him here. The scroll Verena just shredded"—she, Tonio, and Verena all shuddered "—turned up years later in a . . . I guess you'd call it a raid? On some kind of rogue inscription house?"

"Yeah." Verena peered over her shoulder. "The scribe might know who hired him to kill Highfelling."

Sophie handed over the pages. "It says the scribe was reverted to the innocence of childhood."

"That means he had an accomplice wipe his memory," she said. "Pretty typical if you're afraid of getting interrogated."

"So much for that." Bram was going through a trunk of clothes and shoes, methodically checking the pockets of the garments and then handing them to Parrish, who felt along the seams, checking for . . . what? Diamonds? Cocaine?

He came up with Highfelling's Sylvanner sash, faded to no color at all, with all its badges.

"He was married—we could follow that up," Bram said.

"Piper said his kin were dead," Sophie replied.

"Ha. Strike two."

The third crate held an assortment of satchels, inside which were carved pieces of clockwork: gears and curled wooden springs and other pieces that were, unmistakably, machinery, under a layer of oily dust. They gleamed with a strange luminescence, as if they'd been varnished in gasoline.

"Same stuff as these hinges," Bram said, indicating the remnants of the trunk he'd torn in half. "And swords."

"Stonewood," Parrish explained. "The varnishing process makes it hard enough to use for machine parts."

"Parts of what?" Bram was already fitting the pieces of their find together.

"Plans," Sophie said. "Highfelling said, 'Find my plans.'" She dove back into the now-empty trunks, looking for anything that might look like blueprints, coming up dry. "Parrish, take a look at the linings of his coat and whatever, will you?"

"We've done so, Sophie."

Highfelling had no notebook, no papers of his own, no letters but the official correspondence concerning his murder.

Think. Sophie leaned deep into the largest trunk, comparing outer height and inner depth, and pushed at the corners. The bottom shifted. False?

She pried it up. Underneath were a leather tobacco pouch and a rolled oil painting of the Butcher's Baste, the passage of water between Sylvanna and Haversham, a beach washed in ghostly whites and grays.

"They do love to paint on Sylvanna," Tonio said.

Sophie looked at the back of the canvas and then held it up to the torch-light. Lines shone through the thin fabric.

"Blueprints," she said. They unrolled it over the illuminated pool. The room dimmed, but the drawings emerged.

"Looks like an old-fashioned watch," Verena said. "Gears and cogs."

"Bigger," Bram said.

"Some kind of automaton," Sophie said. The plans hidden within the painting showed a faint schematic of what looked like a clockwork toy, four-limbed, low to the ground, almost a dinner plate with legs. An animal?

She shot it twice, taking long exposures to compensate for the dimness of the lines. Her brother looked at it fixedly. After about a minute, he said, "Okay, I've got it."

"Got it what?" Verena said.

"Memorized." He stirred through the bits and pieces of machinery, the cogs of stonewood. "We're missing some parts, not to mention all the cosmetic finishes, but I can put this about halfway together. Verena, give me those paddles—they're its feet."

Sophie returned to her examination of their other finds.

Why hide your smokes? She opened the pouch, which smelled of pipe tobacco. Inside were coarse-haired seedpods, dried to a nearly brown color. Some were embedded in desiccated bits of fruit, rubbery material that smelled of pear.

"I've seen these before; I think they're throttlevine seeds," she said.

"Cly's vegetable nemesis," Bram said. "Are you sure?"

"We'll have to germinate a couple."

Sophie thought of the transformed slaves in the swamp. "All those years ago, Cly had been trying to prove the Havers were sabotaging the Sylvanna lowlands. If this means they're guilty, it's partly Haversham's fault, those goat-people being forced to spend their lives gnawing at the infestation."

I'll remember this, she vowed.

Fenn thought Cly might get rid of his slaves, if the throttlevine infestation was sorted. He hinted as much himself—when Sophie said slavery was a deal breaker, he had asked what would happen if he got rid of them.

"Sold," he said "sold."

It implies he really wants a relationship.

She had no actual evidence that he'd slept with one of the slaves. And she'd been wrong about his betrothing her.

This was a way to test some assumptions about Cly, wasn't it? To find out how far he'd go to make things up with her? If he didn't need the goat transforms, would he really divest the slaves at Low Bann? If she demanded that, and asked that he let Beatrice slide out of the fraud suit . . . how much did this case, and his daughter, really mean to him?

As Sophie gnawed on the problem of her birth father, Bram assembled the machine pieces within the plate that was their case. He stirred a gear around in a circle and the four paddles made a lazy flapping motion, in sync.

"That looks familiar."

"There are chambers here in the top plate that could hold a quantity of seedpods," Bram said.

"It's a delivery system," she said. "It's how they're infecting the lowlands with throttlevine. This might do it, Verena—Cly wants this case won."

"More than he wants Mom?"

"Have to prove it," Bram said. By which he meant: *I'm working, shut up.*

They did, watching him fiddle with the various parts, working for so long that Parrish vanished, returning with a tray containing bowls of tasteless whitefish soup. Sophie photographed every stage. Verena fell into playing mechanic's assistant, handing him pieces and keeping quiet.

"It is afternoon," Tonio said, finally, when Bram came up for air and soup. "Unless we want to spend a second night here . . ."

"I'll wrap up," Bram said immediately.

"Let's see if the monks decided to do anything to punish Brother No Name," Verena said.

They hadn't. He'd whistled his way through an aggrieved complaint about having done the moral thing, sermonizing about the wrong of raising the dead. Half the monks clearly agreed. And when it turned out that the stuff in the trunks had proved useful to Sophie and the others—the rest looked tempted to call "no harm, no foul."

One of them even castigated Brother Piper for authorizing the resurrection without sifting through the evidence first.

"It's not a bad point," Sophie said.

"We may as well pack up and leave," Parrish said. "They'll be arguing about this for years."

"*Bene*," Tonio said brightly. "They could use a break in the tedium."

Parrish pealed laughter, a bright and joyous sound that earned him glares from the monks as it echoed off the monuments and the walls.

"Let's go home," he said, meaning *Nightjar,* and Sophie felt happiness burst through her at the mere thought.

CHAPTER 27

They got down the mountain without getting eaten by specters—the insects were another story—and were aboard ship soon after. Fortunately the medic, Watts, had approved of the cat or perhaps been approved by it. He had packed up his pharmacy and moved into the doctor's cabin while they were gone, and now he was ready and waiting to slather a sweet-smelling oil on their bites, a minty unguent that killed the itch.

By nightfall they had put Parrish's boyhood home, stone skulls, crows, and all, most positively in the rearview. The specter skulls seemed to watch them go. Their eye sockets and mouths were edged in bioluminescence—giving the impression of a hundred feline somethings staring after them, hungrily, as they took an easterly course under a sluggish wind.

Bram had re-created a copy of Highfelling's schematic from memory, then checked it meticulously against the images Sophie had taken in the waking chamber. Now he was working on building the automaton, molding pieces from clay to reconstruct the parts he didn't have to hand.

The general shape and the specific locomotive heave of the automaton's paddles made it clear soon enough that the thing was meant to pass for one of the turtles who turned up annually on the Sylvanna beaches to lay their eggs. The hollow chambers in the casing were indeed for throttlevine seeds—Sophie sprouted samples easily, preserving them as evidence.

"Will it be enough to convince His Honor he can resolve the case?" Verena had stopped sulking, instead taking to hanging around helping every minute.

"Knowing the delivery system should make it possible to stop the sabotage. We'll trade that much information for a promise to get the goat transforms out of the swamp." Sophie looked down at their makeshift turtle and frowned. "As for winning the case—this is just another circumstantial thing to add to the argument . . . it's not proof. What objections would a lawyer raise if we gave him this? We have to answer them all."

"We need to figure out why the Sylvanners never found one on their shoreline. They've been pulling it off for decades."

"No windup toy's going to swim eighteen nautical miles," Bram said. "And it doesn't appear to be magical."

"The plans said nothing about enchanting them. Anyway, they're generic objects—they wouldn't have names."

"So they're releasing them in the water close to the Sylvanna shore."

"The passage between Sylvanna and Haversham is heavily guarded," Parrish said. "In case of slave escapes."

"There are lights ashore and patrols asea," Sophie agreed. "Plus the rocks and navigational hazards. But if it's a patrol ship releasing the automatons . . . I mean, they must know how to avoid their own defenses."

"You studied the Baste, didn't you?" Verena asked.

Parrish nodded. "I meant to race its intervals, before I was expelled from Fleet."

"So we build a case," Sophie said. "We have to document where they're dropping them off, how they're making it to shore, and what happens to them after."

"I have a theory about why they never found a fake turtle," Verena said. She tapped the mix of throttlevine seeds. "Most of these are tucked into a piece of dried fruit, right? So that animals will eat them and carry them into the swamp?"

"Right."

"But here's a chamber just for seeds. The ones not wrapped in a tasty bit of fruit would stay with the original gadget, wouldn't they?" She lifted one of the spare cogs.

"That follows," Sophie agreed.

Verena tapped the cog against the wooden table, making a sharp *clonk*. "Stormwrack has almost no iron or refined metals. Stonewood varnish inscriptions come from Layparee. The pieces are hard, but once the glaze breaks, they fall apart pretty quick. I've been thinking about that trunk Bram destroyed. Throttlevine's got those tough little roots—"

"Genius!" Sophie said. Verena flushed with pleasure. "So the vine grows around the turtle's remnants, the glaze gets cracked by the root system, and soon it's just a pile of biomatter at the base of a throttlevine plant."

"Good in theory," Bram said. "It still isn't proof."

"Ah, but this theory we can test," she said. "We've already germinated two of the pods. Now we just add bits of stonewood to the pots. We watch the plant grow—we've got time—and document the degradation. Verena can sign the notes every day. You're official enough for that, right?"

"I got the shiny badge," she agreed.

They were at sea for ten days before the first new throttlevine root cracked the glaze on the first gear. Sophie cut it free of the plant and added the piece to her growing supply of bagged evidence. A second sample they left, continuing to document the decay of the stonewood gear.

It became apparent almost immediately that Verena's sudden shift to a bright and perky be-everywhere, do-everything demeanor was a new stratagem for keeping Sophie and Parrish from further dating.

The grown-up thing to do would be to tell Verena she was sorry she was hurting but to back the hell off. But after the long stretch of sulking, Sophie couldn't bear another reversal, and she didn't want more hurt feelings. Parrish apparently felt the same—he kept his distance.

But she couldn't leave it alone. Who could?

Finally she slid a note under the hatch to his cabin: *I don't know what you mean by courting.*

By breakfast the next day, Bram had his model finished.

"It descends slowly, carried by the current," he was saying. "At a depth of about fifteen feet, water pressure compresses the midsection, here." He pressed on his model and they heard a click. "This starts the clockwork."

The automaton rolled its flippers forward, inching itself across the galley table toward a bowl of deep-fried fish balls. The ferret, which had been cadging small bites from the safety of Verena's lap, startled and then put out a paw, as if it thought it might rap the device on its carved head.

Bram shut off the mechanism, stilling the gadget. "The automaton then begins to swim for shore. Presumably it's part of a crowd, since they're doing this at laying time. They're somewhat lighter than the actual turtles, so they'd be near the top of the . . . what's the collective noun, Sofe?"

"Dule. A dule of turtles."

"So they ride in piggyback?"

"I'd think if it was right in, swimming with the hundreds, it'd get knocked around and damaged."

"My guess is it swims above the rest, at least until they're pretty close to the beach."

He reached across the table, snagged her book of notes, and doodled a bunch of turtles breaching the water. The automaton, styled with head bolts, like Frankenstein, was riding on the backs of the thousands of individuals scrabbling onto the sand.

Sophie touched the doodle thoughtfully. Bram was one of those people who could sketch in fonts.

"This is all conjecture," he said. "Without an intact sample, we can't be sure."

"No," Verena said. "We'll have to figure out the currents—where they're being released to meet up with the dule."

"I can work that out," Parrish said.

"So you do remember the chart?"

He nodded.

"As for all this conjecture," Sophie said, "what if we dress it up a little?"

"What are you going to do," Verena said, "build a Powerpoint presentation?"

"Basically, yeah." She dug out the second notebook she'd bought weeks ago. It was blank, filled with a collection of now-pressed leaves she'd collected on Sylvanna. She transferred the samples to the book of questions, freeing up the blank notebook, and told them what she had in mind. "Would you mind, Bram?"

"Something to do while we sail east, right?" Bram said, cheerfully enough.

"Would it hold up in court?" Verena said.

"There are no solid standards of proof," Sophie said.

"Yet."

"Still, this doesn't constitute evidence," she said.

"Yeah, but if we dress everything up right, make it glitzy, the Havers might settle the case."

"True." Sophie nodded. "But I don't want to fool around with just bluffing. We'll dress it up because the courts don't respect facts, but we want them to start respecting facts. More importantly, so does Cly. The point is to buy off Cly, remember? Free Beatrice, get the goat transforms out of the swamp?"

Verena frowned. "How are you gonna do that?"

"*We.* Cly was all for having me set up a Stormwrack Institute of Forensics. Here be science, hear us roar! So we write up a charter. Make it pretty enough, I bet they'd accord us just as much legitimacy as the astrologers."

Verena chortled.

"Could you write the document?" Sophie said. "Do the legalese?"

"If we figured out basic principles, I guess. Those would be about the difference between proof and . . . making assertions?"

"Documented experiments, reproducible results." Sophie nodded. "Annela and Cly would slice through the red tape on approving us, wouldn't they?"

"In a second, if it benefited them."

"All well and good, Sofe," Bram said. "But even with a charter, the plans, and this model . . . that's not enough."

"Agreed," Parrish said. "If you want absolute proof, we'll need a clockwork turtle."

"I know."

"Then what's the point?" Verena threw up her hands. "Where are we supposed to get that?"

"That's where I come in," Sophie said. "Bram makes the presentation, you write up a forensic institute charter, and I catch an automaton in the Baste."

There was a silence. Then Parrish got to his feet. "We'll need fair winds to make the turtle migration."

He brushed past her on his way up to the ladder that led to the sailing deck. Touching her hand briefly, he left a piece of paper tucked into her palm.

She felt a ludicrous buzz of delight.

Verena was contemplating the half-made turtle, which looked less like an animal and more like a serving tray for a frozen entrée, full of clock parts and surrounded by the breakfast dishes. Her face had fallen out of its wilfully perky cast and was pensive. Bram was already doing preliminary sketches.

"Excuse me," Sophie said, ignoring a stab of guilt as she ducked out so she could unfold her note.

It read: *I hardly know what I mean by courting myself. Issle Morta, as you may have divined, does not encourage what you call pair bonding. What do you do on Erstwhile?*

Oh yeah, Sophie thought. Dinner and a movie should be easy to pull off on a seventy-foot boat with a heartbroken teenage chaperone.

Verena was, even now, headed up to the sailing deck to join Parrish.

She went back to her cabin, hunting up another scrap of paper. *Usually dating involves cafés and restaurants and entertainments. Long walks in the park, hand-holding.* She felt a thrill, under her skin, and found herself remembering a dozen TV shows about kids at drive-ins in the fifties. Kids cuddling, making out . . .

Oh, this was crazy.

She was, nevertheless, beaming when she folded the note in the pocket of her sweater and went back up.

The crew had raised all three sails and the jib, and the ship was running fast. Sophie got the speed from Tonio, at the helm, and converted it from Fleet units into about ten knots.

"What if we don't make it?"

"Wait a year?"

"Suboptimal," she said. "No. We'll have to conduct a search on Turtle Beach, after the migration, a search for automaton parts."

Prowling a heavily patroled, ecologically sensitive beach. Rees's ecologically sensitive beach at that. She remembered Rees trying to intervene before she embarrassed herself at the festival.

Parrish walking up, just as she was telling the assembled Sylvanners she was hugely promiscuous.

I wonder if that's why it took him so long to make his move?

Cringing inwardly, she touched the note in her pocket.

Verena and Parrish were climbing the rigging, deep in conversation.

"I gather there's a plan?" Tonio asked.

She nodded.

"*Bene.* Feels good to have wind in our sails. A little race. *Miamadre,* forgive me, these last few months have been dull. I've missed being in danger."

"I don't know there's much danger," she said. "Compared to last time, anyway. All we have to do is work out where they're dropping the clockwork turtles."

"And what? Scoop one out of the water within view of the vessel that launched it?"

"Oh. Good point."

The cat, Banana, chose that moment to climb out on deck. Watts had been giving it treats packed with fish oil and herbs, and it was filling out. There was a shine to the tabby's coat, though his ears hadn't outgrown their peculiarities. One was permanently mashed forward, the other back, giving him a pugilistic appearance. He shoved his head against Sophie's hand and began to purr like a little freight train.

"You should write to His Honor," Tonio said.

"Should I?"

"Tell him you expect to have something worth trading. We'll reach Sylvanna days ahead of the Fleet. He could spend that time expediting your mother's release."

"If he will."

"You could update Kir Gracechild while you're at it."

"I'll leave that to Verena." They had to come up with an official-looking forensic institute charter anyway.

Tonio pursed his lips. "Verena is no Gale Feliachild."

"Yet! She's seventeen. Was Gale born good at all this?"

He looked faintly surprised. "How old should she be?"

"Come on, when did you start working?"

"I took up sailing as a second career at fifteen. Before that, I helped keep the books in my family store."

"Seriously?"

"The nations of the Fleet aren't the outlands," Tonio said. "On Erinth, one is expected to make oneself useful."

"At home, if a lovestruck seventeen-year-old behaves stupidly, you give them time to get over it."

He shrugged. "Verena has chosen being a Fleetwoman over being outlandish. Now she must sail that course."

Sophie felt a pang: that made it sound so simple. "As a rude, crude outlander myself," she murmured, changing the subject, "I might ask what info you went seeking on Issle Morta."

"A necessary and terrible burden," he whispered, then seemed to catch himself. "One I may yet share with you."

"May?"

"Do you need another burden at present, Kir?" He smiled. "Give it some thought."

She squeezed his shoulder affectionately, then climbed up the rigging to join Verena and Parrish. The exercise was gratifying: the strength she'd spent all those months building was there at her beck and call. "What are we looking at?"

"Watching for sea specters," Parrish said.

"Orcas," Verena translated.

She turned her eye to the water. They were well east of Mount Rainier now, sailing over what should have been Nebraska. Was the corpse of the state below them—highways, bones, and buildings, sheet glass and I-beams, all submerged and waiting?

She'd have to read up on underwater archaeology techniques. If anything of Erstwhile could be found after millions of years, it might be fossilized in sedimentary layers under the depths.

She imagined splitting a couple layers of shale and finding a Coke bottle or tire treads between them. It was an oddly depressing thought.

"There!" Parrish pointed. What broke the water wasn't an orca but a sea lion, first one and then dozens, a whole curse of sea lions racing eastward.

The orcas would be in pursuit, then, she guessed, and in time the sea revealed them, a pod back behind the flashes of brown fur, both species arcing through the water as they exchanged old air for new, their bodies breaking the surface.

Sophie touched the note in her pocket. It was gone.

Parrish twinkled at her from nearby.

She found a reply in her cabin that night. *Three bells,* it suggested. *In the hold?*

When else would they date but when Verena was finally asleep?

She lay awake and agitated until the appointed time, then made her way down, fifteen minutes early, flinching at every thump and creak of wood.

Parrish was waiting, laying out a small meal on a tablecloth he had draped over a trunk. It was simple fare—a few of the savory breads that closed out each meal, a sliced sausage. Two marionettes lay to one side.

"Puppets?" She kept her voice low.

"You mentioned entertainment."

"You're gonna entertain me?"

"We might entertain each other—what is it?"

"Nothing," she said, knowing she'd cracked another huge smile and hoping it didn't look too lascivious.

"It's the best we can do, under the circumstances."

Sophie sighed. "The best we can do is be honest with Verena."

"I have discussed this with her."

"On the hike up to the monastery? So that is why she was so pissed?"

"Her distress has been building for some time. Losing Gale, then struggling to fill her shoes. I always believed she would outgrow her infatuation with . . . that she'd find someone."

"Before you did?" She sat, picked up a slice of sausage in one hand and a marionette—a sailor—in the other. She fiddled with making it dance.

He picked up the second, a lady—from the hair—in Fleet uniform, maneuvering it through a low bow.

What to say? Her mind churned up possibilities: *Tell me about your affair with Langda Pike, what'll you do if Verena gets fired, does Annela really think I'm a spy?*

Parrish looked similarly at a loss for a topic.

They covered it by concentrating on the marionettes. Sophie tried to copy Parrish's bow, then dance-hopped over to the uniformed woman. She managed to lay her marionette's hand on his.

Their eyes met and Sophie suddenly decided that petting by proxy was not enough.

I'm allowed to want things.

She set the puppet aside, wiped her fingers on her napkin and stood, skirting the makeshift table. Imitating the marionette's abrupt movement, she caught at Parrish's hand.

A little jolt ran through him, and a muscle twitched in his cheek.

Don't overthink this, she told herself, but as she stepped closer she felt it again, some stiffness, a sense of hesitation.

"Do you think I'm a slut?" The question rose, unbidden, to her lips. Parrish's jaw dropped.

"I—"

"I wouldn't necessarily blame you. I mean, I had that fling with Lais Dariach, and—"

"I may have envied Kir Dariach a little."

"That's weirdly gracious of you."

"It is . . ." He seemed to founder. "It is Verdanii custom to have numerous—"

"You're okay with me having *numerous*?"

"No!"

Why was she pursuing this?

He bit his plummy lips. "Is that what you want? Many lovers?"

She shook her head emphatically. "Wow, this is so not first-date conversation. This is sleepless, middle of the night after the third time we—"

She barely managed to run that sentence aground. From the look on his face, Parrish had followed her thought just fine.

"Don't you just have some kind of out-of-the-box boyfriend-girlfriend, spend-time-together, discover-if-we're-compatible kind of customs?"

"Compatible. Are you talking about pheromones again?"

"Why does that bug you? We should be Tru Luv Always, like Corsetta and Rashad?"

"I—" Then he said, "You must feel, at the least, some emotional pull?"

Jeez, now he's broken out a can of extra prissy.

"All I asked is aren't there any see-if-it-works, give-it-a-try, don't-date-anyone-else-in-the-meantime relationships here?"

He nodded stiffly. "If that's what you want."

Now her temper, unaccountably, was rising. "Yeah, put it all on me. What do you want, Parrish?"

"I do. Want." He swallowed. "You."

"You seem pretty damned unhappy about that. Is it guilt? Over Verena's crush on you?"

"No. It's unfortunate, but . . ."

This was silly, Sophie realized. The government might well pack her off home whether she did or didn't get Beatrice out of the jam she was in. She'd lost her feather-light claim on Stormwrack citizenship, and getting to know Cly had been a bust. Now this thing with Parrish was alienating the only remaining biological relative she'd found who'd shown any interest in getting to know her.

I should declare this a mistake and go back to bed, she thought, but instead she just stood there, fists clenched, feeling just about ready to hit him. "Well?"

Parrish was visibly struggling for control. "I have a hunch this isn't first-date talk, either."

"Tell me what's wrong, Parrish, please."

He sat, reached for one of the puppets, and frowned at his hand. It was—no, he wasn't trembling, he couldn't be. "I am guilty."

"Not over Verena."

"When your aunt Gale was born, her relations worked an intention on her; the Verdanii Allmother wanted to know her future."

"This is the thing about how she was supposed to be murdered."

He looked surprised.

"The old onionskin guy mentioned it, remember? It was predicted at her birth?"

"Who else has discussed this with you?" Sharp tone now.

"Nobody. Jeez!"

Again, he seemed to need time to master himself. "It was something of a self-fulfilling prophecy. Gale's parents scripped her inconspicuous, to lower her profile."

"Make her less of a target?"

"It made her perfect for a career in espionage. Where the hazards are considerable, obviously."

Sophie fought an urge to actually wring her hands. Whatever she'd expected, it wasn't one of Parrish's long and wayward parables. She was acutely stressed. And he, he was fighting to bring this . . . whatever this was to the surface. It was like he was vomiting glass.

"When she first set out on *Nightjar,* the ship was captained by a fellow named Royl Sloot. From Tallon, not that it matters." A faint, pained smile. "I'm not sure what's wrong with me. What's your Anglay word? Babbling."

"About Sloot," Sophie said, just to break in.

"None of her family expected Gale to live to adulthood. Once she joined the Watch . . . well, of course she wouldn't see her twentieth birthday. Her twenty-fifth. Her thirtieth."

"But she did."

"The fetes kept coming. Her idea had been that Captain Sloot would be there, when it happened, when she was—" He swallowed.

"Was killed." It had been so fast. The mezmers breaking in through the balcony of the apartment in Erinth, the brawl, the stink of them. Gale's neck, snapping—

Okay, stop crying, just listen to him.

"Sloot retired," Parrish said, as if this were the saddest thing that had ever befallen anyone. She could almost hear violins in the background. "Gale was in good health, still working, and so far, no murder."

She wiped her face. What was wrong with her? "And so—you."

"Me." His eyes were swimming. "Sophie, I—"

This was crazy. She kissed him.

It was a good move, as far as it went: her Ping-Ponging emotions slammed over into lust and he grabbed her almost roughly in response. Their lips locked, tongues met, and there was real heat there—

Rattling at the hatch made them both jump apart, guilty as killers standing over a body. Bram leaned in from the deck above, taking in the tablecloth and puppets.

"Jeez," he said. "I'm sorry."

"Not at all." Parrish drew in a shuddery breath that was almost a sob. "Join us?"

"What, for your intimate tête-à-tête in the basement?"

"It's called the hold. What do you want?" Sophie said, feeling enraged and bitchy. "Are you seasick again?"

"I heard something."

"Like us *talking*?" She emphasized the "talking."

"You're not quiet, you know," he said. "But no. Music. Don't you hear it?"

"Teeth!" Parrish was suddenly in motion, running past her to the ladder, climbing past Bram hastily. "All hands on deck, all hands on deck! Sound the alarm!"

A bell began to toll.

"So," Bram said, into the clamor, "Good date?"

"I asked if he thought I was a slut, he countered with the Commitment Talk—"

"Never your best event, traditionally."

"Shut up. It all segued into the history of Gale's career in the Fleet, complete with prenatal death threats from beyond."

"Yeah, it looked like a history lesson."

"Keep it up. I'll leave a cockroach in your bunk." She was more irritated than was reasonable.

"Nice. Very mature, Ducks."

"You need to stop—"

Now she could hear it, too, the high-pitched, sweet, and faintly metallic chord she had taken for imaginary violin music. It was wordless, almost a combination of human choir and the call of cicadas. The whole crew was tramping up to the sailing deck. Parrish was shouting, "All hands on deck, now, *now!*"

"Guess he means us, too."

They were practically the last up the ladder. Tonio had an upbeat, roguish look to him. He tipped Sophie a wink and leered, just a little, at Bram.

Sophie felt the change as soon as she hit the open air. Her horror over Gale's murder freshened, like a scab torn off a recent wound, and at the same time her desire for Parrish notched up to an intensity that bordered on the painful. The knife's edge of stress about how pointless and stupid it would be to pursue anything with him got worse, as did the heat of how much she wanted to.

That feeling of being torn, wanting to be here on Stormwrack without hurting her parents or abandoning San Francisco, battered her like a typhoon.

"Are you kidding me?" Bram said. "You have sirens here?"

Parrish and Watts were going from crew member to crew member, peering into their eyes, grilling them, rapid-fire questions in a mixture of languages.

"Find Verena, Sophie," Parrish said. "Find her now."

"There." Tonio pointed. She'd climbed the rigging again and was edging out across the mainsail's top spar.

Sophie scrambled after her.

Her sister was atop the mainsail, hanging out over the edge, looking down at the black waters.

"Verena, you okay?" In the light thrown by the ship's lamps, Sophie saw faces in the water—round, lamprey-like mouths, faces that reminded her of the Chinese dragons that danced every Lunar New Year in Chinatown celebrations.

"Leave me alone!"

"You showed me these," she said, "in the pet market in Fleet. They were the size of fingers."

The animals surrounding them were as big as beluga whales, with huge, lash-fringed eyes the color of citrine, and sharp teeth. Some waited just below the surface, barely visible. As she watched, one rose, frothily clearing its blowhole before adding another note to the hum.

"I was five when they told me," Verena said. "I was going into kindergarten. My best friend from play school was moving to Australia and I was heartbroken. Mom and Gale brought me here. Forget Sally, they said. This is your sailing ship, that's her captain. . . ." Her voice trailed off. "My mom says I'm special. What a joke, right?"

"Verena," Sophie said. "The siren things are messing with your head."

"They're called bevvies."

"They're dialing up our emotions, aren't they?" Sophie edged closer. Verena's eyes flicked to her feet.

I need to bring her toward me, not away. Make her mad, not sad.

"I knew it was pointless," Verena said. "I've always known. But as long as Garland didn't care about anyone else, I could imagine . . . pretend. Now here's you: older, prettier, smarter. And a Feliachild. The whole package, practically custom-made. Bam, look at him. Smitten."

"Not true," Sophie said. She looked down at Parrish. He had three of the crew tied and was doing something to block their ears with cotton. "We're attracted, sure, but—"

"Gale was dead five minutes after he first laid eyes on you!"

Sophie felt the shock of the accusation—hurt, defensiveness, guilt, and all of it enhanced by the song pounding at all her membranes—before she realized it didn't make sense. "What?"

"You're the one. Fall in love and Gale meets her doom. That's what the Allmother told him."

"You don't believe in predestination."

Gale said, she said if I came back to Stormwrack I'd bring down doom on all my kin. . . .

Beatrice in jail, Gale dead. Now, thanks to the bevvies, Verena was suicidal.

She meant Cly. Gale didn't want Cly to find out about me, it wasn't some magical fate thing, it was just the law. . . .

"I knew she was supposed to get murdered, but I thought . . . you know. The other nations of the Fleet think the Verdanii are cracked when it comes to prophecy. But Annela showed me both transcripts. . . ."

Three of the *Nightjar* sailors stretched a ratty-looking fishing net off the starboard side.

"'Gale will be safe until Parrish loses his heart,'" she quoted, bitterly.

The crew's trying to clear a little space in case Verena jumps, Sophie guessed. It wouldn't be enough. The bevvies were too agile.

She could easily imagine the creatures devouring Verena if she fell or jumped. The image cleared her head a little.

What would Cly say? He was always pretty infuriating. "What, precisely, is this tantrum getting you?"

Verena's head whipped round, snakelike, and her grip on the rigging tightened.

Man, yeah! Managed the patronizing tone pretty good there. "Perhaps if you fling yourself overboard and get devoured, Garland will realize he's made a terrible mistake?"

"Shut up, Sophie."

"Ooh! And Annela will give you a posthumous medal?"

Okay, kid, you're supposed to be running across the spar now to deck me. She was out of mean comments. She tried to adopt Cly's puzzled, *How are you so dumb and still breathing?* expression.

For a second, Verena stood there, quivering like an electrified squirrel on a high wire. Then she whisked her sword out of its scabbard and came at her.

Oops, bad strategy, forgot the bladed weapon.

But at least Verena was off the edge of the spar now. If she fell, she'd either hit the rigging or the deck. Suboptimal, but she didn't look like she was thinking of flinging herself into the sea anymore.

"We were fine before you came," she hissed. "Now Gale's dead and Cly Banning has Mom jailed. Garland's head over frigging heels—"

"Gale's not my fault!"

"She was safe until he fell in love."

"He's not—"

"And for what? Garland's just another notch on your bedpost. Crook your finger, that guy Lais jumps into your pants. You just assumed you'd gotten engaged on Sylvanna—"

"Yeah, and that was such a barrel of fun." She was getting angry. "Know any five-year-olds, Verena?"

Verena's overwide brown eyes, so like her own, were just inches away. "What?"

"Your neighborhood, in Bernal. Pretty family-oriented, right? Any little kids?"

"So?"

"Any first-grader boys you might consider dating, say in twelve years' time?"

"It's different here."

"Really? It's that different?" She leaned in a little, and Verena did withdraw the blade before it could cut her. For just an instant, Sophie felt a terrible urge to give her a shove. "You sent Garland after us when Lais and I were—"

"Slutting it up?"

"You invited that woman Langda aboard *Nightjar* because you hoped I'd get jealous."

Damn, this is dumb, it's the critters. I gotta dial this down, gotta calm us both.

She whispered through gritted teeth, "Listen. I've never managed to make a relationship work for even eighteen months."

The change of direction caught Verena before she could reply: her mouth opened, and she looked quizzical.

"So," Sophie finished, "chances are good you're gonna get another shot."

An edgy laugh. Then, bursting into tears, Verena sheathed her sword.

To the stern, the school of bevvies was surfacing, one after another, wailing.

Despair rolled through her. *Gale died because Parrish fell for me? That's just—if it's true and they can predict the future then the future is fixed and I had no choice. And if it's not and it was just a coincidence, but oh jeez, what if Gale died and Parrish thought: That does it, Sophie's the one I must be in love with, and deep down he doesn't even—*

Stop it, it's the bevvies, just the weird effect of the bevvies—

She reeled Verena into a hug, just in case her mood swung back to suicidal. "It's gonna be all right," she said, and she was almost crying herself. "Somehow or another, it's all gonna be okay."

"How?" Verena said.

She didn't know.

CHAPTER 28

The bevvies followed them for a day and a half, giving the new medic, Watts, an excuse to ply the crew with a "relaxing" ginger-laced tea that Sophie suspected was a placebo—or, at best, a delivery system for nutrients. The creatures' pursuit left everyone dispirited except Bram, who just tucked his nose into his notebook, finishing their presentation.

"Why aren't they cranking you up?" Verena asked. She was red-eyed and keeping to her cabin.

"I'm more relaxed than I've ever been," Bram said. "All this time to think without the clutter of—"

"Human contact?" Sophie suggested.

"If you're going to heckle, get out," he said, tone amiable.

They made the rest of the sail without any more trouble, or any more dating. Verena's disclosure about Gale's death had left Sophie confused and raw.

It didn't help that the whole crew had been on deck, that Verena's shouted declarations, about prophecies and fate and Garland being a notch on Sophie's bedpost, meant all of them, Parrish included, had heard every word.

As they neared the Butcher's Baste, they laid all their data out on the galley table, once again turning the dining room into a shared workspace as they set out everything from a chart of the currents to Rees Erminne's migration graph, the calendar he used for setting gambling odds on when the turtles would arrive.

"We've missed the first night Kir Erminne listed as a possibility," Parrish began.

"Not a good one," Bram put in.

"The currents at this time of year make it likely the auto—atom—"

"Automatons," Sophie said. "Mindless gadgets with no volition of their own, sowing destruction wherever they wash up."

Bram gave her a slight frown.

"Automatons." Parrish savored the cadences of the English as he repeated the word, then marked a position on the chart. "They should go into the water near here. There's a strong current; it would carry almost anything to Sylvanna in a matter of hours."

"That means there will be a Haversham ship in the area. Since we don't want to be seen, the optimal location for a dive would be about—"

"How about here?" Sophie said, tapping the page. "It's about midway between both nations. Maybe this big islet will offer *Nightjar* some shelter?"

"You would be hard put to resist the current," Parrish said.

"I'll say." Bram had been doing figures on the table, converting the Fleet units to numbers the Americans would understand. "It's about six miles an hour, Sofe."

"So I wash up on the lowlands." She spoke with more boldness than she felt. Thoughts of soot vipers and quicksand—*oh, and let's not forget the fire leeches*—ran through her mind. "Turtle Beach is close to Low Bann. If worst came to worst, I could walk up to Cly's house."

Parrish shook his head. "There will be people on the beach: guards, and someone to time the turtles' arrival for the betting pool—"

"Rees," Sophie said.

"And you organized a scientific experiment, didn't you? To settle another of the lawsuits. So . . . observers?"

"Okay," Sophie said. "No washing ashore."

"I'm serious," Parrish said.

"You're always serious. I'll have to take a tether, that's all."

"I'll run her out in a rowboat," Tonio said. "Same as when she went diving for the Heart of *Temperance*."

Late that night, they sailed into the Baste.

She had heard that the Baste was tricky sailing—the passage had dangerous shallows and was filled with real and man-made islets. As he had on the approach to Issle Morta, Parrish took the wheel, paying close heed to a stopwatch as he took them around three of the islets before weighing anchor near a ponderous hump of rock that Bram, for some reason, had named Elvis.

By night, Sophie could see evidence of border security—a line of watchtowers along the Sylvanner lowland shore, their tops ablaze, drenching the beaches with light. Escapees fleeing to the beach would be hard put to get to the water.

The Haversham navy had responded in kind: brilliantly illuminated warships patroled the waters to the northwest.

Sophie got her gear on and, with Tonio's assistance, launched a small rowboat into the heart of the shorebound current. The boat was tethered to *Nightjar;* Sophie had an additional hundred meters of rope tied to the smaller craft.

"Ready to go?" Tonio asked.

She nodded.

"What about these?" He indicated her tanks and regulator.

"Not until I find the turtles," she said, dropping into the sea.

Diving, finally. She spent a moment getting used to the water, which was chillier than she'd expected. Summer was waning, but who knew what was normal at this time of year?

She'd been on shoots where they'd set up and then been forced to wait for weeks for the animals to show, and one where they'd never put in an appearance at all. Here, she was relying on Rees's gambling odds and on Parrish's knowledge of the currents. Plus a bit of luck.

Concentrate. She adjusted her snorkeling mask—as she'd told Tonio, she couldn't afford to use the air tanks until she absolutely needed them—and set about getting to know the water. She had a good LED dive light and her camera, and as she sank below she turned into the current, submerging her lantern and looking for the turtles, looking for anything.

Staying even with the current was a significant effort. She fell into a rhythm: submerge, search, kick back to the rowboat, submerge again. Her light was faltering and she was exhausted when Tonio indicated it was time to give up for the night.

She climbed into the rowboat. He immediately gave her a flask of hot tea. Feeling chilled and disappointed, she helped him row back to *Nightjar.*

"You rarely score the first time out," she said, as cheerily as she could. Parrish took them around Elvis and out to open sea. She spent the next day recharging her lamp and her camera batteries using the solar panels, and sleeping off the night's search.

The second night was a repeat of the first except that they had to break off a little earlier, when one of the Haver navy vessels seemed to be heading their way. Had they been spotted? Nobody was sure.

On the third afternoon, a chilly rain began to fall, cool wet drops with a hint of autumn in them. They went over the tide charts again.

"It seems to me the rain offers a chance to get closer to one nation or the other," Parrish said. "Visibility will be poorer, and with the clouds there will be no moon or starlight."

"If we aren't tucked in behind Elvis, aren't we more likely to be seen?" It turned out Bram had so named the islet because it was located about where Memphis should be at home.

"I can find a similar berth." Parrish shook his head. "The question is: Closer to Sylvanna, where Sophie might be taken for an escaped slave or someone trying to aid same? Or closer to Haversham, where they could try to sink us to hide what they're doing?"

"Haversham," Sophie said. "More chance we can catch them if we find the ship doing the dumping."

"Sylvanna," Verena said at the same time. "Sophie's sort of one of them. If they don't kill her immediately, she can drop Cly's name. And we can show we're acting in their interests."

Bram squinted at the chart. "You picked a good spot here, Parrish. The turtles will show. Let's not increase the risk."

They were evenly divided.

Tonio said, "I guess you're deciding, Garland."

He looked at the chart, assessed the rain and wind, and thought it over. "We'll defer to Verena's expertise."

"More risk—" Bram objected.

But Sophie was already looking at the line of the beach, the marked currents. "It gets shallow here, right?"

Parrish nodded. "We'll be gone long before low tide."

"Are you sure?" Bram said.

If they were southeast of the deeper part of the Baste, the outgoing tide would lower its depth by—what? Twenty or thirty feet?

You will bring doom on all your family, Gale had said.

Shut up. I don't believe in predestination.

"I studied the Butcher's Baste extensively when I was younger," Parrish said to Bram.

"You know, it looks like it might get choppy." Sophie spoke without premeditation. "What if Verena ran you home tonight?"

Everyone looked at her as though she'd grown a second nose.

"Excuse me?" Bram said.

Sophie persisted. "Why not? You've made up the model turtle, and you're finished with the evidence we're going to present. You're obviously nervous about the Butcher's Baste and there's no reason to spend the night puking your guts out if the wind comes up."

"You're saying you don't need me now, so I should take my toys and go home?"

"Come on, Bram. You hate the cold, you hate being damp, you know you're gonna get nauseated—"

"I hated the cold when I was *four* and my gut has been improving."

"It'd give you a chance to reassure the parents. We'll have this wrapped up in another week, maybe? Then—"

"Then what? Are we back to the 'I'll come home to Earth for good?' thing?" he demanded. "Because I don't think any of us believes that."

They were glaring at each other when Verena spoke. "She's not wrong, Bram. I don't appreciate being treated like a taxi service, but this might get hair-raising."

Bram rose. He closed his eyes and took one of those long breaths that, had he still been a toddler, would have preceded a sustained and piercing shriek of rage. Instead he said, "Surrounded by idiots," and slammed his way off to his cabin.

They retreated to the corners of the ship, waiting for nightfall—it was already plenty dark. Parrish took them into the passage, despite the downpour, steering the ship with his watch once again.

The distance from where they had been diving the previous two nights was less than five miles, but Sophie could feel the difference as soon as she got in the water. The current was stronger. It felt as though it wanted to suck her right down to the bottom.

Should've gone up toward Haversham after all, she thought, but she was here now and tethered to the rowboat, where Tonio waited.

"Okay, Sophie?"

"Keep your eyes peeled," she said.

"In this?" Water was falling in great sheets.

She shrugged.

"Don't worry about Bram," Tonio said.

She groaned. "I should've kept my mouth shut. I should've known I'd just set him off."

He shrugged. "Nobody at home wanted me to go to sea, you know. They saw that I had to—had to go with Garland and Kir Gale."

"This was your preadolescent career change?"

"Only time and proof stopped *amia madre* and my sister from trying to reshape me into a bookkeeper."

"Meaning?"

"I was a sailor. It was inconvenient—painful. But *Nightjar* called me. Your life, Sophie, it's here now."

"That simple, is it?"

"Verena, I think, needs you. As for Bram, that's not up to you."

She felt a sting of actual anger, had to fight an urge to make an obscene gesture at him as she slipped below. But she took the higher ground: she waited until she was underwater, well out of sight, before giving him the finger.

Glowering down into the black, she saw the turtles.

There were thousands of them, shadows in the dark, invisible but for the shine of her lantern off their shells. They were swimming at a depth of maybe twenty feet, an easy distance.

She kicked up, breaking the surface.

"Your light!" Tonio clapped a hand over the LEDs before they could advertise their presence.

"Sorry," she said, shutting it off. "Got that net?"

"They're down there?"

"They so are." She switched her snorkel for her regulator and tanks, took two knotted net bags from Tonio, and double-checked her safety line.

"Good luck." He was shivering today—it was warmer in the ocean than on the surface in the rain and breeze.

"Thanks." She submerged again, checked her breathing and the tanks, reminding herself not to rush. Bram's analysis of the automaton design indicated the decoys would be near the top of the dule, riding the current above them. She kicked slowly, maintaining a depth of fifteen feet, shining the light in the direction they were coming from.

Just observe, she told herself, taking easy breaths. All the time in the world.

When the automaton came, she almost had to chase it—the mechanism was imperfectly balanced. It was high in the dule but paddling sidewise, belly pointed left, shell to the right. She had to dive quickly, scoop at it with the net.

She half-caught it—and caught a live turtle, too. And then she had to grab as the automaton, with a surprisingly powerful *tick-tick-tick* of legs, almost came free of the net. Her light went flying, out to the edge of its safety line. She got the automaton, plunged it into the sack of net, and set herself to kicking against the current and reeling the light in before detangling the live turtle.

Sorry, she thought at it. Go lay your eggs.

The animal resumed its swim, seeming undisturbed. Drawn on to the beach, by instinct's irresistible pull.

Another turtle swam into her with a brisk *bonk*—the current was pulling her toward Sylvanna and down toward the bottom and the dule.

Okay, that's one. But even as she contemplated waiting for a second automaton, there was a yank at her line.

Sophie turned, checked the net and her equipment, then began to swim toward the rowboat while slowly gathering her safety line.

She was only about twenty feet below when she hit a powerful rush of water, a current that threatened to pull her back to the limit of the rope.

She shut off the safety light and focused on swimming. The automaton was kicking against her, within the net, beating an artificial pulse on the rubber-clad skin of her hip.

It was as close as she'd come to true solitude in weeks. Her mind hashed through the unanswered questions she'd yet to research: Was this a future Earth? How did magic—any of it—work in both worlds? And now this new question, about Parrish and Gale having their futures set out for them.

Here in the water it seemed, suddenly, as if all the worrying and flailing had been so much wasted energy. Tonio was right: she'd been called here.

She had to know.

We have to, she thought. Bram as much as me.

That meant whatever it took—trading science favors to Annela and Cly, figuring out how to use Gale's old watch to sneak back and forth to Stormwrack illegally—they'd have to find a way. Pretending she wasn't going to try to stay here was . . . well, it was lying.

As for Parrish and destiny and Gale being doomed, she'd have to prove to his satisfaction that the prophecy was nonsense. If he was still attracted to her after that, well . . .

She broke the surface about ten feet from the rowboat. The ship was reeling them in. She could feel the water resistance against her body, her diving gear.

Tonio was there, rowing hard in the lashing rain, no tea on offer this time.

"Did you get it?"

She nodded. "What's wrong?"

"Don't know." He yanked mightily on the lines.

They scrambled back to *Nightjar,* climbing aboard.

Parrish had all the crew at their stations. "Get below and warm up."

"What's going on?"

"We've been spotted." He pointed into a curtain of rain, presumably to indicate someone after them. Squinting, Sophie saw nothing.

"By which side?"

"Unknown. But with wind and tide and a battleship out there, the route past . . . past Bram's Rock of Elvis is blocked. I'm taking us through the Butcher's Baste."

"Through the passage? Is that possible?"

He nodded. "I know the intervals."

"In a downpour?" The wind was up to ten knots at least. Hardly gale force, but . . .

"Yes."

"Could we be panicking? I mean, *Nightjar*'s inconspicuous, right? Like Gale was?"

"Inconspicuous, not invisible."

Bram was hovering, eager to get his hands on the automaton. "Did you get it?"

She handed him the net. He picked out the automaton carefully, setting it out to dry. It was still *tick-tick* paddling.

"Tag it," she said. One of the goals they'd set out for their forensic institute was to try to establish the idea of a chain of evidence and some form of continuous custody.

"Done," Bram said.

"Fake it until you make it," Verena muttered.

"Sophie, Tonio, go warm up," Parrish said. "I'll need all hands."

She went to her cabin, stripped and dried off, and gulped tea until she stopped shivering even as she loaded up on warm-weather gear. Wool socks, base layer, jeans, sweater, Gortex raincoat overtop. It all looked faintly foreign.

Her legs were shaky from the effort of kicking against the current: she hit the galley for two of the savory scones, just to raise her blood sugar. Then she went up top, plucking at Tonio's sleeve.

"How can I help?"

"Help Sweet install the horn, then join her with the starboard crew," he said, indicating a crew readying, even now, to lower and reef the mainsail.

She did as ordered, helping Sweet lift and then bolt a sturdy-looking brass gadget to the rail.

"What is this thing?"

"Speed gauge. Usually we estimate, but for the interval navigation . . ."

"Precision counts. Got it," Sophie said. They tightened the bolts and went to their separate stations, Sophie taking a place on the starboard team, following orders, hauling ropes, belaying. Rain poured down steadily, the drops slapping coldly at the exposed skin on the backs of her hands, on her face, as the ship sailed through them. The wind was light, and the seas weren't running all that high.

The air was soupy, the passage full of rocks and shallows.

By now Sweet had climbed into the rigging with a spyglass, acting as a lookout. Parrish was at the wheel again.

"I need constant speed," he told Tonio, who had taken a position by the gauge. "Six—keep it to six."

It was better to be up top and pitching in than below. They raced through the hazard-filled water in the murk, with no idea if they were truly being hunted, if their presumed adversary might catch up.

"Hard starboard," Parrish rapped out, as a warning, and Sophie braced along with the others on her rope crew as the ship heeled over in a sharp turn. A tower of rock slid by on the port side, maybe twenty feet away.

Parrish fixed his gaze on the stone as they passed, reset his stopwatch to zero, and aimed *Nightjar* port, into the unseeable black.

Rat-a-tat. A distinct, mechanically regular series of taps, near the bow, raised the hair on her neck.

"What was that?" a crewman asked.

"Baste's a-haunted," came the reply.

"Great," Sophie said. "Now we have ghosts to contend with?"

Rat-a-tat-a-tatta—

This time it was more of a burr, a series of impacts against—the deck?— like a woodpecker's tapping or a very small jackhammer.

"Did anyone see?"

"What is it? What hit us?"

"Turning to port," Parrish announced, as if nothing had happened. Sophie saw another islet looming at a safe distance, but only just. He was cutting it fine.

Can he do this? she wondered. Zoom us through blind just by counting the distances between rocks?

Tonio was absorbed with the speed gauge. She was reminded, again, of
an air horn, and as he maneuvered it, it made a low humming sound.

"It's an exercise they gave the most talented cadets," the crewman beside her said. "Captain learned the intervals for the Baste before he was
expelled from—"

Rat-tatta-tatta. This time it was followed by a shriek.

"Krezzo, take the speed gauge. Call speed for Cap'n Parrish every thirty
seconds." Tonio waited until the massive cannoneer had taken over his
station. Then: "Sophie, with me."

She followed him across the deck.

Beal had fallen into a coil of rope. He was thrashing, obviously in pain.

"Smashed the thing," he managed to say. "But—ow!"

He had been sewn to the coil of rope, fixed there with a strand of what
looked like animal sinew—a trio of red stitches were looped into and
through the rope and his coat. They glistened with fresh blood. The coat
had been punched through, back to front, and on the way something had
passed through the meat of his hip, had even nipped a little piece out of
his leather belt.

The "it" Beal had smashed lay on the deck in broken pieces. It looked
like a bone needle, six inches long.

Tonio gave Beal's pants an unceremonious yank, exposing the twin
punctures and a good deal besides. "Sophie?"

"I think it got muscle, not organs," she said, feeling to be sure. "Watts
will know."

Tonio cursed. "I forgot we had a medic again."

"Want me back to my rope?"

"Not until—"

Rat-a-tatta-tatta—

This time they saw it, a vertical whisk of bone, bouncing across the deck
in a straight line . . .

. . . like a sewing machine needle, thought Sophie . . . until it struck
her swim fin, which was sitting, abandoned, next to the lifeboat. The

needle began bouncing wildly, stitching through the rubber, balling it in sinew.

Something above yanked it then, whisking the fin away. At the same time the thread through Beal's hip tightened, the loops of stitching cinching his wound, clamping the coat around him, and the coil of rope. His midsection rose off the deck and Sophie half-threw herself over him so he couldn't be yanked right off the ship.

He groaned.

"Sorry," Sophie said.

Tonio produced his glass stiletto. It wasn't meant for sawing, but he tried to get a grip on the sinew, to slice it free of Beal's punctured hip.

Sophie wound a hand in what slack she could gather, amid the rope and coat, making a loop he could thread his blade through. She felt the tug from above. There was something aloft, well above the ship, tethered by the greasy sinew and jerking upward, like a big kite.

She squinted at it, but rain blew into her eyes.

Tonio got the strand cut and the sailor fell back to the deck.

"Help Beal—I have to clear this." With that, Tonio began chopping into the slack bits of thread that had bunched up the rope, then pulled it clear and began, painstakingly, to re-coil it.

For an instant, Sophie felt a flash of anger at his priorities. But everything on a ship depended on its lines: if they had to loose a sail now, with its rope stapled together, they'd be dead.

"Speed check," Parrish called.

"Holding six, Captain, breeze is fair," Krezzo replied.

"Sweet, what do you see?"

The bosun's voice came from well above them. "Frigate's well to the stern, Captain."

"Within cannon range?"

"No, and not currently gaining."

"Of which nation?"

"Haversham."

Sophie returned her attention to Beal, pulling the thread of sinew. It was rubbery, with a greasy texture that made it hard to grip. The blood helped a little—it made it sticky.

"Sorry about this," she said, thinking, suddenly, of the transfusion specialist on Sylvanna. *Wish we had one of those.*

"I'm inscribed to heal fast, Kir," Beal assured her. "Just get this witch stitchery out of me."

The ship turned close round another islet and a bell began to toll.

"Losing speed," the canonneer bellowed. "Get that sail up."

Another burr. A third bone needle tatted across the deck, seeking whatever it could puncture. Sophie saw it flash past, bouncing up a spar and striking a sail, then frenzying as it lashed big, looping random-looking stitches into the fabric.

There was a yank and the whole ship shuddered. The sail puckered, bunched, and she heard a ripping sound.

Cursing in Erinthian, Tonio darted after the thread.

"One of those things hits the captain, we're on the rocks for sure," Beal muttered. Pouring rain had diffused his blood across the deck.

And the more of those strings we end up dragging, the harder it is to maintain speed. Could Parrish recalculate his time intervals on the fly if they decelerated?

All they could do was put up more sail, giving the needles ever more cloth to sabotage.

Watts came spidering across the deck just then, trying to keep his long body low. "Sorry," he whispered. "Hatch got jammed by one of those things."

Sophie showed him Beal's wound, which had indeed stopped bleeding, then took a moment to scan the deck.

Her thoughts had slowed, as they tended to in emergencies. The cold air, whipping over her wet face, clarified things further. Tonio almost had the fouled sail straightened. An ugly triangular rip hung loose, but it was mostly intact. She wasn't needed there.

The source of the needles was above them.

"Turning port!"

Parrish brought the ship around in another sharp correction. He looked terribly exposed up at the wheel.

Sophie was barely able to make out the shadow of the islet he was using as a marker, a spire of rubble, human-made. But then the rock lit up, spearing them with incandescence, revealing them to their hunters . . . and also revealing two more sinewy threads, bound to *Nightjar* like bloody kite strings.

Above them, maybe a hundred feet above the water . . .

It was big, maybe fifteen or eighteen feet from toe to crown. It had the face of a porcelain doll and was clad in a billowing dress whose shape reminded Sophie of christening gowns. Black in color, ornately pleated, it was tattered at the hem. Measuring cords dangled around its neck, and its mouth held bone needles and sharp stickpins.

The thing held a live pincushion, a wriggling lamb with bloodied wool.

The floating figure tugged on the two lines it already had in *Nightjar*, then pulled a bone needle from between its lips and stitched it through the bleating, struggling lamb. The needle went into the lamb attached to nothing and came out drawing one of the sinewy threads. The monster then tossed the needle at the ship, at Sophie, with a motion reminiscent of a dart player.

Verena stepped into view just then, stomping the needle's trailing, sinewy thread. Her boot slowed the needle just enough for Sophie to grab up Beal's mallet and bring it down, with a slam, onto the thing. The bone shattered.

"If they get Garland," Verena said. She was carrying her practice dummy under one arm.

"Yeah."

Parrish was haloed in the beam from the receding rock pillar. They'd be shooting for him, wouldn't they? He was standing confidently at the wheel, hand resting lightly on *Nightjar*, head cocked as if he were listening for the rocks rather than looking for them.

"Go protect him," Sophie said.

Verena handed her a serrated knife made, like Tonio's, of Erinthian glass. "Keep 'em from fouling the rigs."

"Kir, we're down to five and a half," Krezzo shouted.

Krezzo's the cannoneer. He should be firing at that thing. But someone's gotta watch our speed, too—doesn't anyone else know how to read the speed horn?

Sophie kept her eye on the sewing monster, up above. It flung another needle, then another. She pressed herself against the deck as one bounced past, then sliced the sinew of another that had punched its way into another coil of rope.

A cry.

Tonio.

She looked up. He was halfway to the top of the mainmast, ill balanced and caught on a sinew.

Sticking the cold, heavy weight of the glass knife in her mouth—very piratical of me, she thought absently, Sophie began to climb.

"Hard to port," Parrish warned, and as the ship tilted she was suddenly skimming over the water. Tonio was no longer above her so much as he was out in front, higher on the sail as the masts dipped toward the sea.

The ship came out of the turn; the mast rose skyward again.

Hang on, she thought. She couldn't say it with the knife in her mouth.

Good advice for them both. The ropes were wet, rough to the touch, and her hands were cold. She could make out that shape in the sky, bound to them, hitching a ride even as it crippled the ship. And was that another ship, sailing to their rear?

Tonio had gotten stitched, just near his collar, to one of the mast's rings. On its return trip, the needle had pierced the web of flesh between his finger and thumb. He'd caught it with his fingertips and was holding it off with the punctured, blood-slicked hand—the grip was precarious—while clinging to the rigging with one arm, hugging the rope as the sewing monster yanked, yanked. The vibrations, as she pulled, could be felt through the whole of the mast.

Sophie mirrored Tonio's position, climbing as close as she could, winding her own arms into the rigging so that she was holding on to the ropes with her elbows and thereby freeing her hands so she could get the knife out of her mouth.

"It feels alive," Tonio said, disgusted. The needle was flexing in his uncertain, blood-soaked grip. Its point was all but scratching at his throat.

"Sophie," he said. "That burden I mentioned."

"Don't," she said. "I've got this." The trouble was that if he let go of the needle so she could cut the sinew, the point would pierce his throat.

"Garland's middle name was hidden before he was born—hidden from everyone, on Issle Morta. It's why he can't be enchanted. A number of years ago, I found out—"

"Don't go all drama queen on me, you're gonna be fine."

The needle jerked hard, fighting the awkward grip of Tonio's fingers and scoring a shallow cut into his neck.

Commit, commit. Sophie pushed her own hand between the point of the needle and his neck, scraping her palm and protecting his jugular, then folded her fingers over his, pressing the needle back against the mast. She slid the obsidian knife point into the needle's eye, pinning it to the mast. She'd hoped that would cut the sinew, but no. The needle wiggled, fighting imprisonment—now it was Sophie who couldn't move.

"You should be able to let go now," she said.

Tonio sighed, flexed his hand, then drew it backward, letting the gory thread pull through the puncture in his hand but taking time to shake out the cramp. Moving carefully, he found his stiletto, sawed off the thread, then cut it free of the mast ring.

The needle went limp, as if it had died.

There was an enraged shriek from above . . . and behind. The sewing monster was falling behind them.

"Someone must have cut her other strings." Sophie shifted, taking a better grip on the wet ropes. She could feel the ship accelerating.

Tonio surprised her by pulling her close.

"Kerlin," he breathed into her ear, before she could object. "If it's ever life or death—no other reason. Garland Kerlin Parrish. Don't tell anyone you know. Don't tell him. Now let's get down, before we both get sewn to the mast."

"Hard to starboard now, now!"

They stayed where they were through the turn, waiting out the tilt of the mast. The sewing monster tossed away its lamb in a gesture reminiscent of a tantruming child and finally began flinging threadless pins, little missiles that rattled across the deck randomly. One punched through the mainsail, leaving a pinhole a foot from Sophie's head. Another, she thought, struck Sweet—at least, she heard a curse from that direction.

There was a loud cracking sound, as of rock on rock. The ship turned sharply. Below them, on the deck, Watts and Beal slid in a slick of blood and water. Sophie and Tonio hung together up top, clinging.

She turned to look down at the wheel. Parrish was safe. Verena stood on his port side, brandishing the practice dummy. Bram was starboard, with a cooking pot. Parrish's bicorne hat had been stitched to the jib.

"Climb down now!" Tonio hissed. "Slow and careful."

She obeyed, matching his pace in case his injured hand cramped or his grip slipped.

"What's our speed?" Parrish said. "Our speed, Krezzo!"

"Kir, I don't—I'm not sure. Five, last count. We lost the horn to that thing up there."

Parrish straightened, narrowed his eyes, and ran a hand through his curls, spraying water everywhere. He took a deep breath and raised his nose into the wind, as if he could smell the rate at which they were barreling through the dark and rain.

He looked at the stopwatch.

"More sail," he said. "More sail now."

"Oh, crap," Sophie said. "He's guessing."

Tonio gave her a pat, attempting to be reassuring.

"Rise, rise, rise!" Krezzo bellowed. At home they'd say "heave." The mainsail was jerking upward, past them, fast and messy. Broken remnants of sinewy stitching were pulling through the fabric here and there. The fabric caught the wind and the ship shuddered.

Now Sophie was down, her feet on the deck, holding a hand up to steady Tonio.

"Keep your eyes open," Parrish said, with all the confidence of a man who was certain of success. "They'll have ships coming round to intercept as we break the Baste."

"Yes, Cap'n."

"Sweet, you still with us?"

"Yes, Kir." Her voice was a little strained.

"Come on down," Parrish said.

"I may need an assist."

"Hold, then. Hard to port, one last time." Parrish said it as calmly as if he were speaking to himself, but his voice carried—everyone braced.

He turned the wheel and just then Sophie saw the islet they'd been aimed at, a long knife of rock rising from the sea like a mammoth shark's fin. Had they turned soon enough?

She heard a hiss and felt a shudder run through the deck. The ship had kissed bottom.

Nightjar slowed a little, dragging.

As they passed the tip of the islet, a lighthouse on its peak flared to life, illuminating them from bow to stern in something akin to daylight. Sophie was momentarily blinded.

They raced out of the beam, which held them as long as it could, and out to open water.

"Two," Sweet called. "Frigates, very fast, lots of cannon, I'm guessing."

"Can we outrun them?" Tonio asked.

"We've got a decent lead."

"Should we make for a Sylvanner port?" Bram set his stewpot on the deck. The slaloming between rocks had left him a little green, but he gave Sophie a game thumbs-up.

Parrish shook his head. "There could be Havers between us and the Winter capital, Hoarfrost—they might even persuade the Sylvanners to hand us over."

"Why flee west?"

"The Fleet is on its eastward procession right now," Parrish said. "We'll meet them."

Verena searched his face. "Are you sure?"

"Positive," Parrish said. "There's nothing we can do now but treat the wounded, repair the sails, and prepare your case for presentation."

CHAPTER 29

They shot out of the Baste moving as fast as *Nightjar* could move. Once they were out in open water, Sweet had each of the torn sails hauled down in turn, laying the tears flat and hastily patching them. She painted a white substance with the texture of melted marshmallow over the rips, then lay a thin sheet of fabric overtop. Linen, cut to fit, went over this, and the whole area then had to be gently ironed dry before they could flip the sail and do the other side.

There was nothing to hide them on the open sea: no fog, not even a wisp of heat mirage. The rising sun brought the view of two ships from Haversham in pursuit of them, big frigates with acres of sail.

Parrish had set a straight course east, running for what he said was the Fleet's position.

Their pursuers started out as specks, then grew into little toy boats on the horizon. It took them a while to clear the Baste; they were bigger and couldn't make a swift course through the dangerous shallows Parrish had taken. By noon they were devouring *Nightjar*'s lead.

We're not gonna be able to lose them unless a heck of a souper comes up. Sophie felt as though they had a bull's-eye painted on their stern and sails; she could almost see the red circles on *Nightjar*'s pearly sheets.

Parrish barely gave their pursuers a glance. He'd seen to the wounded sailors—checking whether the new medic knew his stuff, Sophie suspected—and given orders to inspect the lines for knots or damage while they were on the fly.

Tonio had taken the opportunity to put an ornamental gold hoop through the needle hole in his hand. "I always liked the idea of piercing but lacked the stomach for it," he told her.

"You're making serious lemonade out of that lemon," she said. To her surprise, he seemed to understand what the colloquialism meant.

By midafternoon, Parrish had the crew run up a ship-in-distress flag. "They'll think we've spotted the Fleet," he said, and sure enough the Havers fell back for about an hour, until they saw through the ruse.

"Don't you have something official? Like a watch flag?" Bram asked.

"No," Verena and Parrish said simultaneously.

Verena added, "I benefit personally if we pull this off. It's best if we don't use my position."

Parrish gave them all a confident smile. "We'll make the Fleet. My word on it."

What could anyone say to that? He'd got them through the Butcher's Baste.

Instead of watching the cannon-laden warships as they closed the distance to *Nightjar,* the three of them went below and assembled their case materials—the charter for the forensic institute Verena had drafted, the notebook Bram had been slaving over, the exhibits showing how the stone-wood automaton components were broken down by throttlevine roots. They inventoried the diagrams and the bits and pieces of the half-assembled turtle. Their crowning piece of evidence was the intact automaton Sophie had caught on her dive.

The wood frame of the turtle she'd recovered was covered in a thin, green-painted cloth. It wouldn't fool anyone but the most casual observer, but the devices weren't meant to last long. Bram found a way to detach the eggshell-fine fake shell on one side, swinging it up, almost like the trunk door of a car, to reveal the throttlevine pods within, tucked into the large compartment, each seed carefully inserted into a bit of dried fruit. There were two others in a little glistening bubble of fresh water, encased by wax, already germinating.

"Should we hide all this?" Bram asked. "In case they board?"

"Parrish says we'll beat them to Fleet, we'll beat them," Verena said. Her voice held less conviction than her words.

"Then all we have to do is sell Cly on this. And Annela," Bram said.

"They'll go for it," Verena said. "People here don't watch TV. By local standards, what we've put together is pretty slick. They'll be impressed. Gale ran shakier bluffs than this."

"It's no bluff," Bram said, nettled. "It's facts."

"I don't bluff," Sophie said in the same instant. "That was Gale—I'm no Gale."

"No," Verena said. "None of us is Gale."

"Maybe—" Sophie stopped herself. For once, she wasn't going to stick her foot in it.

"What?"

Tonio had said, *Verena needs you.* She shrugged.

Verena finished the thought. "Maybe with a little luck, the three of us could amount to . . . say, half of Gale?"

"Works for me," Bram said.

Verena looked half hopeful, half wary.

"I just want to do science, Verena. Look around, see the world, understand where and when we are—"

"That's not all you want."

No, it wasn't. Science and exploration and giving Beatrice a chance to maybe like her one day, all of that. *I'm allowed to want things.*

She wanted Parrish.

It sat there, unsaid and unresolved.

Verena let out a long sigh. "You're lucky he can't be enchanted. I'd love-spell him in a red hot smoking minute."

I could enchant him, or Tonio could, and nobody else knows. Sophie's flesh crawled and she felt the weight of it, suddenly, the burden Tonio had talked about. "What's that, your blessing?"

"More of a promise not to stab your eyes out in the night." Verena put up a hand, bringing an end to the conversation, then strode away.

"That was almost heartwarming," Bram observed.

"I can really feel the love. Now if I can avoid getting deported again, maybe we can all get to work on each being one-third of half of Gale."

"More than the sum of our parts," he mused, running a finger over the fake turtle's flipper.

"Fleet ahead! Fleet—*fer le saysa!*" Tonio's cry was echoed by shocked exclamations in a half-dozen languages. There was a rush of feet on the deck above.

They took the galley ladder up to the main deck.

The Fleet was traveling in two distinct convoys, separated by, roughly, a nautical mile. On one side was *Temperance*, the Tallon warship that served as the navy's big gun against piracy. On the other, two Sylvanner ships, *Excelsior* and Cly's *Sawtooth,* were at the fore.

"What's up with that?" Sophie asked. Her mouth was dry. "Is it this war everyone's so scared of?"

"Not quite," Parrish said. "The port and starboard nations line up so, when the Fleet is divided. It means governance is deadlocked."

"I've never seen this," Verena said. "It's happened, like, twice in the past century?"

"This is over Beatrice? Beatrice and Cly and me?" *Holy crap, I'm a diplomatic incident!*

The Havers frigates pursuing *Nightjar* put on an extra burst of speed as the two convoys came into view. Cannoneers were taking positions on their gun decks, lining up with military precision. They'd be making their gunpowder snowballs, she thought.

"Uh, Parrish?"

"Everything's all right, Bram."

"How is this okay? Is a divided Fleet gonna rescue us or watch us burn? You've got some rabbit to pull out of your hat before they blow the crap out of us?"

"In a manner of speaking," he said, "we do."

There was a familiar mirage-shiver, and a mammoth caravel, the one that had seemed far away just moments ago, grew suddenly huge. A cloud of steam puffed upward around it.

Sawtooth. Zita was waving from the starboard rail. She blew past them on the starboard side, putting herself between the two Haver ships and *Nightjar's* stern.

"That's your rabbit, Kir," Parrish said.

They held their breath. Would the Havers fire on Cly?

"Someone's up there with him," Verena said.

Sophie reached for her camera, using the telephoto to zoom in. There were indeed three people up in the bow of *Sawtooth,* presenting a handy target to the cannoneers. Cly's form, whippy and long-boned, was unmistakable.

"One of them's Lena Beck, his captain," Sophie said. "The other, I'm not sure . . ."

"It's Convenor Gracechild," Parrish said, and to her surprise he gave in to that boyish laugh of his. "Unless they're prepared to fire upon both the duelist-advocate and Her Honor, it's over."

"For now," Tonio and Bram muttered in unison, right down to the fatalistic tone of voice.

But Parrish was right. The ships from Haversham reefed their sails, dismissed their weapon crews, and headed home.

CHAPTER 30

With the Havers retreating, *Nightjar* fell into position next to *Sawtooth*, the two ships setting a course for the Fleet even as Parrish issued an immediate invitation to Annela and Cly to come aboard.

Annela arrived clad in long white robes. "The whole Convene's officially on sick leave," she said. "All of governance is on hold because of this tempest."

She was too much the politician to say, *I hope you're happy*, but the implication was there. *You caused this, Sophie*, she seemed to be saying.

"Time to fix it," Sophie said.

Cly, too, was dressed in civvies—Shakespeare outfit, black Sylvanner sash, and no sword. Instead of his dashing cloak, he seemed to wear an air of weariness. Despite her fears and doubts, Sophie felt a stab of sympathy. There was something about him that made you want to . . .

What? Compromise? Forgive? Make him soup?

Annela drew herself up. "How do you propose to fix anything?"

"Pure unadulterated bribery. I offer Cly something tasty in exchange for Beatrice being forgiven. Just as you offered him a cruise with me."

"Bribing an adjudicator, mmm? How do you think that will go?" asked Cly.

"Depends what we've got, right?"

He inclined his head, indicating willingness to listen.

"Should we set up the conference room again?"

"I can forgo pomp if His Honor can," Annela said.

Cly made a gesture that essentially said, *Lead the way.*

Annela may have seemed a little too grand to plunk herself down in the galley, but that was exactly what she did, taking a seat at the table where they'd laid out all their exhibits.

Verena started with the forensic institute charter, giving due credit to Cly for the idea and laying out their starting principles—use of the scientific method, reproducible results, no magic. She explained expert witnesses and chain of evidence.

"You're proposing to set up in competition with the court aetherists, then?" Annela said.

Cly tsked at her. "Tell me there's no use for this, Convenor."

"We can show the use if you'll let us," Sophie said. She left the charter on the table, for Annela to approve or not, and gestured for Bram to move on to the meat of their proposal.

"If Cly lets Beatrice off the hook—" he began.

"—and frees the goat-people in the lowland swamps," Sophie interrupted, earning a glare from her father.

"Right, that's first," Bram said. "Sorry. Then we'll submit the case evidence to the courts on Sylvanna's behalf, proving Haversham's responsibility for the throttlevine infestation."

Cly was all business. "The evidence would have to be persuasive."

"It will be," Verena said.

He ignored both Verena and Bram, leaning in and looking straight at Sophie. "And if I refuse your proposal, child? The throttlevine and the goat-people, as you call them, are to continue in their present balance?"

"I—" Sophie balked. What was she going to do, leave them in their current situation?

Cly gave her that sharkish grin.

"Everything's a duel with you, isn't it?"

Verena laid a hand on hers. "Your Honor. We're going to tell you right now how the throttlevine is being seeded. You won't need the goat transforms once the vines are eradicated."

"Fair point."

"However, if you want us to present the evidence that will win your case in court—"

Sophie finished for her, in a rush, "Then you let them go, and you let Beatrice go!"

"Better," Cly purred.

"The Fleet is on the verge of a major break, Your Honor," Annela reminded him. "Largely because of your domestic problems."

"Your deceiving Sophie by sending her asea with no knowledge of Sylvanna didn't help," he said.

"Which would be why I came aboard *Sawtooth* to help with negotiations," Annela replied.

Ah, so that's what she's doing there! Trying to extinguish the fire her own orders ignited, Sophie thought.

Annela said, "Even so. This is hardly the time to try to teach your daughter the finer points of haggling."

"Hey! What if instead of doing the rhetorical tap dance about whether or not this is a teachable moment, we stay on point. In fact, let's all agree that everyone here's been an utter jerk at one point or another," Sophie said.

"I haven't," Bram said. "I've been angelic."

"Garland's behaved pretty well," Verena put in.

Don't get me laughing. She glowered at them both.

Cly showed his teeth in something that might have been a smile. "Show me what you have. And it better not be petrodemonic mummer images."

Is that what we're calling photographs now? She fought the urge set off another round of snarky banter. Bram held up the second notebook Sophie had bought in the floating mall, all those weeks ago. He had made it official-looking, sketching on a Forensic Institute of Stormwrack logo and adding the official throttlevine case number.

"We call this a dramatic reconstruction," Bram said, demonstrating.

Sophie held her breath. Her big idea for a presentation had amounted to nothing more than having Bram draw a flipbook, stop-motion animation, drawings that moved as you flipped the pages.

Within the notebook was an animation of the turtle automaton. It began with a quick demonstration of its assembly and launch.

Bram's line drawings showed the automaton swimming within the dule of turtles, reaching the beach, and releasing the throttlevine pods. Birds carried the fruit-wrapped seeds into the swamp to take root as the pieces of the automaton were, finally, destroyed by the plant itself.

The flipbook was a kid's trick: Sophie had one, back home, that her grandparents had played with as kids. But Cly watched it twice, three times, taking in the animation intently before handing it to Annela.

"A powerful image—"

"They're not petrodragon-whatever tainted mummer images," she said. "You show this to a judge or jury—do you even have juries? Anyway, it instantly communicates how the Havers have been pulling this off. When the Havers see this, they'll know the game's up."

"Fine in theory, but what if they don't immediately settle the case?" Cly asked.

Annela was watching the animation. "You know they probably will."

Cly flicked the "probably" away. "Sophie, you would need to offer me more than just this . . . assertion. If it came to trial."

"We have copies of the plans of the turtle. The originals belonged to Weyvan Highfelling, and they're in the keeping of the monks on Issle Morta. Who are unimpeachable, right?"

A slow nod. "Yes."

"We and they have pieces of Highfelling's mechanism, and we have a whole automaton, plucked out of the Butcher's Baste. If you have Rees Erminne search Turtle Beach quickly, he might find others. It's only been forty-eight hours."

Cly leaned back in his chair, examining first the documents and then, when Bram produced it, the automaton itself.

"Well?" It was Verena, for once, who couldn't wait out the silence.

"I'll set up a ritual duel with Beatrice immediately. Kir Gracechild?" He set a hand, very deliberately, on the forensic institute charter and slid it across the table toward her. "I believe you'll have to sell your friend Kir Salk at the Watch on this."

Annela shifted in her chair, eyeing the document, then lifted it as though it were a dirty rag.

"Well?" Verena demanded. "Do we want Mom freed or not?"

"If I agree to certify this, Sophie, you will incur obligations to the Fleet and the Judiciary. Are you prepared to fulfill them?"

"Staying's what I've wanted all along."

"The question now may be whether you'll be allowed to go home."

"Wait—" Bram said.

Sophie raised a hand and he fell silent. She opened her mouth to reply to Annela, found her throat and mouth were parched, and made herself take a swallow of water. "We'll work something out. You'll see you can trust me."

"Understand me, girl. Until I do, you'll stay here and work at this forensic. Sail out of formation and you'll find yourself on the wrong end of the Judiciary," Annela said. "Please don't assume that because of your father's position that would be an . . . what's your term? Easy fix?"

"I hardly think you need worry that Sophie expects anything benevolent or easy from me," Cly said, standing abruptly. "Tell my wife I'll see her on the dueling deck."

With that parting shot delivered, he bowed and was gone.

CHAPTER 31

It turned out that the Judiciary had one ship full of courtrooms and documents and clerks—real court, as Sophie thought of it—and another just for settling cases via combat.

The dueling deck was aboard *Martial,* the member ship from Haversham. It was a wide-draft ship, almost as big as a container ship from home, propelled not by sail power but by a combination of magic and steam. It had big screws and a tiny boiler, no bigger than Sophie's hands, that burned minuscule amounts of coal dust. This was sifted by a strange old "loader," a woman in her eighties who kept the boiler in her lap, cradling it almost like a child.

The wide deck of the ship was laid out in fighting rings—boxing rings, fencing rings, wrestling rings—all with seating for court reporters, witnesses, and referees.

About two days after they'd struck their agreement with Annela and Cly, Beatrice was brought aboard and given a sword. She exchanged one token clash of blades with Cly and then surrendered.

After sailing around for a month and a half, trying to help her birth mother with her legal woes, this was the first time Sophie had actually laid eyes on Beatrice.

She was clad in Verdanii robes and her hair had grown. Her skin was tanned.

"Here," she said, after her surrender. She handed Cly and Sophie each a big Verdanii coin stamped with the image of *Breadbasket*. "Damages paid for harm done."

"We're finished, then," Cly said. He appeared to be planning to go back to work as soon as it was over; a minion was hovering, holding out his duelist-advocate's cape and the big ceremonial sword.

"We're not divorced," Beatrice said.

"How could I forget? I've run our case past Sophie's fellow, Bimisi. My heart stopped in a fight, for a few minutes, nine years ago. He seems to think we might invoke the 'till death' clause of our vows."

"You died? That sounds promising."

"I need to ensure that acknowledging it doesn't damage my legal status elsewhere. I wouldn't want to lose Low Bann. It may be that I have no heir."

Beatrice nodded. "I don't expect it matters all that much."

"Perhaps you prefer bigamy, my haughty angel, but I need to get on with my life. Sophie, may I write you?"

Sophie swallowed. "Of course."

"Fair winds, then." He bowed, sheathed his sword, and strode off.

"Come on, this way," Beatrice said to her. "Otherwise I'll have to talk to that frightful reporter, Pyke."

The dueling deck had preparation rooms for people who were fighting; Beatrice had been assigned one, and now they retreated there. It was small, barely bigger than a dressing room.

Oh, this isn't awkward. The first time Sophie had approached her birth mother, it had gotten her nothing but a screaming fight—Beatrice had been horrified to see her. And why not? Sophie turning up was what had ultimately gotten her arrested.

Now, she looked relaxed and tan and remarkably fit; her chestnut hair had grown and she'd put on some muscle. She had a tattoo Sophie hadn't seen before: a species of red fox that seemed to be watching the world from under the gauze of a green scarf wrapped around Beatrice's shoulders.

"I suppose I ought to thank you for getting me off the hook," she said in English, in her typically ungracious manner but, somehow, with less rancor than usual in her voice.

Sophie shrugged. "I got to see more of Stormwrack. Besides, all the international tension over your arrest—my fault, right?"

"I may have to own some of that," she said. "And don't inflate our impor-tance overmuch. The free nations would never go to war over you and me."

Sophie looked out a portal at the two lines of ships, separated by a mile, stretching to beyond sight.

"It's posturing, I tell you. They're closer, but I don't think they're quite ready yet."

"That's a relief." It was, too. Bad enough to have bumbled around sowing trouble for her relations. Starting some kind of inter-island war.

"The Fleet's tense," Beatrice said. "Gale told me it was getting worse, but . . ."

"But?"

"Who ever takes their little sister seriously?" Beatrice said.

Was that a hint about Verena?

"Eugenia Merrin Sawtooth says hi," Sophie said, to break the silence that followed from that.

Beatrice smiled. "That old ghost was very good to me."

"I don't understand why she isn't out on the front of the ship."

"She blabs her full name to anyone she meets. Some kind of curse. Makes her vulnerable to inscription. They'd have scuttled her long ago, but Cly took it into his head to save her."

"Why?"

"He basks in gratitude?"

"You think he's a sociopath, don't you?"

Her mother drew in a long breath. "High functioning, perhaps. Possi-bly amended by magic. But . . . yes. When I got to San Francisco, I found out about sociopathy and serial killers—from a TV thriller, I admit. Even so, I very nearly threw up."

"He didn't hit you or anything. He says."

"No."

"But he's horrible in some way?"

Beatrice pursed her lips, seeming to think. "You've seen Clydon fight. Really fight?"

Crossbow bolt through the throat. Sophie nodded.

"That's how he used to argue, too. Maliciously. Unmercifully. I hope you never . . ." She shuddered.

Sophie remembered nearly heaving on the parade float. "Does he sleep with slaves?"

"No!" Beatrice said, seeming genuinely shocked.

Oh, I was wrong, I was wrong, what a relief! She could feel the tears coming.

They stared at each other, again stuck on what to say. Finally, Beatrice started going through her purse. "I'd kill for a burrito. Have to get Merro to spring for Mexican when I get home."

"That'll be nice," Sophie said.

"You going right back?"

"No. Annela seems to think I need to hang around and make this institute legitimate. If she can't keep me from studying Stormwrack, she may try to keep me here."

"Yes, she dislikes you," Beatrice said. "Don't take it personally. She's got remarkably little patience for me. The emotional outbursts, you know. Not trademark Verdanii."

"I thought if I got Sylvanner citizenship it would help with all this residency stuff."

"Just keep making yourself useful," Beatrice advised. "Nella can't resist a good tool of statecraft. Besides, if she thinks you might take up resolving Sylvanna's thousand lawsuits as a hobby, she'll find other puzzles to keep you busy." Her mouth pinched as if she were sucking a lemon. Thinking of Cly again, probably.

"I thought I needed a nation. People were refusing to sell goods to me in the market."

"You need a *position*. A job in the courts puts you halfway there. Get someone to take you on as crew of their ship. So-and-So of the sailing vessel Whatever is a barely respectable designation."

"I didn't know that."

"People don't offer up information here. You have to claw for it."

"So—a ship. A paycheck, basically?"

"A captain who'll take responsibility for you. That sexy Tiladene still owes you one, doesn't he?" She stood. "I've had it. Someone can send for me when the divorce papers come through. You'll tell 'em?"

"Sure."

Beatrice drew out a thumbnail-size pocket watch and looked at her cannily. "You wouldn't know what became of Gale's brass watch?"

Sophie's heart sank. "She lost it behind a Dumpster. It's at my house. Um, it's broken."

"Get it repaired and bring it by sometime. Odds are you can't make it tick. Supposedly, you need the Allmother's blessing. Still . . ." She spun the watch on its chain. The sounds it made were fine musical plinks. Then she vanished. No poof, just gone.

I have to find out how that works. She felt heartened.

"Sophie?"

Parrish was tapping on the dressing room door.

He must have been meeting with official types. He was shaved, combed, uniformed, every inch the fancy captain.

On a whim, Sophie curtsied. This got her a mildly bemused look and a bow.

She took his arm like an old-fashioned lady, kissed his cheek, and said, "What's up, beautiful?"

"Well," he said. "There's an entertainment tonight."

"Puppets?"

"Music. Would you . . . prefer puppets?"

"We've done puppets," she said, mimicking Annela's frosty tone. "Kir."

A startled laugh. "I beg you, don't ever get caught mocking the Convenor."

"Understood," she said, feeling merry. "So . . . music?"

"Music," he said.

"Like, dancing music? Or opera?" She imagined a scene out of Jane Austen, young ladies in Regency dresses performing on pianofortes.

"Drummers from Zingoasis," he said. "How are you?"

"I suddenly appreciate my sane, normal, super-supportive parents."

A little deflation in him. "You'll go home, then, when Annela says you may?"

"Not permanently. I love—" She faltered. "I need to be here. I can't explain it."

"Pheromones?"

"For a planet? You really weren't listening when I laid that out for you." She nudged him, to show she was kidding, and walked on.

Tried to, anyway, but he was as impossible to move as a statue. He turned so they were facing, looking into her eyes so very seriously.

"Pheromones?" he said again.

"Chemistry," she said, but he didn't smile. He thought she meant, you know, *chemistry*. The science.

"Look, I'm not saying—"

He kissed her, once, long. Let her go and said, "Chemistry?"

It took a second to catch her breath. "Not just chemistry."

"Powerful pre-programmed biological instincts?"

"Now you're quoting Bram, not me. Besides, what about you and destiny and Gale's fate resting on your—"

He laid a finger on her lips.

"Mmphree movfff—"

"Sophie, if you think the heart can be weighed, measured, paced out, timed like the World Clock—"

She pushed his hand away, taking the opportunity to clasp it. "I don't think that."

He looked, of all things, suspicious.

"Jeez, Parrish, don't you know I'm nuts about you?"

"Nuts?"

"Just because I don't buy into this whole maudlin love-at-first-sight thing, or big-*D* destiny, or that iron and lodestone twaddle of Corsetta's, two hearts beating as one—"

"Ah. Sophie, perhaps you should—"

But she wasn't going to let him stop her now. "—just because I don't excuse my feelings with superstition doesn't mean I'm not completely, stupidly, annoyingly infatuated with you. I think about you all the bleeping time. It's . . ."

He waited.

Don't say "obnoxious," don't say "obsessive," oh great, how did I get into this? "It's a lot, okay?"

He nodded gravely, seeming to examine her. "What if I do believe in some of those things? Fate? Or true love?"

"Superstitious. That's a character flaw."

"Indeed?" He was still holding her; now she felt him relax fractionally.

"It's okay. I think . . . you have to have one or two."

"Flaws?"

"*Courting* someone perfect would be exhausting."

A ghost of a smile. "No danger of that."

"Definitely not. Jerk."

"That's an insult, isn't it?"

"I'm not apologizing."

"No?"

"Are we going to see the drummers or not?"

"We are," he said, offering her his arm again, leading her through *Martial* and toward the ferry deck as, behind them, the ships of the Fleet of Nations began, with a slow and formal intricacy, to knit themselves back into a single formation.

ABOUT THE AUTHOR

A. M. Dellamonica is a recent transplant to Toronto, Ontario, having moved there in 2013 with her wife, author Kelly Robson, after twenty-two years in Vancouver. She has been publishing short fiction since the early nineties in venues like *Asimov's, Strange Horizons,* and *Tor.com,* as well as numerous anthologies. Her 2005 alternate history of Joan of Arc, "A Key to the Illuminated Heretic," was short-listed for the Sidewise Award and the Nebula.

Her first novel, *Indigo Springs,* won the 2010 Sunburst Award for Canadian Literature of the Fantastic; she is also a Canada Council grant recipient.

Dellamonica teaches writing courses through the UCLA Extension Writers' Program. *A Daughter of No Nation* is her fourth novel.